W9-BFG-511

Titles by Janet Chapman

HIGHLANDER FOR THE HOLIDAYS
SPELLBOUND FALLS
CHARMED BY HIS LOVE
COURTING CAROLINA

Courting
Carolina

Janet Chapman

JOVE BOOKS, NEW YORK

THE BERKLEY PUBLISHING GROUP
Published by the Penguin Group
Penguin Group (USA) Inc.
375 Hudson Street, New York, New York 10014, USA
Penguin Group (Canada), 90 Eglinton Avenue East, Suite 700, Toronto, Ontario M4P 2Y3, Canada
(a division of Pearson Penguin Canada Inc.) • Penguin Books Ltd., 80 Strand, London WC2R 0RL,
England • Penguin Group Ireland, 25 St. Stephen's Green, Dublin 2, Ireland (a division of Penguin
Books Ltd.) • Penguin Group (Australia), 250 Camberwell Road, Camberwell, Victoria 3124, Australia
(a division of Pearson Australia Group Pty. Ltd.) • Penguin Books India Pvt. Ltd., 11 Community
Centre, Panchsheel Park, New Delhi—110 017, India • Penguin Group (NZ), 67 Apollo Drive,
Rosedale, Auckland 0632, New Zealand (a division of Pearson New Zealand Ltd.) • Penguin Books
(South Africa) (Pty.) Ltd., 24 Sturdee Avenue, Rosebank, Johannesburg 2196, South Africa

Penguin Books Ltd., Registered Offices: 80 Strand, London WC2R 0RL, England

COURTING CAROLINA

A Jove Book / published by arrangement with the author

ISBN: 978-1-62090-418-3

JOVE®
Jove Books are published by The Berkley Publishing Group,
a division of Penguin Group (USA) Inc.,
375 Hudson Street, New York, New York 10014.
JOVE® is a registered trademark of Penguin Group (USA) Inc.
The "J" design is a trademark of Penguin Group (USA) Inc.

PRINTED IN THE UNITED STATES OF AMERICA

To Delbert Byram
(April 13, 1918–October 1, 2011)
Bye, Daddy. Have fun, and say hi to Mom from all of us!

Chapter One

Alec heard the distinct rumble of thunder over the gush of the cascading falls and tossed his shovel onto the stream bank with a muttered curse before vaulting up behind it. He picked up his shirt and used it to wipe the sweat off his face, then turned to glare at the dark clouds rolling across the fiord toward him. "Go around!" he shouted, pointing north with his free hand as he wiped down his chest. But the storm gods didn't have any sense of humor, apparently, and the hair on his arms stirred just as lightning flashed on a sharp crack of thunder. "Well, fine then!" he shouted with a laugh as he bolted toward camp. "Take your best shot, you noisy bastards!"

Alec slipped into his shirt when the wind pushing ahead of the storm took on an ominous chill, and lengthened his stride when he realized he was losing the footrace to the sheet of rain sweeping up the mountain. How had he been caught by surprise? There hadn't been a cold front forecast to come through, or even any clouds in the crisp September sky ten minutes ago. Another crack sounded to his right just as the wind-driven rain hit with enough force to make him stagger, and Alec scrambled to catch himself with another laugh.

But he came to an abrupt halt at the sound of an unmistakably feminine scream, followed almost immediately by an enraged shout that was also human—and male. He held his breath through several heartbeats trying to discern its direction in the downpour, then took off at a run again, leaving the trail at a diagonal down the mountain. He weaved through the old-growth forest even as he wondered who was out here, as this section of the resort's wilderness trail was closed to guests until he had all the footbridges and lean-tos in place.

Alec came to a halt again next to a large tree and lifted his hand against the rain as he quickly calculated his odds of saving the woman without getting himself killed in the process. The two brutes attacking her weren't much of a worry, whereas the large dog racing up the mountain toward them might be a problem.

The woman gave another bloodcurdling scream as she bucked against the man straddling her, and twisted to clamp her teeth over the wrist of the guy kneeling at her head, pinning down her hands. The ensuing shout of pain was drowned out by a vicious growl as the dog lunged at the man on top of her, the animal's momentum sending them both tumbling to the ground.

Okay then, the dog was on her side. Hoping it realized he was also on the woman's side, Alec drove his boot into the ribs of the man she'd bitten, sending him sprawling into a tree just as lightning struck so close, the percussion knocked Alec to his knees. And since he landed next to the woman, he caught her fist swinging toward him, grasped her waist with his other hand, and lifted her to her feet. "Run! Up!" he shouted as he gave her a push. "God dammit, go! The dog and I will catch up!"

She hesitated only a heartbeat, but it was long enough for him to see the uncertainty in her eyes as she glanced at the dog before she turned and ran uphill. The guy he'd kicked lunged at her on the way by, and Alec leapt to his feet when he realized the bastard had a knife.

The woman scrambled sideways, crying out as she grabbed her leg and kept running. The man started after her again, but suddenly turned at Alec's roar. Alec caught the wrist holding the knife and drove his boot into the man's ribs again, twisting the guy's arm until he felt it snap before plunging the blade into the bastard's thigh. He then spun around when the dog gave a yelp to see it regain its footing and lunge again at the other man, this time going after the arm holding a goddamned gun.

Alec slammed into the guy, grabbing his wrist just as the weapon discharged. The dog tumbled back with a yelp, and Alec snapped the bastard's arm over his knee, causing the gun to fall to the ground. He then shoved the screaming man headfirst into a tree, watching him crumple into a boneless heap before he turned and rushed to the dog that now had its teeth clamped down on the other man's neck.

"Hey, come on!" he shouted over another sharp crack of thunder. He grabbed the dog by the jowls and pulled it away. "That's enough," he said, holding its head from behind so it couldn't turn on *him*. "I know you'd like to see them both dead, but they're not worth the hassle it's going to cause us. Easy now, calm down," he said loudly over the raging storm, guiding the dog uphill several steps, then giving it a nudge with his knee. "Go on. Go find your lady."

The dog hesitated just as the woman had, its eyes narrowed against the rain and its lips rolled back, then suddenly took off in the direction she'd run and disappeared into the storm. Alec looked down at the man cradling his broken arm against the knife in his thigh, knelt to one knee, and drove his fist into his face. "Sleep tight, you son of a bitch," he muttered, glancing over to make sure the other guy was still out before he also headed uphill at a run.

Only he hadn't gone two hundred yards before he found the woman lying facedown on the soaked forest floor, the dog licking her cheek. Alec approached cautiously, crooning calm words loud enough to be heard over the pounding rain, and slowly knelt on the other side of her. He laid a firm hand on the dog's raised hackles when it stiffened on a warning snarl. "You're going to have to trust me, ye big brute. Your lady's hurt, and I need to see how badly."

He felt the dog—which he suspected was a wolf or at least a hybrid—tremble with indecision, and Alec slowly reached out with his other hand and touched the woman's hair plastered to her head. "Easy now," he said when the snarling grew louder, moving his fingers to her neck to feel for a pulse. He breathed a sigh of relief to find it strong and steady, and carefully rolled her over. "There we go," he said, releasing the dog when it lowered its head and started licking her face again. Alec slid an arm behind her shoulders and a hand under her knees and stood up.

He carried her uphill until he came to the trail and turned toward camp. "No, heel!" he snapped when the dog stopped and looked back down the mountain. "They're not going anywhere." The animal fell into step beside him, and Alec repositioned the woman's head into the crook of his neck to keep the driving rain off her face and blew out a harsh breath to tamp down his own anger. Christ, it had been all he could do to keep from killing the bastards himself when he'd caught them brutalizing her.

What was she doing out here? Had the men brought her into the wilderness to rape and kill her and bury her body? The nearest old logging tote road was six miles to the south, and the resort he worked for was over ten miles away on top of the mountain. But she'd been running up from the fiord—just a mile below his camp—which meant they'd probably come by boat.

Alec scaled the lean-to steps, then dropped to one knee and carefully set the woman on the plank floor beside his sleeping bag, keeping her upper half cradled against his chest. He slid his hand from under her knees, then had to shove the dog away when it started licking her again. "Nay, ye let me check her out," he murmured as he smoothed the hair off her face—only to suck in a breath.

She was beautiful but for the angry welt on her pale

cheek and the darkening bump on her forehead that ran into her hairline. Alec looked down at her endlessly long legs and saw the bastard's knife had drawn blood. Realizing she was shivering violently, he started undressing her, but stilled in surprise again when he pulled her soaked blouse out of her pants and saw the dark bruise on her side. It ran over her ribs into her sheer blue bra, and he recognized that it was two or three days old. Filled with renewed rage, he carefully worked the blouse off her shoulders, only to find her arms also covered in small bruises, some of them appearing to be fingerprints.

It was obvious the woman had been struggling against them for several days, and he started rethinking his decision not to kill the bastards as he continued exposing the full extent of her nightmare. Feeling much like the storm raging directly overhead, Alec fought back the darkness that had been his life for eight years when he caught himself thinking there wasn't any reason he couldn't bury the *men* out here; quietly, efficiently, and with the calm detachment he'd once been known for.

The woman had been bound, as evidenced by the raw chafing on her wrists. He found more bruising on her legs when he carefully peeled down her slacks, and she was missing a shoe. Alec pushed the dog out of the way, lifted back the edge of his sleeping bag, and carefully set her inside it.

He pulled over his duffel bag and dug around until he found a T-shirt. "Sorry, sweetheart," he murmured as he sat her up and unhooked her bra. "But I'm afraid getting you completely dry trumps modesty at the moment." He worked the T-shirt over her head, carefully slid her arms into the sleeves, and smoothed it down over her utterly feminine, rose-tipped breasts all the way to her thighs. He pulled her heavy mess of long, wet hair out of the collar and laid her down, then grabbed a towel hanging on the back wall of the lean-to and wrapped it around her head. Setting his jaw determinedly, he slid his hands under the T-shirt and carefully worked off her matching blue panties, but stopped when he reached the knife gash. "Damn," he growled, pulling off the panties and tossing them beside the discarded bra. He tucked the sleeping bag over her upper half and opposite leg, then dug through his duffel for the medical kit.

The dog settled against the woman's side and rested its chin on her shoulder, keeping a guarded eye on him. "You're a good friend," Alec said conversationally as he examined the wound on her thigh. "Ye can guard my back anytime you're wanting."

It wasn't a deep gash that needed stitching, he was relieved to see as he carefully cleaned it with gauze then started placing butterfly bandages along the length of the cut. He dabbed it with salve and covered it with another piece of gauze, taping it into place before tucking the baby-soft leg into the sleeping bag.

"Had ye reached the end of your strength or is that bump on your head making you sleep?" he asked the unconscious woman, carefully lifting first one and then the other of her eyelids. Again relieved to see her pupils appeared normal and even, Alec sat down and took off his boots. He then stood up and started stripping off his own wet clothes as he studied what was definitely a full-bred wolf, its long guard hairs muted black over a soft pelt of gray, with piercing eyes of hazel-gold watching him from a broad wet face. "Aye, you're a good partner in a fight," he said as he shoved off his pants and boxers. "And I thank you for not going for *my* throat."

The wolf's brows were all that moved as its gaze followed Alec around the shelter as he dried off with another towel and slipped into clean clothes. He pulled the band off his wet hair, toweled it dry as well, then combed his fingers through the shoulder-length waves before tying it against the nape of his neck again. He crouched down and laid a hand on the woman's forehead, gently smoothing her brow with his thumb. "She's going to be okay," he promised the wolf as he stood up and walked to the front rail of the three-sided lean-to that sat twenty yards up from the trail.

The storm was finally making its way north between the mountain they were on and the one at the end of the fiord, leaving in its wake an almost obscene silence but for the water gently dripping off the leaves. Alec glanced in the direction of the men and blew out a sigh, then walked to the rear wall and pulled down a small backpack. He placed a coil of rope inside, along with the resort's satellite phone and the medical kit, and slipped the pack over his shoulders. He sat down and dug two pairs of socks out of his duffel, putting on one pair followed by his boots, then rolled to his knees and peeled back the bottom of the sleeping bag.

He slid off the woman's socks—one of them shredded from her running in only one shoe—and covered her feet with his hands to take away some of the chill. He then slipped his oversized socks on her and tucked the bag around her legs before moving to her head. Alec reached inside the sleeping bag, pressed his palm just below her collarbone, and felt her steady heartbeat and even breathing.

"Ye stay here and keep warming her up," he told the wolf, tucking the bag tightly around the woman before standing up, "while I go tie our two sorry friends to a tree and call the sheriff to come get them. And I'll call the resort to come get your lady." He grinned down at the wolf. "I hope ye like riding in a helicopter."

Alec started to leave, but stopped when the woman suddenly moaned, and he turned to see her lift a hand from the confines of the sleeping bag when the wolf licked her face. He crouched down beside her again, laying a steadying hand on her shoulder when she tried to sit up. "Easy, now. You're safe. No one's going to hurt you."

She pressed back into the pillow, confusion clouding the deepest green eyes he'd ever seen. "Who are you? Where am I?" she asked, her gaze darting around the shelter. She started to pull her other hand free, only to gather the oversized T-shirt she was wearing into her fist, her gaze snapping to his. "You undressed me."

He nodded. "I needed to get you dry to warm ye up," he explained, stifling a grin when her other hand moved inside the bag and she gasped. "Don't worry, I kept my eyes closed," he said with a wink when her emerald gaze narrowed, her indignation assuring him she was well on the road to recovery. "What's your name, lass?"

She blinked up at him, saying nothing.

Alec shrugged and stood up. "If you'll excuse me, then, I have some trash I need to deal with. I'll call the sheriff and then the resort to have their helicopter come pick you up." He nodded toward the wolf. "Does your tenacious protector have a name, at least? Because I'm thinking he deserves a few slobbering kisses in return for the way he ran to your rescue."

She pulled the sleeping bag up to her chin, again saying nothing.

"Okay then, I guess I'll be on my way."

"Wait," she said when he walked down the steps, making him turn back. She rose up on one elbow, causing the towel to fall off her hair. "I don't . . . Could you please not . . ." She took a deep breath. "Please don't call the authorities. I don't want anyone to know I'm here."

"You can't be serious," he said, scaling the steps to crouch down beside her again. "Your family must be going out of their minds looking for you." He touched her bruised wrist. "You've obviously been missing for several days."

"But nobody knows I'm missing," she whispered, clutching his arm. "Please, could you let me stay here with you for a few days, just until I get my strength back and can decide what I need to do?"

Was she serious? "Hell, woman, for all you know I could be more dangerous than the bastards who had you. You don't know a damn thing about me."

"I know you didn't hesitate to save me from two armed men."

"The wolf took care of one of them," he snapped, standing up. Why in hell was she asking him to stay? Was someone still after her? Or was that bump on her head making her delirious? "What's your name?"

Her gaze lowered. "Jane."

"Jane what?"

"Smith," she said, her cheeks darkening with her obvious lie.

"Well, Jane Smith," he muttered, walking off the platform again. He stopped and looked at her. "We'll discuss your staying when I get back from dealing with the trash before it crawls away."

"You could just kill them," she said quietly, "and bury their bodies under a rock."

Okay then, *he* must be delirious, because he'd swear she'd just asked him to commit murder. "No, I can't," he said just as quietly, "because then I would have to kill any witnesses."

She didn't even bat an eyelash. "I won't watch."

At a complete loss as to how to respond, Alec strode off—only to stop when she called to him again. "I have a couple of bags," she said. "But I had to leave them when I realized the men were gaining on me. Could you get them for me, please?"

"Are they full of gold? Stolen art? *Drugs?*"

"No," she said, startled. "They're full of my clothes." She reached behind her and gave the wolf a shove. "Kitty knows where they are."

Alec closed his eyes. "Please tell me ye didn't just call that noble beast Kitty."

"And could you feed me when you get back from dealing with the . . . trash? I haven't eaten for three days."

She was a rather bossy victim. "I'll see if *Kitty* and I can't hunt down a squirrel or two while we're at it," he said, turning away to hide his grin and jogging down the trail before she thought of something else she'd like him to do—other than commit murder and find her clothes and rush back and feed her.

Oh, but he was tempted to let her stay, if for no other reason than to keep himself entertained for a few days. That is, until he remembered her battered though otherwise flawless body and felt his groin grow heavy. Hell, spending even one night in the same lean-to as the beautiful woman would likely test the noble intentions of a saint, much less a man who'd been all alone in the woods all summer.

Alec followed the wolf into the forest from where they'd emerged onto the trail earlier and tried to remember when the last time was that he'd been so immediately captivated by a woman. Especially an obviously high-maintenance princess who'd given him a fictitious name, who didn't want anyone—including her family—to know where she was, and who woke up from a nightmare and started issuing orders.

He found the men right where he'd left them, the only problem being the bastards were dead. Hell, one of them was actually smoldering, as was the exploded tree he was crumpled against. The other guy was riddled with shrapnel, a large piece of wood so forcibly driven into his chest that it was sticking out of his back.

Alec crouched to his heels and rubbed his face in his hands, then stared at the men in dismay. This ought to be interesting to explain to the sheriff: two fried corpses that upon closer examination would show cracked ribs and broken arms and a knife wound, and also a discharged gun nearby. Oh, and a battered, not-missing woman in his sleeping bag going by the name of Jane Smith, who also happened to have an illegal pet wolf named Kitty.

Speaking of which, where was Kitty?

Alec scrubbed his face again, undecided what to do, then suddenly stilled. Well hell, it wasn't his fault these two idiots had chosen this particular piece of wilderness to settle their differences, was it? In fact, he could think of several scenarios for their being out here, from a drug deal gone bad to a botched smuggling trip to . . . to an execution interrupted by a thunderstorm that had killed both executioner and executee.

As for the beautiful princess in his sleeping bag . . . well, what princess? He could let her stay a few days to get back her strength, then run her down to Spellbound Falls in his boat in the middle of the night, hand her a few dollars, and kiss her saint-tempting mouth good-bye. After all, he used to make his living orchestrating damage control—on damage he'd caused, usually. In fact, he'd been so good at it that he'd had to leave the game before he'd irrevocably damaged himself.

Alec went over and started carefully rifling through their pockets, only to come up empty-handed. He didn't find a wallet, money or loose change, or even any lint—which meant they weren't going to tell him what was going on any more than the woman was. But just as he started to stand, he noticed the odd-looking burn mark on the smoldering bastard's shirt, unbuttoned a couple of buttons, and pulled away the material.

"Bingo," he murmured, taking his knife out of its sheath. He cut the leather cord and peeled the medallion off the charred skin before buttoning the guy's shirt back up and standing.

He studied what appeared to be an ancient coin of some sort as he walked to the other man and crouched down, used the tip of his knife to snag the cord around the bastard's neck, and lifted another medallion out of his shirt. He sliced the cord then held the coins beside each other, frowning at the identical symbols crudely stamped into what he suspected was bronze, before turning them over to see writing in a language he didn't recognize.

Okay then; these weren't telling him anything, either, since he didn't have a clue what the symbol was. Could it be the calling card of some criminal organization? Or judging by the men's plain, almost crude clothes, maybe a cult? Or for all he knew, these two bastards could be members of an arcane fraternity he'd heard about a few years back that got its jollies pulling elaborate international crimes, and Jane Smith could be nothing more than the innocent victim of a pledge prank that had gone bad when she'd escaped.

Alec shoved the medallions in his pocket as he walked a short distance away, deciding to keep them secret until he got more pieces of the puzzle to put together. He sat down, slipped off his pack, then reached in past the now useless rope and medical kit and pulled out the satellite phone—because the resort owner and his boss, Olivia Oceanus, had decided *cell* phones ruined the wilderness experience for her guests and had talked her wizard husband into blocking reception in the resort's backcountry. He dialed 911, dutifully reported the *accident* he'd stumbled across—because he really didn't want to bury the problem under a rock—and gave the dispatcher the coordinates. He also gave his satellite phone number, saying the sheriff could give him a call when he arrived so Alec could lead him to the bodies.

He shoved the phone back in his pack, then started walking the area looking for wolf and smaller shoe tracks in the scattered patches of mud. He erased them all the way up to where she'd collapsed before he backtracked through the scene and headed down to the fiord, again leaving only the tracks the men had made. He eventually found where they stopped—or rather, had started—at the inland sea's high tide line; the problem being that he didn't find the boat they had to have used to get here. He saw only his boat, which was pulled into the trees and turned over, its motor stowed beneath it. He looked out at the fiord, wondering if the storm's waves had set their boat adrift. But if the men had been chasing her, then there should be two boats floating out on the water instead of none. That is, unless she'd escaped the moment they'd stepped ashore and the storm had sunk their boat.

Alec faced the looming mountain at the end of the fiord and frowned. He knew the water was over two thousand feet deep in the unnatural waterway, and that the underground saltwater river ran up from the Gulf of Maine before it continued north all the way to the St. Lawrence Seaway. The twelve-mile-long fiord had been added to Bottomless Lake when an earthquake had pushed several mountains apart two and a half years ago, at the same time turning Maine's second largest freshwater lake into the new Bottomless Sea—all compliments of Spellbound Falls's resident wizard, Maximilian Oceanus, who also happened to be Olivia's husband and Alec's other boss.

None of which explained how Jane and Kitty and the two dead men had gotten here. But at the moment he honestly didn't care, as he had damage control to see to, a woman to hide—and feed—and two bags to find. He'd found her missing shoe when he'd followed their trail down, making him realize that she'd traveled over half a mile wearing only one shoe.

Which meant Jane Smith was one hell of a *tough* princess.

Alec gave a sharp whistle then waited, and smiled when Kitty—Christ, he needed to find a better name for the noble warrior—silently stepped out of the woods less than forty feet away. "Well?" he asked, lifting his hands in the universal gesture of question. "Did ye find your lady's bags or not?"

The wolf trotted to the overturned boat and scratched at its gunwale.

Okay then, he guessed that settled that mystery. Jane had stashed them under his boat, which implied she'd had enough lead on the men to take the time to hide her bags. Correction: Her *luggage*, Alec discovered when he pulled out two heavy satchels.

Oh yeah, the lady was definitely high maintenance.

He shoved the wolf away and opened the smaller of the two bags and started pulling out . . . girly stuff. Toiletries, mostly: a silver brush and comb and mirror set, two ditty bags full of makeup and lotions, some pretty expensive perfume, then an iPad and an iPod, and a . . . She'd brought an alarm clock on her great escape?

But on closer inspection, he saw it was also a sound machine. Honest to God, the label said it had fifty digital recordings to lull you to sleep, including a waterfall, a heartbeat, thunderstorm, nighttime woods, ocean surf—complete with seagulls—and the gentle sound of a crackling fire, just to name a few.

Alec tossed the machine onto the growing pile with a snort, then picked up one of the ditty bags again. "Let's see what's in your medicine cabinet, sweetheart," he murmured, unzipping it. Nothing interesting, he discovered as he pawed through the tubes and containers of makeup. He found more of the same in the second bag. Hell, the woman didn't even have aspirin. He picked up another small tubular bag and unrolled it to expose several clear pouches, about half of which were filled with jewelry. He unzipped one and pulled out a necklace, giving a soft whistle. Just the center stone—which was an emerald and definitely real—could feed a small nation for a year.

Okay then; Jane Smith was rich.

Or else a very expensive date.

He replaced the necklace and started to roll the tube back up, but stopped when one particular item caught his eye. He unzipped the pouch and pulled out the small packet and started to smile, only to suddenly frown when his years of training to notice even the smallest detail kicked into gear. That seemed a bit odd; why keep a condom with her jewelry instead of in her toiletries bag?

A nagging little warning alarm went off in his gut, telling him it just didn't fit. He wouldn't have thought anything of it if he'd found it anyplace else, but there was only one, and the woman appeared to be treating it like a precious jewel.

Alec placed the packet back in its pouch and rolled the bag back up, deciding to catalog the condom in the back of his mind along with all the other peculiarities about his beautiful guest that didn't add up. He peered down into the satchel again, pulled out the tall boots lying across the bottom, but stopped in the act of throwing them to the side and looked inside one of them. "Bingo," he said, pulling out a thin leather wallet.

He dropped the boot and opened the wallet, then sat back on his heels with another quiet whistle at the sight of no fewer than ten credit cards. He pulled one out; *Jane Smith*, he read. He pulled out another one and saw it was issued on a European bank. He fingered through the other cards until he found *three* driver's licenses belonging to Jane Smith, who was five feet eleven and thirty years old, had lied about her weight he knew from carrying her, and who apparently lived in New York City—at a very uptown address—as well as Monte Carlo and South Africa.

Well, at least she was keeping her lies somewhat simple.

She had about a thousand dollars in cash in various currencies, the bulk being American. But no photos of family or anything of a personal nature other than a sales receipt for the boots—which she'd apparently had custom made in New York for the tidy sum of twenty-nine hundred bucks.

Hell, his entire wardrobe hadn't cost three thousand dollars. Alec stuffed everything back in the wallet, shoved it back in the boot, then repacked the bag. He sighed, willing to concede that his hunting rifle had cost him several grand, so he supposed spending was a relative matter. He gave a quick glance at the sun to see it was nearing noon, then hauled over Jane's other monstrous satchel and pulled back the zipper—only to have its contents explode free. "For the love of Christ, is there anything you *didn't* bring?" He swiped a pair of purple lace panties off his arm, plucked the matching bra—noting the rather full cup size—off his thigh, and smiled.

Damn, he had a thing for sexy underwear.

Just as his mysterious guest did, apparently.

Alec drove his hand down through the clothes in the satchel, feeling around until he was satisfied Jane hadn't brought anything practical to her kidnapping, like a knife or handgun or Taser or bazooka. Nope, she hadn't even packed any hand grenades.

He stuffed everything back in the bag, then had to press his knee down on the damn thing to get it zipped closed. He straightened with a long-suffering sigh and stared in the direction of his uncle's home halfway up the fiord on the opposite shore. Should he let Duncan know what was going on?

Probably not. A little over two years ago, Duncan had become a husband and instant father to four little heathens—which had turned into five exactly nine months later—and the man didn't seem to be anywhere near to recovering yet. Alec decided he shouldn't say anything to Mac and Olivia, either, as he didn't want anyone making him turn over the order-issuing, straight-faced lying, beautiful gift the storm gods had seen fit to present him with this morning. Because, hey, he was just tired enough of his own company that he was actually looking forward to camping out with a princess. And all that really mattered was that she was safe, right?

Well, safe from anyone who might still be chasing her, Alec decided with a grin as he picked up her bags and headed toward camp. Because safety was also a relative matter, and he wasn't making any promises to the storm gods *or* Jane about keeping his hands off her.

And he definitely wasn't making such a foolish promise to himself.

As for Kitty . . . well, considering he'd survived being shot twice, blown up to hell and back once, and stabbed more times than he cared to remember, Alec figured the wolf would just have to get in line if it wanted a turn at him.

Chapter Two

———————

Alec arrived back at the lean-to to find Jane sitting up with the sleeping bag tucked around her legs, wearing one of his flannel shirts over his T-shirt, stuffing her mouth with trail mix as fast as she could chew and swallow. Her dark hair was more dry than wet now, hanging in wild knots to her waist . . . in places. In other places the odd hairstyle reached only halfway down her back. The welt on her cheek definitely looked like a handprint, the bump on her forehead had darkened, and her expressive green eyes instantly brightened when he dropped her two heavy bags beside her.

She immediately set down the tin of trail mix and started digging through the smaller satchel—only to stop and glare up at him. "You went through my belongings."

Alec arched a brow as he pointedly looked at the mess she'd made rifling through *his* stuff. "I was trying to decide if I wanted to harbor a criminal for the next few days," he drawled, walking to the rear wall to hang his pack on a peg.

"I'm not a criminal," she said, her voice muted as she dug through her satchel.

Oh, yes she was; the woman was criminally beautiful, even or maybe especially minus all the makeup he'd seen in her arsenal. "Did you know the men who were chasing you?" he asked as he started picking up the mess she'd made. He looked up when she didn't answer. "Or were you simply a victim of opportunity?"

Her chin lifted. "I'm not a victim, either. Where's Kitty?"

He grinned. "Hunting squirrels for our supper."

She reached in the tin of trail mix, grabbed a fistful and shoved it in her mouth, then started working the knots out of her hair with the silver brush.

"Ye know," he continued, "it's been my experience that when I'm wanting a favor from someone, it helps to be nice to them. And cooperative."

"What's your name?"

"Alec."

"Alec what?"

"Smith."

She dropped her gaze to her fistful of hair as her cheeks turned a dull pink, and went back to working out the tangles. "Where are the men?" she asked softly.

"Dead."

She snapped her head up. "You *killed* them?"

He arched a brow. "Didn't you ask me to?"

"But I didn't mean it!" Her face went as pale as new snow and she leaned away. "You really killed them?" she whispered.

"No," he said, shoving some of his clothes into the duffel bag. "A lightning strike beat me to it."

He heard her release a soft sigh. "I hope they rot in hell." She touched his arm when he reached for a shirt lying beside her. "Did you call the authorities, Alec?"

He nodded. "I put a call in to the sheriff. But," he rushed on when he saw her shoulders slump, "I told the dispatcher only that I'd stumbled onto two dead men, and I wiped away all traces of you and the wolf." He reached out and lifted her chin. "So we have about two hours to get you settled farther up the mountain before the sheriff arrives. That is, if you still insist on hiding out here for a few days."

Her eyes started to brighten, but then suddenly turned suspicious. "Why?" she asked softly. "Why are you letting me stay?"

Finally the woman was realizing she very well could be jumping out of the frying pan into the fire. Alec shrugged and gathered up more of his clothes. "I figured that if I didn't let you stay there was a good chance you'd run straight back into trouble," he said instead of admitting he was a masochistic idiot. But who was he to question the storm gods' decision to send him a beautiful woman?

She beamed him a smile that outshone the sun. "Thank you. I promise to be a perfect guest." She looked around the shelter at all his gear. "You appear to be settled in here somewhat permanently. Are you also hiding out? But doesn't this land belong to the resort on top of the mountain?"

Alec stood up and stowed his duffel bag against the rear wall. "I've spent the summer out here building a new hiking trail." He turned to her. "For the resort that you appear to be familiar with," he added. "Yet I've never seen you around Spellbound Falls or Turtleback Station, although I've spent the last two summers working in the area."

She returned to untangling her hair. "I'm . . . familiar with the resort."

Okay then, that certainly narrowed things down. Alec used his foot to push the larger satchel toward her. "Grab some clothes to wear, put everything you own back in the bags, and I'll take you up the mountain a few hundred yards."

The brush stilled in a knot and her eyes widened. "You can't mean to make me camp out in the open. Why can't I stay here?"

"Because there's a chance the sheriff might come *here*, and I prefer he doesn't find you or your lacy underwear while I'm lying through my teeth about what happened to those men." He pulled down the bra and panties and shirt and slacks she'd hung over the railing to dry, and tossed them on the sleeping bag. "Or have you finally come to your senses about letting me call someone to come take you home?"

She dropped her gaze to the clothes. "No. I can't ever go home again."

Alec crouched down beside her. "What kind of trouble are you in, Jane?"

He saw her pull in a shuddering breath. "I believe those two men, and one other, kidnapped me for ransom." She shook her head. "Apparently they hadn't heard that my father disowned me two years ago, so they didn't know he wouldn't have paid them anything."

Alec gave her a warm smile. "Daddies don't ever disown their daughters, lass. They might blow and bluster and put on a good show, but there isn't a man alive who's immune to his little girl's cry for help."

She looked down at the brush she was holding in a death grip. "It was the most terrible fight we've ever had. We both said things we regret, I know, but . . ." She looked up at him. "But even if he did take me back into his heart I couldn't return, because nothing will have changed. He'd still be dictatorial in his determination to see me settled into a life of *his* choosing, and I'd still be his . . . his clueless daughter," she growled, waving the brush in the air. Her chin lifted. "And in my two years of freedom, I've discovered that I prefer making my own choices."

"Are you an only child?"

"No, I have a brother."

"And is your father dictatorial with him?"

She snorted and went back to brushing her hair.

"Who's been bankrolling your exile?"

Her chin lifted. "I have."

Alec remembered the half-empty jewelry bag. "And who's been helping you stay one step ahead of your father these last couple of years? Your brother?"

She dropped her gaze as she went back to brushing, but not quickly enough for him to miss the stab of pain in her eyes. "No, a . . . friend has been helping me."

Alec stood up. "You can finish fixing your hair once I have you stashed out of sight. Pack your bags and get dressed while I go fill some canteens at a spring not far from here. And if you're still hungry, I'll feed you before we go," he added, trying not to sound too dictatorial himself.

He gathered together snacks she could take with her while Jane found the clothes she wanted to wear and repacked her bags in silence, then he headed up the trail to the spring—pointing out this was her chance to get dressed without him peeking.

So, it appeared Jane Smith had two problems and nowhere to run, since solving her more immediate problem by telling Daddy that kidnappers were after her meant walking right back into the very problem that had made her leave the safety of home to begin with. As for hanging out here with him . . . well, either Jane's father had good reason to watch over his clueless daughter with a heavy hand, or the woman didn't know her biggest problem was six foot four and quite eager to get her pretty little panties off her again.

Damn, he really needed to stop being attracted to women with kissable mouths, legs that ran up to their armpits, and sexy bedroom eyes—especially when they came with a whole lot of *heavy* baggage.

Either damage control no longer held the thrill it once did, Alec decided as he watched the sheriff's small flotilla finally speed off down the fiord, or else he'd lost his legendary patience since getting out of the game three years ago. "Goodbye, you long-winded bastards," he called after them, cheerily waving an obscene gesture.

The sun had already set and, realizing the light of dusk was quickly fading, Alec turned and headed up the mountain at a flat-out run. Not knowing if Jane was afraid of things that went bump in the night or not—remembering the woman traveled with a sound machine—he did know darkness had a way of turning even the bravest soul into a cowering ball of sweat in the aftermath of a trauma. And to his way of thinking, being kidnapped and held for several days was one hell of a trauma.

He found Jane and Kitty right where he'd left them, stashed under an outcropping of ledge; the only difference being that instead of fighting the tangles in her hair, Jane was hugging the wolf with her face buried in its fur, softly sobbing.

"Hey. Hey," Alec said, sitting down and prying her away from Kitty—only to have her throw herself at him and start sobbing harder. "Easy now, it's okay," he crooned, stroking her back as he held her protectively. "You're safe now, Jane. I'm not going to let anyone hurt you. What was that?" he asked, lifting her chin to look at him. "What was cut? Your leg?" He clasped her to him again. "I know it probably stings, but it's not going to leave a scar, sweetheart. It wasn't all that— What?" he asked, leaning away when she muttered something again.

She immediately grabbed a handful of her hair and held it up for him to see. "Th-they cut my hair," she sobbed. "I'd forgotten the other man had taken a large ch-chunk of it when he cut off my ankle bracelet." She pressed the hair to her eyes with a shudder. "He just hacked it off with a knife!"

"Hey now," Alec said, urging her forward to hide her face in his shirt instead of her butchered curls. He stroked his hand over what he thought was still a lot of hair. "It'll grow back in no time, lass." Unless this wasn't about the hair at all, but about the full force of how helpless she'd been finally hitting her.

Nope, it was about the hair. "But it's my crowning mantle," she cried, pulling out some of *his* chest hair when she balled her fist in his shirt. "I've been growing it for *forever*." She suddenly sat up. "You have to fix it, Alec," she said, making him grunt when she pushed off his lap to go after her smaller satchel. "You have to make it even. I have scissors."

Alec scrambled to his feet, grabbed the satchel out of her hand and closed it, and gave her a tight smile. "It's too dark to see what I'm doing," he said, having no intention of going anywhere near her *crowning mantle* with scissors. "Let's go back to the shelter where I've got some lanterns, and I'll see what I can do about . . . fixing it."

She swiped her damp cheeks and squared her shoulders on a lingering sob. "Thank you," she said, gathering her hair and pulling it over one shoulder as she started down toward the trail.

Alec looked at the wolf looking up at him with its head canted, one side of its face wet with Jane's tears. "You don't happen to have opposable thumbs on any of those paws, do you?" He picked up the other satchel with a muttered curse and followed. Damn, what if he made an even bigger mess of her hair? Women were touchy about that sort of thing. "We probably won't need the sound machine tonight," he continued when Kitty fell into step beside him, apparently all Janed out. "As I fear we'll be going to sleep to the sound of sobbing."

Alec noticed Jane was limping slightly as she walked the trail ahead of him, but he also couldn't help but notice that her wonderfully feminine bottom—the one that sat at the top of those really long legs—formed a perfect upside-down heart. Speaking of legs, he'd been rather startled when he'd returned from filling the canteens to discover that Jane really was nearly six feet tall in her stocking feet. And after slipping on her custom-made boots and standing up again, she'd looked him almost level in the eyes.

Sexy underwear, endless legs, a heart-shaped bottom, bedroom eyes, the warmest smile this side of Bermuda; damn, the storm gods were a benevolent bunch.

She'd already pulled his food trunk away from the rear wall by the time he walked up the lean-to steps, and was sitting on it combing her fingers through her endless miles of hair that flowed around her pretty much like an actual mantle. "Hurry and light the lanterns," she instructed, looking around for them as she squirmed expectantly.

Alec set her small satchel on her lap and the other one beside her feet, half-tempted to hold out his hand for a tip for lugging her luggage up and down the mountain several times today. "Would you like something to eat first?" he asked, gesturing at the locker she was sitting on.

"Maybe later," she said, pulling her ditty bag out of the satchel.

"Would you mind if I had something to eat first?"

She stilled with the scissors in her hand, and then he saw her cheeks darken and her shoulders slump. "No, of course not."

Alec stifled a sigh and took down one of the lanterns hanging on a rafter. Hell, even though he hadn't had anything to eat since breakfast, he seemed to have lost his appetite. *Might as well get this massacre over.* He lit the lantern and hung it back up, then lit two more before walking over and taking the scissors out of her hand. "Never mind," he said, getting down on his knees behind her. "I might as well fix your hair first."

She squirmed again but then went very still when he reached through her mess of curls to the nape of her neck, and Alec closed his eyes and bit back a groan as he slowly slid his fingers through her hair.

"Um . . . I just need you to . . . I want . . ." *She* groaned and drew in a ragged breath. "Okay, just do it, Alec."

He couldn't do it, because he was pretty sure every blood cell he owned was pooled below his belt, and that was why his hand was trembling when he lifted the scissors only to find that his fingers wouldn't fit in their tiny holes.

"Is . . . is it bad?" she whispered when he continued to hesitate.

Not as bad as it's going to be, he felt like saying. "No," he said instead. He pressed a finger to the middle of her back at the height of the hacked-off hair. "Do you want me to cut it all this length? Or should I try to . . ." Hell, he didn't know anything about women's hairstyles. "Isn't there something called layering or . . . something?"

Jane started trembling worse than his hands were. "Make it all one length," she rasped, her voice husky with what he was afraid were unshed tears.

Alec dropped his head in defeat. "Okay, here's the thing: I can't use these scissors because they're too small for my fingers. But I have a razor-sharp knife," he rushed on when he saw her shoulders quiver on a silent sob. "Only I don't want you to freak out when you see me coming at you with a knife. Or Kitty to go for my throat," he muttered, eyeing the wolf eyeing him.

Jane stilled again, her backbone going ramrod stiff. "I won't freak out. I'm not a hysterical female."

No, but she was an easily offended one, apparently. Alec slid his knife out of its sheath, set his jaw determinedly, and flattened a lock of her long hair between his fingers, slowly running his blade across it. He let the cut hair fall to the floor and eyed his work. That didn't look so bad. He ran his fingers to the nape of her neck again, slid them down with more of her tresses flattened between them, and made a slice at the same level—only to have her hair spring into a curl that went halfway up to her neck.

Damn. Now what?

He slid his fingers through more hair—making sure to capture some that he'd already cut to judge the length by—and stretched it out and sliced. Okay then, they just might both survive this. "Where did the men kidnap you from?" he asked, his tone conversational as he slowly amassed a pile of long, wavy hair on the floor in front of him. Aw, hell, over half her hair was going to have to come off.

"I was . . . um, in Boston," she said after a long hesitation. "Yes, I was in Boston when they broke into my hotel room and snatched me."

"Then how did you end up in Spellbound Falls?"

He felt her go perfectly still again. "I have no idea." She shrugged—making the slice he was taking at the time a little higher than the others. "A good deal of the last three days is a blur to me."

"And Kitty; did they kidnap the wolf, too?"

An even longer hesitation, then, "I escaped and made my way to . . . to the kennel and got Kitty, then just headed north. Yes, I think that's what happened."

Alec stopped slicing. "After you went back to the hotel they'd snatched you from and got your belongings," he continued for her, seeing how the poor woman couldn't seem to concoct a lie on the fly. "And you stole a boat in Spellbound Falls and drove up the fiord, and your kidnappers stole another boat and chased you. Is that how you all happened to end up in my neck of the woods?"

"Yes!" she cried, pivoting to grace him with one of those saint-tempting smiles.

Alec nudged her back around to hide his own smile, then curled his fingers around the hair hanging in front of her shoulders and drew it back.

She immediately snatched it out of his grasp. "No, wait. You can't pull it back and cut it the same length, because it will be longer when it falls forward again," she explained. She turned on the food locker so that she was sitting sideways in front of him. "You have to cut your way around my head."

"Okay. But just remember that you're not a hysterical female when you see the knife coming at you."

Her chin lifted and she stared straight ahead without saying a word, and Alec immediately felt bad when he saw the handprint on her cheek. Damn, she was resilient. He had no right to be baiting her after what she'd endured. Jane Smith might be telling the mother of all lies, but those bruises certainly were real. He slowly started slicing off her hair again, working all the way around to her other side until, near as he could tell, every hair on her head was the same length— sort of.

He slid his knife into its sheath and leaned back to sit on his heels.

Jane turned on the locker to face him, the lantern light reflecting off the moisture in her questioning eyes. "W- well?" she whispered.

"You . . ." He cleared his throat. "You're beautiful, lass." He touched one of the tendrils cascading down the side of her face. "Strikingly beautiful."

"Oh, thank you, Alec!" she cried, throwing her arms around him and planting her mouth dead center on his.

Her kiss was so unexpected that Alec reared away in surprise, only to realize too late that away was *not* the direction he wanted to go. So he wrapped his arms around her and simply brought her with him. He landed on the planks hard enough to make the entire lean-to shudder, and Jane landed on him with a startled yelp.

Kitty landed beside him with an ominous growl.

Alec turned to stone, and Jane sat up straddling him to shove the wolf away as if it were a pesky pup. "Kitty, stop that. Alec was just being gallant, catching me when we fell so I wouldn't get more bruises."

The wolf sat down, instantly contrite, and actually hung its head.

Okay then, if that's what the lady wished to believe then who was he to burst her bubble? Alec rubbed his face with his hands, partly to hide his smile but mostly so Jane wouldn't see him run his tongue over his lips to savor her taste. But then he snapped his hands to her hips when she squirmed, and jackknifed upright as he lifted her off his groin. He plopped her back on the food locker, immediately stood up, and walked to the rear wall so she wouldn't seem him tug on his pant leg.

Yup, either dear old Daddy had every reason to be dictatorial or the woman was one hell of an actress. But the scariest thing was he was beginning to suspect that Jane didn't even realize she was acting. It was as if she'd been playing an airhead for so long—for some arcane reason only she knew—that she'd forgotten she was strong and resilient and . . . well, not clueless.

Damn, why did he always have to analyze people the same way he used to take apart every toy he'd ever been given to see what made it tick? That little habit may have served him nicely when he'd been serving his country, but it was hell on his love life.

"You've had a rather eventful day," he said, fiddling with

his backpack until his jeans stopped feeling two sizes too small. He finally walked to his sleeping bag and picked it up along with the mat. "You must be tired. I'll set you up in the back corner so you'll be out of the breeze. Leave that, I'll get it," he added when he saw her hands trembling as she gathered her cut hair off the floor.

She straightened. "But you only have one sleeping bag. Where are you going to sleep? How will you stay warm?"

He shook out the bag and settled it over the dense camping mattress. "I'll throw on my long johns and a jacket. Don't worry, lass," he said when he saw her stricken look. "I've camped out in a lot colder weather wearing a lot less. I'm used to roughing it."

"But when I asked to stay, I didn't mean to take your bed!" She drew herself up to her full height—which was damn impressive. "I'll dress in several layers of clothes and sleep . . . over there," she said, pointing to the opposite back corner. "I can unpack everything and use my bags as a sleeping mat. And maybe you have an extra blanket?" She was wringing her hands at her waist now, and dropped her gaze to stare at his feet, her cheeks a dull red. "I'm sorry, Alec, I didn't think this through."

He was standing in front of her in one stride, and smoothed back several tendrils of hair off her face. "But I did think it through before I agreed to let you stay," he said with a warm smile. "And I'm not bruised from my nose to my toes. I swear, Jane, that once I'm horizontal I could sleep naked on a rock and not care."

Her eyes flared slightly, and her cheeks went from dull red to rosy pink.

"However," he said softly, "a sweet kiss from a beautiful woman would probably keep me warm all night."

One corner of her mouth lifted ever so slightly, and her eyes took on a bit of a sparkle. "You had all afternoon to figure out how to charm a kiss out of me, and that's the best you could come up with?"

Oh yeah, Jane Smith was all act. Loving that she stood

almost tall enough to look him in the eyes, Alec gently pulled her into his embrace. "It was either that or simply steal a kiss," he said quietly.

She palmed his face in her hands, pulled his mouth to hers, and kissed him sweetly as she pressed her body against the length of his. Then she leaned away just enough to smile at him. "That was for saving my life today," she whispered, just before she kissed him again—this time lingering a bit longer. "And that was for letting me stay." She canted her head, her eyes glittering like emeralds in the lantern light. "Does my forwardness shock you, Alec?"

"Not as much as it probably should." He sighed. "But I'm fairly certain you'd learned your effect on men by the time you were two months old, and that you've spent every year since perfecting how to use it to your advantage."

Which she proved by pouting. "You make me sound manipulative."

"Nay, lass, I'm just stating a fact. And Miss *Smith*?"

"Yes, Mr. *MacKeage*?"

He merely arched a brow.

Jane's pout turned into a full-blown, saint-tempting smile again. "It would appear that while you were down at the water going through my belongings that I was going through yours, including the wallet you left in your wet jeans. So yes, Mr. MacKeage?"

For the life of him, Alec couldn't remember what he wanted to tell her. Not when she looked him directly in the eyes like that, her own eyes shining with amusement. So he simply kissed her. But where Kitty didn't seem to mind if his lady was the one doing the kissing, the wolf apparently didn't like it when men kissed *her*, and gave a warning growl low in his throat. Only this time instead of scolding her pet, Alec felt Jane's lips smile against his.

Nope, there wasn't one clueless bone in the woman's body.

Which was why, not half an hour later, Alec lay on the plank floor on the opposite side of the shelter with Kitty stationed between them curled up against Jane's side, hating to ask about something that had been bugging him all day but really needing to know. "Were you raped, Jane?"

"Of course not."

He lifted his head. "Why 'of course not'? You make it sound as if the thought never even crossed those bastards' minds."

"It probably didn't, likely because they were too greedy."

"Excuse me?"

He heard her sigh. "They didn't want to devalue me because they wanted to get as much money from my father as they could."

"Excuse me," he repeated in a growl, sitting up to glare into the corner. "What in hell do you mean *devalue* you? Are you saying they were afraid your father would have paid less for . . . soiled goods?"

She also sat up. "In my world, an unmarried woman's value is in her chastity."

"Are you serious?"

He saw her chin lift. "Producing heirs is very serious business. *Wars* have been started over a man discovering that he just married . . . soiled goods."

"Where in hell are you from?"

She lay back with another sigh, and he saw her give a negligent wave. "The whole world is my home." He sensed her smiling, or maybe heard it in her voice when she said, "But at the moment I am content to be tucked safely in this beautiful corner of it with you." She gave a loud yawn behind her politely raised hand. "Good night, Alec."

He flopped back against his duffel bag with a muttered "good night," confounded but not really all that shocked. He knew there were entire cultures still clinging to the antiquated notion that women were commodities, the most blatant offenders often being wealthy business tycoons who built their dynasties on power marriages. For the love of God, was Jane's father one of those men? No wonder she was reluctant to go home, if dear old Daddy saw her only as an asset instead of a grown woman with a mind of her own.

Hell, now there was a man he wouldn't mind burying under— Wait; did that mean Jane was a virgin?

Seriously? The woman was thirty. And in this day and age, thirty-year-old virgins were as rare as . . . well, as *real* princesses.

Damn. Jane's sexy little lace panties had just turned into a chastity belt, and the next few days had just turned into his worst nightmare. And here he thought the storm gods didn't have a sense of humor, when what could possibly be funnier than gifting a horny red-blooded male with a beautiful virgin.

But it was just as he was finally drifting off to sleep that Alec remembered the lone condom in Jane's jewelry pouch, and he snapped open his eyes when that warning alarm went off in his gut again. Was Jane planning to trump dear old dictatorial Daddy by *devaluing* his most lucrative asset before he could marry it off?

Well, Christ Almighty; if his worst nightmare of having a beautiful woman all to himself and not being able to do anything about it had just come true, he was damned well making sure the kiss-bestowing princess suffered right along with him.

Chapter Three

―――――――

The salacious dream-turned-nightmare began at dawn the next morning when Alec cracked open his eyes just enough to see Jane crawling out of her sleeping bag wearing only his T-shirt—she apparently hadn't had room to pack pajamas—looking so damned sexy, he just barely bit back a groan. She held a finger to her lips—that he now knew tasted as sweet as they looked—signaling the wolf to be quiet as she tiptoed to her larger satchel. Alec watched her take out a pair of fire-engine red panties and slowly slip them up those really long legs, then wiggle into a pair of jeans that looked painted on by the time she finished fastening them. She sat down on the food locker and pulled on socks, then glanced over to make sure he was still asleep and quietly put on her boots. She grabbed a matching bra and heavy sweater out of the satchel, and he actually stopped breathing when she started to lift the hem of the T-shirt but stopped in mid-lift with another glance in his direction.

Damn, she didn't quite have the courage, and he started breathing again when she tucked the bra and sweater under her arm and quietly walked down the shelter's steps. After looking around, she stood with her eyes closed and her face bathed in the rising sun long enough that he stopped breathing again. She finally headed toward the outhouse hidden in a stand of young spruce trees fifty yards up behind the lean-to, Kitty dutifully trotting ahead to run interference against any lingering night critters.

Alec sat up and rubbed his hands over his face with a muttered curse. What, exactly, had he gotten himself into? Because other than spending the next few days walking around in pants that felt two sizes too small from watching Jane walking around in her too-tight pants, he was pretty sure he'd be spending more time babysitting the woman than working.

That is, unless he put her to work, too.

Yeah, he should be able to find something the princess could do to earn her room and board. Nothing too strenuous that might cause her to chip a nail or anything, but maybe she could fetch him water, hold the end of the measuring tape, and hand him tools. Stuff like that. He was just warming up to his plan when he remembered the cut on her thigh and her tender foot from running in one shoe, and stood up with a sigh. Maybe she could sit by the stream he was prepping for the bridge and read. First, though, he supposed he should feed her before Jane started equating him with her kidnappers.

"You're up," she said in surprise as she rounded the side of the shelter—carrying his T-shirt rolled around her red bra, he couldn't help but notice.

Now why hadn't she put on her bra, and why did he have to be so damned observant? "Yeah, the sun woke me. You hungry?" he asked, opening the food locker.

She gave a laugh. "Actually, I seem to still be full from last night, and I rarely eat first thing in the morning, anyway." He watched her stuff the bra and T-shirt under her pillow before turning to him. "But I would be happy to fix you something. Do you have eggs? I make a very good omelet."

"You cook?" he blurted out before he could stop himself.

Up went that chin—although it was accompanied by a derisive smile. "In the first month I was on my own, I discovered hunger is all the motivation needed to teach oneself to cook."

"I'm sorry. I didn't mean to imply that I thought you—"

She laughed, cutting him off. "Of course you did, Alec. I surprised myself at how good a cook I've become." She sobered. "Please, I want to earn my way this week by helping out however I can. I can do the cooking and keep the shelter organized, and I can even wash your clothes if you'd like." Her smile returned. "But my first order of business this morning is to go down to the fiord and gather some sweet grass to make you a mattress, so you won't have to lie on those hard planks tonight."

Was she seri— Whoa, a week? A few days had turned into a *week*?

She crowded him out of the way and knelt in front of the food locker. "Go do your morning rituals as if I'm not even here," she instructed as she started rummaging through what was left of his supplies. "I'll have something cooked for you in no time."

"Thanks, but I usually only have cold cereal or trail mix in the morning. I don't like working on a stomach full of heavy food."

She straightened and turned to him. "You have milk?"

"No, I think I used the last of it two days ago. But they're supposed to bring me supplies today when they bring the bridge."

She scrambled to her feet. "People are coming here today?"

"No, they're not coming *here*." He pointed down the trail. "They're bringing the bridge only as far as the falls, which is a quarter of a mile to the south. You don't need to worry, Jane. The helicopter's not even going to land, so if you simply hide in the trees while it's hovering, no one will see you."

Her eyes widened in surprise. "They're bringing a bridge by helicopter?"

He nodded. "We figured the easiest way to build the infrastructure for the trail was for me to give the carpenters working on the resort the measurements, and for them to build the bridges and lean-tos and privies at the shop. Then they fly the structures here instead of lugging in the timber."

"And they just lower them down to you? But how do you set them in place?"

"I guide them down and swing them onto the rock abutments I've built."

She clutched her throat. "You'll stand under the bridge while it's in the air?"

"No, I'll grab the rope dangling from it while the winch operator lowers it to me."

"Oh, I can't wait to see that," she said, clasping her hands together. "What an ingenious way to build a wilderness trail without hurting the wilderness. And they also lower whatever supplies you need?"

"Yup," Alec said with a grin, her smile contagious. "So if there's anything you need, I could have them bring it on their next trip. Except . . . ah, female stuff, because that might be a little hard for me to explain." He felt heat creeping up the back of his neck and turned and headed down the stairs. "If there's something you absolutely have to have, I can make a boat trip into town one of these evenings."

"Alec," she called out, making him stop and turn to her. "Thank you for being so accommodating," she said, her own cheeks turning slightly pink.

"My pleasure, lass. Why don't you pack yourself anything ye might want for the morning? You can use that smaller backpack hanging on the rear wall. Also put the satellite phone in it, would you? And you might want to bring your iPad, in case you don't find watching me shovel dirt to be all that interesting."

"But I want to help you."

"You can't. Not with that cut on your leg and bruise on your side."

"But there must be something I can do. Oh, your mattress; I can walk down to the water and gather sweet grass this morning."

"No, you can't," he repeated, grinning at her scowl. "Someone might see you. The entire fiord is crawling with tourist boats out looking at the colorful foliage and trying to spot whales and dolphins. And I wouldn't be surprised if the sheriff shows up again today with state troopers in tow, trying to figure out what two men wearing street clothes were doing out here. But," he conceded when her shoulders slumped, "I'll give you clippers and you can cut some fir tips to make me a bed if ye want."

She grabbed the small backpack off the peg. "I'll be ready when you get back," she said, giving him a princess-like wave of dismissal.

Not only was she ready, but she was standing in the trail waiting for him, her hair pulled into a ponytail, the back-pack on her shoulders with all four canteens hanging off it, and that saint-tempting smile making another appearance when she saw him. She waited while he went to the lean-to and gathered up what tools he needed, then fell into step behind him.

Speaking of ponytails, he probably should give his own hair a trim, seeing as how it was nearly as long as Jane's. Washing his face this morning, Alec had realized he hadn't shaved in over a week, either. Hell, it was a wonder the woman hadn't run screaming into the forest again when she'd awakened to find herself more naked than clothed, looking up at the hairy giant who'd undressed her. So he'd spent half an hour this morning shaving and trying to tame his own mess of dark blond hair before Jane decided to take her tiny scissors to him while he was sleeping.

"Where's Kit?" he asked over his shoulder, refusing to call the wolf Kitty any longer.

"Probably hunting, as I think he prefers something more substantial than cereal for breakfast."

"Where did ye find him?"

"I didn't," she said with a musical laugh, the sound send-ing a good number of blood cells straight to his groin. "Kitty found me. He just showed up on my doorstep one day and wouldn't leave."

"Which doorstep would that be; the one in New York City or Monte Carlo or South Africa?"

"I . . . I can't remember," she said after a long hesitation. She gave a soft snort. "I guess the bump on my head damaged a few memory cells. So, Alec," she rushed on, "how long have you worked for the resort?"

Okay then, it appeared they were going to talk about *him*. "I don't, actually. I'm what you might call a ski bum from November to late April. My family owns TarStone Mountain Ski Resort over in Pine Creek. Have you heard of it?"

"I have," she said, sounding slightly out of breath.

Alec immediately slowed down, contrite for having forgotten her sore foot. "In the summer and early fall I come to Spellbound to help my uncle, Duncan MacKeage, in his construction business. Duncan built a home across the fiord a little farther up from here two years ago, and he's been doing the earthwork for Olivia and Mac Oceanus, who own Nova Mare. You know them?"

Another, even longer hesitation, and then, "I know *of* them. So how come you're not helping your uncle finish the resort? Only the first phase is completed, isn't it? I think I read that someplace," she quickly tacked on.

"They started taking guests a couple of years ago as they built each of the sixteen planned cottages, and three of the five hotel segments opened just this month. But when Olivia mentioned that she'd like to offer backcountry camping, I volunteered to spend the summer building her a wilderness trail."

"But is it really a wilderness trail if there are bridges and shelters and privies?"

He stopped and turned, disguising his checking on her with a crooked grin. "For city-dwellers, I imagine this is about as roughing it as they care to get. Having a marked trail and lean-tos makes the deep woods less overwhelming." He shrugged. "The true naturalists still have the option of carrying a tent and compass, and stripping off to ford the rivers and larger streams."

Well, she didn't look ready to faint. In fact, except for the handprint, her face was positively glowing. So maybe he'd been a bit hasty labeling her a princess, as the woman actually appeared to be enjoying herself. "How's that bruise on your side?" he asked. "You want me to carry the pack?"

"I can handle it," she said, grasping the straps protectively.

"At least let me take the water bottles," he said, reaching toward her. "They have to be banging against your hip."

"I'm okay," she said, moving past him. "How much of the trail have you finished?"

Damn, now he was forced to watch that luscious heart-shaped bottom. He could see why she'd had the boots custom made, because those were really long legs.

"Alec?" she asked, glancing over her shoulder.

He lifted his gaze in time to see her smile when she realized where he'd been looking, and he'd swear her hips sashayed a bit more as she continued on.

"What was the question?"

"How much of the trail have you finished?"

"About forty miles. I only have this last larger bridge and five small ones left to set in place, two more shelters and privies to find locations for, and a spur trail I want to lay out that'll lead down to a pretty little grotto I found near the end of the fiord."

She stopped and turned. "What do you mean by a grotto?"

"I discovered a small sandy beach hidden at the base of a crescent-shaped cliff, and the only way to get there is during low tide. There's a shallow cave at the back that has a sweet-tasting spring flowing out of it." He used the opportunity to take the lead again. "The place reminded me of a grotto, where a couple of lovebirds could have some privacy or a person could go and think in peace."

"You're a romantic."

Alec tripped on a root and scrambled to catch himself. He'd been called a lot of things in his life, but sure as hell never a romantic. "Here we are," he muttered, setting down his tools.

"Oh, this is beautiful," she said over the gush of the water tumbling down the narrow, boulder-strewn ravine. She turned to look at where the stream continued its descent below. "This is where you're putting the bridge?" she asked, stepping up to the edge and peering down. She looked across to the other side, then back at him in surprise. "The span must be twenty-five or thirty feet! They're going to fly a bridge that large out here dangling from a helicopter?"

Good Lord, Duncan's seven-year-old twin sons didn't ask as many questions as she did. "The resort has two helicopters; one for scenic tours and one's a workhorse designed for heavy lifting, like they use out west to log the steeper mountains."

She looked across the stream to the other side again, then down the ravine and then back up it. "How come you didn't place the bridge up there where the span is narrower? It can't be more than fifteen feet between those ledges, and there would have been less work constructing the abutment," she said, pointing across the stream at the log cribbing he'd spent the last three days building and filling with rocks.

"Because if I'd set it up there, you'd miss the beauty of the falls."

She blinked at him, and then her gaze suddenly dropped and he saw her cheeks redden, as if she were . . . embarrassed. "Oh, yes, that makes perfect sense."

Alec frowned as she walked to a boulder and slipped off the backpack. Now what in hell was she embarrassed about?

"Um, did you remember to bring the clippers?" she asked, turning to him and holding out her hand—her gaze aimed in the vicinity of his chest.

What just happened? One minute she was all excited and the next she was acting like he'd kicked her. He hadn't sounded defensive when he'd told her why he'd placed the bridge down here, had he? "You really don't have to make me a mattress," he said, even as he pulled the clippers out of his hind pocket.

"But I want to." She took the clippers and turned away,

then stood in the trail with her back to him and looked around. "That seems like a good stand of fir. I'll be just over there," she said, walking to where she'd been pointing.

What in hell just *happened*?

Whatever it was, it appeared to have passed an hour later when Jane had amassed a pile of fir tips large enough for all three of Goldilocks's bears to sleep on, and for the last hour she and Kit had been watching him shovel dirt as if it were the most fascinating activity on earth. Jane would make him stop about every twenty minutes, though, and take a drink from the canteen she would hold out to him. During his last break, however, she'd snatched the shovel out of his hand and replaced it with a granola bar. So he was obediently sitting and eating, wondering when the last time was that anyone had treated him like a four-year-old—or worse, a little brother.

"When is the helicopter bringing the bridge?" Jane asked after swallowing the last of her own granola bar.

"Anytime now," he said, looking up at the sky. "The drop is scheduled for ten o'clock, but they'll call when they're on their way to make sure I'm ready."

He saw her stiffen, her gaze snapping to her backpack. "Oh, no!" she cried, her face paling as her eyes met his. She jumped to her feet. "I forgot to bring the phone!"

He also scrambled to his feet to stop her when she started for camp. "It's okay. They'll see me when they get here. It's no big deal," he added at her stricken look. He gave her a sheepish smile. "It won't be the first time I don't have it with me."

"But how will you communicate with the helicopter?"

He guided her back to the rock she'd been sitting on. "We'll use hand signals." Alec lifted her chin to look at him. "Don't beat yourself up over it, okay? You're black-and-blue enough as it—" The chopper was practically on top of them before he heard the thump of the blades over the sound of the gushing falls. "Run," he growled, lifting her off the rock and turning her toward the trail. "Hide."

"My backpack!" she cried over her shoulder as Kit bolted past her.

"They'll think it's mine," he shouted. Alec turned and looked up to see the chopper descending the ridge with the monstrous bridge hanging beneath it, and he couldn't help but grin. Damn, he loved this job; mostly because Mac Oceanus had a bottomless bank account that he didn't mind spending on whatever it took to build his wife an unrivaled world-class resort. Only much to the wizard's consternation, Olivia was determined to keep it rustically simple; the irony being that doing so had turned Nova Mare into the most exclusive resort on the planet at the moment.

"Where's your goddamned phone?" Duncan's voice boomed from the chopper's speaker as he leaned out the cargo door against his harness and glared down at Alec.

Alec waved him a cheery obscene gesture, even as he wondered what Duncan was doing running the crane instead of Pete, the guy who co-owned the chopper with the pilot. Damn, he hoped his uncle didn't want to stay for lunch.

Fighting the rotor backwash as well as the storm of blowing dust and leaves it created, Alec scaled the ravine to halfway up the falls and, after a quick glance to make sure he couldn't see Jane or Kit, reached out and grabbed the rope dangling from one end of the twenty-six-foot-long bridge. He signaled the pilot to start descending, then hopped from boulder to boulder while holding the rope until he reached the trail and gave the pilot the signal to hover.

Duncan took over the bridge's descent, working the winches as Alec swung the wooden structure into place so that the end of it lightly rested on the ledge. He then hopped onto rocks to cross the stream and scaled the other side. But instead of grabbing the rope, he took hold of the bridge itself and signaled Duncan to lower it as he manhandled it just above the log and rock cradle. Satisfied it was dead center, he signaled Duncan to lower the bridge, giving it one last shove as it dropped into place.

He shook the bridge by its rail, then stepped onto it and

jumped up and down. Giving a thumbs-up, he unhooked the cable the moment it slackened, then ran across the bridge and did the same on the other side. Duncan immediately engaged the winches to haul up the cables, then lowered a cooler tied to a rope down by hand. Alec unhooked the cooler and watched the rope retreat, then watched it return with a burlap sack full of more goodies before disappearing again.

"Hey, Grizzly Adams," Duncan shouted from the speaker as he peered down. "Have your phone with you tomorrow morning and be wearing sneakers. We're bringing three of the smaller bridges in one trip, and you're going to have to run to each brook to off-load them." Alec saw him grin behind the mike. "Or hitch a ride on the cable. Oh, and thanks for calling to tell us about those two dead men, by the way."

Alec held his fingers to his mouth and ear in the universal symbol for *I'll call you*, which he quickly followed with the signal for *go to hell, you big bastard*, then picked up his supplies and walked off the bridge to Duncan's booming laughter. The helicopter lifted, hovered briefly again, then shot down the mountain toward the fiord like an oversize dragonfly diving for prey.

"How did he know about the men?" Jane shouted over the fading thump of the blades as she came running up the trail toward him.

Alec set down his supplies. "I imagine everyone in town heard about them when the sheriff landed in Spellbound with two body bags in his boat. Don't worry; if Duncan even suspected there was more to the story, he'd have had the pilot land on the ridge and hiked down to see me." He gave a laugh when she threw herself at him and wrapped her up in his embrace. "Your secret's still safe, sweetheart."

"I'm not your sweetheart," she muttered—although he noticed she wasn't in any hurry to step away. In fact, she snuggled against him with a shiver.

"Sorry, but you are for the next week, *sweetheart*."

She snorted and leaned her head back to look him in the eyes, her own eyes narrowed. "You are not riding dangling in the air from that cable tomorrow."

"I'm not?" He sighed to hide his grin. "You want me to flat-out run seven miles trying to keep up with the chopper? It can't hover all day waiting for me to mosey along from one brook to the other."

"You will call your uncle tonight and tell him to bring one bridge at a time. And you said you guided it down with the rope, but I saw you grab the bridge itself while it was hanging by only two thin cables, and the wind from the blades was making it sway. You could have been hit in the head or pinned up against a rock."

Alec finally let his grin free. "Careful, sweetheart, or I might think you care."

"I care not to be picking up body parts." Her eyes narrowed again. "Is Olivia aware that you're taking such risks while in her employ?"

Alec arched a brow. "The Olivia you know *of*?" Her cheeks flushed, and he tightened his embrace when she tried to step away. "So well, apparently, that you're on a first-name basis with her?"

"You told me she was your boss."

Well, she had him there. Alec glanced around looking for the wolf, then kissed her beautiful scowling mouth—loving that he didn't get a kink in his neck doing so. And although Jane didn't seem real eager to participate, she didn't push him away, either. All by itself, without any encouragement from him, one of his hands slid down and cupped her heart-shaped bottom and pressed her more intimately against him.

Still no reaction, except maybe her shivering stopped.

Okay then; so far, so good. But would it hurt her to kiss him back? Because honestly? He couldn't quite tell if she was happy to have his mouth devouring hers, or just curious, or politely waiting for him to figure out that she wasn't all that impressed.

Hell, he wasn't very impressed with himself, either. Maybe he *had* been out in these woods too long. But just seconds away from giving up, Alec felt her hands slide up his back just as her head tilted to fit her mouth more perfectly against his, and her lips parted and her tongue touched his. Not hesitantly, either, but with the boldness of a woman who knew exactly what she did to men.

As for what she did to him in particular . . . well, he didn't know which was going to give first, his control or the zipper on his jeans. Damn, she felt good in his arms with her unconfined breasts pressing into his chest, her mouth fully engaged now and tasting sweeter than maple sugar, and her smelling like fir sap and fresh air and sunshine.

If this was a nightmare he wasn't in much of a hurry to wake up, he decided, finally breaking their kiss to lean his forehead against hers with a soft growl. "I'm beat. Let's go back to camp and take a nap."

Her husky laugh held a hint of alarm as she slipped out of his embrace and turned away, giving an imperial wave over her shoulder. "You go ahead, then. I wish to sit on this flying bridge and stare at the falling water and . . . think."

Alec shot around her and stood blocking the way, because last he knew, a woman sitting and thinking usually meant trouble for the poor bastard she was thinking about. "It's not safe yet. I haven't finished anchoring it into place."

"*You* walked across it." Her gaze traveled down the length of him and back up, her kiss-swollen lips turning up in a smile. "And you obviously weigh more than I do."

Lord, he was tempted to kiss her again, but was afraid if he did they wouldn't make it back to camp before he had them both horizontal. So he very nobly took hold of her hand and led her onto the bridge, stopping directly in the center to face upstream.

She clutched the railing and looked up at the falls tumbling toward them over the worn boulders, and gasped. "Oh, Alec, it's beautiful!" she cried, lifting her face to the fine mist floating on the air. "This is why you went through all the trouble of building that abutment." She turned to him, her mist-dewed cheeks suddenly flushing as her gaze dropped to his chest. "I'm sorry I questioned you earlier as to why you didn't put the bridge up on the ledges. It's obvious you knew exactly what you were doing."

He started to lift her chin but dropped his hand to his

side, realizing they were back to her looking embarrassed and him not knowing *why*. "It was an intelligent question," he said. "And one I asked myself when I first came across the falls. It took me three days of studying the ravine from every angle to decide to put the bridge here." He smiled when she finally lifted her gaze, her deep green eyes . . . aw hell, now she looked *grateful*. He turned her around so she wouldn't see his frown and guided her off the bridge. "How about we find out what goodies Duncan's camp cook—who also happens to be his mother-in-law—packed for me? I don't know about you, but I'm starved. You check out the cooler while I ransack the sack," he suggested, picking up the burlap bag.

But he waited until she opened the cooler and heard her gasp. "There's mostly beer in here," she said, picking up one of the ice-cold cans.

Alec plucked it out of her hand, popped the top and took a long guzzle, then wiped his mouth on his sleeve with an appreciative groan. "Go ahead," he said, stifling a laugh at her horrified expression as he used the can to point at the cooler. "Have one. It's good for what ails ye." *Whatever the hell that might be,* he silently added.

She closed the cover and stood up. "Thank you, but I believe I'll wait and have one with dinner tonight. Is there any *food* in the sack?" He saw a corner of her mouth twitch. "Other than pretzels?" she drawled as one of her perfectly arched eyebrows lifted. "Beer and pretzels is the preferred diet of American males, is it not?"

He pushed the sack toward her with his toe and downed the rest of his beer. "Personally, I prefer ham and cheese on homemade bread slathered with mustard with my beer," he said, lifting the cooler cover and dropping the empty can inside. He pawed through the ice and pulled out a white paper package. "Ah, Jeanine's maple-glazed ham," he said after tearing open the wrapper.

Jane snatched it away just as he was reaching for a thick slice of the ham, and immediately wrapped it back up. "Your hands are dirty, and once you start eating I'm guessing you're the sort of man who doesn't stop until it's all gone."

"There's at least four pounds there. And I was going to share."

"*After* you wash up I will make you a proper sandwich," she said, setting the ham back in the cooler next to the package of cheese. She straightened and looked down the trail, then back at him. "Do you have mustard in your food locker?"

Alec nodded on a sigh, set the sack on the cooler and picked them both up, and started toward camp. "We'll go make lunch then come back, and you can read or listen to music while I anchor the bridge into place." Dammit, half the fun of a supply delivery was immediately gobbling down some of everything.

Jane gathered up an armful of fir boughs and fell into step behind him. "Alec, can I ask you a question?"

"Aye. What?"

"Can you explain to me why you set the shelter so far from the stream? Wouldn't the hikers like to go to sleep to the sound of the falls and wake up to their beauty?"

"I set it a quarter mile away because the sound of the falls doesn't allow you to hear danger approaching."

"What kind of danger?"

"Like a thunderstorm or helicopter or . . . a woman screaming."

She grabbed his belt with her fingers—poking him in the back with a fir branch—and pulled him to a stop, then walked around to stand facing him, her brow furrowed. "Are you saying you actually consider such things when you're laying out a trail?"

"Not so much the helicopter and woman screaming," he said with a grin. "But a thunderstorm catching a hiker by surprise in the middle of the night can be dangerous. And I prefer to hear a bear nosing around *before* I wake up to find it sitting on my chest." He gave her a wink. "We might close our eyes to sleep, but there's a reason we don't have ear-lids."

Well, she didn't look embarrassed by his answer this time, but she definitely looked thoughtful as she turned away and started for camp again. Not five minutes later, she suddenly started walking backward. "That makes perfect sense." She smiled. "Which is why it's a good thing you are laying out the trail and not me." She turned back around with a decided spring in her slightly limping gait. "Would you mind if I stayed at the shelter after lunch and . . . took a nap?"

Oh yeah, Jane Smith knew exactly what she did to men. "Not at all, sweetheart," he said cheerily through gritted teeth as he watched her sashaying bottom. "I guess if you can scream loud enough, I *might* hear you if that big old bear that's been hanging around follows his nose to the cooler of ham this afternoon."

This time he was ready when she glanced over her shoulder, and he had his eyes trained on her face. "A bear?" she squeaked, looking into the woods on both sides of the trail before turning to him. "There's been a bear hanging around your shelter?"

He nodded, and smiled, and took over the lead again. "That's why I keep all the food in a sealed locker. But don't worry; Kit *might* be able to scare him off. Although," he said cheerily, "it is a really big bear. Speaking of Kit, where is your pet?"

"He ran off when the helicopter arrived," she said as she rushed to catch up.

Alec grinned at the worry in her voice, not the least bit contrite. Two could play her little game. And if the woman was going to drive him crazy, he was going to damn well make sure she did it in plain sight, since he only had her for a week. Hell, maybe he'd have to take off his shirt this afternoon while he anchored the bridge. Yeah, it had grown noticeably hot for mid-September all of a sudden.

Chapter Four

———

Apparently the threat of a big old hungry bear hanging around was enough to turn the tough and resilient Jane into a clinging vine. By the time they made it back to camp later that afternoon, Alec sorely regretted scaring her, as baby-sitting a nervous princess was enough to make even a saint take up serious drinking. He was dog tired; mostly because his poor confused blood cells had spent the day rushing to his groin, only to find out they weren't really needed and had to rush back to his *upper* brain before he said or did something else stupid.

Honest to God, this nightmare just might kill him. But at least he'd die smiling, he decided as he stretched out on the fir-tip mattress Jane had made him with the tarp he'd lugged to the bridge for her after lunch. Well, she'd made it in between bouts of rushing to him at every little noise she'd heard in the woods. Apparently escaping knife- and gun-wielding kidnappers spoke to Jane's braver side, whereas bears had her needing big strong arms to hold her while the big strong man they belonged to whispered assurances that he wouldn't let anything hurt her.

Oh yeah, he'd been thinking with his lower brain when he'd mentioned the bear, especially seeing how Kit still hadn't shown his fur-covered face since the helicopter had spooked him this morning—which implied the wolf also had selective bravery.

"I stink," Jane unabashedly announced as she came up the shelter steps, slightly out of breath from her run to and from the privy in broad daylight. "I haven't had a bath in four days."

He'd been waiting for that announcement, actually, and had spent a good part of the day coming up with a plan to accommodate her—because Jane was always so kiss-bestowing grateful when he did. "I can remedy that, but it will require a boat ride."

She straightened from sitting on the food locker trying to tug off her boots, her expression wary. "I don't wish to go into town."

"Not to town; just across the fiord. Then you have the choice of hiking a couple of miles up to a warm-water pool, or we can stay at the shoreline where the brook spills into the fiord—except the water's cooled off a bit by the time it reaches there."

She stopped tugging on her boot again, her eyes lighting with interest. "There's a pool that's warm enough for swimming?"

He nodded. "It's the temperature of bathwater. But it's a two-mile hike up the mountain," he reminded her. "In the dark."

"Didn't you say your uncle lives on that side of the fiord?"

He sat up, nodding again. "Aye, but Duncan and Peg's home is down by the shore and a good three miles from the pool."

"How far to their house from where the brook spills into the fiord?"

"About a mile."

"And how cool is the water by the time it reaches there?"

"Still warm enough to bathe in." *Without freezing off your luscious little heart-shaped bottom,* he silently added.

She stood up. "If we leave now, we could be there before dark."

Alec lay back against his duffel bag, locking his hands behind his head. "Too risky. Someone might see you in my boat. And since I've used up my monthly quota of lies on the sheriff, I'd rather not have to come up with another one—especially to Duncan—explaining what I'm doing running around with a woman nobody is missing. So, it's either go after dark or heat up water on the camp stove and take a sponge bath."

"Do you take the boat across the fiord to bathe every day?"

He grinned in anticipation. "No, I take a shower in the falls we were at today."

"But that water was freezing when I dipped my hand in it!"

"I'm a first-generation Maine highlander, lass," he said with a laugh. "My father had me and my brothers swimming in cold mountain ponds since we could walk. So, what'll it be: a sponge bath or a boat ride?"

"Are there bears across the fiord?"

He was going to hell for the lies he was telling, but Jane did seem to bring out the best of him. "Nay, I believe the beasts prefer this side of the waterway."

She nibbled her bottom lip, glancing at her larger satchel. "I didn't think to pack a swimsuit," she said, looking over at him, "because it's September in *Maine*."

He arched a brow. "So you were on your way to Maine when they kidnapped you from that Boston hotel?"

She nodded.

"Where in Maine?"

"I had rented a cottage on Mount Desert Island near Acadia National Park. But when I realized the kidnappers must have discovered my iden—my itinerary, I decided to fool them by coming inland instead."

"So you were heading to Nova Mare when they caught up with you?"

She hesitated, then nodded again. "I didn't have reservations for a cottage, though. But I thought they might have the hotel finished since the last time I was there."

"When was that?"

She walked to her satchel and opened it. "About two years ago."

Okay then; either Jane was finally getting her own lies in order, or her tall tale was actually starting to make sense to him. Well, except that she'd changed her mind about going to the resort for some reason and decided she preferred camping out in the middle of nowhere with him. "Right around the time you had your fight with dear old dictatorial Daddy," he said, "and he disowned you. Has he stayed at Nova Mare?"

She looked over her shoulder at him. "That . . . that's where we had the fight."

"Then why come back here?"

"Because this is the last place he would expect me to come."

Alec scrubbed his face in his hands, then dropped them to grin at her. "That was pretty damn smart. But let me get this straight; you came here to hide from both your kidnappers *and* your father? And no one in your family knows you're missing?"

She sat down on the sleeping bag and wrapped her arms around her knees with a nod. "And I don't believe the other man who was in on the kidnapping is aware that I'm missing, either." She looked up at the rafters and frowned. "Well, he might know by now, but he'd left to go set up for the ransom before I escaped."

Alec jerked upright. "Are you saying the ransom demand may have already been delivered? For the love of God, why did you wait until *now* to tell me?"

She went perfectly still, her eyes widening in alarm. "I thought it didn't matter, since I'm no longer kidnapped."

"But the third kidnapper and your father don't *know*

that." Alec jumped to his feet, making her scramble across the sleeping bag to the back corner of the shelter. "Jane," he said softly, reining in his own alarm. "Your father probably has the authorities in twenty different countries looking for you right now."

"I told you, he disowned me."

"And I told you that no matter what the fight was about, fathers do not turn their backs on their children when they're in danger."

She pressed deeper into the corner, hugging herself into a tight ball even as she raised her chin defiantly. "I'm not going back to him, Alec," she whispered. "Not *ever*."

He turned away and rubbed his neck, blowing out a harsh sigh. "Pack your small satchel with whatever you need for your bath," he said, walking down the steps to the trail. "We'll leave in a couple of hours, so fix yourself something to eat while I'm gone."

"Wait. Where are you going?"

"For a walk," he said without looking back. "I need to think."

"But what about the bear?"

"If it comes around, just bang some pots together to make noise," he said with a negligent wave over his shoulder. "It's more afraid of you than you are of him."

Dammit to hell; messing around with a grown woman who *wasn't* missing was one thing, but continuing to hide a kidnapping victim from her father and probably the authorities was an entirely different matter, and potentially dangerous.

Christ, they could eventually trail her here, catch sight of him with her, and shoot first and not ask questions until *after.* Or, if Daddy was as rich as Alec suspected he was, there was a chance the man would just quietly hire professionals to find her, and they wouldn't ask questions before *or* after— just like he hadn't for eight years. He used to get in, get the goods—human or otherwise—and get out; his first concern not implicating his country in the crime, his second getting out alive, and his third effectively dealing with anyone who could mess up concerns one and two.

Alec eventually reached the fiord and crouched down on his heels just inside the tree line to stare at his overturned boat. He was back to his theory that Jane was an innocent victim of a cult or fraternity crime gone bad—except how had the kidnappers known who her father was? Jane's fake IDs had been professionally made, and she'd obviously been taught to use them by someone who knew the intricacies of traveling between countries without raising any red flags. So where was this mentor, and why hadn't Jane run to him—or her—when she'd escaped?

And why Spellbound Falls, other than because she'd been here before, he wondered as he rubbed his face in his hands—only to stop in mid rub. Maybe she had been running to her mentor but hadn't quite reached him. Alec looked back toward the mountain. Maybe that's why Jane had wanted to stay at camp this afternoon; she'd intended to use the satellite phone to call and let the guy know she'd been trying to get to him when the bastards had caught up with her again.

Well, she was all alone with the phone now. And he'd bet his hunting rifle that she didn't realize he could look up the last numbers dialed on the call log. So, okay then; he was finally getting somewhere. Jane Smith, who now was most likely officially missing, obviously had someone in Spellbound Falls—because this was literally the end of the road to nowhere—who could fabricate entire identities and who cared enough about her to help pay her way.

Mac? He had the means—albeit magical—to conjure up some driver's licenses and credit cards, and he certainly had the bankroll to keep Jane in the lifestyle she was obviously accustomed to when her jewelry ran out. But then, Alec wondered with a frown, how come he'd never seen her around town the last two summers he'd been here? Jane wasn't exactly a woman who would have slipped his notice, even in the throng of tourists who'd been flocking to the

Bottomless Sea since its magical creation two and a half years ago.

But if Mac was Jane's *friend*, then why hadn't she just let him call the resort to come get her yesterday? Who else in town might have the knowledge required to invent a whole new identity? Alec stilled again. Sam Waters, Olivia's long-lost father. The moment he'd met Sam, he'd realized there was more to the man than met the eye. Rumor was Sam had abandoned Olivia thirty years ago to protect her from his enemies, and men didn't make enemies who went after daughters unless those enemies were cold-blooded killers— much like his own targets had been. Hell, he doubted Sam Waters was the man's real name. Sam's father was Ezra Dodd, who owned the Bottomless Mercantile & Trading Post in Spellbound, and he'd bet his hunting rifle again that Dodd was also a bogus name.

Christ, he'd been living with a bunch of shadows right under his own damn nose for the past two summers. Had his instincts gone to hell in a handbasket, or what? But then, Waters could have been nothing more than a common criminal and Mac could have simply . . . erased his father-in-law's past transgressions, because the wizard was just that much in love with Olivia.

Alec straightened and walked to his boat and stood staring down at it with another frown. So that meant Jane's ID-forging mentor could be anyone in Spellbound Falls. Or maybe Turtleback Station, which was a larger town on the southern end of Bottomless. Or the guy could merely be a frequent guest of Nova Mare. Jane could have called him when she'd escaped her kidnappers, but in order to keep their rendezvous a secret they could have agreed to meet out on the water. Only the kidnappers had caught up with her first, and she really hadn't had the opportunity to get in touch with him since Alec had kept her pretty well occupied today.

Alec started to turn over the boat, but snapped his head up at the sound of a wave cresting offshore. He dropped onto his belly when he saw the swirl speeding toward the small gravel beach, recognizing the unmistakable head and dorsal fin of a killer whale break the surface. There was a sudden flash of light just as a burst of energy pushed through the air with enough force to make— Sweet Christ, the whale turned into a *wolf* the moment it hit land!

It had been traveling at such great speed that the momentum nearly drove the wolf's nose into the ground as it stumbled to gain its footing, continuing up past him at a flat-out run and disappearing into the forest. Alec straightened to his knees in time to catch a glimpse of it heading up the mountain in the direction of the shelter.

He scrubbed his face in his hands—after using them to close his gaping mouth—then jumped to his feet and ran to where the whale—no, the wolf—had exited the water. His jaw dropped again as he stared down at the wet tracks that went from the dragging imprint of a broad belly and fins to paws clawing for purchase, then slowly lifted his gaze to where it had run into the forest. He swayed at the rush of blood draining from his head, and fell to his knees with a muttered curse.

Kit was an *ocean* wolf—an orca.

Which meant the woman he'd rescued *really was* a princess.

And he was a lust-blinded idiot standing neck-deep in the goddamned *magic*.

Chapter Five

━━━━━━

They walked down to the boat at dusk without talking, Jane finally breaking the silence once he pushed them into the fiord. "Please don't be angry with me, Alec," she said as she hugged Kit to her on the front seat. "I didn't tell you about the other man leaving before I escaped because it never occurred to me that it might be important."

Alec stopped with his hand on the motor cord and blew out a heavy sigh. "I'm not mad at you, Jane. I'm just not being talkative because I still haven't decided what this means for us—for you staying with me without letting anyone know you're okay."

"Is there some way we could get word to my father without revealing where I am? What about your uncle? Could Duncan help us?"

Alec looked her directly in the eyes and nodded. "Tell me your father's name and how to reach him, and I'll have Duncan get word to him."

She mutely dropped her gaze, only to suddenly lift her

head again. "What if you take me to Turtleback Station and I call him myself?"

"If the authorities are already involved, or if your father hired professionals to find you, his phone is set up to trace calls. Even if you kept the conversation short, they'd be able to trace you at least to Maine. And considering two strange men were found dead in the resort's woods, this would be the first place they'd check. And I'm only guessing here, but I'm thinking the moment your father discovers you were kidnapped, your two years of freedom will come to an abrupt end—with or without your cooperation."

She hung her head again.

"Well, I hope Kit doesn't get seasick," Alec growled as he pulled the cord and started the motor. He put it in gear and sent the boat speeding diagonally up the fiord. Dammit to hell, why wouldn't she admit who she really was? She'd been trusting him with her life and her damn *value* for almost two days, so why not her identity? Did she think he'd be so in awe of her father that he'd run up the mountain shouting he had her?

Christ, he was probably the only person in Spellbound Falls who wouldn't know her on sight, likely because he'd been in Pine Creek whenever she'd been visiting.

Had she used the satellite phone while he'd been gone? Who had she called? Certainly not Mac, he thought with a stifled snort, because the princess would right now be bathing in one of the resort's marble soaking tubs instead of heading to a lukewarm brook. He'd brought the phone, but hadn't had a chance to check the call log yet, planning to do it while she was bathing.

Alec dropped the motor back to an idle so they could talk. "What about whoever made your IDs?" he asked, ignoring that her chin tilted stubbornly at his question. "Can you call that person and have him or her contact your father?"

"What do you mean, whoever made my IDs? I am Jane Smith."

He snorted and sped up again. "Only for the last two

years," he muttered loud enough to be heard over the engine. "You do realize that if this all goes to hell in a handbasket, I'm the one who's going to be in the direct line of fire, don't you?"

Her head snapped up again. "What do you mean?"

"I mean that just as soon as Daddy gets over the shock of your being kidnapped and then returned safe and sound and *intact*, he's going to come after me."

"But you saved me."

"And then I kept you."

Up went that chin again. "I believe I kept myself."

Alec wiped a hand over his jaw to hide his grin. Well, she had him there; he hadn't exactly been keeping her tied up in his sleeping bag, now had he? And he much preferred her all stubborn and prickly to acting like a kicked puppy.

So okay then, he just had to figure out how to get them both out of this mess relatively unscathed. But he couldn't really do anything until he found out exactly what had happened two years ago between her and Daddy—preferably from the person who cared enough about Jane Smith to have fabricated her a whole new life.

Because honestly, that person must have balls of steel.

Alec nosed the boat onto the gravel beach ten minutes later and decided they'd bathe down by the fiord instead of hiking up to the pool, as Jane's limp had grown more pronounced on the walk to the boat and he was afraid she was more sore and tired than she was willing to admit. "You want me to check that cut on your thigh?" he asked as he helped her out of the boat. "The gauze can come off, but you should probably leave the butterfly bandages on a while longer."

"I can take care of it."

"Okay then, why don't you splash around first and I'll keep a lookout for two- and four-legged peeping toms," he said with a wink, handing Jane her small satchel.

She arched a brow. "And who's going to keep *you* from peeping?"

"You can," he offered, waving toward a large boulder

down the beach. "I'll be sitting right there in the open, and the full moon will allow you to see my back's turned the whole time." He lifted the backpack he'd brought for himself. "I need to call Duncan, anyway, to talk about tomorrow's bridge delivery." He nodded at Kit. "And your furry friend can stand guard on the other side. It's okay, Jane," he rushed on when he saw her looking toward the dark woods. "I won't let any bears or bogeymen eat ye, lass."

Up went that chin again. "I'm not afraid of bogeymen," she said, turning and walking toward the babbling brook. She stopped at the small waterfall spilling out of the forest into a shallow pool, turned to face him as she dropped her satchel and slipped off her jacket, then very deliberately—with provocative slowness—started undressing.

Alec looked down at Kit looking up at him. "What's the matter, the boat ride mess up your land-legs? Go on," he muttered, giving Kit a nudge with his knee. "At least one of us wolves might as well enjoy the show."

Alec walked down the beach, hopped up onto the boulder, and unzipped the backpack, then pulled out the phone. He turned it on, then held his finger to the call log button—but instead of pushing it, he looked up at Whisper Mountain looming into the nighttime sky. Did he really want to know who Jane had called? Because the moment he discovered the identity of her *friend*, he would have to wake up from his salacious dream and deal with the reality of a runaway princess whose father sane men feared and fools died at the hands of; the only problem being Alec wasn't exactly sure which category he fell into. Because honest to God, he was tempted to simply forget who Jane really was—at least long enough to help her deal with her father once and for all instead of having her spend the rest of her life hiding from the dictatorial bastard.

Aw hell, who was he kidding? What he really wanted was to keep Jane until she was so soundly imprinted on his brain that he'd go to his grave hearing her musical laugh and remembering the taste of her lips and feel her body pressing against his. He'd known her only two days, and already he was willing to throw himself in front of a goddamn bus to help her realize her *true* value.

Alec pushed the log button, took a deep breath and looked down, and frowned at the familiar number. Jane had dialed the Bottomless Mercantile & Trading Post? Had she called looking for Ezra? But the guy was over eighty years old. Sam, then? Had she been trying to reach Ezra's son and Olivia's father, Sam Waters? Alec hit the redial button and heard an equally familiar voice answer on the third ring.

"Trading Post," Grundy Watts barked out. "We're closing in twenty minutes, so talk fast, 'cause I got stuff to do."

"Grundy, it's Alec. I was wondering if a woman called there a few hours ago looking for either Ezra or Sam."

"Alec?" Grundy said, his voice softening. "Well, how the hell are you, anyway? How come you ain't been into town lately? You still owe me breakfast at the Drunken Moose, you know."

"You filled that sea bass's belly with lead when I wasn't looking, you old cheat. Any idiot could see my fish was twice the size of yours."

Grundy made a *tsk*ing sound. "And you're twice the size of me and you're still pouting like a little girl. Pony up, MacKeage, and buy me breakfast."

"Okay, next week," Alec conceded with a laugh. "But only if you tell me if a woman called earlier looking for Ezra or Sam."

Grundy snorted. "I swear I don't know what the ladies see in that quiet bastard. Hell, the guy still gives me the spooks, even after he helped me out with my . . . um, little problem last year."

Bingo. "Did she talk to Sam?" Alec asked, glancing over his shoulder to see Jane splashing around in the pool near the falls.

"No, he'd already left. And when she asked if his cell number had changed because she'd tried it several times before calling here, I told her he was unreachable this evening," Grundy said, his voice lowered in male conspiracy. "I think Sam got his social calendar screwed up and made two dates for the same night, as I saw him filch a bottle of expensive wine and a quart of strawberries out of the cooler before he left." He sighed. "Only this lady sounded a bit young for him."

Alec frowned out at the fiord. "Where is Casanova, anyway? He can't very well entertain his women at home."

"My guess is he's up at Inglenook. I think he's using the old groundskeeper's cottage for his love nest." Grundy snorted again. "It's hard for a grown man to bring his girlfriends back to his daddy's house. Although he might have done so tonight, since Olivia and Mac took Ezra with them and the kids to Midnight Bay for the weekend."

"Okay, thanks, you old cheat. I'll be in later next week to take you to breakfast."

"Early," Grundy said. "Before all the damn leaf-peeping tourists gobble up all of Vanetta's cinnamon buns."

"We'll be at the door when she opens," Alec promised with a laugh just as he hung up. He opened the call log again and scrolled down to see where Jane had dialed another number three times before finally calling the trading post, and then he sat staring up at the resort's lights on top of Whisper Mountain. So, Sam was Jane's *friend*, was he? Holy hell, the man didn't have balls of steel; they were made of titanium if he was helping her hide from her father. "How are you doing over there?" Alec called down the shoreline. "You aren't making the trout blush, are you?"

"The water's too warm for trout," she called back with a musical laugh—which sent several foolishly optimistic blood cells racing to his groin again. "Oh, Alec, this is heavenly. I could just soak here all night."

"You have ten more minutes, and then it's my turn."

Her answer was another laugh, followed by a good deal of splashing.

Alec dialed Duncan's home, only to have one of the twins answer on the second ring. "MacKeage Construction," the boy said in a winded rush.

"That you, Repeat?" Alec asked, taking an educated guess. "It's me, Alec."

"Alec!" Jacob cried. "Are you calling on the satellite phone? Where are you? You coming to visit and bringing me more rocks? I looked up that shimmery one you brought me last week, and the gem book said it was laba . . . labri . . . tite or something."

"Labradorite," Alec clarified. "It's named after the Labrador Peninsula in Canada, where it was first found. What's the book say about its powers?"

"Magic," Jacob reverently whispered. "And protection."

"That sounds like a good stone to carry in your pocket, then. Although it's probably not as powerful as the one Duncan gave you from his mountain, so maybe you should just add it to your collection. Speaking of my esteemed uncle, is he home?"

Alec heard muffled muttering, then, "Why is it you only remember ye have a phone when it suits *you*?" Duncan drawled.

"Because Pete and Clarence and I are a well-oiled team and only need hand signals. Where is Pete, anyway?"

"He flew back to British Columbia two nights ago when his wife decided to go into labor several weeks early."

"Hell, is everything okay? Have you heard anything?"

"Yeah, mama and babies are doing fine. Pete, however," Duncan said with a chuckle, "may not recover. The guy was a basket case when Clarence and I put him on the plane in Bangor, and when he called this morning he still couldn't string a coherent sentence together."

"A girl or—wait, you said *babies*. Pete didn't mention they were having twins."

"One of each."

"They had *twins*?"

"That's what they usually call the little heathens when they come in pairs. So, why aren't ye sleeping already? You're going to be busier than a one-armed paper hanger tomorrow."

"Yeah, about that; how about if you leave the twelve-footer for the next trip? That way I'll only have to run four miles instead of seven."

"How about you hop the cable? You grown soft since Afghanistan, or just lazy?"

"I'd like to think I've grown smarter."

Alec heard a snort come over the phone. "Okay, we'll only bring the bridges for the next two streams," Duncan muttered. "Speaking of pairs, what's up with the men you found, anyway? Talk in town is a lightning strike did them in, and that you're the one who stumbled across them and called the sheriff."

"Yeah, hell of a surprise. Have you heard anything about who they might be? They weren't dressed for hunting or hiking, and I found a handgun nearby. They looked like they'd been fighting each other. One had a knife sticking in his thigh, and when I checked for pulses it appeared as if they each had a broken arm."

There was a hesitation, and Alec assumed Duncan was looking around to make sure he was alone. "An execution?" Duncan said softly, not unfamiliar with damage control himself. "Or a falling-out among thieves, or maybe drug runners? The sheriff's being tight-lipped, but Spellbound and Turtleback are crawling with state police and game wardens and border patrol asking if anyone saw two men hanging around fitting their descriptions."

"And?"

"And nothing. Nobody saw anything."

"What about missing boats or abandoned cars?" Alec asked. "Any speculation as to how they ended up in my neck of the woods? The closest tote road is six miles away. That's a hell of a walk in street shoes for an execution or drug drop."

"Which means you keep your eyes open for trouble, Grizzly Adams."

"I'm hurt you didn't notice I shaved today."

"Maybe tomorrow I'll raise the winch high enough for the rotor blades to give you a haircut. Or are ye finally turning into your old man?"

"You see me running around with two small braids

dangling down the sides of my face, you have my permission to shoot me on sight," Alec growled on a laugh. "Hey, toss a pillow in the chopper tomorrow, would you? I got back to the shelter today and found mine scattered all over my campsite. Anything happening at the resort I should know abo—"

Alec slapped a hand over the phone's mike when Jane let out a bloodcurdling scream, and turned to see her running up the beach toward him.

"What in hell was that?" Duncan's voice boomed from the phone.

"Raccoons," Alec muttered as he hung up and jumped off the boulder just in time to catch the naked woman when she threw herself at him.

"There's something in the woods!" she cried as she proceeded to try burrowing inside his jacket. "Even Kitty was so scared that he ran off. It must be a bear!"

Apparently the only threats Kit felt confident going up against on land were two-legged, Alec decided as he contorted first out of Jane's death grip and then his jacket. He wrapped it around her, then pulled her back into his arms, partly to keep her from thrashing him but mostly because she was so soft and cuddly and all but still naked.

Oh yeah, he was definitely going to hell for mentioning the bear.

"Easy now, there's nothing in the woods that's going to hurt you, I promise." He kissed her forehead. "How about if I—" A god-awful commotion came from a hundred yards past the brook, quickly followed by a snarl that turned into a panicked yelp, which was then followed by a loud splash hitting the fiord.

"Ohmigod, Kitty!" Jane cried, thrashing again, only this time to get free instead of trying to burrow inside him. "We have to go save him!"

Alec took hold of the empty sleeves of his jacket to control her struggles. "The splash was too small to be Kit." Was she afraid the orca-wolf would *drown*? "It's likely only raccoons fighting over dinner." He kissed her forehead with another chuckle. "I swear they sound meaner than wolverines when they're having a family squabble."

Jane relaxed into him, wrapping her arms around his waist and resting her head on his shoulder with a heavy sigh. "I'm not a very good woods-woman, am I?" She leaned back to look him in the eyes. "And I want so very much to be one."

"Why?" he asked, brushing a lock of wet hair off her face. "What's wrong with being just you?"

Her gaze lowered to his chin. "Because I want to be a woman you would like."

Alec pressed his hands to her face and lifted her eyes back to his. "I like you just fine, Jane, just the way you are."

"You . . . you do?"

He nodded and pulled her to him, only to find himself kissing a completely naked woman when she slid her hands around his neck and his jacket fell to the ground.

"Enough to make love to me?" she whispered against his mouth.

Seeing how every blood cell in his body shot straight to his groin, all Alec could do was cup her baby-soft bottom and press her into the evidence of his desire.

"I want you, too, Alec, so much that I ache."

Nearly shouting with elation that he hadn't been the only one who'd spent today in lust-induced pain, Alec swept Jane into his arms and headed for the woods in search of a soft bed of moss. He stepped into the trees, lowered her feet to the forest floor, and popped several buttons on his shirt trying to take it off as Jane kept equally busy kissing him. He tossed the shirt on the ground and dropped to his knees while bringing her with him, then ran his fingers through her wet hair to tilt her head back and pressed his mouth to the racing pulse on her neck.

Her gasp ending with an encouraging little sound of pleasure, Jane clutched his shoulders when he pressed her back onto the shirt and carefully settled on top of her, her legs immediately wrapping around him. Alec found just enough firing cells left in his brain to realize that he not only had to get his own urgency under control, but Jane's as well. The woman might still be a virgin, but she certainly hadn't spent the last two years as a wallflower. And when her attempts to reach his belt buckle failed because she couldn't squeeze her hands between them, she started ordering him to take off his pants. Well, that is when she wasn't using her imperial mouth to drive him crazy by kissing his chin and cheeks and whatever else she could reach.

Christ Almighty, if he didn't slow her down to a reasonable speed, the few remaining cells in his brain were going to abandon their post and join the party in his jeans. He captured her pushing and tugging and kneading fingers and, being mindful of the bruises on her wrists, pressed her hands up over her head with one of his, then carefully eased his tongue out of her mouth before she swallowed it.

He rested his forehead on hers. "Here's an idea," he rasped, only to snap his free hand down to her hip to stop her squirming. "How about if we just do a little necking first, before we rush straight to the good stuff?"

She stilled, and stiffened, and tried to slide out from underneath him.

Alec settled more intimately against her. "I'm one second away from disgracing myself, lass," he whispered against her lips. "And I'd really rather not."

"Oh. Oh, I'm *sorry*," she cried, her eyes going as round as the full moon reflected in them. "I didn't realize!"

He choked back a laugh and rested his forehead on hers again. "Never apologize for holding that kind of power over a man, Jane, because that's where your true beauty lies. Will you let me give ye a small taste of that power tonight?"

She stilled again, a smile slowly lifting the corners of her mouth. "That sounds . . . delicious."

Okay then; permission had been asked for and granted.

Alec took a fortifying breath and allowed his lower brain free rein, its first order of business apparently being Jane's wonderfully full, conveniently naked breasts. "Damn, you're lovely," he murmured, kissing his way toward one of the luscious mounds as he palmed it—only to become so distracted that he lost his grip on her hands. But instead of going for his belt buckle again, Jane pulled the band off his hair and ran her fingers through it, then used her grip to guide his journey.

Oh yeah, the lass was no wallflower.

Alec ran his tongue around her beaded nipple before closing his mouth over it, smiling when she arched into him and abandoned his hair in favor of digging her nails into his shoulders. "Ohmigod, *yes*," she rasped on a moan, unwrapping her sexy long legs to lift her hips into his. "Whatever you do, don't stop."

"Not a worry, lass," he said on his way to her other breast, which he then closed his mouth over and suckled. He settled lower on her body so that his naked chest was touching her mound, which turned her responding moan into another gasp. Alec once more sent his mouth downward, relishing the feel of her heated skin quivering beneath his tongue as Jane grew restless, her hands tugging and pushing and kneading at him as he sipped a path down the tightening muscles of her belly.

She reared up, her hands going to his hair again. "Alec," she cried hoarsely in surprise. "W-what are you doing?"

He lifted his head just enough to smile at her and gently nudged her back down. "Close your eyes and focus only on feeling what I'm doing to you." He settled lower, sliding his hands under her bottom and opening her to him, and kissed her mound before lifting his head again. "Are they closed? I need ye to turn your mind's eye inward, Jane. Can ye trust me enough to take you to a wonderful place?"

"Y-you have to come with me," she softly petitioned, even as her hips lifted in anticipation. "I want us to go there together."

"Not this time," he said thickly, lowering his head to kiss her more intimately, pulling another gasp from her as she stilled on an indrawn breath.

Assured he had her undivided attention, Alec found her bud nestled in a bed of moist warmth, and lightly suckled.

Her responding cry of pleasure went straight to his groin; her thighs quivering against his shoulders as she rose into his intimate kiss. He felt her muscles contracting and slid his hands up to capture her restless fingers as every little sound she made, every shudder of her building passion, brought him closer to the edge of his own control, until Alec feared he really might disgrace himself.

And still he continued, his own mind's eye picturing Jane bathed in moonlight, her head thrown back with abandon as she spiraled headlong into the storm he was creating inside her. She was so responsive, so alive with passion that he nearly lost it when she suddenly crested. She stilled on a keening cry of release that lasted several pounding heartbeats, and Alec gently soothed her breathless journey back to reality until he felt her relax on a ragged sigh.

He slowly sipped his way back up over her heated skin to her breasts, and kissed first one and then the other of her softened nipples. He continued on to the racing pulse in her throat with a deep sigh of his own, then carefully moved to settle alongside her. She immediately rolled into his embrace and buried her face in the crook of his neck, and he pulled his shirt she'd been lying on up over her shoulder as she gave a sensuous shiver. After kissing her cheek, he used his chin to tuck her head against his chest, and grinned at the realization she was fighting back sobs.

Jane Smith might be aware of what her saint-tempting smile and sashaying bottom did to men, but it was obvious she hadn't realized all that a man could do to her. And truth be told, he was rather humbled that she had trusted him to give her a glimpse of what—or at least some of what—she had to look forward to. His brain slowly starting to function again, Alec ran his fingers through her nearly dry hair and tilted her head back. "Ye know," he said thickly, "I do believe I've never been so glad I was born male." He brushed his thumb over her flushed cheek. "Ye don't ever worry about being anyone but yourself, Jane, because you're a treasure to be cherished."

She blinked up at him, pulling in a shuddering breath.

"I . . . I don't want to be some treasure that gets locked away for safekeeping." She smiled sadly. "I want to be an ordinary woman a perfectly ordinary man could love, and live in a house overlooking the ocean that we'd fill with beautiful, ordinary children."

Alec hugged her to him again, his heart aching with the knowledge of just how impossible her dream was. "Would ye settle for camping out in a lean-to with a ski bum for a while before ye go in search of this perfect man?" He rested his lips on her hair. "Because I'm thinking that when you do find him, ye might like to have something by which to judge this paragon of . . . ordinariness." He tightened his embrace, partly to still her trembling, but mostly to tamp down the image of her with another man. And then he took a deep breath and stepped in front of the bus. "And if ye want, I will stand beside you as you stand up to your father."

She reared back. "You can't. No one can fight my father."

"You have, quite successfully for over two years." He shrugged one shoulder. "I've never much cared for the antiquated notion that men have the right to bully women under the guise that it's for their own good."

She leaned as far away as his embrace would allow. "My father's not a bully. He's just . . . he's just being a *father*."

Alec pulled her against him again to hide his smile. So she didn't hate her old man; she just didn't care to have him deciding her fate. "Does that mean you don't want me to help you remain missing?"

She tilted her head back again, her eyes narrowed. "Only if you promise that if he does find me, you won't confront him. This is *my* battle, and I won't allow you or anyone else to become casualties." Her fingers dug into his chest. "You men don't have a monopoly on waging war, you know. I might not have your physical strength, but there certainly isn't anything wrong with my brain."

"Nay." He chuckled. "And that's what really worries me."

She poked him hard enough to make him grunt. "Give me your word that you won't step between me and my father if it comes to that." She poked him again when he hesitated.

"I mean it, Alec. If you don't promise, I swear I'll disappear on you, too. I won't have your damnation on my conscience."

"Did you make the friend who helped you run away swear such an oath?"

This time Jane hesitated. "Why are you men so stubborn? You actually make everything more complicated with all your male posturing." She sighed, pressing her nose into his chest. "I'm never going to find an ordinary man to love me, am I?"

He snorted. "Sorry, lass, but I'm afraid we all become posturing, lust-blinded idiots when there's a beautiful woman watching."

Her poking fingers started stroking his chest. "Speaking of lust," she whispered, "when are you going to finish what you started tonight?" One of her really long legs ran up the length of his and wrapped around his thigh as she pressed forward into his groin. "I thought you were going to make love to me."

"I did," he growled, jerking his hips back.

"But we didn't actually . . . We never . . . And you didn't—"

"Oh, but I did, lass," he lied with a derisive chuckle. "Just like a schoolboy."

Her eyes rounded, her mouth forming a perfect *O*.

Alec kissed her, then rolled away and sat up to stare out at the fiord, noticing the tide had reached the rock he'd been sitting on. "Not that it matters, because my pants will be staying on whenever we're horizon—"

She was on her feet and running before he even finished. Alec jumped up and caught her in three strides, only to have her hand shoot out of the sleeve of his shirt and poke him in the chest again. "You're no different from all the other men," she snapped. "You haven't even met my father and you're too afraid to make love to me."

He pulled her to him before she could poke him again. "This isn't about your father, Jane, it's about *you*. And until you want to make love for all the right reasons, nothing more than what we did tonight is going to happen between us."

"What do you mean, all the right reasons?"

"I mean that until ye see me only as a *man you want* instead of a good way to get out from under your father's rule, your one lonely condom is staying in that pouch with your other precious jewels."

Her mouth opened only to snap shut again, and Alec saw her cheeks flush and her eyes well with tears.

He pressed his hands to her face to keep her looking at him. "I'm sorry for being so blunt, but ye need to know how I feel. You've managed to hold on to your virginity this long; please don't toss it away merely to win a senseless war. Give it to the man lucky enough to earn your love."

"Do . . . do you know why I'm still a virgin?" she whispered, her tears spilling free. "Because all the men I've ever been allowed to be around were too afraid even to hold my hand. And those I've been with since I've been on my own were . . . I didn't . . . I couldn't . . ." She pulled in a shuddering breath. "Never mind, I understand. If you'll be so kind as to let me stay tonight, I'll leave first thing in the morning."

"No," he growled, tightening his grip when she tried to step away. "You can't run forever, Jane. Stand up to your father here and now, with me standing beside you."

"But at what cost? Because you were right, you know; you'll be in the direct line of fire if this all goes to hell in a handbasket, and the price you could end up paying is more than I'm willing to live with."

"I'm not afraid of your father, lass."

"You should—"

He kissed her before she could finish, then swept her into his arms and carried her across the pebbled beach to the stream. "I'll make a deal with ye, then," he said over her sputtering protests, standing her next to her satchel. "Let me worry about finding a way to deal with your father that doesn't involve using your condom, and you worry about finding the best way to deal with me."

She stilled. "What do you mean, deal with you?"

"I mean," he said quietly, getting right in her face and stifling a grin when she didn't back away, "that every time I catch you lying to me or acting clueless, I'm going to kiss you. And every time you look embarrassed or grateful, I'm going to strip you naked right on the spot and do exactly what I did to you tonight."

Her eyes kept widening with every threat he made—only to suddenly narrow. "And if I catch you lying to me, I will return the favor," she snapped, giving him a shove and bending to grab her satchel.

Alec used the momentum to pivot away and headed down the beach toward the boulder. "Ye certainly have my permission to try."

"Wait, where are you going?"

"For a swim," he said without looking back.

"In the *fiord*? But it's freezing!"

"It won't be by the time I'm done. Get dressed and call your pet so we can leave. I have one more stop I need to make before we head back to camp."

Chapter Six

Alec stood several yards back in the woods, waiting to see if Jane intended to keep her promise to stay put, only to be pleasantly surprised to realize she did. He patted the spark plug he'd slid in his pocket after stashing her and Kit a mile down the shore from Inglenook—which had once been a camp for families that Olivia had run for her ex-in-laws, but was now the base for the scientists studying the two-year-old inland Bottomless Sea—and silently turned and ran through the forest to go ask a *friend* some questions. Not that the answers would make much difference, considering he'd already stepped in front of the goddamned bus. But he really couldn't imagine living with himself if he abandoned Jane to her fate despite there being a good chance he could die if he took up her battle—seeing how her father was the most powerful magic-maker on the planet and her brother the second most powerful. Christ, even idiots knew that incurring the wrath of either man was tantamount to suicide.

So what was Sam Waters doing helping Jane?

Alec stopped fifty feet short of Inglenook's groundskeeper's cottage and saw light coming from several of the windows and only Sam's SUV parked in the driveway. He crept through the shadows around the small house, hesitating at the bathroom window long enough to decide that Sam was showering alone, then slipped back to the kitchen door and silently let himself in—only to grin when he saw the table was set with candles, two wineglasses, and a sad-looking bouquet of flowers. And if he wasn't mistaken, there was a distinct smell of burning chicken in the air.

Alec walked over and turned off the oven, grabbed one of the strawberries off the platter and dipped it in the bowl of chocolate, then popped it in his mouth as he crept down the hall. He pressed his back to the wall when the shower shut off, and grinned again when the door opened and Sam came limping out wearing nothing more than a towel around his waist—only to stop mid-limp when Alec came up behind him and touched the blade of his knife to his throat.

"I have some questions to ask you, Waters, and if I don't particularly like your answers, you're going to spend a very long night watching yourself slowly bleed to death. We'll begin with why you told Carolina Oceanus to come to me if she gets into trouble," Alec quietly growled, having already figured out that Jane landing in his neck of the woods had been no accident.

"Have you ever seen my son-in-law angry, MacKeage? Because I think it might really piss him off if you kill me."

Alec pressed the knife deeper. "I'll take my chances with Mac."

Sam Waters very carefully nodded. "Which is exactly why I told Carolina to run to you if she ever found herself in more trouble than she could handle."

"Why me? Why not her brother?"

"For as much as he loves his sister, Mac's hands are ultimately tied, because when push comes to shove, she's still Titus's daughter. And in their world, that makes the old man the boss of her."

"Again, why send her to *me*?"

"Because the way I figure it, the only hope Carolina has

of ever being the boss of herself is to find a champion who understands the magic and isn't afraid of it. And," Sam rushed on when Alec put more pressure on the knife, "if I had to pick the one man who might stand a snowball's chance in hell against Titus, it's you."

"Why goddamn me?"

Alec canted the blade when Sam hesitated and slowly drew it across his windpipe. "Shit. Okay. I picked you because whenever it was decided a mission was doomed to fail from the outset, we simply sent in . . . *the Celt.*"

Alec went as still as stone. "Who the hell are you?"

"Twenty-two missions in eight years," Sam continued. "And that bastard always came back. Sometimes on a gurney, but he always returned successful."

Alec stepped away, dropping his hands to his sides.

"I personally sent him on most of those missions, although back then he was only a thick file to me," Sam went on as he rubbed his throat. He turned with a glare and wiped his bloody fingers on his towel. "But even after getting to know him up close and personal these last two years, I still can't reconcile the carefree, boyishly charming Alec Mac-Keage with the ruthless, utterly focused weapon we just had to aim and pull the trigger on." He shook his head. "Shit, half the time we expected you to blow up in our faces and the rest of the time we almost wished you would, because I swear the more difficult the mission was, the scarier you got."

"You obviously have me mixed up with someone else."

Sam shook his head again. "Your own parents don't know you as well as I do. I bet your mother still doesn't know all those packages she sent to Afghanistan through your three *tours* of duty were being opened and photographed in DC so you could write and thank her for the maple cream cookies and blue socks. And I'm damn certain your father doesn't know you had a vasectomy nine years ago." He arched a brow. "Been rethinking that decision since you got ou—"

Alec was on him before he'd even finished, this time pressing his arm to Sam's throat and the tip of his knife into the towel below Sam's waist. "You know why I always came back?" he quietly asked. "Because I had no intention of dying until I found the bastard who blew our cover on my sixth mission out."

Sam's eyes flared briefly, then suddenly narrowed. "That's why you walked away three years ago without so much as a backward glance. You didn't get out because you botched the job and got your partner killed; it all went down exactly like you planned."

The phone rang and neither man moved; Alec because he hadn't gotten all the answers he wanted, and Sam likely because he still had a knife in his groin.

"Sam, sweetie," a feminine voice said after the beep, "your not answering better not mean you plan to meet me at the door wearing only a towel again." A sigh came over the line. "You promised we'd at least get to light the candles and actually eat this time before we . . ." Her laugh was husky. "Well, I'm just turning onto the Inglenook road. Be there in a few minutes, sweets."

"Ah, do you mind?" Sam said as he carefully lifted away from the knife. "I'd really hate to disappoint my lady friend this evening."

Alec stepped away with a snort. "Now I see why you've been gaining weight this summer." He arched a brow. "You do know that Vanetta's husband nearly beat her to death, don't you, and that he *accidentally* died of carbon-monoxide poisoning when he got drunk and left his car running in their garage?"

"I know," Sam said with a nod as he adjusted his towel. "But what worries me is how you know. Netta told me everyone believes she moved here from Alabama and bought the Drunken Moose because she needed to get away from the fond memories of her dead husband."

Alec turned and walked to the kitchen. "It must be my boyish Celtic charm that makes people want to confide in me."

"Wait," Sam said, causing Alec to stop with his hand on the doorknob. "If Carolina ran to you, she must be in some pretty bad trouble. Is she in danger?"

"Not anymore, or for the time being."

"What in hell does that mean?"

"It means that I took care of two of the bastards trying to ransom her back to her father after holding her for three days before she escaped. But it also means I give her a month before she gets into trouble again."

"Shit, she was kidnapped? But how did they even know who she was? I gave her the best cover possible." He shook his head. "Knowing Carolina, she didn't go quietly." Sam's eyes darkened. "Was she hurt?"

"They were afraid Titus wouldn't pay full price if they didn't return her whole and hearty." Alec shot Sam a warning glare. "I'm nobody's champion, especially Carolina Oceanus's. And when you see her again, you two better have a little talk on how she's going about being an independent woman. Do you realize she's been lugging around a single condom, looking for an unsuspecting schmuck she can trust enough to *devalue* her before her father can marry her off?"

Sam's jaw momentarily went slack, but then his sharp gray eyes lit with interest. "You worried about looking like a trustworthy schmuck?"

Alec snorted. "Look, hell; I've pretty much been acting like one for the last two days. Jane might think that once the deed's done she'll finally be free, but she doesn't have a clue about men. Not if she thinks one condom is all she's going to need."

"No clue about men in general or you in particular?" Sam asked with a grin. "You MacKeages are rather possessive when it comes to your women, I've noticed."

That grin set off a warning alarm in Alec's gut. "Give me one good reason why I shouldn't dump her on the resort's doorstep tomorrow and let her be Mac's problem."

"Because if you do, you'll be condemning her to a loveless marriage." Sam blew out a heavy sigh. "Titus hasn't been all that worried about Carolina's safety because she wears an ankle bracelet that gives her some sort of magical protection and, I suspect, also keeps track of her whereabouts. But he's had enough of her little rebellion, and he's getting serious about— What?" Sam asked when Alec stiffened.

"Jane told me the third kidnapper cut off her ankle bracelet when he hacked off some of her hair to send with the ransom demand. At the time she mentioned it, I assumed it was just a piece of jewelry her father would recognize."

"Holy shit, they were able to cut it off? But Olivia told me no one but Mac could take off the one she wears, because it's supposed to be made of some special metal."

Alec shrugged to disguise the really loud alarm going off inside him. "Apparently the Oceanuses have some magical competition." So okay then; if Jane was no longer wearing the bracelet, that meant she shouldn't have any problem staying missing not only from Titus, but also from whomever had had the balls to kidnap her. "I can buy you one, maybe two weeks by keeping Jane with me while you fabricate a new identity for her. But once you do, she's back to being your problem."

Sam shook his head. "I doubt we have that long. Titus had already reached the end of his patience, but once he realizes Carolina's no longer wearing that bracelet he's going to turn the entire planet upside down looking for her. Hell, I heard he'd already gotten serious about searching for a husband he hopes will make her happy." He snorted, shaking his head again. "I'm pretty sure that's why Mac's planning a fancy ball for Nova Mare's official grand opening next month. And from what Olivia told me, the men are lining up from all over the world from *every century* trying to get an invitation, hoping to become Titus's son-in-law."

"How in hell can a father do that to his own daughter?"

Sam sighed, rubbing his throat again. "He's doing it because he loves her too damn much. How do you think Carolina reached the age of twenty-eight without his marrying her off before she finally found the nerve to run away? But her being on her own these last two years nearly killed him. Even Rana's been so worried that now she's actually agreeing with him that the girl needs to settle down. And if they find out she was kidnapped by someone with the power to . . . Did you really get the bastards?"

"Not all of them. There's still one other man, only now I don't even know what century he's from."

Sam paled again. "When Titus realizes someone not only had the balls but the means to get that bracelet off, there'll be casualties scattered from here to eternity with the war he's going to wage. Carolina told me what he did to his grandson's uncles when they tried to kill Mac in order to keep control of Henry." Sam stepped closer. "You can't turn your back on her, Alec. Do you have any idea what it must be like for Carolina to see her brother given the kind of power he has just because he's male, where she's being treated like a child just for being a woman? It's archaic and oppressive and a ridiculous waste of intelligence, but for Carolina it's a fact of life."

"Titus certainly doesn't treat his wife like a child," Alec pointed out. "I've seen His Royal Highness pale to the roots of his regal white hair when Rana says his name in a certain tone. She defers to him only when it suits *her* purpose."

"Theirs was a love match from the beginning," Sam snapped. "They met long before Titus built Atlantis and sank it into the sea. But what do you think the chances are of his finding a husband for Carolina who'll love her for herself rather than for the power he'll gain the day she gives him a son?"

"Why do you care about her so much?"

"I may have failed to keep Olivia from marrying a bastard the first time around," Sam said thickly, his eyes turning haunted, "but that doesn't mean I have to stand back and watch Carolina get bullied into a loveless marriage."

Alec dropped his head in defeat. "She's got this pie-in-the-sky dream of falling in love with an ordinary man who's never even heard of the magic, and living in a house overlooking the ocean that they're going to fill with babies."

"Vasectomies are reversible," Sam said softly.

Alec shot him another warning glare and finally stepped outside, slipping into the shadows as silently as he'd arrived just as headlights crested Inglenook's last knoll.

Dammit to hell, he didn't care how beautiful and passionately alive Jane was; he was *not* a schmuck—even if her
smiles did make him want to forget the promise he'd made
himself nine years ago.

Alec took his time returning to Jane as he thought about
what he knew and still didn't know as a couple more pieces
of the puzzle fell into place, and wondered if there wasn't
some way he might actually be able to use the magic to his
advantage.

Titus Oceanus was from the time of mythological gods—
himself likely a god or demigod—and had chosen to
champion mankind when his fellow gods had been fighting
over who got to control all the poor dumb mortals. So he'd
built Atlantis on which to cultivate his Trees of Life—
which supposedly held mankind's conscience as well as all
knowledge—and had hand-chosen a small group of mortals he trained as drùidhs to protect them. But when the
gods had realized what he was doing and for once had
joined together to destroy him, Titus had been forced to
scatter his Trees and small army of drùidhs to all four corners of the world and sink Atlantis into the sea.

Alec snorted. Hell, his own cousin, Winter, was a drùidh.
She was married to Matt Gregor—also known as Cùram de
Gairn—an eleventh-century highland warrior who was supposedly one of the most powerful drùidhs of all time, and
together they were protecting a new Tree of Life species
growing right here in Maine. Alec also knew about the magic
from his own father, Morgan, who was a twelfth-century
highland warrior brought to this time—along with nine other
highlanders and their warhorses—over forty years ago by a
bumbling and now powerless old drùidh named Pendaär.

As for the Oceanuses, Rana had given Titus two children,
Maximilian and Carolina. But being born of a time when a
woman's main role was that of producing heirs, Carolina
had been raised—without question, quite lovingly—to be a
wife and mother, whereas Mac had been raised to eventually

take his father's place as king of the drùidhs and protector of man's free will.

Alec finally reached the fiord and saw Jane curled up in the bottom of the boat hugging Kit, both of them bathed in moonlight and sound asleep. He crouched on his heels and scrubbed his face in his hands. Sam was right; denying a woman anything based on gender alone was a terrible waste of intelligence, and he'd bet his hunting rifle that Jane dreamed of more than just marrying an ordinary man and having babies. She'd been so excited about the flying bridge, and so determined to know why he'd spent so much energy placing it where he had, that he'd caught a glimpse of a mind that was interested in far more than producing heirs.

That is, until Jane had remembered she was merely a woman who shouldn't be questioning a man's decision to spend three days shoveling dirt. The bridge, the logistics of laying out a wilderness trail, escaping and then eluding armed kidnappers—oh yeah, there was a keen intelligence lurking behind those sharp green eyes.

And for a while at least, that beautiful body and mind were all his.

He hadn't been bluffing earlier when he'd threatened Jane about acting clueless or embarrassed, and before he was forced to give her up he intended to make sure the woman knew her sexiest asset sat on top of her shoulders. Because he really couldn't in good conscience let her loose on the world believing one lone condom was all it would take to destroy her value.

Alec stood up and started toward the boat, making enough noise to alert Kit so the wolf wouldn't go for his throat.

Only the minute Kit raised his head, Jane did, too. "Alec, is that you?"

"It's me," he said, stepping into the boat and walking past her to the motor as he pulled the spark plug from his pocket. "You can go back to sleep if ye want. It's a forty-five minute ride to the end of the fiord in this old tub, and then we still have a bit of a hike to camp." He turned with the motor cover in his hand to look at her. "Unless you feel like sleeping on a soft, sandy beach tucked in a pretty little grotto instead."

She stopped rubbing her eyes to blink at him. "But we don't have any blankets." She pursed her saint-tempting lips and blew into the air. "And it's already cold enough that I can see my breath, so how will we stay warm?"

He turned to hide his grin and screwed the spark plug back in the cylinder. "I guess we'd have to snuggle." He replaced the cover to absolute silence then turned to her again. "Ye should be warm enough sandwiched between two wolves."

That got him the smile he was looking for. "I think Kitty should be in the middle."

"It's your fanny to freeze," he said, starting the motor. He backed them into the fiord and pointed the bow north. "So, did ye sleep the whole time I was gone?" he asked when she settled against the seat facing him. "Or did ye spend it thinking about my offer to help you get your father off your back for good?"

Her chin lifted. "I spent the time trying to decide where you'd gone. Certainly not to get anything, as you came back empty-handed."

"I went to see a friend." He arched a brow at her scowl. "What, you don't think I might actually have friends?"

"A female friend, who likes you for *all the right reasons*?"

"Careful, sweetheart; I do believe you're turning as green as your eyes."

Her chin rose higher. "I have nothing to be jealous about, because I am *not* your sweetheart."

"So I'm just one more in a long line of potential lovers you've been auditioning?"

Her gaze dropped and her cheeks darkened—nicely confirming his suspicion.

Alec brought the boat to an idle and patted the seat beside him. "Come here, Jane." But when she merely folded her arms under her breasts and continued staring at the floor, he reached out and pulled her onto the seat beside him, wrapping an arm around her stiff shoulders. "The friend I went to see was male, and I swear you're the first lass I've been able to persuade to kiss me in nearly a year."

She leaned away to gape at him. "What? Are all the women in Maine blind? You're handsome and strong and . . . and . . ." The heat in her cheeks kicked up several notches and her gaze dropped. "And smart," she ended in a whisper.

Alec ran a hand down his puffed-out chest. "Ye think I'm handsome?"

A smile tugged at her mouth. "You might be, in a Grizzly Adams sort of way."

"Do you even know who Grizzly Adams is?"

Both corners of her mouth lifted, along with her gaze. "I assume he's a man named Adam who is as big and hairy as a grizzly bear."

Alec gave her a bear of a hug, then tucked her against his side and started speeding up the fiord again. "Ye mentioned that the man who cut your hair also cut off your ankle bracelet," he said as she snuggled into his shoulder. "Did ye see him do it?"

"No, I was always kept blindfolded." She frowned. "And now that I think about it, he never spoke to me directly; in fact, I hadn't even realized there were three of them until he came in and hacked off my hair and ankle bracelet. And even though I was blindfolded, I could tell he wasn't either of the men who'd kidnapped me because he didn't reek of sweat and stale beer."

Alec decided Jane must be still half asleep if she wasn't alarmed that he was asking about her *magical* bracelet. "So how did ye actually escape?"

"On the second night after their leader left the ship where I was being held, the two men went to the next room to have dinner. I know," she muttered, "because I could smell food. I also realized they were drinking, as their laughter grew louder as the evening wore on. I finally shouted that I needed to use the bathroom, and the man who tied me up again was so drunk that he didn't notice I was fisting my hands to make the rope loose. When it grew quiet and I guessed they were asleep, I made my way up on deck, climbed over the side, and swam across the harbor." She tilted her head to smile up at him. "To fool them, as I knew they would assume I would swim directly to shore."

Alec nudged her upright. "You slipped into Boston ocean water in the dark and swam *away* from shore? How far?"

She gave him a haughty princess glare and snuggled back against his shoulder. "I'm a very strong swimmer." She politely covered her yawn. "And the cold water felt good on my bruises."

Alec wiped a trembling hand over his face. Christ, she was tough. Not that Atlanteans could drown, he didn't think, but just picturing her swimming in a cold, dark harbor made him break into a sweat.

Wait; did *Jane* have a strong command of the magic?

Hell, if Kit could transform from an orca into a wolf, maybe Jane had changed into a dolphin or seal or . . . a mermaid and had swum all the way to Spellbound Falls, and that's why he hadn't found a boat. It certainly was possible, since the subterranean river Mac had created two and a half years ago flowed inland from the Gulf of Maine. The wizard had made it surface in five lakes before reaching Bottomless, specifically so sea mammals—such as dolphins and whales and *orcas* and *mermaids*—could breathe.

But if that was how Jane had gotten here, then how had the men followed her?

Unless the bastards really did also have command of the magic. Could that be why they'd been wearing those medallions? Did the symbol have something to do with black magic, maybe?

Alec wiped a hand over his face again at the realization that besides helping Jane escape her father's rule, he also needed to protect her from an unknown and equally magical enemy who didn't seem all that worried about incurring the wrath of Titus Oceanus.

Talk about heavy baggage; Christ, could he pick his sweethearts or what?

Chapter Seven

———

The second full day of his salacious dream began when Alec woke up to find Jane sprawled on top of him, her unconfined breasts nestled into his groin, her mouth apparently drooling all over his chest because his shirt felt wet, her hands tucked into his armpits, and her hair tickling his chin as it tumbled out from under his jacket that he'd thrown over her sometime in the night.

Okay then, it would appear the princess preferred sleeping on a hard—in some places uncomfortably hard—body as opposed to a bed of soft, malleable sand. But if all of Jane's wonderfully sexy body parts were accounted for, then what was wafting the smell of fish over—

Alec snapped open his eyes with a silent curse.

For christsakes, Kit was using his head for a pillow!

Alec carefully slid his hand from under Jane's fleece and took a swipe at the wolf, making Kit scramble away in a shower of sand. Not that any landed on Jane, though, because she was still snuggled under his jacket, completely oblivious. Alec wiped the sand out of his eyes and Kit's drool off his forehead, and grinned out the shallow cave at the puffy white clouds lazily marching toward the rising sun.

Oh yeah, he really didn't want to wake up anytime soon.

He slid his hand back under Jane's fleece while also moving his other hand to palm the sides of her luscious breasts—that were doing a fine job keeping his groin warm—not at all contrite to be copping a feel off the sleeping woman. Because hey, permission had been asked for and granted—and acted on—last night across the fiord.

Lord, he hoped he caught her acting clueless or looking embarrassed or grateful today so he could make good on his threat to take her right on the spot—assuming he could catch her after running flat-out for four miles setting two bridges. He should probably position her at the second drop site, he decided, so she wouldn't try to keep up with him—assuming he could persuade her there wasn't a big old bear hanging around.

Alec wondered yet again how he felt about Sam telling Jane to seek him out if she ever got in trouble. But probably more disconcerting, Waters knew who he was—or rather, who he'd been. And that had him wondering if the bastard might try to blackmail him into *remaining* Jane's champion, figuring even *the Celt* wouldn't dare retaliate against the father-in-law of a powerful wizard.

Alec frowned at the clouds. Mac was probably the least of his worries, though; because if push did eventually come to shove, Titus would likely be the one chopping him into tiny pieces and feeding him to the orcas.

Unless he could find some way around the old man's magic.

Yeah. Everyone had an Achilles' heel, even demigods. So what was Titus's weakness—other than loving his daughter so damn much that he was determined to see her happily producing heirs for some power-hungry bastard?

Alec blew sand off his lips with a stifled snort. Christ, it would appear Jane really had come up with the easiest way to trump her father. Well, except for the poor schmuck she eventually conned into devaluing her, when the guy found himself standing at the altar with a shotgun at his back and then had to spend every night of the rest of his sorry life in Jane's bed.

Dammit; he didn't want an ordinary schmuck to get Jane, especially not some idiot who couldn't stop ogling her long enough to realize there was a sharp, inquisitive mind hiding behind those sexy bedroom eyes. Jane needed a man who saw her haughtiness for the defense it was, who liked that she dared to lie right to his face, and who didn't mind that she came with a whole bunch of baggage. At the very least she deserved someone who wanted her *despite* who her father was, and who would willingly step in front of a goddamn bus if that's what it took to prove her value.

Basically, someone like . . . him.

Except she couldn't have *him*; partly because he couldn't give her a house overlooking the ocean and filled with babies, but mostly because he simply wasn't that cruel. Messing with Jane for a couple of weeks was one thing, but giving any woman happily-ever-after had ceased being an option nine years ago. Hence the vasectomy, for in case he ever forgot what a cold-blooded, murdering bastard he was.

Alec sighed when he felt Jane suddenly stiffen, guessing that not only was she trying to figure out how she'd ended up on top of him, but also how she was going to extricate herself from the decidedly provocative position. So of course, being the bastard he was, he brushed his thumbs along the sides of her breasts—only to jackknife upright with a grunt when she scrambled off him. He managed to keep from being emasculated, but wasn't quite quick enough to catch Jane before she landed on her lovely backside with a yelp of surprise.

Kit, however, was more than fast enough to jump between them with his hackles raised and his lips rolled back—which the scowling princess didn't seem in any hurry to squelch. Half-tempted to finally establish his position in this ragtag little wolf pack once and for all, Alec instead rubbed his face in his hands. He then rolled to his knees and stood up, walked over to Jane, and lifted her chin. "Morning, sweetheart," he murmured, giving her a kiss before turning away to hide his grin when she started spitting sand off her lips. "It's a good thing you woke up when ye did. The tide's coming in, and I really wasn't looking forward to carrying you through two feet of ice-cold seawater."

His grin widened when Jane stood up and silently marched toward the end of the crescent-shaped cliff, Kit dutifully trotting behind her. Alec picked up his jacket and followed. "I've been thinking," he said to her ramrod-stiff back, "that since ye seem to be pretty well recovered from your kidnapping, it might be time I put you to work."

That turned her around. "Women's work?" she said ever so softly. "Like cooking your meals and washing your clothes and polishing your boots?"

Alec continued past her, deciding it was too early in the day to be walking behind that lovely backside. "No, I was thinking more like having you hike the trail I've already marked out and deciding where to place the next shelter." He glanced over his shoulder to see she'd stopped and was gaping at him, then continued along the point of land toward the boat he'd beached several hundred yards up the shore. "Assuming ye have a good sense of distance, as I've been trying to keep them spaced between four and five miles apart."

He heard her running to catch up and let her pull him to a stop and turn him around. "You want *me* to choose the next campsite location?"

He nodded. "If you're feeling up to it. But if you're still too sore to be hiking that far, then I guess you'll just have to spend another day hiding from the helicopter."

"But I don't know any— What?" she said when he suddenly narrowed his eyes.

Alec pulled her into his arms and kissed her quite soundly before heading for the boat again. "I warned you what would happen if I caught you acting clueless."

He heard her footsteps in the gravel rushing up behind him, only this time she poked him in the back. "That wasn't cluelessness, it was surprise." She pulled him to a stop again and Alec turned to see Jane's eyes had narrowed. "You can't just kiss me or do that . . . other stuff whenever you merely think I'm acting a certain way," she ended in a whisper, her gaze dropping to his mouth and her entire face turning a dull red.

Well, it appeared she wasn't saying he couldn't follow through on his threats, only that there needed to be some ground rules. "Okay then," he said just as softly. "What's your definition of acting clueless?"

Apparently hearing the amusement in his voice, her gaze snapped to his and her eyes narrowed again, even as the beginning of a sinister little smile tugged at her mouth. "Well, I suppose I will have to catch *you* acting clueless or embarrassed to give you an example," she said, pivoting away—and taking the lead again, he couldn't help but notice. "Why do you set the shelters only four or five miles apart?" she asked, a decided spring in her step, which sent several of his foolish blood cells heading south. "Surely hikers would travel two or three times that far in a day."

"I'm assuming there's going to be more than one party of guests using the trail at any given time, so there need to be plenty of campsites. But bunching them together sort of defeats the wilderness experience, wouldn't ye say?"

She glanced over her shoulder with a frown, only to catch him lifting his gaze to her face. She marched back and palmed his cheeks, and being so tall was able to kiss him full on the mouth—rather robustly—before heading down the beach again. "I've decided that when I catch you ogling me, I'm going to kiss you," she declared with an imperial wave over her shoulder. "Now, about where the next shelter should be placed; do you swear you're not just humoring me, and that you'll simply change the location if you don't agree with where I think it should go?" She stopped and marched back to him again. "Because if I suspect that's the case, *my* pants are staying on and *yours* are coming off next time," she growled, poking him in the chest for emphasis—which she completely ruined by blushing.

"Ye certainly have my permission to try," he said cheerily, taking the lead again.

*   *   *

Alec MacKeage was a scoundrel, Jane decided later that morning as she and Kitty ambled down the trail looking for the next perfect campsite. Oh, the man might be fast and strong and brave, which was nice if she happened to need rescuing, but that certainly didn't make him condom-worthy.

Not for the first time, Jane wondered why Sam had been so adamant that she run to Alec if she ever got into trouble. Because honestly, the guy didn't seem all that bright. Well, he might be smart about anything to do with the outdoors, but he hadn't even found it strange that she had suddenly shown up in his woods with no reasonable explanation as to how she'd gotten here.

He didn't appear very motivated, either. According to his driver's license, Alec was thirty-two years old, and yet he was a self-admitted ski bum at his family's resort—he certainly hadn't gone far looking for work—and took any old odd job he could find during the summers. And she really couldn't understand why Sam had repeatedly warned her against making Alec angry, considering the rake seemed more interested in kissing her than taking her own warnings about her father seriously.

So what made Sam think an underachieving, oversexed scoundrel could be her champion? Well, besides his being a MacKeage, which meant he understood the magic. And Alec was big and strong and apparently good in a fight. But the man was much too handsome—in a grizzly bear sort of way—and far sexier than any of the full-of-themselves buffoons she'd dated over the last two years. Heck, one of the self-important jerks had actually taken her out into the Mediterranean on his yacht for their very first date, popped the cork on an expensive bottle of champagne at dinner, and boldly stated that he expected her to "put out or get out."

She'd given the jerk a toe-curling kiss for dessert, sent him to his mirror-clad stateroom with instructions to get ready to experience a night in heaven, then jumped overboard and swum back to Monte Carlo—making his night

and ensuing days sheer hell as he tried to explain to the authorities why he'd called in a distress signal when Jane
Smith was seen all over town shopping with friends the very
next day.

Yes, she'd kissed her share of frogs without finding one
who even came close to deserving her. So what if she was
being too fussy—although she preferred to see it as discern-
ing; shedding her virginity didn't have to be at the expense
of her dignity.

But after she'd awakened in Alec MacKeage's sleeping
bag wearing only his T-shirt, and considering how he'd gallantly come to her rescue and fixed her hair and given her his
bed, Jane had thought she'd finally found a man she could
trust not only with her body but also with her tender feelings. Only he'd turned out to be nothing more than a scoundrel; first for making her want him with every fiber of her
being, then for giving her a taste of unbelievable pleasure—
only to then tell her he was keeping his pants on until she
wanted him *for all the right reasons*.

Sweet Athena, this was the twenty-first century; what
more reason did a woman need than simply being attracted
to a man? If she'd wanted a noble atavist, she would have
spent the last two years searching *previous* centuries.

Jane stopped at the brook cutting across the trail, slid off
her backpack, and knelt down to cup her hands in the crystal
water. She splashed some on her face but stopped short of
taking a sip, remembering Alec's warning to drink only
from a bubbling spring if she didn't want to find herself
spending the night making several trips to the privy.

"Kitty, no," she said, pulling him away when he started
lapping the water. "There might be tiny bugs in there that
could make you sick." She sat down right in the middle of
the trail and hugged the wolf, rubbing her cheek on his fur.
"You are such a good friend, Kitalanta, for leaving your
watery world to come keep me safe in mine. But just think
of all the wonderful tales you'll have to tell your pod-mates
when you return," she murmured, giving him a squeeze.
"And I will make sure your heroics are known far and wide

throughout all the oceans." She gave him a kiss and straightened away with a laugh. "And all the lady orcas will be vying for your attention, and you'll turn into a vainglorious old lug just like Leviathan."

Jane rested back on her hands, closing her eyes and lifting her face to the noontime sun with a heavy sigh. "I still don't know what to do, Kitalanta, as I'm beginning to think that hiding out here is only postponing the inevitable." She pulled over her backpack to use as a pillow and lay down, running her hand over Kitty's fur when he flopped down beside her and rested his chin on her stomach. "Alec seems to think he can help me get free of Father." She snorted. "Without using my condom. But if you ask me, he's the one who is clueless. Oh, he knows who Titus Oceanus is, since he's familiar with the magic, but I would bet my emerald necklace that he'd be singing a different tune if he knew *my* real name." Jane lifted her head so Kitty could see her scowl. "Sam made a mistake sending me to him. Alec won't take my virginity, and he's going to get himself killed if he tries to stand up to Father." She flopped back with another snort. "So I guess it's up to *me* to protect *him*. By the gods, men are—"

Jane stilled at the sound of heavy thumping. "Oh no, the helicopter! Come, Kitty," she cried, grabbing her backpack and jumping to her feet. "We were supposed to be well past this brook by the time they got here," she said, splashing through the knee-deep water and running farther down the trail.

Certain that she'd gone far enough, Jane pulled Kitty behind a large tree and looked up at the sky, only to gasp at the sight of Alec sitting on the bridge dangling beneath the helicopter. "You idiot!" she half shouted, half growled over the loud pounding of the blades. "You were supposed to run here, not fly!" She crawled over to a moss-covered boulder closer to the brook. "I swear I will kill him myself for pulling such a stupid stunt," she muttered, hauling Kitty behind the rock with her. "The lazy bum wasn't being thoughtful letting me locate the next shelter; he only wanted me out of the way so he wouldn't have to run four miles."

She flattened against the rock and had to raise a hand to protect her face when the rotating blades created a windstorm of dust and blowing leaves, then she had to grab Kitty when he tried to run off. Jane's heart rose into her throat when she saw Alec was now hanging off one end of the bridge as it slowly descended through the trees, and she stopped breathing altogether when he suddenly reached out and snagged a wildly blowing branch to maneuver the bridge past a bent tree—only to then grab another branch and use it to swing himself to the ground!

Jane decided killing the idiot was too kind, and vowed to find a way to scare twenty years off his miserable life for scaring ten off hers.

Ignoring the rope dangling beside him, Alec grabbed hold of the bridge itself with one hand while signaling with the other; she assumed first to the crane operator when the structure stopped descending, then to the pilot when she saw the bridge moving upstream through the wind-battered trees. He signaled again and the bridge stopped, hovered momentarily, then slowly descended toward two large, flat rocks positioned on either side of the brook a dozen paces up from the trail. Alec then started pushing and tugging on the bridge, his muscles straining against his shirt as he wrestled the swaying structure into place.

Jane hugged Kitty to her, undecided which warring emotion was making her tremble: abject horror at the risk Alec was taking, sheer awe at how effortlessly he made it appear, or blatant envy of his obvious joy. She turned to lean her back against the boulder and buried her face in Kitty's fur, no longer able to watch. Sweet Athena, what she wouldn't give to experience that kind of passion, where time stopped and the world receded to nothing but the excitement of the moment.

Was that what Alec was doing out here in the wilderness, experiencing the joy of simply being alive, with no obligations to anyone but himself? No rules to follow but those of Mother Nature, no clocks saying it was time to get up or eat or go to bed, no reason to shave or even bathe if he didn't wish to?

With no one constantly reminding him who he was and how he should act?

Was Alec MacKeage really not very bright, or was he wise beyond his years?

Jane pulled in a shuddering breath as she looked toward the brook—only to gasp again when she saw Duncan Mac-Keage descending through the trees on the cable. "Ohmigod," she said, crouching lower and pulling Kitty down with her. Why was he here? And more importantly, how long was he staying? Could the cable pull him back into the helicopter, or did he intend to spend the night? Because she was fairly certain that had been a pillow dangling from his belt.

She had to get out of here, as Duncan would immediately recognize her even from a distance. And then he'd ask his nephew what he was doing with Maximilian's sister, and she really would discover what Sam meant about not making Alec angry when he realized the full scope of her lies to him.

Jane's heart sank when the helicopter lifted away and she heard the men talking above the fading thump of the rotor blades. She glanced over the rock again when Duncan gave a deep laugh and saw him clap Alec on the shoulder hard enough that Alec stumbled toward the stream. Only instead of retaliating, Alec jogged up to the bridge and gave it a shake before stepping onto it and jumping up and down.

"Have ye noticed any other odd happenings in the woods since finding those two dead men?" Duncan asked, tossing the pillow on the ground and following. "Because I've been feeling a strange energy around here lately."

Alec walked off the bridge and knelt down to look underneath it. "It's probably just Leviathan. Now that the kids are back in school, that love-struck old whale is depressed because he isn't getting his daily dose of gummy worms."

"No," Duncan said, stopping beside Alec and crossing his arms. He shook his head. "This energy feels . . . aggressive."

Alec stood up. "Where have ye been feeling it, and for how long?"

"Out on the fiord, mostly. The first time was the day after that freak thunderstorm killed those two men." Duncan shrugged. "Since then it's been coming and going in pulses, like a wave that's moving closer." He rubbed the back of his neck. "I don't know what in hell it is, just that it doesn't feel . . . right."

"What does Mac say about it?"

"Only Olivia and the kids and Ezra came back from Midnight Bay yesterday, because Mac and Trace Huntsman headed out in Trace's lobster boat to go visit Titus when he suddenly called them. I did manage to get through to Mac on his cell phone before he and Trace left, and when I told him I've been feeling a strange energy around here, he said I'm probably just overly sensitive to the magic—which isn't uncommon, apparently, as he claims it takes years to master the kind of power he gave me. Then he got a bit aggressive-sounding himself," Duncan said with a grin, "saying it was probably leftover energy from his parents' last visit, which they've grown too fond of doing lately. But when I told him it was getting stronger, not weaker, he decided it must be some of the *more distant* guests trying to get here for Nova Mare's grand opening ball." He shook his head. "Apparently some of them haven't quite mastered the art of breaching time."

Jane sucked in a breath, hugging Kitty so tightly, he gave a soft whine. Father and Mother kept visiting Nova Mare? Sweet Athena, did they keep coming here hoping she'd cave in and finally come see Mac? She pulled in another shuddering breath, realizing that for as hard as her exile had been on her, it likely had been even more heartbreaking for her dear mama. And precious baby Ella; she hadn't even held her new niece, having only seen pictures of Mac and Olivia's sweet baby girl that Sam had texted her—pictures that had been in the cell phone the bastard who'd cut her hair had tossed on the floor and ground under his boot.

Jane peeked over the top of the boulder again in time to see Alec shake his head at Duncan. "Then if Mac's not worried about the energy, why are you?"

"Because apparently it's my *calling* to protect this area," Duncan growled, waving toward Bottomless, "because His

Royal Pain-in-the-Ass is too busy protecting everyone else's goddamn free will but mine."

Jane saw Alec break into a grin. "That'll teach you to ask for a mountain."

"I didn't ask! The bastard just up and gave me one." Duncan strode onto the bridge and stopped on the other end to point across the fiord. "And every time I need its energy, the contrary thing is *napping*." He reached in his pocket and pulled out a tiny piece of red material and waved it like a flag. "Just like it was sleeping last night, when it should have been scaring off the owner of these panties."

Jane slapped a hand to her mouth to stifle a gasp.

"I found them snagged on a rock in the brook where it comes out onto the beach when I was walking the dog," Duncan continued. His eyes narrowed. "Didn't I hear that rattletrap old boat of yours go by the house last night around eleven o'clock?"

Alec snorted and got down on his knees at his end of the bridge. "Sorry, uncle, but that lovely bit of lace isn't my style—or my size."

Jane leaned back against the rock again and covered her flaming cheeks with her hands. Uncertain of Alec's mood last night when he'd finished his swim in the fiord, she hadn't dared mention not being able to find her panties. She peeked over the boulder again to see both men on the upstream side of the bridge, stacking rocks against it at each end—she assumed to keep the flowing water from undermining the large, flat rocks Alec had set into place as abutments.

Their conversation continued, only now she no longer could hear what they were saying, and Jane wondered if she dared creep closer or if she should make a run for it while they were occupied. "Let's go, Kitty," she whispered, pushing the wolf toward the woods on the downside of the trail. She crawled on her hands and knees as silently as she could, hoping the babbling brook covered the sound of the crunching leaves.

Dammit to Hades, how long was Duncan staying? Because she really didn't want to spend the night sandwiched between Kitty and a rock, trying to hear a bear before she woke up to find it sitting on her chest. Jane stopped mid-crawl. Oh no; if Duncan went back to the shelter he'd see her satchels!

She started crawling again, only this time at a diagonal back toward the brook until she was far enough down the mountain that she could stand up without being seen, then started running through the forest toward camp.

Chapter Eight

His patience gone and his mood as black as the cloud-covered night, Alec waved an obscene gesture over his shoulder as he opened the throttle on his brand-new shiny boat and headed across the fiord. Christ, his uncle could be long-winded sometimes, and he should have anticipated that Duncan would insist he come up to the house when Alec had taken him home. And that, of course, had led to his staying for supper, then to his having to smile his way through a campfire with Peg and the kids if he didn't want to look suspicious, because they *always* had a campfire when he visited. Then he'd had to act all excited when Duncan had pulled a tarp off the bigger, faster, heavier boat he'd needed at the *beginning* of the season, not the goddamn end of it.

And the entire time he'd been basking in the glow of family, all he'd been able to think about was Jane alone back at the lean-to, curled up in the corner with all the lanterns blazing, hugging Kit as she held two pots to bang together.

He'd spent the afternoon working himself into a good fit of frustration, starting when state troopers had shown up to ask more questions about the dead men since the rain had wiped out any usable evidence. Then he'd worried that Jane would suddenly come strolling down the trail, all while he kept finding excuses to keep Duncan away from camp. And he still didn't know if his uncle suspected anything or not, because even without the magic he had now, Duncan had always been a little too astute—which certainly kept Alec on his toes and his lies to a minimum, especially when they talked about their respective *tours* of duty. That's why he'd served occasional months in the Afghan mountains between missions, just so he could sound like he knew what he was talking about with his cousins and brothers and long-winded uncle.

Duncan had flown Black Hawks in Afghanistan and Iraq, their cousin Robbie MacBain—who also happened to be their clans' magical Guardian—had spent several years in special ops, and another MacBain cousin was in the coast guard. Alec had supposedly been a marine, and his three brothers had been equally diverse: Ian had also been in special ops, Hamish had served on a carrier, and their younger brother, Seamus, was right now trying to make sense of the truckload of documents they'd found in Bin Laden's lair. All of which made for some interesting conversations whenever they all managed to be home at the same time.

But every MacKeage and MacBain male was expected to serve at least one stint in the military, because they were first and foremost *warriors*. After that they were college-educated businessmen, expected to take over the ski resort and the MacBain Christmas tree farm when their fathers finally retired—which at the rate the elders were aging probably wouldn't be for another thirty years. And all first-generation highlanders, male and female, were expected to help rebuild their respective clans to the greatness they once were, albeit in twenty-first-century Maine instead of medieval Scotland.

And Jane thought *she* had a dictatorial patriarch; near as Alec could tell, eleventh-century highlanders determined to hold on to the old ways were just as inflexible. Hence his quiet vasectomy nine years ago, as he couldn't quite see a cold-blooded bastard having little heathens of his own after murdering someone else's child.

Instead of going to the small beach where he usually stowed his boat, Alec aimed for the rugged shoreline directly below camp, only slowing down at the last minute to allow the backwash of the transom wave to push him onto the ledge. He tilted up the motor and strode over the seats, jumped onto the ledge and grabbed the bow, and pulled the heavier new boat completely out of the water. He tied it to a stump for added insurance, then headed into the pitch-black forest.

And while dodging trees, he ran several apologies through his mind.

He probably should start by apologizing for not anticipating that Duncan might need an afternoon of male bonding, then move on to his having a belly full of venison roast while Jane had likely finished off the tin of trail mix. Yeah, then he'd cook her a big plate of pan-fried potatoes and ham, and dig out his bottle of Scotch and coax her to down a couple of shots to take the edge off her haughty princess anger.

Lord, he hoped she'd been far enough down the trail that she hadn't seen him flying to the second brook, or he'd be apologizing for that, too. And last but by no means least, he was going to admit he'd made up that goddamn bear.

He'd just reached the trail not a hundred yards south of camp when he felt the first raindrop, and broke into a run with muttered a curse. But the fine hairs on his neck stirred when he didn't see any light coming from the lean-to, and a chill ran up his spine at the absolute silence but for the rain hitting the dried leaves still clinging to the trees.

"Jane," he called out. "It's just me, lass, and I'm all alone," he thought to assure her on the chance she'd seen Duncan with him earlier and was hiding. "Jane? Dammit, woman, say something!" he snapped as he scaled the lean-to steps. He lit one of the lanterns and hung it back on the rafter, then dropped his jaw in disbelief as he gazed around the neatly organized shelter—which he noticed *didn't* include Jane's satchels.

He squatted onto his heels and rubbed his face with a growl. Where in hell was she? She'd obviously caught sight of Duncan this afternoon and snuck back to hide her belongings and then herself; but where? He rose to his feet, grabbed the headlamp out of one of the pouches on his larger backpack, and ran down the steps and up the trail toward the ledge where he'd hidden her the afternoon the sheriff had come for the men. Christ, she had to be cold and hungry and scared to death, and probably soaking Kit's fur with her sobs.

That damn wolf had better not have abandoned her, or he was skinning it alive.

He slid the lamp onto his head as he ran, and adjusted the straps and turned it on just as he left the trail to once again weave up through the trees. "Jane!" he shouted as he approached the ledge. "Answer me, lass."

Only the beam of his light revealed nothing—no woman, no satchels, no wolf. He stepped under the outcropping to get out of the rain and took a steadying breath when he felt himself start to shake either in fear or anger—or both. Had she gotten lost? Or found someplace else to hide? Or had she finally had enough of camping out with a lust-blinded idiot and had hiked up the mountain to the resort?

Give me your word that you won't step between me and my father, or I swear I'll disappear on you, too, she'd threatened when he'd offered to help her stand up to Titus. Alec wiped a hand over his wet face. Sweet Christ, had she *swum* away?

But Carolina Oceanus, aka Jane Smith, had arrived on an unnatural storm. And he hadn't heard any thunder today, and this rainstorm was a plain old everyday cold front moving through.

Then where *was* she?

He suddenly stilled. The grotto; the intelligent woman had figured out it was the one place a big old bear wouldn't be able to reach her. And the shallow cave offered shelter from the rain and wind, and it had a bubbling spring and a floor of soft sand.

It was a hell of a hike carrying two heavy satchels, though, and there weren't any trees so she couldn't build a campfire to keep warm. There wasn't even any driftwood, because the point of land that kept the cove hidden protected the beach from waves.

Alec scrambled back down to the trail and started running again, realizing it was high tide, and by the time he made it to the grotto he'd still have to wade through several feet of cold seawater to reach it. He took the lean-to steps in one stride, pulled down the large backpack he always kept packed, and stuffed some dry clothes on top of the small camp stove and mess kit and dehydrated food. He then wrapped his bottle of Scotch in one of his shirts and shoved it on top of his clothes with a snort, figuring he was going to need a couple of shots himself before this night was through.

Hell, maybe he'd get them both drunk.

He rolled up his sleeping bag and attached it to the pack's frame, then dug the rain shield out of one of the pouches, slipped it on over the pack, and secured it in place. He put on a dry shirt and his jacket, then settled the heavy pack over his shoulders and cinched the waist belt, took one last look around before dousing the lantern, and headed down the stairs. Reaching the trail, he adjusted his headlamp with a heavy sigh and started north at a steady but ground-eating pace. He estimated it would take him maybe ninety minutes to reach the turnoff, then another full hour to reach the point of land—assuming he didn't slip in the mud during the steep descent and break his neck.

By God, Jane had better be rehearsing a couple of her own apologies, first and foremost for making him run up and down the mountain several times because she couldn't be bothered to leave him a clue as to where to find her. Why hadn't he thought to make a plan for in case they got separated? Apparently he *had* been out of the game too long, or else he wasn't used to planning anything around anyone else. After his murderous sixth mission, he'd insisted on operating alone—that is until his last time out, when he'd agreed to take along an old partner.

Oh yeah, he definitely hadn't looked back when he'd walked away.

Two hours later, figuring he was about a mile past the last bridge he and Duncan had set, Alec bent at the waist and braced his hands on his knees to fight the heaving in his stomach. Damn, running flat-out on a full gut while carrying a forty-pound pack was hard on a body that had spent the day wrestling flying bridges. He could already feel his muscles threatening to cramp, and he still had over an hour of treacherous going.

Yeah, well, he better find the smart little princess tucked safe and sound in the grotto, or she was going to discover that dear old dictatorial Daddy was actually a saint compared to an angry Celt.

Seeing the power gauge start to blink, Jane shut off her iPad with a sigh, hoping the sun came out long enough tomorrow to use her solar charger. "I guess it's time we call it a night, Kitalanta," she murmured, giving her friend a pat when he lifted his head off her thigh. She looked out at the cove and sighed again, realizing she couldn't even see the dark outline of the point because it was raining so hard. "I guess Duncan did spend the night after all." She snorted. "Or else Alec couldn't be bothered to hike—"

Jane stilled and pressed a hand to her suddenly pounding chest when Kitty gave a soft growl at the sound of splashing coming from the cove. She snapped off her flashlight and scrambled deeper into the cave, then stilled again when she saw the shadow of an unnaturally tall man wading through the waves.

Sweet Athena, had her father somehow discovered she was here and come after her? Because the only men she knew who ever made themselves that tall where Titus and Mac, and then usually only when they were using the magic. But she sighed in relief when the dark figure called out, realizing he was hoarsely shouting *Jane*, not *Carolina*. "Alec!" she cried, jumping up and rushing into the driving rain. "I'm here!"

She stopped at the water's edge, but then scampered back when he stepped onto the beach and dropped whatever he'd been holding over his head and collapsed to his knees. His hands suddenly shot out and snagged her waist, and he pulled her down to him and folded her into a crushing embrace. Jane stopped struggling when she realized he was shaking uncontrollably, his chest expanding on ragged pants as he buried his face in her hair, and she wrapped her arms around him to find he was freezing and his jacket was soaked through.

"Alec, come," she said, struggling to get free. "We need to get you dried off. Alec," she whispered, touching her lips to his ice-cold face when his embrace merely tightened. "Sweetheart, come on," she gently urged just as a tremor shot through him, jerking them both. "Come into the cave with me. I'll have you warmed up in no time."

But he still refused to let her go, muttering something about a bear, his rasping breaths heightening her alarm. For the love of Zeus, had the bear been chasing him? She kissed his drawn cheek. "It's okay, I won't let that mean old bear hurt you. You're safe now, I promise."

She was finally able to wiggle enough to loosen his hold, and ducked under his arm and shot free, only to jump to her feet and grab hold of his jacket when he nearly fell flat on his face. "Alec!" she snapped, giving him a tug. "Stand up!" She lifted his arm over her shoulders and helped him to his feet. "Now walk!" He staggered forward and Jane slid a hand under his jacket and grabbed the back of his belt. "That's it," she urged more gently, guiding him up the beach and stumbling into the cave when his knees started to buckle. "No!" she snapped. "Keep going."

She waited until they were well out of the rain before she dropped to her knees with him, easing his fall as he rolled onto his back. But then she immediately pulled him onto his side and held him steady as he coughed up seawater. "Sweet Athena, did you swallow half of the fiord? Oh, Alec," she whispered, gently wiping his mouth with her wet sleeve. "You really are an idiot. Why didn't you stay at the shelter?"

"Damn b-bear," he said through another fit of coughing. "S-sorry."

"Yes, I'll just bet that damn bear is sorry it tangled with you" she soothed, brushing back the hair plastered to his face, only to realize there was blood mixed with the rain and seawater when she felt the oozing bump on his forehead. "Stop talking and help me get you undressed."

Only she'd had an easier time dressing up her pet seal when she was three than she did getting Alec out of his soaked clothes. First the laces on his boot were so swollen tight that she ended up pulling his knife out of its sheath and simply cutting them. And he was shivering so violently that getting him to roll one way and then the other to get his jacket off proved nearly impossible. She eventually managed to peel off his shirt along with the jacket as she pushed and pulled against him, but knowing she'd never sit him up to get his T-shirt over his head, she simply cut it off also. It then took her several attempts to unbuckle his belt and unzip his jeans when he started in on another fit of coughing; although once she did she was able to use his restless twisting to pull off his pants and boxers.

But now what? Was she supposed to dress him in *her* clothes?

Remembering that he'd been carrying something over his head, Jane blindly felt around in the dark and found her flashlight, turned it on, and angled it toward Alec—only to suck in her breath at the sight of him fully naked.

Holy Hades, the man made Hercules look like a mere boy. Alec didn't seem to have an ounce of fat on him; his body long and lean and powerful-looking as his muscles tightened with shivers, his broad chest and wide shoulders appearing to be made of stone, his thighs and hips sharply sculpted into his . . . his . . .

Jane dropped the light and jumped to her feet, realizing her *blush* could probably warm him up as she ran back out into the rain. Sweet Prometheus, it was a good thing he *had* left his pants on last night, or she very well might have fainted dead away. She walked back and forth across the beach looking for what he'd been carrying while remembering the movies she'd downloaded onto her iPad, and decided that although she might have blushed the whole time she'd watched, the men in them were nothing compared to the real thing. She slapped her hands to her cheeks as she stumbled to a halt. Had she really threatened to do to Alec what he'd done to her last night?

Jane took a deep breath and lifted her blistering face to the rain. By the gods, she was no shrinking violet. She'd watched women performing oral sex on men in those movies, and both parties had appeared to be having a wonderful—

She snapped her head around when Kitty let out a soft woof.

Alec was freezing to death and here she was about to burst into flames! Jane stumbled around until she nearly tripped over the large rectangular object, and finally realized it was a backpack. She grabbed one of the shoulder straps and nearly fell again when she tried to lift it, then simply dragged it to the cave. She let it go once she was well out of the rain, then angled the flashlight toward it and tried to take off the rain shield. She finally found the ties just short of deciding to cut the material, and peeled it back to reveal his sleeping bag.

"Yes!" she cried, untying the bag off the frame. She crawled over and shook it out behind Alec, unzipped it, then tucked one edge of it down the length of his back. She started to roll him onto it, but stopped when she realized he was covered in sand. She grabbed her small satchel and took out the spare fleece she'd brought and carefully wiped him down, *then* rolled him onto the open bag. She pulled it over his shivering body with a derisive snort, realizing that he probably hadn't had half as much trouble stripping her off and getting her in his bag three days ago.

Jane grabbed the light, returned to his backpack, and looked inside. "Oh, thank the gods," she said when she saw one of his shirts. Only when she pulled it out, she had to scramble to catch the bottle that tumbled out of it. "Scotch?" she read from the label as she held it in front of the light.

She set it down with a snort, aimed the light into the pack again, and pulled out two entire changes of clothes—including thermal underwear—several small packets of dehydrated food, what appeared to be a smaller version of his camp stove, two bottles of fuel, and some nested pots.

She grabbed one of the thermal shirts and rushed back to Alec, angled the flashlight toward him, peeled back the sleeping bag, and slipped the shirt over his head—being careful of the cut on his forehead. But then she sat back on her heels, staring at him in dismay. That is, until she remembered how well he'd responded to her snapped instructions on the beach, and softly snorted at the realization that no matter what century it was, warriors always obeyed orders barked at them.

"Alec, sit up," she commanded, using the shirt around his neck to pull him upright. "You will help me," she growled, wrestling his shivering arm into a sleeve, only to have him flinch with an equally threatening growl. Realizing his wrist was tender, she carefully worked the sleeve up his arm, did the same with the other arm, then pulled the shirt down to his waist—jerking away when he collapsed onto the bag and her hand brushed him intimately.

Jane took a steadying breath and suddenly wanted to smile, remembering the lying scoundrel saying he hadn't peeked when she'd awakened in his sleeping bag wearing only his shirt. "Yes, well," she said, taking a good long peek even as she fought to contain her blush, "my mama didn't raise a fool for a daughter." She sighed when he started coughing again, and pulled the edge of the sleeping bag around him and zipped it up. "Kitty," she said, waving her pet over, "come cuddle against Alec to help get him warm." She urged the wolf into a position that wouldn't allow Alec to roll onto his back as he continued to give occasional coughs, then grabbed the flashlight and positioned it to shine on the items she'd pulled from the backpack.

Her first order of business was to get the stove running,

she decided as she picked up the small burner and studied it. She rummaged through the side pockets of the pack until she found what looked like a flashlight she could attach to her head, as well as a plastic bag filled with goodies—including several lighters.

She put on the headlamp, adjusted the straps, and turned it on, then held the stove up and squinted to read the instructions etched on the side. She turned the knob, then immediately tightened it again when fuel hissed out. She set it level on the sand, then flicked the lighter just above the burner and turned the knob, only to rear back when it ignited with a *whoosh*.

Jane held her hands over the small but surprisingly intense flame, realizing she was also shivering. But she couldn't change into dry clothes just yet. She jumped to her feet and ran back out into the rain, gathering rocks the size of her fist until she had an armful. Loving that the light shone at whatever she looked at, she ran back into the cave and dumped the rocks beside the stove, then opened the nesting pots, grabbed the largest one, and ran to the back of the cave. She dipped the pot in the bubbling spring to fill it with water, went back and added as many rocks as the pot would hold, and set it on the burner, being careful not to let the sloshing water put out the flame. Only then did she take off her boots and stand up to start stripping off, all while watching Alec. His breathing had calmed to nearly normal, and he was holding the sleeping bag tightly around his shivering body, his eyes closed as if in pain.

Jane stilled with her jeans halfway down at the realization that he might have other injuries besides that bump on his head and sore wrist. If he really did tangle with that stupid old bear, had she missed something in her haste to cover him up?

She pulled her pants back up and knelt down next to him, unzipped the sleeping bag after wrestling it out of his grip, and peeled it back. She carefully pulled his thermal shirt up his chest and slowly ran her hands over his torso—stopping when he gave a violent shiver. "I'm sorry," she whispered, blowing on her hands to warm them as she ran the beam of her headlamp over his body—gasping in surprise when it landed on the angry patch of red running up the length of his ribs and around to his back. "Oh, Alec," she whispered, palming his clenched jaw and bending to kiss his cheek. "Why didn't you stay at the shelter until morning, or at least until the rain stopped?"

"G-goddamn bear," he rasped. "S-sorry."

She kissed his cheek again, guessing the bear must have given him a terrible fright. "Hush now. You're safe, sweetheart. I promise you that bear will definitely be sorry if it shows its hairy face around here."

After changing her clothes—putting on the other warm-looking thermal shirt belonging to Alec—Jane went to work tucking the heated rocks against his torso inside the sleeping bag, then gave his body a more thorough inspection.

He'd taken a really bad tumble, she decided, seeing that he'd skinned one of his shins, his right wrist was swollen and possibly sprained, and the palms and fingers on both his hands were scratched raw as if he'd repeatedly grabbed at rocks and bushes trying to break his fall. As a precaution in case his wrist was broken instead of just sprained, she immobilized it with a pair of her knee-high stockings—making sure not to wrap it too tightly in deference to the swelling. She put his wool socks on his feet, found a medical kit in one of the pack's pouches and cleaned the cut on his forehead, and changed out the now cooled rocks for warm ones from the pot again.

Jane then crushed three aspirin from the medical kit into a small tin cup, added some spring water, and poured in a rather large dose of Scotch. It took her five full minutes of coaxing to get him to drink every last drop before she gulped down her own dose of the breath-robbing liquor. She smiled, imagining Alec was also experiencing the warmth spreading through his limbs when she saw him relax onto the fleece she'd balled up as a pillow and let out a soft sigh.

Jane stood up and slowly swept the beam of her headlamp around the cave, then out at the cove—only to see huge snowflakes mixed in the rain. She quickly repacked the backpack, shut off the stove, and spooned the rewarmed rocks into another pot to carry over to Alec.

"You're doing a wonderful job, my valiant friend," she whispered, giving Kitty a pat when he lifted his head to rest it on Alec's shoulder. "And I will see that you have a grand ceremony when you receive your badge of honor." She laughed. "And when Leviathan calls you a nasty name, you will know he's only jealous of the attention you're getting."

Satisfied that she'd done all she could after she changed out the rocks one last time, Jane lifted the edge of the sleeping bag, settled along the length of Alec, and carefully wrapped her arm over his shivering shoulder with a tired smile. Alec had gallantly trudged through a nighttime rainstorm, battled a mean old bear, and gotten himself beaten up getting to her, so she supposed that made the underachieving, oversexed scoundrel *her* sweetheart.

Lord, she hoped he acted embarrassed tomorrow for *her* having to rescue *him* tonight. Because wanting to make him moan and groan and carry on like the men in those movies was *all the reason* she needed to show the kiss-stealing, backside-ogling man that he wasn't the only one capable of giving unbelievable pleasure.

And anyway, she needed the practice for when she did find a condom-worthy lover who wanted *her* for all the right reasons.

Chapter Nine

Alec woke up to the uneasy feeling that he'd lost control of his salacious dream, most likely right around the time he'd found himself lying at the bottom of the hundred-foot, nearly vertical fall he'd taken. He'd been in roaring pain from what felt like cracked ribs, his wrist and left leg throbbing, and the rain pounding his face as he'd watched the beam of his head-lamp wildly swinging from a bush halfway back up the ridge.

Yup, that's when he'd known that a cold and frightened princess was probably the least of his worries. By sheer will alone, he'd managed to make it to the grotto before collapsing into Jane's arms, and then he'd . . . well, things were a bit blurry after that. Except he was pretty sure he'd apologized for making up that bear, and was fairly certain—or rather, afraid—that he may have thrown up on her.

Alec mentally took stock of his situation, trying to decide if he could salvage at least some of his dignity. His entire side still hurt like hell, he couldn't close his right hand into a fist, and he had a headache threatening to turn into roaring pain again if he opened his eyes. On the upside, however, he was warm as toast, naked but for a thermal shirt, and comfortably nestled in his sleeping bag. Well, comfortable except for all the hard lumps poking into his sides and back.

What in the name of God was he lying on? Had Jane made him sleep out on the rock-strewn beach instead of inside the grotto on the nice soft sand?

Hell, he *must* have thrown up on her.

Alec heard whispering and carefully cracked open his eyes to sunshine and saw Jane kneeling at the entrance of the cave fiddling with something on a large boulder, Kit listening with rapt attention as he sat beside her.

"I need you to stay here and keep an eye on Alec for me, Kitalanta, so you can let me know if he wakes up. But you must stay in the cave with him, as I'm going to be throwing branches onto the beach from the top of the cliff so we can have a campfire."

"No, you're not," Alec said through gritted teeth, fighting against the pain of lifting his head to glare at her.

Jane immediately stood up and walked over to him, her smile outshining the sun peeking over the point of land protecting the cove. "You're awake." She knelt beside him and adjusted the semisoft lump under his neck to prop up his head. "How are you feeling this morning?" she asked as she gently pressed her palm to his cheek and smiled again. "You're not feverish, so I predict you'll live."

"You're not climbing the cliff and tossing anything over the edge of it."

She sat back on her heels and looked down to brush several specks of sand off her jacket. "Odd, but I don't recall receiving an invitation to your coronation." She shot him a sassy smile. "So I guess that doesn't make you the king of me."

Oh yeah, he'd definitely lost control of his dream. "You can build a campfire when we get back to the shelter," he said on a growl, using the pain to propel himself upward just as Jane caught hold of his shoulder and held him down. Not that he could fight her, since his ribs started roaring louder than his pounding head, and he dropped back with a hiss of pain. What in hell was poking his sides?

She ran her knuckles over his cheek. "We're not returning

to the shelter today and likely not tomorrow, either. You're a mess, Alec. You'll never make the hike up to the trail, much less back to camp." She smiled again. "And I'm not carrying you."

Damn; apparently princesses didn't get mad—they got even. He wiggled off one of the back-poking lumps, only to land on another. "What in hell am I lying on?" he muttered as he felt around with his left hand. He pulled out a rock, incredulous. "Why did you fill my sleeping bag with rocks?"

She unzipped the bag and started tossing them onto the sand. "To warm you up. I heated them in a pot of water on the camp stove, then tucked them around you."

Alec relaxed back against the lumpy pillow with a heavy sigh. "That was smart. And I'm sorry for growling." He tossed the rock away and captured her hand. "Jane, I want . . . Last night I . . ." He sighed and gave her a squeeze. "Thank you."

She brushed at her jacket again, her cheeks flushing. "Yes. Well. I didn't do half what you did for me three days ago." She shot him another brilliant smile. "But if that mean old bear that chased you had dared to show its furry face here last night, Kitty and I would have dispatched it to hell with my kidnappers."

Okay. Not only *hadn't* he told her he'd made up the bear, but apparently he'd led her to believe it had attacked him. Wait; did that mean he *hadn't* thrown up on her?

"Are you thirsty?" she asked, standing up and walking to the back of the grotto. She came back carrying a tin cup and the medical kit. "I think you should have a few more aspirin to fight the swelling in your wrist and ribs." She knelt beside him again. "And then we'll see if you can stand, and I'll help you down the beach so you can"—her face flushed again—"do your morning rituals," she muttered, becoming very busy rummaging through the medical kit. "Then I'll feed you before I leave."

He closed his hand over her fist holding the bottle of aspirin. "The ground's still wet, making the hike to the top of the cliff too dangerous. We don't need a campfire."

"Maybe not today," she countered, pulling free and opening the bottle. She shook three aspirin into her palm. "But we'll need one tonight when the temperature drops below freezing." She shoved the pills in his mouth when he tried to speak, then lifted his head and pressed the tin cup to his lips. "Drink."

Alec obediently drank all the water that didn't run down his chin, then gently nudged her away, gritted his teeth to keep from growling again as he lifted onto his elbow, and pushed himself upright.

Jane scrambled out of his way. "Wait, you're not wearing pants."

"Then I suggest you close your eyes," he hissed, deciding that if he didn't stand up now he might not stand at all. So he rolled to his knees, braced his good arm on the jagged wall of the grotto, and pushed himself to his feet—only to have Jane jump up and try to steady him even as she tugged down the hem of his shirt.

"I'm okay," he assured her as he straightened, finding that breathing was a lot easier standing upright. He spotted his backpack. "Just hand me my thermal bottoms before ye go for a walk down the beach while I . . . ah, do my morning rituals."

Keeping her eyes locked on his—even though his shirt hung to midthigh—she stepped away and gave him a mutinous glare. "You end up flat on your face and I'm leaving you right where you fall."

He ran a battered finger down one of her flushed cheeks. "I'm okay now that I'm standing, and I'll loosen up once I start moving around. Why don't you and Kit go see if any driftwood washed ashore beyond the point before the tide comes back in? You might be able to gather enough for a small fire tonight."

She strode to his pack at the rear of the grotto, dug out his thermal underwear bottoms, and came back and handed them to him—her gaze never straying lower than his chin. She strode to the pack again, pulled the small folding wood saw out of the side pouch, and headed past him toward the beach.

Alec dropped his pants to snag her arm on the way by. "A fire's not worth risking your neck over, Jane. So I'm *asking* that ye please not hike to the top of the cliff."

"I don't take foolish chances, and I know my limits." She canted her head. "If our positions were reversed, would you not do everything in your power to keep me comfortable while I healed?"

"Not worrying about your breaking your beautiful neck is all the comfort I need."

Up went one of her brows. "So it's okay for you to dangle from a thin cable beneath a helicopter as it flies over the treetops, but it's not okay for me to walk up a hill and toss down branches?"

"That's different," he growled, feeling heat creeping up the back of his neck. He took a steadying breath. "I knew what I was doing because I've done it dozens of times before, and the risk was minimal," he said more softly.

She turned away to stare out at the water, but not before he saw the spark of challenge leave her eyes. "Yes. I see. You men always know exactly what you're doing, and we women are clue—are to be protected and cared for."

Dammit, if she fell he might not be able to get to her in time. "Please don't go."

She pulled in a breath and held it for several heartbeats, and Alec didn't release his own breath until he saw her shoulders slump. "I won't climb the cliff," she said softly, walking out of the grotto and turning to follow the beach around the cove, Kit dutifully walking beside her.

Alec bent down and picked up his thermal bottoms, then slipped them on with a muttered curse. Christ, he couldn't have wounded Jane more if he'd kicked her. But he'd rather hurt her feelings than have her break her beautiful neck— because then they'd both end up dead when he killed himself trying to reach her.

And he'd be damned if he was letting Jane Smith die a virgin.

*   *   *

Not about to add insult to injury, Alec had very nobly refrained from telling Jane to watch for boats on the fiord when she'd headed out again after dumping an armful of neatly sawn driftwood next to the grotto entrance. And he'd merely smiled and nodded when she'd politely asked if she could strip the frame off his backpack, and had handed her a granola bar as she'd left carrying the frame and a short length of rope. He might be a bastard, but he wasn't an idiot. If the woman wanted to gather enough fuel to build a bonfire that could be seen from space, who was he to stop her?

Certainly not the king of her, that was for sure.

Hell, he wasn't even king of himself at the moment.

Alec absently blew on the steam wafting up from the cup of soup he'd heated on the stove, and stared at the shrinking beach across the cove as he wondered if it was his throbbing side or the goddamn bus sitting on his chest that was making it hard to breathe. When in hell had his innocuous dream of messing around with a beautiful, not-missing woman for a few days turned into a raging desire to possess her completely?

Dammit, he didn't want to care.

No, that wasn't true; he *couldn't* care.

Carolina Oceanus was so far out of his league that they might as well be living in different universes. And Jane Smith was definitely beyond his reach, because he'd bet his very life that the sexy, intelligent woman had never once dreamed of being devalued by a child murderer.

He had no business messing with her at all. And if he had anything resembling a conscience left, as soon as he could make the climb he should drag her up the mountain and dump her at Nova Mare before she suddenly vanished in a thunderstorm when she finally figured out what a bastard he really—

Alec stilled at the soft, electronic chime coming from the front of the grotto, only to realize that Jane was using a tiny solar panel to recharge her iPad. After glancing toward the point of land, he set down his soup and carefully got to his feet, slowly walked over and unplugged the iPad from the charger, then hobbled back to the sunbathed boulder. But instead of sitting on it again, he carefully lowered himself to the sand and leaned against the rock instead.

He found the power button and turned on the tablet, grinning when the screen lit up with a picture of a beautiful ocean sunset. He studied the device, having been contemplating getting himself one when he went home this fall. The sleek tablet was definitely lighter than his laptop, and he figured an iPad was his next step on the technology ladder, since TarStone Mountain had wireless Internet in the hotel and lodge, and even up at the summit house.

He gave another glance toward the fiord, then slid a battered finger across the screen to unlock it and grinned again when a variety of icons appeared. Not the least bit contrite to be snooping through Jane's virtual world, since being nosy was probably the least of his sins, he lightly tapped the e-book icon—then softly whistled at the sight of her extensive library of books on nuclear fission, quantum physics, sustainable energy, and solar and hydro and wind power.

Jane Smith was into some heavy reading.

His eyes widened as he continued scrolling through the virtual bookcase: *The Joy of Sex . . . The Happy Hooker . . . Kama Sutra . . . The Idiot's Guide to Oral Sex . . .*

Seriously? Somebody had written a book on oral sex?

And Jane had *bought* it?

Alec wiped his sock-wrapped hand over his face. Well, that should teach him to snoop. Except instead of having learned his lesson, he kept right on snooping—only to nearly drop the iPad when he tapped the movie icon.

Holy hell, the woman had an equally extensive *video* library of pornography!

He stared out across the cove, more confounded than shocked. Why would Jane have downloaded a bunch of dirty movies and sex manuals? He understood the energy and physics books, since she obviously was into that kind of stuff, but *The Happy Hooker* and *Debbie Does Dallas*? What sort of mind mixed pornography with quantum physics?

Alec snorted. An intelligent and inquisitive mind did,

especially if it belonged to a sheltered princess with dreams of being more than a wife and mother and beautiful asset to some power-hungry husband.

But *The Happy Hooker*? Was Jane studying up on how to lose her virginity?

For the love of Christ, she was learning about sex from a prostitute!

Kit suddenly came barreling up the beach, spraying Alec in a shower of sand when the wolf slid to a halt, dropped a large piece of driftwood, and looked at him expectantly. Really? The killer whale wanted to play fetch?

"You're an orca," Alec muttered, picking up the driftwood. "You're supposed to be terrorizing helpless seals." He awkwardly tossed the stick toward the water, only to immediately regret the action and cradle his ribs on a hiss of pain.

"Kitty, I told you Alec is too sore to play," Jane scolded as the wolf raced past her after the stick. She stopped at the entrance and slid off the pack frame—that probably had forty pounds of driftwood lashed to it—then rushed onto the beach. "Kitty, no!" she cried, catching the wolf by grabbing one end of the stick and bracing her feet to stop him. Using her grip on the stick, and apparently not the least bit worried when Kit gave a protesting growl, Jane got right down in the wolf's face. "I only showed you that game so you could show your pod—you're pack mates," she whispered, darting a glance at Alec to see if he'd caught her mistake, only to straighten with a gasp when she saw him holding her iPad.

The woman should be blushing to the roots of her wind-tangled hair, Alec decided as he gestured at the boulder near the entrance. "It started beeping and . . . ah, I've thought about buying myself one, so I . . ." He snorted and held the iPad out to her. "Do they come already loaded with all those books and movies?"

Her complexion went from pink to dull red as she hugged the tablet to her chest, even as her chin lifted defiantly. "It's not a crime to be curious, and I've always been interested in various energy sources."

"Yeah, right; you—" Alec snapped his mouth shut when the last of her sentence sank in. She was embarrassed he'd discovered that she read *science* books? "I wasn't referring to your scientific library," he drawled, "but your collection of pornography."

"Oh, that," she said with a smile of obvious relief. She waved a hand in dismissal and sat down across from him to lean against the grotto wall. "No, the iPad doesn't come with any books or movies on it. You not only have to buy the pornography, but you have to download the app you wish to use based on which online store you plan to buy from." She beamed him a saint-tempting smile. "Then you go to that store and simply type in *SEX* and *thousands* of books and movies pop up." She shook her head. "Some of the titles are really quite comical." She held the tablet toward him. "You're welcome to peruse my libraries while you're recuperating if you wish, and that way you can decide if this is the brand of tablet you might want to purchase."

Was she *serious*? Alec gestured for her to keep the tablet and took as deep a breath as the bus sitting on his chest would allow. "Jane," he quietly began, despite not knowing where he was going with this conversation, "you can't learn how to make love from reading books about sex or watching a bunch of actors going at . . . pretending to . . . Pornography is misleading." He nodded curtly. "Yeah, it's nothing but fantasy."

She arched a brow. "So the reason it even exists is . . ."

Well, she had him there. Alec disguised his urge to grin with a snort. "It exists to keep beautiful women safe from lust-blinded idiots."

"And only *men* experience lust?" she asked, her eyes lighting with challenge. "And women mustn't be curious about such things?" She canted her head. "Tell me; would you expect a doctor who hadn't spent years studying the human body to operate on you? Or would you send a soldier into battle without any training?"

"Sex isn't a battle," he growled. "It's a natural, spontaneous occurrence between two people."

Her eyes crinkled with amusement. "So are you saying

that if neither person has any experience, they will both still find pleasure?"

Damn, her smile was contagious, and Alec finally gave his grin free rein. "Well, okay. It helps if *one* of them knows what they're doing."

That brow lifted again. "Preferably with the man being the experienced one?" She sobered. "Knowledge is power, Alec. And ignorance about sex puts a woman at a disadvantage—and at a man's mercy."

Alec scrubbed his face in his hands, wondering what had possessed him to get into a conversation with her about sex. "Okay, point taken. I suppose if I were running around audition—looking for an ordinary man to marry, I'd at least want to know how to keep things from getting out of control. But," he rushed on when she started to say something, "pornography has absolutely nothing to do with lovemaking." He gestured at her iPad. "Those movies are visual exaggerations, Jane, aimed at a *male* audience. Did you see any displays of affection when you watched them? Or tenderness, or any real emotion? Hell, they don't even kiss."

She looked down at her lap, her cheeks darkening. "No, I saw no affection." She lifted uncertain eyes to his. "But if those movies are designed for male entertainment, couldn't a woman watch them to learn what men like?"

"Men like women to be themselves."

She looked down at the iPad again, although not quickly enough for him to miss the wistful look in her eyes. "But everyone appeared to be having such a good time," she murmured, more to herself than to him, he suspected. She stood up, took a deep breath, and gave him an overly bright smile. "Thank you for explaining it to me, Alec, as I did wonder at some of the things I saw in those movies." He also didn't miss the sparkle that returned to her eyes as she turned away. "Particularly some of the positions. Now, I believe I'll build a fire and cook the fish that Ki—um, that I found trapped in a tidal pool."

She set the tablet down on the boulder next to him, then went over and pulled several long thin saplings from the firewood lashed to the pack frame, as well as the already gutted fish dangling from it. She walked over and handed him both the saplings and the fish—that appeared to have teeth marks in their sides—and yup, that was definitely a sparkle outshining her smile. "If you don't know how to whittle a spit to roast the fish on, I believe there's a book on my iPad that explains how to do it."

For the love of— She'd studied up on camping, too?

Well of course she had, because Jane Smith had wanted to be prepared when she got into trouble and came running to the biggest schmuck on the planet. "Thanks, but I think I can manage," he drawled, taking his knife when she handed it to him.

Hell, had he *ever* been in control of this dream?

The scoundrel; Alec had snooped through her iPad and then had the audacity to be scandalized that she'd downloaded movies and books about sex. Yet she'd bet her emerald necklace that *he* hadn't been living like a monk for the last twenty years, or that she was the only one going around auditioning lovers.

Jane got down on her hands and knees next to the campfire she'd constructed, deliberately facing her backside toward the ogling scoundrel, and blew on the smoking grass to coax it into flames—stifling a smile when she heard him muttering something under his breath about a goddamn bus.

Yes. Well. Alec MacKeage didn't have a monopoly on lust—as he would discover tonight when they went to bed. Because after finding some way to trick him out of his underwear, she intended to crawl in the sleeping bag with him—fully clothed, of course—and finally see for herself what all that moaning and groaning and carrying on in those movies was all about.

Oh, her condom might be staying in her jewelry bag, but as the very happy Madam Xaviera Hollander had vividly expressed in her candid book, there were quite a few ways to curl a man's toes.

Chapter Ten

Alec woke up to day five of his apparently on-again dream and smiled at the water's reflection dancing on the grotto ceiling as he rubbed Jane's sex-tangled hair between his battered fingers. Control, he decided, was a relative matter depending on which side of it a person was on. And handing control over to a sexy, intelligent, very determined princess could prove quite interesting—especially if she also happened to be quite passionate.

Lord, he couldn't remember ever being so captivated by a woman. He could live to be a hundred and two and never grow tired of messing around with Jane, and if he died tomorrow, Alec suspected even the posies he'd be pushing up would be smiling.

For someone rebelling against a dictatorial father, Jane sure wasn't above making a few demands of her own. She'd all but ordered him out of his clothes last night, using some lame excuse about needing to put salve on his shin and check the swelling on his ribs, only to *accidentally* spill an entire pot of water on his thermal bottoms and shirt so he couldn't put them back on. Then she'd added a couple of logs to the campfire and crawled—fully clothed—into as much of his sleeping bag as she could, considering he was already occupying most of it.

She hadn't even waited sixty seconds before she'd pounced.

And being the lust-blinded idiot he was, Alec had not only let her, but had helped.

Yes, Jane was a very passionate woman, and what she lacked in experience she made up for in enthusiasm. She was also a quick study, surprisingly bold, and really quite inventive. He'd been so overwhelmed by her determination to give him pleasure that he'd come dangerously close to forgetting who *he* really was and *she* really was, and nearly taken things past the point of no return.

Forget the damn bus; Jane Smith had somehow managed to get past all the barriers he'd erected and smashed headlong into his heart. And although that would ultimately be a problem for him, Alec didn't see any reason it had to be a problem *today*. Until Sam established a new identity for Jane, they could simply finish laying out the wilderness trail together, all while continuing to explore their seemingly well-matched passions. Hell, he was even willing to disappear with her when the time came, just to make sure she got safely settled in her new life, seeing how *the Celt* was really good at that particular game.

Alec kissed the top of Jane's head when she stirred, and smiled again when he felt her stiffen, willing to bet his hunting rifle that she was blushing to the roots of her sex-tangled hair. "Good morning," he said, his voice thick with some emotion he wasn't quite willing to identify. He gave her hair a tug, partly to get her to look at him, but mostly to see her blush. Except that when she tilted her head back, the only pink in sight was where her cheek had been nestled against his naked chest, and she gave him a pleased-with-herself smile that crinkled the corners of her sleepy bedroom eyes.

Damn, he was in trouble—because if he remembered correctly, confident, passionate women really turned him on.

"Good morning," she whispered, her voice also thick with . . . yup, that was definitely passion, evidenced by her hand sliding down his stomach.

Alec captured it before she could reach anything important, even as he felt heat creeping into *his* cheeks. He brought her palm to his lips and kissed it. "Have mercy, lass," he said on a derisive snort. "If I get any more weak in the knees, I'll never make the hike back to camp today."

She gave him a really impressive pout. "Poor baby. Did all that moaning and groaning and carrying on last night wear you out?" She kissed his chest—her lips lingering a bit long, he couldn't help but notice—then snuggled back against him with a sigh. "Can't we just stay here in the grotto forever?"

"We'd eventually run out of food, I'm afraid."

"Kitty could hunt for us." She lifted her head to smile at him. "I'm certain I downloaded a book of recipes for venison and rabbit and partridge."

"Ah, lass, but ye tempt me," Alec said, giving her a squeeze. He touched his lips to her hair. "But last I knew, hiding from a problem never made it go away." He tilted her head back and smoothed his thumb over her wrinkled brow. "Your week of getting your strength back and deciding what to do is almost up. So, have ye decided to let me help you deal with your father?"

She rolled away and sat up to stare out at the cove. "Nobody can *deal* with my father," she said softly.

"I can. All ye need do is ask, Jane, and I'll be your champion."

She looked over her shoulder at him, her obvious surprise at the word *champion* turning to a sad smile as she gazed out at the water again. "I can't ask, Alec, because I find myself caring about you too much." He saw her release a shuddering breath. "And I will return home and be a dutiful daughter before I'll let anything happen to you."

Not caring for the direction this conversation was going, considering the night of passion they'd just shared, he reached out and pulled her into a fierce embrace. "With or without your permission," he growled, tugging on her hair so she could see he was serious, "and as long as there's breath in me, your father will not bully you into a marriage ye don't want."

The sudden sparkle that came into her eyes completely ruined her threatening glower. "There you go again, sounding like the king of me," she drawled, her fingers lazily running through his chest hair. "Really, Alec, you need to have a word with your royal mailman about misplacing my—"

He kissed her; partly to shut her up but mostly because her sassiness turned him on. The little minx didn't even try to protest, her answering kiss immediate and hot and making every damn one of his blood cells rush straight to his groin at the memory of their passion-filled night. And when her hand slid down his stomach again, this time he didn't stop her.

Jane had fallen into step behind Alec to judge for herself how well he was feeling, only to decide within the first ten minutes that the stubborn man was struggling despite having left his heavy pack at the grotto and cutting himself a walking stick to help with the rougher parts of the climb up to the trail. But because the satellite phone was at the lean-to, he was determined to reach camp before the helicopter left Nova Mare with the next two bridges, wanting to call Duncan and postpone the delivery for a few days.

Jane felt guilty it was her fault that Alec felt rushed because she'd all but attacked him again this morning—although only a little guilty, considering he had attacked her back. Right after she'd collapsed beside him—her breathing as ragged as his—the man had somehow managed to find the strength to dress himself, undress her, then give her another wonderful taste of unbelievable pleasure.

Jane had never been so glad she'd been born a woman. Oh, she might technically still be a virgin, but she certainly didn't feel like one. Alec MacKeage might still be an under-achieving ski bum of a scoundrel, but after last night she no longer could deny he was *her* scoundrel. "I do believe I finally understand what sex is all about," she said just as they finally reached the trail.

Alec turned to her with a chuckle. "You're only now figuring out how babies are made?"

Jane started past him toward camp, walking backward. "I'm not talking about procreation; I'm talking about sex. Or more specifically, the *pleasure* of sex."

"I'm pretty sure mankind wouldn't have gotten past the Stone Age if making babies weren't pleasurable," he said, returning her smile with a thoroughly male grin. "It's needed to counter the stress of raising all the little heathens it produces."

Jane stopped walking. "The drive to procreate is in every plant and animal on the planet, but having sex for the sheer joy of it even *after* a baby's been conceived is almost uniquely human." She canted her head. "And do you know why that is?"

He stopped walking when he reached her and grinned again. "To make sure all the lust-blinded idiots hang around long enough to provide food and shelter and safety for the mothers and babes."

She nodded. "Exactly. Sexual pleasure creates intimacy between a man and woman, and bonds them as a couple."

"So we're a couple now because of the pleasure we've shared?"

Jane patted his chest, then left her hand there. "Well, I do find myself feeling rather proprietary toward you this morning." She tilted her head in question again. "And I wonder what your reaction would be if a man walked up to me right now, pulled me into his arms, and kissed me quite passionately. Would you shove your hands in your pockets and casually stroll away—whistling?"

His already deep green eyes darkened. "I might," he said ever so softly, "after I beat the bastard to a bloody pulp." He threw his walking stick into the trees and pulled her into his embrace, then leaned in until their noses were nearly touching. "But my hands wouldn't be in my pockets; they'd be holding ye tossed over my shoulder as I strolled away—whistling."

Jane closed the two inches remaining between them and kissed him full on the mouth, then pulled away with a laugh. "Will you be my boyfriend, Alec?" she asked as she headed down the trail again so he wouldn't see her holding her breath.

She nearly suffocated waiting for him to answer, and then he only asked another question. "Would having a boyfriend get your father off your back?"

"Probably not," she said, stopping but continuing to look straight ahead.

"Would being your boyfriend give me the right to stand beside you when you finally do face him?"

"No."

"Jane."

She turned to see that he hadn't moved from the spot where she'd kissed him, and beamed him the brightest smile she could muster. "Being my boyfriend would give you the right to share my bed every night, though." She held up a hand to stop him from speaking. "Providing we always stop short of using my condom."

He dropped his gaze to the trail between them and remained silent so long, Jane realized she was holding her breath again when she started feeling dizzy.

He finally looked at her. "We came dangerously close to needing it last night, lass," he said quietly. "But the bond I believe you're talking about is only realized with that final act of intimacy." He slowly shook his head. "And I'm sorry, but that's not going to happen between us. It can't, Jane, because you're an all-or-nothing woman, and I . . ." He lifted his arms from his sides and let them fall back. "I have nothing to offer you."

She was suddenly so angry she almost stamped her foot. "I'm not asking you to marry me," she snapped, spinning on her heel and marching down the trail again—only to squeak in surprise when he pulled her to a stop and turned her around.

"Give me your word that you won't suddenly disappear."

Jane lowered her gaze to escape the intensity in his and brushed at nothing on her jacket. "I believe only a boyfriend may ask for that kind of promise." She pulled in a steadying breath and lifted her eyes to his. "So what's the point of my staying? If I can't even look at you without wanting to rip off all your clothes and lose myself in your body until time stops and the world ceases to exist but for the passion you ignite inside me, then why stay?"

He dropped his hands and stepped back. "For the love of God, woman, ye can't say something like that to a man." He grasped her shoulders and got right in her face again. "Don't do this, Jane; don't drive an all-or-nothing wedge between us. Please, lass," he said more softly, pulling her into a breath-robbing hug. "Just promise me ye won't suddenly vanish."

She balled the back of his jacket in her fists at the feel of his heart pounding against hers. "I promise not to vanish." She leaned away. "But I can't promise not to want you."

He hugged her to him again on a deep sigh. "I'll consider myself warned, then. And in return, I promise to let you trick me out of my clothes anytime ye want."

"Don't do me any favors," she snapped, trying but failing to get free because she didn't want to hurt his ribs.

He gave a sinister-sounding chuckle. "Trust me, the *pleasure* will be all mine," he said with a final squeeze before letting her go and heading down the trail—forcing her to stare at his big broad shoulders, she realized with a sigh as she followed.

And so began five of the most magical days of Jane's life, where time stopped and the world receded until only the excitement of the moment remained, as she and Alec worked together laying out the wilderness trail by day and lost themselves to the pleasure of their passions every night.

Well, magical until the afternoon everything went to hell in a handbasket.

Chapter Eleven

Alec didn't know which he looked forward to more, spending his nights *almost* making love to Jane or spending his days working beside the smart and sassy woman. Then again, teasing Jane had its own rewards, considering how easily she rose to the bait, making her striking beauty nearly blinding when she was riled. Besides, he figured he owed her for deciding the next campsite *simply had* to be situated on a knoll overlooking the fiord, which meant he'd had to relocate two miles of trail to reach it. It didn't help that she was absolutely right, Alec decided as he stared out at the fiord, because it really was one hell of a view.

He stifled a grin when his last comment was met with silence, and turned to see Jane straighten to her knees to better glare at him. "You take that back," she growled. "Henry Oceanus is a *darling*. The moment I met him I fell in love with that unfailingly polite, deeply intelligent, wise-beyond-his-years little boy."

Alec snorted and went back to placing rocks in a circle. "Like I said, he's a prig."

Apparently not caring to have Mac's nine-year-old son—who also happened to be her nephew—referred to as anything but a *darling*, Jane jumped to her feet to loom over him, her hands balled into fists. "He is n—"

"He can also be a downright pain in the ass sometimes," Alec said, cutting her off for the simple pleasure of watching her eyes fill with fire. "Just like his prig of a father," he added, pulling her back down to capture her gasp in his mouth. "In fact, the only Oceanus I know who isn't a petty little tyrant is baby Ella," he said the moment he came up for air, referring to Mac and Olivia's nineteen-month-old daughter—that he just now realized Jane probably hadn't even met yet. Alec shrugged. "But I'm sure it won't take the little heathen long to catch up. Hell, even Olivia gets on my nerves sometimes, and she only married into the family just over two and a half years ago."

Alec worried he may have gone too far, apparently having rendered Jane utterly speechless. But being the bastard he was, he gave a derisive snort and said, "None of them comes close to Mac's old man, though. I swear, Titus acts as if God himself crowned him king of the world."

This time Jane gasped so hard that Alec barely caught her from falling in the pit when she reared away. "You think the Oceanuses are . . . that they're *all* prigs?"

"Just most of the ones I've met," he said, fighting a grin. He looked past her shoulder. "But Mac's supposed to have a sister—Carolina, I think her name is." He looked back at Jane. "Did ye happen to meet her when you stayed at Nova Mare? Talk in town is she's quite a looker." He sighed. "Although I'm guessing that being a beauty would only make her spoiled rotten." He tightened his embrace when she tried to turn away. "So, did ye ever meet Carolina?"

Her face blazing red, she merely nodded.

"And?"

"She *is* beautiful. And she's personable and intelligent and not the least bit spoiled. And Henry is a remarkable young man, and Mac's a wonderful husband and father, as well as a good brother to Carolina. And their mother, Rana, is the embodiment of love."

"And Titus?" Alec quietly asked. Seeing the fight leave her as suddenly as it had arrived, he touched his forehead to hers. "What was your impression of the old man?"

"He appeared to love his family very much." She wrapped her arms around him and buried her face in his neck. "Titus only gets stern and dictatorial when he cares deeply about something, especially if it concerns his family."

Alec leaned away so she'd see his smile. "You mean like *your* father gets?"

She hid her face in his neck again, apparently horrified at her near blunder—except he'd swear he heard her snort. "My father and Titus could be twins," she said, her breath fanning—hey, did she just lick him?

And that sure felt like her hand cupping his ass when Alec suddenly found himself falling sideways until he was flat on his back and Jane sat straddling him, sending all of his well-trained blood cells rushing to his groin. She pinned his hands down—thoughtfully holding his forearm instead of his nearly healed wrist—and lowered her nose to nearly touching his. "Will you willingly say you're sorry for calling Henry a prig, or must I make you beg for mercy?" She wiggled intimately against him when he hesitated. "Have you not come to know me well enough to realize you needn't bait me, Alec?" she whispered huskily. "You need only look at me to stir my passion."

Well, she had him there. "I, ah . . ." He cleared his throat when she wiggled again. "Aye, Henry's a remarkable young man, and Mac is only a pain in the ass some of the time." Lord, save him from sexy princesses. "And I'll take your word for it that Carolina is as sweet as she is beautiful," he ended with a threatening growl when she wiggled again. He bucked her off and rolled until their positions were reversed, not missing that the fire in her eyes was no longer angry. Aye, he simply should have asked. "And I've had the pleasure of meeting Rana," he continued, "and I agree the world could

use more women like her. And lasses like you," he added
thickly, swooping in for a kiss—only to stop in midswoop
when he caught the distant but unmistakable sound of a shod
hoof striking a rock at the same time Kit gave a soft warning
growl.

Alec lifted a finger to his lips signaling Jane to be silent,
then cocked his head to listen to what was definitely several
horses heading toward them, noticing that Jane was also
holding her breath, also listening, her eyes widened in
alarm.

"You and Kit go hide," he whispered, lifting away and
pulling her to her feet. He clasped her head in his hands to
hold her facing him. "There's more than one rider, but it's
likely just Duncan and Mac checking to see if I really did
beat myself up in a fall or if I'm playing hooky," he said, not
wanting to alarm her further that there were more than two
horses approaching. "You know the drill; head to the grotto.
It's set up for you to spend the night if ye have to, so just sit
tight until I come get you or you hear my signal." He waited
until she nodded, then kissed her before looking her in the
eyes again. "Don't panic and vanish on me, okay?"

Mimicking his hold, Jane clasped his face, the only difference being her smile. "I'd be more worried about *never*
getting rid of me if I were you," she whispered, just before
she kissed him—lingering a bit longer than he had, he
couldn't help but notice.

In fact, he had to unwrap her arms from around his neck
and step back, hearing her mutter something about how time
was supposed to be stopped as she grabbed her small backpack. "Go," he said when she hesitated to look up the trail.
"And no matter what you might hear, you *keep* going." He
caught her arm when she turned away without nodding
agreement. "Jane, you don't *exist*."

She beamed him a saint-tempting smile and patted his
cheek. "Then I guess you've been having one heck of a wet
dream all week, haven't you?"

Nearly strangling himself stifling a bark of laughter,

Alec turned her around and gave her heart-shaped bottom a robust pat to get her moving. Jane, however, didn't even try to stifle her snicker as she shot down the knoll and disappeared into the trees.

Kit stood watching her before turning at the sound of men talking, his hackles rising with his soft growl. "Nay, you go with her," Alec said, nudging the wolf with his knee before turning to face the campsite they'd been preparing for the lean-to. Satisfied the ground was too littered with leaves and pine needles for distinguishable footprints and that Jane hadn't left anything behind that said he had a woman with him, Alec knelt down and casually began placing more rocks on the half-finished fire pit. He sat back on his heels and made sure to disguise his alarm when *six* men rode into the small clearing—four of whom he knew and two he didn't.

Damn; he didn't see this ending well.

Duncan was the first to dismount, his face grim and his eyes narrowed in anger as he approached. "I've been calling your goddamned phone all morning," he said under his breath when he reached him.

Alec dusted off his hands and stood up. "I forgot to recharge it. Are ye out giving scenic tours of the fall foliage?" he asked cheerily, nodding toward Mac and the two strangers dismounting. Titus Oceanus, however, was apparently content to glare down his imperial nose at Alec from his saddle, and Sam Waters was . . . hell, the bastard looked like he was attending a funeral.

"This is serious," Duncan said quietly. "Carolina was kidnapped two weeks ago."

"She apparently escaped within a few days," Mac added as he stopped beside Duncan. "But instead of running to safety, she's been missing for the last ten days."

Alec made a point of looking at each man before locking his gaze on Mac—who seemed taller than usual, his eyes unnaturally bright. "So it took six of you to come ask me to help go look for her?"

"No," Mac said, a decided edge in his voice. "The others are here to make sure you don't interfere when I leave with her."

Alec crossed his arms over his chest. "Carolina's not here."

Titus prodded his horse forward, his also unnaturally bright eyes narrowed. "You dare lie to us?"

Alec shrugged. "I've committed worse sins."

"Alec!" Duncan snapped.

"By the gods, MacKeage," Mac growled, "we've just spent several centuries scouring four continents looking for Carolina and our tempers are short. Give her up and you may continue breathing." He stepped closer and lowered his voice. "Assuming you were wise enough to keep your hands off her."

"What makes you think I even have her to give up?"

Mac reached in his pocket, pulled out a pair of red lace panties, and slapped them down on Alec's folded arms. "You know damn well *who* you've been hiding for the last ten days, yet you didn't have the decency to let us know she was safe? You have sixty seconds to hand her over before I rip you to shreds."

Duncan at least had the decency to pale when Alec looked at him. "Rana's sick with worry," his uncle said. "She needs to know her daughter's safe and . . . unharmed."

Having little hope that Jane was well on her way to the grotto instead of hiding in the woods within earshot, Alec spoke directly to Titus. "If Carolina were here, she'd be perfectly safe." He dropped his arms—letting the panties fall to the ground—and stepped closer to Mac. "And she'd be unharmed," he quietly growled. He looked past Mac at Titus again. "But it's been my experience that when a *grown woman* goes missing, she usually has good reason."

"Alec," Duncan cautioned under his breath.

Alec kept his eyes locked on Titus. "Considering your daughter's obviously intelligent and resourceful enough to escape kidnappers, I imagine she'll show up when she's ready. I prefer you not touch that," he said, turning to the stranger who'd been quietly working his way around the campsite and was just bending to Alec's backpack.

Alec started forward when the man ignored him, but ran into Mac when the wizard stepped in his path with a lethal-sounding growl and gave him a hard shove—which brought a lethal *feminine* growl from the woods.

"You leave him alone, Mackie!" Jane shouted, rushing into the clearing. "He didn't know who I—"

She was cut off in midshout when the stranger dropped the backpack and snagged her around the waist on her way by, then lifted Jane off her feet when she started struggling against him. "No, Nicholas, let me go!"

"Let her go," Alec snapped as he started toward them, only to explode in a blur of motion when Mac grabbed his shoulder and swung him around. Using the momentum of his turn, Alec elbowed the wizard in the gut, then followed through with a fist to his jaw before spinning to plant his boot in the stomach of the second stranger rushing toward him. He then went after the bastard carrying the now cursing as well as struggling Jane tossed over his shoulder as he headed for the horse beside her father.

Only Alec hadn't taken two strides when he was slammed from behind. "No, don't hurt him!" he heard Jane shout as he went down. "His ribs are sore! Father, make them stop! He didn't know! Alec, stop!" she cried when Alec sprang to his feet, managing to land another blow to Mac's jaw before ducking his shoulder to rush the other stranger with enough force to send him staggering into Duncan.

Alec went after Jane again as her captor mounted his horse, her struggles nearly making them fall. "Let her g—"

Titus cut him off by slamming his horse into Alec at the same time Duncan tackled him from behind. "Dammit, cut it out!" Duncan shouted as Alec went down again—thanks to Mac and the other man's added momentum.

"Don't hurt him!" Jane screamed. "Father, make them stop!"

"Enough, Maximilian," Titus said calmly. "We have what we came for; leave him to Trace and Duncan."

Being a dutiful son, Mac pushed himself to his knees by giving a hard shove to Alec's ribs, and the last thing Alec saw was the wizard's bloody mouth twisted in a feral grin just as an oversize fist slammed into his face.

Alec woke up feeling like he'd been run over by a goddamn bus, and kept perfectly still as he thought about how *not* well things had ended. He supposed it was nice he was still alive, but every one of his muscles was roaring in pain, he was lying on the cold forest floor with his hands tied behind his back and his feet bound, and he wasn't alone. He could hear a fire crackling, men softly talking several yards away, and horses about twenty yards behind him. He slowly cracked open his eyes to see Duncan, Sam, and the other man responsible for his roaring pain lounging against their saddles next to a fire blazing in the half-finished pit.

Alec closed his eyes again, barely stifling a snort at the stellar champion he'd turned out to be, seeing how he'd almost literally been caught with his pants down but for the men arriving five minutes later, and Jane was right now back in the loving arms of her dictatorial father. Hell, *she* had saved *his* sorry ass. "Could someone untie me before my arms fall off?" he asked, making three sets of glaring eyes turn to him—not one of the bastards rushing to fulfill his request.

Duncan snorted. "Why, so you can pummel us again?" He rubbed his swollen jaw, his glare intensifying. "Where in the name of God did ye learn to fight like that?" Duncan got up and walked over to crouch down in front of him. "You've always been anything but serious, but I don't recall your ever being an outright idiot. Mind telling me what possessed you to hide Carolina from Titus?"

"I don't like bullies."

"He's her father," Duncan snapped. "And you're a goddamn idiot."

"Thanks for the help, by the way, *uncle*."

"Somebody had to stop you from committing suicide."

Duncan leaned closer. "Christ, man, ye don't piss off the most powerful magic-makers on the planet."

"You're lucky Mac didn't rip you to shreds," the stranger interjected. "Considering the ten days of hell we just spent looking for her." He visibly shuddered and shook his head. "I don't think I've ever seen either of the Oceanus men quite so . . . crazy."

"And you are?"

The guy rubbed his stomach where Alec had planted his boot earlier. "Trace Huntsman, Mac's friend from Midnight Bay."

"The lobsterman *friend* who coldcocked Mac and locked him in the cellar when his son's uncles were trying to kill him?"

Trace nodded. "If you know the story, then I suggest you take note as to how Titus deals with people who mess with his family."

"What in hell were ye thinking?" Duncan repeated. "Why didn't you drag Carolina up the mountain the day you found her?"

"Because I don't like bullies. Are you going to untie me sometime tonight?"

Duncan got up and walked back to the fire. "As far as I'm concerned, one idiot in the family is already one too many," he muttered, sitting down and reclining against his saddle. "So I'm thinking ye should stay right where you are until ye find a little wisdom." He rubbed his swollen jaw. "Or until I cool off."

Alec dropped his head, trying to relax his muscles. Christ, he hurt; several of his ribs felt cracked for real this time, he was pretty sure he had two loose teeth, and his nearly healed wrist was swelling into the rope and throbbing. "Who was the bastard who rode off with her?" he asked without lifting his head. "Jane called him by name, so she must know him."

"Jane?" Trace said, sitting up. "You mean you really didn't know who she was?"

Duncan snorted before Alec could answer. "Of course he knew." He took a sip from a bottle of Scotch—*his* bottle,

Alec couldn't help but notice—then used it to point at him. "My nephew might be an idiot, but he's not stupid."

Alec also couldn't help but notice that Sam Waters didn't have much to say about anything—just like he hadn't earlier when everything had been going to hell in a handbasket. Not that he blamed the man, considering Mac's mood at the time.

"So, who was the bastard?" Alec repeated.

"Nicholas," Trace said, motioning for Duncan to hand him the Scotch. "I don't recall hearing a last name. He's supposedly Carolina's bodyguard from *mythological* Atlantis." He took a swig from the bottle and handed it to Sam before wiping his mouth on his sleeve. "And after spending the last ten days scouring four continents through five friggin' *centuries* with him," Trace continued with another visible shudder, "I figure the bastard gave fighting lessons to Attila the Hun." He shot Alec a nasty grin. "Mac told me Titus is encouraging Nicholas to court Carolina over the next few weeks, since they've known each other since they were kids." Trace snorted, taking the bottle when Sam handed it back. "Assuming he won't get lost in the crowd of competition arriving at Nova Mare this weekend."

Alec gritted his teeth to propel himself upright and leaned against the tree behind him. "What competition?"

Trace handed the bottle off to Duncan before looking at Alec again. "The way I understand it, six men from various centuries, all chosen by Titus for their skills on the battlefield, are coming to Spellbound Falls to vie for Carolina's hand in marriage. According to Mac, his old man personally hand-delivered each of them an engraved invitation to Nova Mare's grand opening ball that's taking place in three weeks, along with enough power to breach time to get here. Mac said Titus instructed them to arrive no later than this weekend, to come alone, and to leave their weapons at home."

"The old bastard's made his daughter a goddamn prize?" Alec growled. And the crazy woman had rushed to save *his* sorry ass? "Christ, no wonder she changed her name and ran away."

"Mac said Titus let her run away, thinking to give Carolina a chance to find a husband on her own." Trace pushed himself to his feet and, after snagging the bottle from Duncan on his way by, crouched in front of Alec and grinned. "But apparently the best she could find was *you*." He held the bottle to Alec's mouth and let him take a swig before lowering it to look him in the eyes. "I figure you have two choices the moment the ropes come off; you can head home to Pine Creek and forget you ever heard of Carolina Oceanus, or you can wrangle yourself an invitation to Nova Mare's grand opening ball."

"Or," Alec said quietly, "I can steal Jane back and make sure she disappears for good this time."

Trace apparently had to think about that before he slowly nodded. "You could try," he said just as quietly, "if you don't have an aversion to dying." He shrugged. "Titus doesn't strike me as the sort of man who makes the same mistake twice. He lost Carolina to kidnappers two weeks ago; I doubt he'll lose her again. The energy he's going to expend securing Nova Mare will probably suck the sun dry."

"Did you catch the third kidnapper?"

"No."

"Did Titus figure out how they were able to cut off her ankle bracelet?"

"No."

Alec smiled. "Do ye suppose my bringing him the head of the third kidnapper will get me invited to the ball?"

Trace gave a chuckle and started untying Alec's feet. "Hell, you do that and you could probably walk in the front door, toss Carolina over your shoulder, and walk back out again without anyone stopping you." He pulled Alec forward and untied his hands then straightened, his ice-blue eyes stone-cold sober. "It was a hell of an ugly ten days when we didn't know if Carolina was even alive. Mac and Titus are still pissed that they can't figure out who had the balls to take her, so I doubt either of them is going to let her out of their sight anytime soon." He grinned again. "I wouldn't be surprised if the old man tags along on her honeymoon."

Alec carefully rubbed the circulation back into his hands. "Assuming Jane hangs around long enough to get married."

Trace turned and sat down against a tree, picked up the bottle, and waved it toward the campfire. "Help me out here, Duncan. Since your nephew is obviously another one of you MacKeage throwbacks, will you please help me explain to him that Carolina isn't leaving Nova Mare without a wedding band on her finger. And Sam, if you get any quieter, I'm going to start digging your grave." He looked over at Alec. "Titus predates *history*, for christsakes; marriage isn't an option for the daughter of the king of the drùidhs, it's a requirement."

Having noticed the bottle was nearly empty, Alec snatched it away from Trace and lifted it to his lips, not lowering it until he'd coaxed every last drop down his throat—after, that is, he'd swirled it over his loose teeth and the inside of his swollen jaw.

"You could do worse than Carolina," Duncan said softly.

Alec glared at him. "Aye, and she could do a hell of a lot better than me." He shook his head. "I'm never getting married."

Duncan snorted. "I seem to recall telling myself that very thing not so long ago. Marriage isn't a death sentence, Alec; it's a rebirth."

"It would certainly solve Carolina's problem," Sam interjected, finally finding his voice. "And yours."

Alec turned his glare on Waters. "I wasn't aware I had a problem. Or I didn't have one until Jane Smith suddenly showed up in my neck of the woods—uninvited, I might point out." He looked down at the bottle, pushing at the label with his thumbnail. "So I'm guessing that particular problem's over now."

"But *hers* isn't," Sam growled. "In fact, based on what Trace just said, she's got seven problems." He nodded when Alec snapped his head up. "Or are you forgetting the six invitations Titus personally delivered, as well as Nicholas?" He cocked his head. "You spent, what, ten days getting to know Carolina? Tell me, do you think she'll make a good warrior's wife and enjoy living in some ancient century?"

"She's from mythological time," Alec said on a hiss, feeling like he'd just taken another punch to the gut when he remembered Jane's iPad full of science books. "Any century later than the one she was born in will seem modern to her."

Sam eyed him for several heartbeats, then leaned back against his saddle with a shrug. "Yeah, she'll probably be too busy having babies to miss technology, anyway."

"Actually," Trace said, drawing Alec's attention again, "you do still have a problem; namely, those very ten days you spent alone out here with Carolina, not to mention knowingly hiding her from her family. I'm not all that certain Titus is going to let that slide." He snorted. "I sure as hell know Mac won't." He shook his head. "You have no idea what we went through trying to find her. Hell, I wouldn't be surprised if Titus offers Carolina to whichever of those seven men brings him *your* head." He ran his gaze over Alec and suddenly grinned. "You think you can survive running a three-week gauntlet of epic proportions?"

"Over my dead body," Duncan growled, getting to his feet—to better glare at Trace, Alec assumed. "No one is hunting anyone for sport on my watch, especially not one of my clansmen. And a couple of pissed off, pain-in-the-ass wizards sure as hell aren't turning my nephew into a means to win a goddamn princess wife. MacKeages are warriors, and *we* do the hunting."

"This isn't your fight, Duncan," Alec said softly.

Duncan pointed at him. "I'm driving ye back to Pine Creek tonight."

"Last I knew, MacKeages don't run, either." Alec set down the bottle and slowly pushed himself to his feet, stifling an urge to cradle his ribs. "Assuming there's even anything to run from," he continued, gesturing down at Trace. "He's just speculating on what Titus and Mac might like to do—which I'm betting they won't. They'll calm down now that they have Jane back *unharmed*."

"Carolina!" Duncan snapped. "She's *Carolina Oceanus*." He pointed at Alec again. "And if ye don't want to spend the next three weeks rotting in that goddamn hole in the belly of my mountain, you'll stay the hell away from her."

"Not a problem, uncle," Alec said, walking over and snagging the strap on his backpack. He slid it onto his shoulders and turned to him. "I'll call you when I'm ready for this site's lean-to and privy to be delivered." He started down the trail in the direction of his old campsite. "Enjoy the view when you wake up in the morning, gentlemen," he said, waving an obscene gesture over his shoulder as he walked into the night. "Ye have Jane to thank for it."

Chapter Twelve

Jane—she really didn't feel like Carolina anymore—knelt in front of the chair with her arms wrapped around her mother's waist, unable to stem the flow of tears that had started the moment Nicholas had deposited her inside the door of her parent's private cottage. "You have to help me, Mama," she said on a sob, straightening to wipe her eyes. "I need to go after Alec. He saved my life, and instead of rewarding him, Mac beat him up and Father left him at the mercy of Trace and Duncan."

"Hush, baby," Rana crooned, pulling her back into a fierce hug. "Duncan will protect his nephew."

"But his ribs are still bruised from a fall he took, and the men pummeled him." Jane straightened again. "Alec didn't know who I was. He thought he was helping an ordinary woman named Jane Smith. I have to go back and explain why I lied so he won't hate me. Oh God, I hurt him worse than Mac did," she sobbed, burying her face in her mother's bosom again. "Please help me, Mama."

"I'm sorry," Rana said thickly, her lips touching Jane's forehead. "But I doubt the combined power of the gods could get you out of here now." She threaded shaking fingers through Jane's tangled hair and tilted her face up. "We didn't know if you were dead or alive, Caro," she whispered, her own tears spilling free. "Or what unspeakable horrors you were experiencing. Why didn't you come to us? Why did you run to Alec MacKeage instead of Maximilian?"

"This is why! I didn't want to be locked away like a mis-behaving child, then given to the first man brave enough to ask for my hand in marriage."

"I've managed to keep that from happening so far, haven't I?" Rana said calmly, brushing her thumbs over Jane's cheeks. "My word, Caro; I won't let your father force you into marriage. But," she said, dropping her hands to grip Jane's shoulders, "I'm afraid I couldn't stop him from scour-ing the world looking for warriors to bring here to court you in the weeks leading up to Nova Mare's grand opening ball." Jane reared back with a gasp, but her mother's grip was unbreakable. "Listen to me," Rana said firmly. "It's time for you to get serious about settling down. You're nearly thirty-one years old, and your childbearing years are wan-ing." Her eyes softened. "Don't you want babies, Carolina? Beautiful sons and daughters who will fill your heart to near bursting as you and Maximilian have filled mine?"

"Not if it means I have to marry a man I don't love." Jane jerked away and jumped to her feet, hugging herself. "Mama, please, you have to make Father stop this insanity. This is the twenty-first century," she cried, gesturing angrily. "Fathers do not force their daughters to marry in this time." She gasped when her mother lowered her gaze. "No! No, I refuse to live in any other century!"

Rana lifted beseeching, pain-filled eyes. "I persuaded Titus to give you two years to find a husband in this century, Carolina." She stood up and walked over to touch Jane's cheek. "Two long, heartbreaking years with the entire world at your disposal, and you still couldn't find anyone to love."

Jane threw herself into her mother's arms again. "I promise to stop being so fussy! I just need more time."

"Hush now," Rana crooned, holding her tightly. "You mustn't ever stop being fussy, Daughter, or settle for anything less than true love." She leaned away, smiling tenderly. "You deserve a husband you absolutely adore. A man who steals your breath away and makes you glad you were born a woman."

"But I did find such a man," Jane said, dropping her head to her mother's shoulder again on a lingering sob. "Alec makes me feel smart and strong and feminine and alive."

"Then why didn't this wonderful man bring you home to us?"

She straightened. "Because he doesn't believe in treating a grown woman like a mindless child. He was waiting for me to decide how to handle Father, and offered to stand *beside* me instead of fight my battle *for* me."

Rana tucked a lock of Jane's hair behind one ear, her eyes crinkling with her smile. "Then you did indeed find a rare treasure, Caro. But," she said, gripping Jane's shoulders again, "I'm afraid Alec MacKeage is not one of your father's or Maximilian's favorite people at the moment. You might see him as an exciting, modern male, but they see him as the bastard who put us through ten days of hell. It wasn't until Olivia finally told Duncan what was going on that Duncan said he suspected you were right here in Spellbound Falls."

"Then that makes Duncan the bastard," Jane hissed, pulling away. "He betrayed his own nephew."

"No, he most likely saved Alec's life." All the tenderness left her mother's eyes. "I swear I wanted to kill him myself for the terror we lived through. We thought you were *dead*, Carolina. Or worse, that our enemies had you. Did you not care how worried we would be after receiving that fistful of hair and your ankle bracelet?"

Jane dropped her gaze. "Yes, I cared," she whispered. "I just didn't . . . I was afraid . . ." She lifted her chin. "I knew once Father got hold of me again that he'd take away what little power I have and marry me to the first man he could find." She pulled up her pant leg. "And I was right, wasn't I? Before I even dismounted, Nicholas held me still while Father replaced my shackle."

"That's not a shackle," Rana snapped. "It's your protection."

Jane dropped her pant leg with a snort. "It is until someone else comes along and cuts it off."

"Trust me, Caro, Zeus himself couldn't get this one off." Rana cupped Jane's face, her eyes turning tender again with her smile. "How about if we form a pact, you and me, in which I will continue to ensure that you don't have to marry a man you don't love, and you give me your word that you will at least try to give the six warriors coming here a chance to take your breath away?"

"Alec MacKeage already stole it—as did this century and all of its wondrous possibilities." Jane smiled sadly, already knowing the answer to her question. "Are any of Father's hand-chosen warriors from this time?"

Rana rolled her eyes as she turned away and walked to a small table beside the chair, then picked up a piece of paper and started reading. "Ranging from the tenth to the fifteenth centuries, there's a knight of the Round Table, a Bedouin, a Crusader, a Prussian prince, a Norseman, and . . ." She looked up, her expression turning wary. "And a highland laird named Niall MacKeage." She lifted her hand questioningly. "I can only assume Titus must have felt that one of Duncan's ancestors would be a good match for you." She brightened. "Which means there may be hope for your Alec." But then she shook her head, tossing the paper back on the table. "No, I might be able to persuade Titus to give your young man a chance, but when Maximilian heard who was hiding you, he became . . . Well, let's just say your father threatened to leave him behind when they went after you if he didn't calm down." She shrugged. "I don't know why Mac feels as he does about the MacKeages, considering how close he is to Duncan, but when he saw Niall's name on the list he tried to talk Titus out of inviting him."

"Mac doesn't like the MacKeages?" Jane asked on a gasp.

Rana shook her head again. "I don't believe he dislikes them, exactly; I think he simply doesn't want you marrying one of them."

"But why?"

"I guess that's something you'll have to ask him." Her mother walked over and grasped her shoulders. "So do we have a pact? You'll open your mind to the men coming here to court you, and in return I'll make sure your father opens *his* mind to the fact that you're a grown woman capable of knowing what you want?"

"What I want is to live in this century, not the tenth or any one in between. And I *don't* want to spend the next three weeks being polite to a bunch of ancient, full-of-themselves warriors expecting to win a quiet, demure, *obedient* wife who will give them a dozen baby princes and princesses."

Rana closed her eyes on a sigh, and Jane leaned away when her mother opened them again and actually gave her a shake. "I'm asking you to *try*, Caro. Because if your father sees you're finally taking a sincere interest in marriage, I will have an easier time persuading him to let *you* choose your husband instead of him choosing for you." She gestured toward the table. "If not one of these six, then we'll let him scour the world for six more he approves of, preferably from a more recent century or even this one. And another six, if that's what it takes." She clasped Jane's head to look her directly in the eyes. "But your father has to see you *trying*."

"Well, fine then," Jane growled. "I will be the epitome of grace and demureness for these six kowtowing buffoons."

Rana pulled Jane to her with a laugh and gave her a fierce squeeze. "Now that's the daughter I raised." She turned with her arm still around Jane and started toward the hallway. "So let's get you cleaned up and dig through my closet for something you can wear, as I believe two or three of your buffoons have already arrived, and I feel it's imperative we begin our campaign immediately." She stopped to run her gaze over Jane and frowned. "And I'll see what I can do to disguise the mess you made trying to fix your hair. I swear it looks like you finished hacking it off with a knife. First thing in the morning we'll have Olivia drive us to Turtleback Station to buy you a temporary wardrobe while I send Leviathan to get what's left of yours at home, and we'll find a salon and see about getting your hair styled."

Jane gathered her tangles in a protective fist. "I like my hair the way it is. And I didn't finish hacking it off, Alec did. And I think he did a wonderful job."

Rana leaned away to gape at her—that is, until a sparkle suddenly came into her eyes. "I must say that on the few occasions I've had the pleasure of seeing Alec MacKeage, I never once realized there was a hairstylist hiding behind all that roguish charm," she said with a laugh, heading them down the hallway again. "I wonder what other hidden talents your modern, breath-robbing man has."

"Oh, the scoundrel has all sorts of amazing talents," Jane said, only to rush in the bathroom pulling her fleece up over her head to hide her blush when Rana gaped at her again. Sweet Athena, she had to be careful what she said! Her mother might be her greatest ally, but the poor woman would have a heart attack if she knew just how *passionately* her daughter had embraced the twenty-first century.

Jane began her campaign immediately following her bath; her first order of business being her refusal to sleep under the same roof as her father. And when her mother suggested she could stay in the main lodge with Mac and Olivia and the children, Jane had simply given her a hug and headed down the wooded path—having absolutely no intention of sleeping under the same roof as her brother, either.

Nicholas had immediately fallen into step behind her. And although the man had wisely remained silent, Jane had not, letting him know exactly what she thought of his actions today. She'd abruptly shut up, though, when she'd looked over her shoulder to see him grinning.

Nicholas was . . . well, Nicholas. And dammit, she loved

him. Even when they'd been kids running carefree all over Atlantis, the more she had railed at him the wider his grin had gotten. He'd grown into a man of few words who had the patience of a saint, the body of a gladiator, the mind of a scholar, and the social skills of a hermit. And that's why when Jane had suddenly stopped in the middle of the trail and turned to see his grin grow tender, she'd thrown herself into his big strong arms and soaked his shirt with tears.

Once finished, she'd pushed Nicholas ahead of her to knock on the door of the massive log-and-stone lodge with instructions to ask to speak to Olivia—while she had safely hidden behind a tree. Olivia had run outside and then proceeded to soak *Jane's* blouse with tears as they'd hugged each other fiercely, after which her sister-in-law had insightfully offered Jane a cottage of her own before she'd even asked.

They'd gotten into one of the cute little electric carts in front of the resort's office, with Nicholas opting to jog to the cottage instead. "I swear those were the most words I've heard that man utter since he arrived," Olivia said once they'd driven out of earshot. She reached over and squeezed Jane's hand. "Damn, Carolina, you gave us a scare. I don't think I've ever seen Mac so crazy."

"Me, either," Jane said, shaking her head. "And I am truly sorry for selfishly not letting someone know I was safe."

Olivia patted her hand, then turned the cart onto a path that wove up through towering oaks covered in burnished leaves glistening in the setting sun. "I guess what I can't believe is that Alec didn't tell anyone, not even Duncan."

"He thought I was just an ordinary woman named Jane Smith."

Olivia glanced over at her. "Yes, I was told you claim Alec didn't know who you were, but Mac believes he *did* know and simply didn't care." She gestured at nothing. "Mac thinks all the MacKeage men are contrary that way, and that having even one of them on the payroll is sometimes one too many."

Jane grabbed Olivia's arm. "But Alec didn't do anything

wrong, Olivia. I *lied* to him. Oh please, you have to talk Mac out of firing him. Alec loves his work."

Olivia stopped the cart in front of a small log cottage sitting on a wooded knoll with an expansive view of the Bottomless Sea. "I don't have to talk Mac out of anything, because as my dear sweet husband keeps reminding me, Nova Mare is mine. I do the hiring and firing, and Alec isn't going anywhere until he finishes my wilderness trail." She leaned closer and lowered her voice as Nicholas came walking up the path. "Tell me truthfully, Caro; do you look at Alec's big broad shoulders and charming smile and suddenly feel your insides clench and your mouth go dry and your heart start pounding so hard, you think you might to pass out?"

Jane blinked at her, even as she felt her cheeks flush with heat. "I . . . um . . ."

Olivia got out of the cart with a laugh, dragging Jane with her. "Never mind, I don't want to know." She guided Jane up the stairs. "Because I don't want your dear sweet brother drilling me for details of how you spent the last ten days."

"Princess."

Jane pulled away just as Olivia opened the cottage door, turned to Nicholas standing at the bottom of the stairs, and arched a brow. "Yes, Nikki?"

One corner of his mouth twitched slightly. "I have to go help Titus settle in some newly arrived guests." He gestured back down the path. "You may move about freely, but I'll know the moment you step off the resort grounds." That hint of amusement disappeared. "Don't force me to come after you."

"Why, I wouldn't dream of it, Nikki," she drawled, giving a dismissive wave as she turned and walked in the cottage.

"Princess?" Olivia repeated, peeking out the door at Nicholas's retreating back. She looked at Jane. "He calls you *princess*?"

"Only when he's trying to get a rise out of me. And just so you know, he really hates being called Nikki—which I unwittingly discovered when I was eight." Jane shook her head. "I didn't work up the nerve to call him Nikki again until I was nearly twenty."

"That's right; when I asked who the scary-looking guy was with Titus and Mac and Trace when they arrived this morning, Rana told me you and Nicholas had grown up on Atlantis together." Olivia walked to the fieldstone hearth taking up most of one wall, grabbed a box of matches off the mantel, and lit the kindling already arranged in the firebox. "Aeolus's Whisper is open from breakfast through dinner, so you're welcome to eat there," she continued, setting a couple of logs on the snapping fire. She replaced the screen and brushed off her hands. "Or you can raid its walk-in cooler if you want to lug stuff back here and cook your own meals."

"Thanks, I just might take you up on that offer," Jane said, walking to one of the two interior doors at the back of the cottage. She peeked inside the bathroom, then shot a grimace over her shoulder as she walked into the bedroom. "I imagine I'll have to eat at the restaurant with whichever one of my suitors has captured my attention that particular day, but I'm going to need breakfasts here to prepare myself for long days of pretending to be sincerely interested in the full-of-themselves buffoons."

Olivia rushed into the bedroom just as Jane hopped up on the large bed made of hand-hewn logs. "Your *what*?" she said on a gasp. "Those men are here to *court* you? But I thought they were just friends that Titus had invited to attend our grand opening."

Jane snorted. "My father doesn't have any friends. There will be other guests arriving for the ball, but the men coming here this weekend are hand-chosen candidates vying to become Titus's son-in-law." Jane pulled the clearly nonplussed woman onto the bed and wrapped an arm around her. "It's okay, Olivia," she said, giving her a squeeze. "I have three weeks to figure a way out of this mess. But in the meantime, I've given Mother my word that I will act sincerely interested in these men while she persuades Father to stop this insanity."

"He can't actually make you get married, Caro."

"Actually, he can." Jane folded her hands on her lap and looked down at them. "I realize this is probably beyond the understanding of a twenty-first-century woman, but in our world, Father's word is law. My refusal to marry someone he approves of would mean immediate banishment—without any of my powers." She pulled in a shuddering breath. "I would no longer be able to travel through time or shape-shift or conjure even the simplest spell, and would age naturally and die an old woman in whichever century I was trapped in."

"For the love of God," Olivia whispered, leaning away. "Titus wouldn't . . . He *couldn't* do that to you, Carolina. Your father loves you."

"This isn't about love," Jane quietly explained. "It's about the king of the drùidhs holding on to his authority." She shrugged. "If Titus Oceanus can't even rule his daughter, then how can he command the respect of mankind?"

"Mankind doesn't know he even *exists*," Olivia growled. "Nobody believes in the magic anymore."

Jane slid off the bed and turned to face her. "The drùidhs certainly know, as do Father's enemies. The gods have been waiting thousands of years for Titus to falter so they can finally destroy Atlantis. Don't you understand, Olivia? If Atlantis ever falls, so will mankind."

Olivia also stood up, her face flushing in anger. "Are you saying that everything sits on *your* shoulders? That if you don't marry one of those men, the world as we know it will cease to exist?"

Jane shook her head. "Not on my shoulders; on Father's. I'm only saying that as his daughter, I have a duty to uphold his authority."

Olivia's cheeks darkened even more. "I thought his authority was protecting people's free will. So what happened to *your* right to choose your own damn husband, or even remain single if that's what you want?"

Jane captured Olivia's fisted hands and gave them a squeeze. "But I am free to do whatever I please, as long as I don't mind living with the consequences."

"But what kind of choice is that!" Olivia pulled away and

ran out of the bedroom. "By your stupid gods, we'll just see what Mac has to—"

Jane ran into the main room and pulled her to a stop. "You are not getting involved in this, Olivia. Mac has no more say about this than I do, and I won't have you at odds with your *dear sweet husband* over something none of us can control." She shook her head. "I can be mad at Mackie for beating up Alec, but you can't be mad at him for being caught in the middle of a fight that he and I both knew was coming. Why do you think I ran away two years ago? You and Mac were newlyweds and about to have a baby together; did you think I was going to wage my battle against my father here in Spellbound Falls and rip your new family apart?"

"But it's not fair," Olivia whispered. "You deserve to marry for love just like your brother did."

"I love you for loving Mac, Olivia, and am truly happy for you both. But you know he was facing the same dilemma when he came here, and would right now be in a loveless marriage but for your courage to love him for who and *what* he is." She smiled sadly. "I spent two years searching for what you two have, only to discover there are buffoons in every century." Jane walked to the hearth and stared into the fire, balling her own hands into fists. "That is until ten days ago, when a handsome scoundrel saved my life and ignited in me a passion that outshines the sun."

"Then tell your father that you *have* found a man you can love."

Jane turned to her. "I don't believe Alec feels the same way, Olivia."

"He must feel something for you, Carolina. He kept you hidden for ten days."

"No, he was hiding Jane Smith."

Olivia shook her head. "Alec might act carefree and fun-loving, but he's a *MacKeage*. Trust me; he knew exactly who you were." She canted her head. "In fact, I bet that's precisely why he didn't tell Duncan or anyone else about you."

Jane spun to face the fire again. Could that be true? Could

Alec have known the dictatorial father she was hiding from was Titus Oceanus, and he'd hidden her anyway?

"Maybe the question you should be asking," Olivia said, walking up behind her, "is why *did* Alec risk everything to help you?" Olivia turned her around. "If he knew you were Carolina Oceanus, and that hiding you would bring him nothing but trouble, then why did he?"

"He . . . Alec said he has nothing to offer me."

"Well, of course he said that. He knows you're a *princess*, and he's a—"

"A scoundrel!" Jane blurted out, throwing her arms around her insightful sister-in-law. "An underachieving ski bum who thinks he can't even be my boyfriend. Oh, Olivia, thank you," she said, giving her a squeeze—only to suddenly step back, shaking her head. "He's also maddeningly noble. If he's made up his mind that he doesn't—no, wait. He *deceived* me. All this time he's been—"

"No, *you* wait," Olivia said on a laugh, snagging her arm when Jane started for the door. "It was your lie, Carolina; Alec was just playing along. You can't get all huffy—"

"Auntie Caro!"

"Ohmigod, Henry!" Jane pulled open the door just in time to catch her nephew when he threw himself into her arms. "Henry-Henry-Henry!"

"Oh, auntie, I missed you," he said, hugging her fiercely. "You've been gone two whole years."

"Aunt Carolina!" Sophie shouted, running up the steps carrying a small toddler. "You're back!"

"Sophie." Jane pulled away from Henry just in time to catch the little girl hurling herself out of Sophie's arms. "Oh, you must be Ella," she said on a laugh, catching the gurgling bundle of energy. "Sweet Athena, is there not a shy bone in your precious body, you sweet little cherub?"

Olivia plucked her daughter away from Jane, causing Ella's gurgles to turn to shrieks of protest. "Shy?" Olivia said with a snort, clasping the squirming child. "Try *pushy.*" She kissed Ella's head when the little imp gave an intrinsically feminine pout. "I swear we spend all our time peeling the sweet little cherub off complete strangers." She snorted again. "Ella thinks our guests come from all over the world to see *her*, not the Bottomless Sea."

Jane touched one of the girl's riotous blond curls. "Oh, Olivia, she's beautiful." She turned and started to kneel to Henry, only to remain standing when she realized he'd grown quite tall. "And you, young Mr. Oceanus," she said thickly, cupping his face with a trembling hand. "And Sophie," she added, pulling the girl against her side. "I can't believe how much you've both grown."

"I knew you would come, auntie," Henry said, looking up with a beaming smile. "I told Mum we must have a grand ball to celebrate the opening of our hotel, because that would surely bring you back to us." He looked at Olivia, giving her an intrinsically male wink. "And I was correct, wasn't I? She came."

Jane ruffled his hair with a laugh. "Prometheus himself couldn't have kept me away, Henry."

"Did you bring a pretty gown to wear, Aunt Carolina?" Sophie asked—only to suddenly step back with a gasp. "You cut your hair!" She frowned. "Is that some sort of new style they wear in South Africa? It's sort of . . . uneven."

Guessing Olivia had told the children she'd been living in South Africa for the last two years, Jane tucked a stray lock behind her ear and shrugged. "It was becoming too much to care for, so last week I finally dug out the scissors and cut away." She sighed dramatically at Sophie's horror. "I'll find a stylist tomorrow and have it evened out. I can't believe how much you've both grown," she repeated, touching Henry's shoulder.

Olivia shifted Ella to one hip and herded Sophie and Henry out onto the porch. "Come on, people, we need to let Auntie Caro get settled in." She shot Jane a cheeky smile over her shoulder. "She's probably going to need a nap before we put her to work taking guests out on trail rides to view the fall foliage."

"Oh, yes, auntie," Henry said, stopping at the bottom of the stairs, a distinct Oceanus gleam in his deep green eyes.

"Grampy must have told several of the male guests that he expected you would be here, because one of the gentlemen brought a beautiful Arabian mare with him, and another one arrived with a large hunting falcon. And when I told Grammy, she said they were likely gifts to impress a princess." That gleam intensified. "I believe your dance card will be filled long before the ball."

"They'll all have to get in line behind you, Henry."

The boy suddenly bolted back up the stairs and threw himself at her, making Jane stagger as she caught him. "I missed you so much," he said against her shoulder.

"I missed you, too, little man," she whispered thickly, pressing her mouth to his hair. "And I promise I won't ever stay away that long again."

"I have to go help Mr. Nicholas now," he said, giving her one last squeeze before he ran down the steps and past the cart Sophie had driven here. "I believe another one of Grampy's guests is arriving." He turned and walked backward, beaming Jane a huge smile. "I'll be by to take you to dinner at Aeolus's Whisper this evening," he said with a wave as he turned and broke into a run.

Sophie watched him disappear down the winding path, then frowned first at Jane and then at Olivia. "Do you have any idea how popular I could be at school if I brought Grampy's guest with the falcon in for show-and-tell?" She eyed Jane again. "Or I could bring you, Aunt Carolina; you're an honest to gosh *princess*."

"Of a mythological island," Jane said with a laugh, "which makes *me* a myth."

Sophie blew out a sigh, her shoulders slumping as she climbed in the passenger side of the golf cart. "What good is spending the whole month of July in Atlantis if I can't even mention it in my essay about what I did over summer vacation? And the SD card in my camera was completely blank when I got home," she muttered, shooting a glare at her mother as if it were somehow Olivia's fault. "And when I told my friends at school that Nova Mare means *New Sea* in Latin and that we named the restaurant Aeolus's Whisper because

Aeolus is the mythical god of the winds, they thought I was just making it up to sound smart," she said, turning her glare on Jane, as if it were somehow *her* fault. Sophie suddenly broke into a smile again, nicely demonstrating the wind god's fondness for changing directions on a whim. "Is your boyfriend coming to the ball, Aunt Carolina? I hope he's really handsome and smart and everything, because a horse and falcon are gonna be hard to compete with."

"What . . . what makes you think I have a boyfriend?"

Sophie shrugged. "When I asked why you weren't coming to visit us anymore, Grammy Rana said you were traveling the world looking for your own Prince Charming." The girl went back to smiling. "I bet the frogs all lined up hoping you'd kiss them because you're so tall and smart and beautiful. So, did you kiss one and he turned into your prince? Is he coming to the ball?"

At a complete loss for words, Jane was saved from responding when Olivia slid in behind the wheel of the cart and plopped baby Ella on her daughter's lap with a laugh. "You're going to have to wait and see just like the rest of us, Sophie, because it looks as if Carolina still has a few more frogs to kiss."

Chapter Thirteen

⁓

Alec came awake with a groan, then used a growl to propel himself upright only to go perfectly still at the sight of five— no, *six*—wolves sitting scattered around him in the lean-to, their wet fur glistening in the rising sun.

Son of a bitch, where was his knife? He was still dressed— because undressing had been too much effort after limping back to the lean-to last night—but he was pretty sure he'd pulled the sheath off his belt so the hilt wouldn't keep jabbing his ribs while he'd slept. But where in the name of God had he put it?

Making sure not to show any outward sign, Alec inwardly tensed in preparation of defending himself, despite knowing he didn't stand a snowball's chance in hell of surviving. Six goddamn wolves. Christ, talk about pissing off Jane's father; the old bastard really was going to feed him to the orcas.

Where in hell was his knife?

Hearing soft thumping, it took Alec a moment to realize the closest wolf was wagging its tail. "Kit?" he whispered, squinting into the rising sun trying to make out its features. The thumping grew faster and the wolf ducked its head with a soft whine, then suddenly stood up, walked over, and gave him a smelly lick on the face. Alec didn't move so much as a muscle, uncertain if that had been a friendly hello or a taste. One of the other wolves tilted its head back on a huge yawn, then lay down and rested its chin on its paws with a heavy sigh—the other four following its lead and dropping like dominoes. Kit flopped down and rested his broad snout on Alec's thigh, his lupine brows puckered over soulful eyes as he gazed up at him.

Okay then; either he had six new buddies or the orca-wolves needed a little nap before they ripped him to shreds. Still, he'd feel better if he could get his hands on his knife—which he finally saw sticking out from under Kit.

So now what was he supposed to do? Because he was pretty sure going back to sleep was out of the question. Nor was he inclined to pick his way over a small herd of wolves and bolt for the safety of the privy only to get trapped there. Alec started to lift his hands to rub his face, but stopped in midlift when all six heads rose.

Christ, just what he needed; six spies. Or jailors, maybe? Had Titus sent them to make sure he stayed away from Nova Mare?

Well, he supposed it beat becoming bait chum. Alec finished raising his hands and rubbed his face—gingerly, in deference to his swollen jaw—then gazed around the lean-to. Damn, it felt empty despite being full of wolves. It was also too damned quiet.

Keeping an eye on his *guests*, Alec slowly reached for his duffel bag and slid it over, unzipped it, then shoved a hand inside and felt around. He pulled out a plastic bag and opened it, gathered up a fistful of Jane's hair, and held it out to Kit.

"Smell familiar?" he asked when the wolf pressed his nose into the hair. Alec reached in the bag again and pulled out more of the tresses he'd cut off Jane that first night—that he'd secretly hidden instead of putting in the trash—then spent several minutes weaving the strands together until he had a braid almost two inches thick. "Ye want me to make a smaller one you can wear like a collar?" he asked Kit as he pulled more hair out of the bag. He softly chuckled. "Or I could attach it to your mane and let it dangle behind one of your ears like my old man, if ye want."

Kit belly-crawled closer and pressed his head against Alec's chest with a soft whine. "Aye, I miss her, too," he murmured as he carefully wove a thin braid of Jane's hair into the wolf's fur. "Just a minute, don't move," he said, reaching in his duffel again and pulling out his ditty bag. "I need something to tie it off so it doesn't come undone."

He found a small rawhide lace and secured the braid, then reached under Kit for his knife, unsheathed it, and cut off the ends of the lace. "There, now ye look like a true highland warrior." He chuckled again; partly because he was talking to a wolf as if it understood him, but mostly because Kit canted his head trying to see his lady's token.

Two of the wolves got to their feet as they eyed the dangling braid, making Alec stiffen with his knife half-sheathed when they moved closer—only to feel the hairs on his arms raise when Kit rolled back his lips on a soft snarl, which effectively sent the pair scurrying back to their spots near the front rail.

Okay then, Kit was apparently the boss of this ragtag pack. Good to know—assuming the wolf didn't try to be the boss of *him*.

So . . . what to do now?

Being careful to treat Kit with respect in front of his buddies, Alec carefully pushed the wolf off his lap and slowly rose to his feet, taking a relieved breath when the other wolves didn't stir. He pressed a hand to his ribs and took a deeper breath, then blew it out on a sigh as he decided nothing was cracked or broken, which meant he should be back in fighting form in no time.

Alec spent the day lazily tidying up the already neat shelter, napping, repacking his larger backpack to make it lighter, gathering firewood for the increasingly colder nights, napping again, and generally keeping himself limber without overdoing it. The wolves spent the day following him around, although he noticed a couple of them would silently slip away only to return a few of hours later as two more disappeared. They were running down to the fiord to feed, he figured, rotating shifts so there were always at least four with him at any given time—which brought him back to wondering if they were guards instead of simply liking his company. Then again, maybe Kit had told his pod-mates all about his little adventure with Jane and was upping his popularity by giving guided tours of land life.

He'd have to see if he couldn't scare up a big old bear to give them a real thrill.

Waking up from his most recent nap, and after checking the position of the waning moon and figuring it was nearing midnight, Alec slipped into his boots and pulled a dark sweatshirt on over his sweater. He grabbed the larger one of Jane's satchels—that had been stashed under the back of the shelter in case Duncan showed up unexpectedly again—and walked down the stairs to the trail, the six wolves silently falling into step around him as he headed toward Nova Mare.

"I thought we agreed you wouldn't make me have to come after you."

Jane spun around with a shriek, which she quickly followed with a heated curse aimed at the far end of the porch. "Dammit, Nikki, you scared ten years off my life."

She saw the dark figure shrug as he sat on the floor leaning against the front of her cottage. "Ten years off thousands isn't so bad."

"What are you doing out here?"

"Enjoying the crisp night air."

She snorted. "So much for trust between friends," she muttered, bending down to pick up the blankets and pillow she'd dropped.

"What brings you outside tonight, Lina?"

Jane walked to the center of the porch and dropped the bedding, then got down on her knees and grabbed the feather mattress topper she'd stolen off the bed. "I came out to enjoy the crisp night air," she drawled, folding the topper in half lengthwise and smoothing it out. She plopped the pillow at one end, flopped down with a dramatic sigh, then pulled the quilt she'd also taken off the bed over herself. "Go away, Nicholas. I'm not going anywhere."

"I'm not your jailor, Lina; I'm here to protect you."

She shifted onto her stomach and bunched the pillow under her chin. "He's not going to come after me."

"I would, if I were him."

"Yes, but only because we both know how much you hate losing. You would come after me just on principle."

"I've been led to believe the men of his clan live by a similar code."

"Go away, Nicholas."

"It's not really MacKeage I'm worried about," he continued as if she hadn't spoken. "Or are you forgetting there's still one kidnapper unaccounted for?"

Jane lifted her head in surprise. "Do you honestly think anyone would dare try to snatch me from Nova Mare?"

"We *honestly* didn't think anyone would dare snatch you at all. Hell, Lina; the gods themselves won't go anywhere near you." It was too dark to be sure, but she thought he grinned. "Or hadn't you noticed they were unusually silent during your little two-year tantrum?"

Jane dropped her head. "Go away, Nikki. I need my beauty sleep."

He gave a soft snort. "You can't improve on perfection, princess."

"Yes, I love you, too," she muttered into the pillow. "Look, I have to be up at the crack of dawn to go rabbit hunting with . . . with either Aaron of someplace or what's-his-name, the Bedouin—whichever idiot brought the falcon."

"Devonshire," Nicholas said with a chuckle. "The Arab brought the mare. You're not really sleeping out here tonight? It's nearly freezing."

"I have on warm clothes and plenty of blankets," she said without looking up. "Now *go away*."

She heard him get to his feet, sensed him drop to one knee beside her, then felt the blanket tuck tightly around her just as his lips touched her hair. "I'm well acquainted with how hard it is to go from sleeping under the stars to having four walls and a roof close in around you." He gently squeezed her shoulder and stood up. "Sweet dreams, Lina," he said quietly.

And then he was gone.

Jane gave a heavy sigh that ended on a sob. Dreams, hell; she'd more likely have nightmares of seeing Alec's bloody face and hearing the thud of fists pummeling him as he valiantly—and foolishly—tried to protect her. Dammit, she'd had no right to involve him in her stupid war with her father. Alec had been nothing but kind to her, and in return she'd deceived him and gotten him beaten up.

Sweet Athena, she missed the scoundrel. How could she have known the man less than two weeks, yet feel like flotsam drifting without direction or purpose after being separated only one day? When she'd awakened in that empty, too-soft bed this morning still exhausted from having cried herself to sleep, and realized she'd never again wake up to Alec's beautiful smile or feel him pulling her intimately against the evidence of his desire, she had come very close to dying inside.

And she just might have remained wallowing in despair and self-pity if not for the realization that she had some pretty powerful allies—two of whom were married to some pretty powerful men. And Sam; she had to believe Sam wouldn't abandon her. She'd thought at first that he might have, when he'd come after her with Mac and her father. That is, until he'd stayed behind with Duncan and Trace, and she'd realized Sam intended to quietly continue working *within* the family as he championed not only her but hopefully Alec as well now.

No, she simply couldn't give up; not with her mother and sister-in-law and Sam fighting beside her. And Alec; if the scoundrel had known all along who she was and had risked his very life so she could live *hers*, then she refused to concede defeat. So she'd spent a good part of today in Turtleback Station and Spellbound Falls with her mom and Olivia and princess hugs-a-lot—with Nicholas quietly shadowing them—shopping for clothes, getting manicures and their hair trimmed, and stopping into the Drunken Moose for pie before heading back to Nova Mare in time for dinner.

Dinner had been . . . interesting. All six time-traveling suitors had arrived and were settled in, all looking overwhelmed by the wonders of the twenty-first century but by no means put off their goal of catching her interest—all while giving each other narrow-eyed glares.

What in the name of Zeus was her father thinking to bring six powerful warriors together in the same place at the same time, with each of them knowing there could be only one groom? Because if the prospective bride didn't murder them in sheer frustration, they'd likely start murdering each other to better their odds.

So while eating dinner at Aeolus's Whisper with her mom and Olivia and Henry and Sophie—her father and Mac wisely deciding to babysit the cherub—Jane had politely smiled through Nicholas's introductions as her various suitors had each come rushing into the restaurant upon hearing she was there, after which she had coyly ignored them. Well, that is until Aaron—she was fairly certain he was the infidel-killing Crusader, judging by the looks the Bedouin had been giving him—had boldly fallen into step beside her as she'd strolled to her cottage with Nicholas silently falling back to stroll several paces behind them.

Thus, her first outing was falcon hunting for rabbits at the crack of dawn.

Yes, she intended to pour all of her considerable princess talents into appearing sincerely interested in each of the buffoons to make her mother's role in their pact easier, and as an added bonus, Jane hoped her sudden turnaround drove her father crazy trying to figure out what she was up to.

As for Mackie . . . well, if her heavy-fisted brother dared

to say one disparaging thing to her about Alec, she intended to blacken his other eye.

Too excited to take one of the slow electric carts, Jane exited Nova Mare's registration pavilion and ran flat-out toward the large barn set back in the woods at the far end of the resort. She gave smiled nods as she dodged guests in carts headed to the restaurant to have breakfast with the rising sun, and took only cursory notice of the three separate hotels—that eventually would be five—staggered at varying elevations over the resort's hundred-acre campus. Only a single story high and consisting of eight guest rooms flanked by two suites, each hotel was carved into the rise of the mountain with only the front facade of floor-to-ceiling windows exposed.

The entire resort, from the hotel to the cottages to Mac and Olivia's private lodge, had been carefully designed to blend in with the forested terrain yet give each guest an unobstructed view of the spectacular forty-mile-long Bottomless Sea. From any vantage point below, whether looking up at Whisper Mountain from town or from a boat, a person would see nothing but a natural landscape with only occasional hints of man-made structures. The architecture was nothing short of inspired, and Nova Mare was already well on its way to becoming one of the world's more fashionable destinations.

But if someone without deep pockets wished to have a rustic Maine-woods experience, Olivia had plans to accommodate them as well. Besides buying most of the timberland around the newly formed inland sea two and a half years ago, Mac had also secretly purchased the family camp Olivia had run for her ex-in-laws—that *she* had secretly been planning to buy, it turns out. Inglenook sat on the shore of Bottomless, consisting of a main lodge and ten weathered cabins that Olivia hoped to open to budget-minded families just as soon as the scientists moved to the permanent facility they were building in Spellbound and she could refurbish all the cabins. And the wilderness trail was slated to open next spring for the true nature enthusiasts—providing Alec finished it before he had to leave to go be a ski bum again.

Jane had been thrilled when she had approached Olivia with the idea of running both Nova Mare and Inglenook on clean, sustainable energy and her sister-in-law had not only embraced the idea but asked her to be in charge of making it happen. So Jane had spent that entire spring and summer locked away on Atlantis with several of the island's more brilliant minds, and by the time the road Duncan was building up Whisper Mountain reached the summit, she'd been able to present Olivia with detailed blueprints for a synergetic wind and solar and geothermal energy system. She'd even included plans for indoor and outdoor saltwater swimming pools, where tidal-powered turbines would pump seawater up from the fiord through shafts cut in the granite mountain. The water would be heated by geothermal exchange before entering the pools, then would naturally cool off again on its return journey to Bottomless.

Granted, her pool design had required a bit of wizardry to create the shafts in the mountain, but apparently Olivia wasn't above asking her dear sweet husband to use his own powerful energy when she felt the end justified the means. And Mackie apparently wasn't above doing anything to please his wife, who had been very pregnant at the time. But only the pools had required the use of the magic—well, for *her* part of the construction, at least—because Jane had wanted Nova Mare to be a shining example of what was possible on a global scale *right now*, using twenty-first-century technology that was already available.

So she'd proudly returned to Spellbound Falls in November with blueprints in hand and quite eager to make it happen, except that her father had suddenly become unreasonably adamant that she instead turn her attention to finding a husband—hence the fight-of-all-fights that had sent her into hiding as Jane Smith. She still wasn't sure why Sam had insisted on helping her, but she loved him dearly for aiding and abetting her defiance, as she would probably right now be living in some ancient century, married and with a baby or two, if he hadn't.

Jane approached the barn, still at a flat-out run, and gave a winded snort at the realization that all she'd managed to do was postpone the inevitable by two years.

"Nicholas!" she called out as she ran inside. "They told me you were here."

He stepped out of a stall leading a horse. "I'm here."

So was the Crusader, Jane discovered when he poked his head out of a stall farther down. She waved at Aaron, then grabbed Nicholas's arm and started dragging him—and the horse he was leading—out of the barn. "Are you the one he gave my satchel to?" she asked in a winded whisper. "Did you talk to him? Did he look okay?" She stopped well away from the barn just as the sun broke over the mountains across the fiord. "Did you go to him, or was he well enough to make the hike up here?"

"Who are you talking about?" Nicholas asked, only to suddenly stiffen. His hands shot out and grabbed her shoulders when she took a step back. "MacKeage? He was here, on the resort grounds?" He gave her a slight shake when she didn't immediately answer. "Did you actually see him?"

"No, I didn't see him; that's why I'm asking you. I found my satchel with most of my belongings on the bottom step of my porch this morning when I woke up. I thought you had put it there."

Nicholas snapped his gaze toward the resort. "That's impossible." He looked back at her, his eyes narrowed in suspicion. "There's no way he could have gotten within half a league of the resort without my knowing it."

Realizing she'd just made a serious error, Jane shot him a broad smile. "Maybe Alec gave my satchel to one of your guards and *they* set it on my step. You did bring a small army from Atlantis to secure Nova Mare for the next three weeks, didn't you?"

He nodded, even as his gaze scanned the surrounding

woods. "They would have given the bag to me, not you." He brought his ice-blue eyes back to her again. "You heard nothing? You just woke up and it was there?"

Growing alarmed at *his* alarm, Jane tried smiling again while this time patting his chest reassuringly. "It must have been Duncan, then. Alec must have given his uncle my belongings, and Duncan brought them to me early this morning."

"I would have *known* it." He lifted one of her hands and slapped the reins in it. "Take the horse back to its stall."

Jane dropped the reins and ran after him when he started toward the resort. "Nicholas, no," she said, pulling him to a halt. "You leave Alec alone. He's not trying to cause any trouble; he simply returned my belongings."

He gently pulled free. "I'm not worried about Mac-Keage," he growled. "I'm worried about how he got on the grounds *without my knowing it*." He reached out and touched her cheek, his eyes suddenly softening. "I won't hurt him, Lina, unless he forces me to. I just need to find out how he got—"

"You're right on time, princess," Aaron said, leading another horse past the one she'd abandoned. "It looks to be a fine morning for our hunt. I'll help you mount then go get your hawk, so you two can become acquainted before we leave." He stopped and gave a slight bow, the rising sun making his beady brown eyes appear golden. "I don't doubt you'll find her beauty and spirit matches your own, princess."

"Please, last evening I asked you to call me Caroli—"

"The hunt's off," Nicholas interrupted.

"Off, you say?" Aaron snarled, his eyes shooting to Nicholas before he obviously remembered he probably shouldn't act like a buffoon, and looked back at Jane with concern. "Are you not feeling well this morning, princ—Carolina? I must say you do look rather flushed."

Nicholas grasped her arm and started leading her toward the resort. "Take care of the horses, Devonshire," he said with only a cursory glance over his shoulder. "And she's *highness* to you."

Chapter Fourteen

―――――――

Seemingly endless days of smiling and nodding, batting her eyelashes, politely laughing at lame jokes, and demurely avoiding sometimes blatant but more often awkward attempts to lure her away from Nicholas's watchful eye were starting to take their toll on Jane's resolve. Damn, she'd forgotten how tiring acting clueless could be.

Speaking of which, she was one second away from either punching Nikki in his rock-hard belly or deliberately sneaking off the resort grounds just to wipe that stupid grin off his face. The man was enjoying her command performance way too much.

By the gods, her father's hand-chosen warriors were ancient-minded. Well, except for Niall MacKeage. Jane didn't know if Niall was deliberately avoiding her to pique *her* interest in *him* or if he had accepted her father's invitation simply to get to this century. Oh, three days ago he'd dutifully taken his turn alone with her—and Nicholas, of course—but instead of expounding on her beauty and pleasant demeanor,

Niall had spent their entire four-hour ride talking about automobiles.

The man was fascinated by anything with an engine, apparently, and had been sorely disappointed when they'd taken horses instead of one of the "amazingly silent little carts" that he was constantly zipping around in. And she'd noticed that not only was Niall spending more time with his Mac-Keage descendent than trying to catch her eye, he'd somehow managed to persuade Duncan to let him drive one of the large earth-moving machines working up on the site of the fourth hotel.

Jane figured that after the ball, Nicholas was going to have to ambush Niall in order to send him back to twelfth-century Scotland—assuming the highlander didn't run off to Pine Creek to seek sanctuary with Winter MacKeage Gregor. Winter was a powerful drùidh—who just happened to be married to Matt Gregor, a nefarious magic-maker better known as Cùram de Gairn. In fact, Winter was the first *female* drùidh, and if not for her intelligence and courage and womanly insight, the Trees of Life would be facing extinction—much to Titus's consternation. But apparently Providence didn't have her father's worry about putting such powerful magic in the hands of a woman.

As for Niall MacKeage . . . well, he was over an hour late for their picnic.

Jane absently tapped her fingers on the steering wheel of the amazingly silent little cart she was sitting in—the picnic basket stowed in back and starting to smell of pungent cheese—as she glared at Nicholas grinning at her from atop his horse. He had opted for *one* horsepower instead of several, because he claimed the carts couldn't race and weave through the woods if he needed to whisk her to safety.

"You know what I think, Nikki?" Jane said through a tight smile.

"I usually prefer not to know what you're thinking, princess."

"I think you're afraid of modern technology."

He merely arched a brow.

"And that's why I haven't seen you driving or even *riding* in a cart."

He dismounted and walked over. "You want to know what I think, Lina?"

"Not particularly."

"I think you're more pissed that your highland suitor hasn't been completely taken in by your little performance than you are that he's not really interested in courting you." His grin turned tender as he ran a finger down her cheek. "You're not losing your touch, Lina; Niall is just more enamored with this century than with marriage."

Jane gripped the steering wheel with both hands, hunching her shoulders on a sigh as she stared out the windshield at the restaurant. "He's the only one of them who's not a buffoon. I actually enjoyed our ride the other day. We conversed as equals, and not once did he brush off anything I said as mere woman-talk. I can't believe he's from the twelfth century."

"There's a reason Providence decided its first female drùidh would come from the clan MacKeage; they've always been forward-thinking and open-minded for their time. And from what I understand, they still are."

Jane glanced up at him from the corner of her eye. "Do you know where Father's gone off to? I haven't seen him around for the last two days, and Mom was vague when I asked where he was."

"If Rana's not saying, what makes you think I will? I serve both of your parents."

Jane suddenly straightened. "Please tell me he's not seeking revenge on Alec."

He smiled, even as he shook his head. "He's not."

She dropped her forehead to her hands on the steering wheel. "I miss him."

"Your father or MacKeage?" Nicholas asked with a chuckle.

She rolled her head just enough to shoot him a glare, only he didn't see it because he was looking toward the other end of the resort.

"I guess it's true that nature abhors a vacuum." He gestured in the direction he was looking. "If one suitor stands you up, then another one rushes into the void."

Jane lifted her head, only to growl in frustration when she spotted Jacoby—the Prussian prince—smiling like the village idiot as he strode toward them leading two horses. "Damn, he's a full-of-himself horse's ass." She glared up at Nicholas. "I swear if I hear his whiny voice say 'Oh, highness, you mustn't exert yourself like that' one more time, I'm going to punch him right in his whiny nose. What in the name of Zeus was Father thinking to invite him? I thought he wanted my husband to be a fearless *warrior*." She gestured at Jacoby, lowering her voice as he drew closer. "I'm tempted to plant a big hot kiss on the toad just to watch him faint dead away."

"You're not the only proficient actor in this little drama, Lina," Nicholas said quietly, turning and mounting his horse.

"Good morn, highness," Jacoby chirped in old-world German—which Jane didn't have any problem understanding because every Atlantean spoke and read all the languages, including varying dialects. Heck, they'd *invented* some of them.

Jacoby gave a slight bow. "It's come to my attention that Laird MacKeage had some pressing matter he needed to attend to this afternoon, and fearing you would be left at loose ends, I thought I might interest you in a gentle ride through the lovely autumn foliage." His grin tightened as he looked up at Nicholas. "Assuming your stalwart protector approves."

"You're in luck, Jacoby, as her highness just happens to have a food basket already packed," Nicholas said far too cheerfully, making Jane stifle a smile when Jacoby's eyes narrowed at her stalwart protector's refusal to address *him* has highness.

But heck, Nicholas called the king and queen of the drùidhs by their first names, because the man had *earned* the right—and had the scars to prove it.

Jane jumped out of the cart far more cheerfully than she

felt. "Why, I do believe I would love a gentle ride through the foliage." She grabbed the basket out of the back of the cart and shoved it at Nicholas, then quickly spun away when she noticed something leaking out of the bottom of it. "Nikki will carry our lunch for us. Can you help me mount, please?" she asked sweetly, batting her lashes as she walked to the fidgeting stallion instead of the half-asleep mare. "I hope you chose a gentle horse for me."

"No!" the prince snapped as he grabbed her arm and pulled her away, only to immediately let go as he shot a concerned look at Nicholas. "I mean, this is your mount, highness," he said, moving the mare up beside her. He cupped his hands together and bent toward her left foot. "Your safety will always be my first concern."

Jane let him lift her full weight as she slowly swung her leg over the saddle, taking note that Nicholas was probably correct about Jacoby's performance, as the man certainly didn't lack physical strength. Yes. Well. He could act like a simpering buffoon until the sun burned out; she was not living in the fifteenth century. She took the reins he handed her, gave him a coy smile as she gave the mare a kick, and realized it really was going to be a gentle ride when the horse couldn't even work up a trot.

Jane shot Nicholas a speaking glare as she plodded past, then sucked in a fortifying breath. "So, Jake," she said as the prince trotted up beside her while working to control his prancing stallion. "I'm just dying to hear all about the vast kingdom you're in line to inherit."

Because Nicholas wasn't about to leave her alone with Jacoby—even though the prince was in no condition to make a pass—and because he wouldn't let her gallop back to the resort alone to get help, either, Jane ended up riding the stallion and leading her mare—since the damn stallion kept trying to *mount* the mare when she tried leading it— while Nicholas held a groaning and hissing Jacoby in front of him on his horse.

She still wasn't sure what had happened, but one minute the prince had been leaning quite far toward her—after they'd ridden around a bend in the trail far enough ahead of Nicholas that the buffoon felt safe to boldly steal a kiss—and the next minute all hell had broken loose.

Jacoby's stallion had suddenly . . . exploded, rearing up with a loud scream of what appeared to be surprise. And already being off balance, the prince had gotten slammed into a tree as the horse bolted down the trail. Somehow managing to stay with the startled beast, Jacoby had then pulled back on the reins so hard, the stallion had slid to a halt on its haunches, and Jane had watched with her hands over her mouth as her Prussian suitor went flying over the horse's head with an equally startled scream—which had ended abruptly when he slammed into another tree.

Nicholas shot past her at a flat-out gallop, and Jane didn't know which surprised her more: what had just happened or that her stalwart protector had a large caliber, very modern-looking pistol in his hand. Nicholas had pulled his own horse to a sliding stop—his butt not even lifting an inch off the saddle—between her and the unmoving Jacoby as he scanned the woods on both sides.

"What in hell happened?" he growled, still scanning.

"I have no idea. One minute he was trying to steal a kiss, and the next minute his horse suddenly bolted, like something bit its ass."

He finally looked at her, and in the blink of an eye Nicholas went from warrior to childhood friend, one side of his mouth lifting. "*Something*, Lina . . . or you?"

She shook her head. "I swear on Prometheus's toes, I didn't do anything. Um, do you think we should go see if Jacoby is still breathing?"

Nicholas went back to scanning the woods around them. "Did you happen to hear anything before something bit his horse's ass?"

"Only a whiny voice whispering that my beauty makes Venus a hag."

His mouth twitched again as he finally slid his weapon

inside his jacket—into a shoulder holster, she assumed. "The guy was comparing you to a *Roman* goddess? Maybe he is a buffoon." He shrugged. "Titus must have invited him out of respect for his father, knowing Jacoby didn't stand a chance of your picking him."

Jane stood up in her stirrups to look past Nicholas at Jacoby's still motionless body, then sat back down. "You intend to leave it to me to tell Jake's father his son is dead because we were too busy discussing what happened to save his life?"

Nicholas gave a sigh and dismounted, then walked down the trail to the fallen prince. "He's still breathing," he said as he rolled him over. He shook his head. "But I don't think you're going to see his name on your dance card. His left knee is busted." He suddenly stilled, then pulled out his gun as he rose to a crouch, his gaze going to the woods off to Jane's right. "Dismount," he quietly hissed without looking at her. "And lay flat on the ground."

Jane immediately slid off her horse and lay down, putting a large tree between her and where he was looking, and stopped breathing to listen. They each held their positions for several pounding heartbeats, and then Nicholas suddenly stood up with a snort and shoved his gun back inside his jacket.

"Call your pet, Lina," he muttered, gesturing toward the woods.

Jane rose to her knees and gasped in surprise. "Kital-anta!" she cried, jumping to her feet just as the wolf suddenly sat down a good twenty paces away, his gaze darting from her to Nicholas then back to her. "No, it's okay. Nicholas is proud of your role in helping me escape the kidnappers. Come on, Kitty," she petitioned, patting her knees when the wolf still didn't move. "Nicholas, tell him what a good orca he is."

Nicholas turned away and knelt down to Jacoby. "Kital-anta negated his good deed when he didn't immediately come tell us where you were."

"He's my friend," she snapped, rushing to the wolf. "Yes,

my loyal friend," she murmured, dropping to her knees and giving him a fierce hug. "You don't listen to Nikki; he's just grouchy because he has to lug Jacoby back to the resort." Jane leaned away to clasp Kitty's face but stilled in surprise. "What's that you're wearing?" she whispered. She glanced over her shoulder to make sure Nicholas was occupied, then touched the braid of hair—which looked like *her* hair—woven into Kitty's fur. Jane shot her gaze to the woods behind the wolf, her heart pounding with a mixture of excitement and dread as she gave another quick glance at Nicholas. "Did Alec put that there? Is . . . is he here?" she asked softly, looking around again.

Kitty leaned in and gave her a lick, then ducked his head with a grumbling whine, but Jane clasped his face again. "Listen carefully, Kitalanta; you must keep Alec away from Nova Mare. Can you do that, my friend? I'm afraid of what will happen if he's caught trying to sneak onto the resort grounds, and Nicholas doubled the guards after Alec brought me my belongings. You have to keep him—"

"I could use some help over here."

Jane stood up and turned to see Nicholas lifting Jacoby onto his horse. "What do you want me to do?"

"Go get his horse," he said, nodding at Jacoby's stallion pulling against its reins tangled around a branch down the trail.

Jane turned back to Kitalanta and nudged him with her knee. "Go on, now. Go keep an eye on Alec for me," she said softly as the wolf took two steps then stopped and looked at her again. "And . . . and tell him I'm sorry," she whispered, spinning away and running to the trail—only to glance over her shoulder to find that Kitty had vanished.

So that was how Jane and Nicholas and a groaning and hissing Jacoby ended up returning to Nova Mare later that afternoon, and Jane subsequently learned that Niall Mac-Keage had apparently decided picnicking with a princess didn't hold a candle to sneaking off to Pine Creek with Duncan to meet more of his descendents.

It was also when, much to her delight, Jane realized that

of her six original suitors, she was down to four and a half—
if she counted that Niall was only half-interested in becoming Titus Oceanus's son-in-law.

Aeolus's Whisper's private dining room was abuzz the following evening as to why the five remaining warriors had
been collectively invited to eat with the Oceanuses, as well
as speculation about what had really happened to cause
Titus to send Prince Jacoby home that morning. Jane sipped
her wine to hide her wince as she remembered seeing Jake's
ribs wrapped so tightly it was a wonder he could breathe, his
right eye swollen shut, and his left leg trussed up in a crude
splint that wouldn't raise any eyebrows when he showed
back up in the fifteenth century.

   She'd felt bad—but only a little bad—this morning when
she'd given the Prussian a kiss on his battered cheek as he'd
repeatedly petitioned her father to please let him stay. And
she'd felt only a little more bad when she'd heard Jake actually break into sobs as Nicholas had carried him into the
woods—only to return shortly after a loud clap of thunder
had pulsed through the air and shaken the ground.

   "It's just as well," Titus had said on a heavy sigh as he'd
turned and walked away. That was all; *it's just as well*.
Those had been the only words he'd said to Jane since coming after her in the woods five days ago. No, he hadn't spoken to her then, either—not that she'd gone out of her way
to give him a chance.

   It had been while she'd been watching him walk away
that Jane had heard the helicopter start up, and nearly
dropped to her knees when she saw it rise into the air lifting
a huge lean-to. On the one hand that meant Alec must be
well enough to work, but the ache Jane had felt knowing he
was so close but so far beyond her reach had nearly crushed
her. She hadn't heard Nicholas when he'd walked up behind
her, and had broken into huge sobs when he'd wrapped his
arms around her. "I'm sorry, Lina," he'd murmured into her
hair before turning her around and holding her face to his

chest so she'd quit watching the chopper flying away. And then he'd simply let her soak his shirt, his silent understanding doing more to help her weather the storm than any words could have.

Jane took another sip of wine as she glanced around the long table taking up most of the private upstairs dining room—the restaurant being the only two-story building on the resort—and found herself feeling sincerely sorry for the five remaining men, knowing they were all going home losers.

She suddenly stilled, realizing only four warriors were present. So who had been foolish enough to ignore an imperial invitation to dine with the royal family? Niall was there, so despite being only half-interested he obviously wasn't stupid. Sir Garth of the Round Table was there, and the Bedouin, and Aaron of Devonshire—which meant Soren the Norseman was missing.

Come to think of it, she hadn't seen him all day. And that was unusual, since the Viking usually looked her up most mornings and tried to entice her to join him for a swim—in the freezing *fiord* instead of the nicely heated outdoor pool, the idiot.

She leaned toward Nicholas. "Have you seen Soren today?" she whispered.

Nicholas let his gaze travel the length of the table, his eyes stopping at the empty chair on the opposite side. "I saw him heading down the mountain just after dawn. *Alone,*" he said with a chuckle. He shook his head. "You would think he'd catch on and just swim in the pool with you."

Jane leaned away, widening her eyes in mock horror. "And concede defeat to a mere woman?" She looked around the table again and sighed. "Why do you suppose Daddy put on this little feast?"

"Daddy?" Nicholas repeated, arching a brow.

Jane shrugged one bare shoulder and tugged on the front of her black strapless dress—that she'd worn just to scandalize the ancient-minded buffoons. "Henry's been bugging me to call Father *Daddy*, claiming it's more modern and . . . affectionate."

"And have you called him *Daddy* to his face?"

Instead of answering, she took another sip of wine.

Nicholas merely chuckled.

Jane never did find out why her daddy had called everyone together, because not five minutes after Titus had entered with Rana on his arm—causing everyone to rise to their feet—and Mac had entered with Olivia—causing everyone to rise again—all hell broke loose for the second time in two days when the Norseman came staggering into the dining room, his face a bloody mess.

And in another clap of thunder, Jane was down to three and a half suitors.

Chapter Fifteen

―――――――――

The mere hint of sound was enough to awaken Alec in a state of battle-readiness, although he was careful not to show any outward sign. But what really worried him was that the wolves weren't alarmed, which led him to believe he probably wasn't going to like his late-night visitor.

Cracking open his eyes to see the unusually tall man bathed in moonlight sitting on his food locker, Alec spread his arms out from his sides and slowly sat up. "Take your best shot, old man, because if your first blow isn't fatal, it may well be your last."

"I didn't come here to kill you, MacKeage."

"Then you're a bigger idiot than I am."

"My daughter wants you."

Alec dropped his arms on a heavy sigh and pushed back to sit leaning against the rear wall of the shelter he'd set onto the site yesterday afternoon. "Look," he said, "I was just a safe place for Jane to land for a little while."

"Yes, safe," Titus said gruffly, brushing at nothing on his pant leg, "and obviously quite caring." He looked back at Alec and arched an imperial brow. "So much so that you willingly risked your life protecting her, first from the kidnappers and then from me."

"The way I hear it, you're hoping your man Nick will take over where I left off."

"Nicholas will marry Carolina if I ask him to, despite his feelings for her being those of a brother to a sister." The old wizard leaned forward to rest his elbows on his knees, his slightly glowing eyes somber. "And if another option doesn't present itself *soon*, I will have no choice but to ask him."

Alec stiffened. "Why? What's happening *soon*?"

"If Carolina's not married and with child by her thirty-first birthday in three months, she will become fair game for my enemies."

"What in hell do ye mean, fair game?"

"Every immortal—god *and* demon—will be free to pursue Carolina the day she turns thirty-one, with the sole intention of seducing her in hopes of getting her pregnant with *their* child."

"Christ, who in hell is she?"

"My daughter," Titus said quietly. "And the only real weapon my enemies have against me." The wizard stared down at his hands. "Enemies I made when I built Atlantis," he continued without looking up, "who will use any means at their disposal to destroy it." He straightened, his eyes clouded with pain. "And that is why it's imperative that Carolina marry a strong and fearless mortal who can protect her."

"You're a goddamned wizard," Alec snapped. "Use *the magic* to protect her."

Titus shook his head. "It's exactly their hope I'll expend so much energy protecting Carolina that I'll leave Atlantis vulnerable to attack. And if Atlantis falls, they will then go after the Trees of Life, and they won't stop until all of mankind's knowledge and free will is destroyed." Anger flared in his eyes. "And if that happens, the entire planet will be at the mercy of the gods again."

Alec just stared at him. Seriously? The fate of mankind depended on protecting Jane from being—"Wait; you said they'll be free to *seduce* her. Does that mean she can just say no? That an immortal won't—or can't—force himself on her? Well, hell," he went on when Titus nodded. "Forewarned is forearmed; all she has to do is say *no*," he repeated.

"You would think it's that simple. But since the beginning of time, men—gods and mortals alike—have used everything from flattery to trickery to successfully seduce even the most astute and resilient woman."

"And here I thought it was the other way around," Alec drawled.

One side of the wizard's mouth lifted. "It's an affliction that runs both ways."

"Why thirty-one?"

Titus sobered. "I was certain I would have Carolina safely wed by that age. So in return for leaving my daughter alone until her thirty-first birthday, I promised that my army of powerful drùidhs would only protect the Trees of Life instead of my focusing their energy on destroying my enemies." His eyes took on a triumphant gleam. "Upon realizing I had the power not only to build Atlantis but to keep it hidden from them all these thousands of years, they've been content to wait me out."

"*They* don't actually exist."

The wizard looked down, brushing at his knee again. "Yes, we're only a myth."

Alec scrubbed his face in his hands, hoping like hell he was having the mother of all nightmares. "Does Jane know any of this?"

"No one but Maximilian and Nicholas know, not even Rana."

Alec stared at him for several heartbeats, hating to ask because he knew he wasn't going to like the answer, but asking anyway. "Why are ye telling me, then?"

"Because I am just as desperate to see Carolina happy as I am to keep her safe."

"I can't make her happy."

"You already have, Alec."

"And I can't keep her safe, because I can't get her pregnant."

"That can easily be remedied."

"Dammit, your daughter deserves better."

Titus was silent so long that Alec figured he was finally getting through to the old bastard. That is, until the wizard smiled sadly. "The boy whose neck you broke nine years ago; did you know that if you had hesitated but a second longer, you would have been his fifth murder?" He nodded when Alec stiffened. "His mother was his first, when he was twelve. She tried to stop him from going with his father to join the rebel fight, and the boy bludgeoned her to death with her own frying pan."

"How do you know what happened nine years ago?"

Titus arched a brow. "Did you think I wouldn't look into the background of my daughter's self-appointed champion? Your partner and lover at the time, Sabrina," he continued solemnly, "was the boy's fourth murder. His father deliberately sent his son in his stead to meet the two of you, knowing Americans wouldn't think one so young would pose a threat since you keep your own children sheltered into their twenties."

"The kid was *fourteen*," Alec growled. "He was barely old enough to shave."

Titus nodded again. "But as you learned that night and subsequently during your years as the Celt, children grow up more quickly in other parts of the world, especially when fed a constant diet of hatred by fathers raised the same way." He hesitated, tilting his head. "Do you know the difference between a murderer and his victim, Alec?"

"There is no difference, as they're both dead, except one is still breathing."

"The difference," Titus said quietly, "is intent, or the predominant emotion at the moment of the fatal blow. Murderers are ruled by their hatred and walk away feeling empowered, whereas the true victims are the ones who walk away believing they've lost their souls." He undid the top two buttons on his jacket and slid a hand inside. "You've been living with what you perceive is an unforgivable sin, Alec, but what you haven't taken into account are the lives you saved by stopping the boy when you did," he finished softly, his hand emerging holding a thick vellum envelope.

Damn. "I don't want your daughter."

Titus leaned over and set the envelope on his sleeping bag. "That's too bad, as I believe she wants you."

"And whatever the princess wants, she gets?"

"You tell me," the wizard said with a soft chuckle. He set his hands on his knees and pushed himself to his feet—which brought the wolves to their feet as well. "Exactly how many battles did *you* win during your ten days together?"

"The important one," Alec snapped. "You got her back at full *value*."

The old bastard arched a brow. "And would that make you a saint . . . or an idiot?"

"Wait," Alec said when he turned away. "You mentioned Jane has to marry a mortal. Why? Wouldn't she be safer with a husband who has command of the magic?"

Titus turned back, a strange light flaring in his eyes. "It's a misconception that we magic-makers hold all the power, whereas it's actually the man who understands the source of that power who is the true force to be reckoned with."

Alec glared at him, wondering what in hell sort of answer that was.

Titus started to turn away again but hesitated. "I would ask that you not mention this evening's conversation to anyone, including Maximilian." He grinned. "It does my old heart good to see my son passionate about something other than building his own version of Atlantis," he said, gesturing in the direction of Nova Mare. "And Carolina needs to know that she can rely on her brother in the future instead of running from him." His grin turned to a glower. "Should her husband prove to be a blackguard."

And just that quickly Titus grinned again and gestured at the wolves. "If you happened to be wondering, they're here of their own choosing, not mine." Up went one of those imperial brows. "It would appear that just like my intelligent daughter, Kitalanta also recognized the real man behind all that . . . Celtic charm." The old bastard actually gave a slight bow. "I wish you good luck in the coming weeks, Mac-Keage, should you choose to follow your heart instead of your hard head. Although I do believe Maximilian will prove to be your greatest obstacle, as he's still . . . What is the term you moderns use? Ah yes, he's still too pissed off at you to see what his sister sees."

He turned away when Alec said nothing, and silently walked down the steps, only to turn again when he reached the bottom—the moonlight revealing his slightly hunched shoulders. "Would you happen to have any suggestions as to how I can get my daughter to stop crying, Alec? She is the face of politeness and grace in the company of others, but the night breeze carries her sadness to her mother and me."

"I can't—" Alec went silent when he saw the desperation of a father aching for his child, and softly sighed. "I'll see what I can do."

Titus gave another slight bow. "Thank you." But then he canted his head. "I doubt you could be aware of it since you've been isolated out here building your trail, but my hand-chosen field of suitors is now down to four—not counting Nicholas." He shook his head. "Prince Jacoby met with an unfortunate accident two days ago that broke his leg, and I felt compelled to send him back to fifteenth-century Prussia, as I couldn't see a man who couldn't even control a startled horse protecting my daughter."

Alec shrugged. "It's probably just as well, as I don't think Jane would have been happy living in fifteenth-century Prussia after experiencing the wonders of this time."

"Yes, you're probably right. And just today," Titus said, sounding confounded—or maybe that was barely contained amusement—"a renowned Viking hiked down to the fiord for a morning swim, but came staggering back to the resort after dark. Soren was battered and somewhat addled in the head, and couldn't account for the missing hours." Titus gestured at the trees. "He believes he fell down a steep ridge when something—an acorn, he thinks—hit him in the temple just as he was leaping onto a boulder."

"It sounds to me," Alec said, deadpan, "as if traveling

through time has thrown some of your strong and fearless mortals off their games."

The old man shook his head. "It's really quite disheartening that a mere acorn and what was likely nothing more than a bee stinging a horse has forced me to send two great warriors home. At the rate they're dropping out of the competition, there won't be anyone left by the grand opening ball."

"There's always brotherly Nick."

"You can rest assured," Titus said with a chuckle, "that the remaining four will be on their toes over the next two weeks as they each try to capture Carolina's interest. And Nicholas assures me that he's tightened security around Nova Mare despite having made it . . . well, *almost* impenetrable the day we arrived."

"Then maybe ye should send your remaining fearless mortals home and simply award Jane to Nicholas, if he's so good at what he does that he can protect her from falling acorns and bee stings."

The wizard's eyes hardened. "My daughter is not a prize in the sense you're implying. And I could do a lot worse than having Nicholas for a son-in-law."

"Aye, ye could."

The old bastard stared at Alec for several heartbeats, then turned and walked up the trail. "Enjoy these next two weeks of your carefree lifestyle, MacKeage," he said with a suspiciously cheery wave over his shoulder, "as they very well could be your last."

Alec watched the wizard disappear into the night, then looked at the six wolves settling back down around him. "Thanks," he muttered, "for the warning." He dropped his gaze to the vellum envelope on his sleeping bag and blew out a sigh. Dammit to hell, he didn't want to go to a goddamn ball. He hated having to smile and nod and pretend he was having a good time eating pretty food and drinking weak punch.

And besides, he didn't have anything to wear.

What in hell was Jane doing camping out on her porch and crying herself to sleep every night, anyway? She was an intelligent, tough and resilient, kidnapper-escaping, porno-watching woods-woman, for christsakes, not some spoiled-rotten princess who burst into tears when she wasn't getting her way. Alec reached under his pillow and pulled out the braid of Jane's hair, then rubbed it between his fingers as he stared at the moonlight reflecting off the fiord below. She had no business wanting him. Hadn't he told her—several times, actually—that they didn't have a future together?

He dropped the braid on his lap with a snort, wondering what made him think she'd been listening any of those times, and reached inside his duffel bag, took out her iPad, and turned it on. He spent the next twenty minutes wiping out Jane Smith's extensive libraries of pornography, then another half hour studying the details of the elaborate wind and solar and geothermal systems she'd designed for Nova Mare—which had saved Olivia from having to run power lines up the mountain, smartly making the resort completely self-sufficient.

He grinned as he made one more adjustment on the tablet before finally shutting it off and staring out at the fiord again, undecided if he was awed or really quite frightened that Jane had inherited her father's brilliant mind. Because just as Titus's acumen for world-building had allowed him to create Atlantis and successfully keep it hidden all these tens of centuries, Jane appeared to be just as passionate about getting the entire planet running on clean energy. Hell, he thought as he slipped on his boots, she'd probably have nuclear fission perfected in less than ten years—providing she got to stay in this time.

Alec pulled on a heavy sweatshirt, then dug through his duffel bag again and pulled out Jane's sound machine. He grabbed the iPad before walking down the stairs and headed up the trail as the wolves silently fell into step around him, figuring he might as well go give Jane something other than her own misery to dwell on—as well as punch another hole in brotherly Nick's *almost* impenetrable security.

Chapter Sixteen

Jane pulled the quilt over her nearly frostbitten nose when the rising sun hit her face, but then sat up with a gasp when she realized that instead of dreaming, she was hearing the song for real. She gasped again when she spotted her iPad leaning against the front wall of the cottage as it played "Good Morning Sunshine," the giant clock on its screen proclaiming it was six forty-two A.M. Jane scrambled for the iPad and stuffed it under her sweater even as she glanced over her shoulder looking for Nicholas—only to yelp in surprise when the cold tablet touched her bare belly. She jumped to her feet and ran in her cottage, pulled out the iPad, and frantically tried to remember how to shut off the stupid alarm.

"You *idiot*," she growled into the sudden silence broken only by . . . What was that noise? It sounded like rain coming from—Jane ran into her bedroom just as a rumble of thunder filled the room, and stood gaping at her sound machine sitting on the nightstand. Sweet Athena, what was Alec doing? She ran to the window, saw it was locked, and peered out at the woods. How had he gotten in? Or more importantly, how had he gotten onto the resort grounds?

No, even more importantly, *why*?

What was he hoping to accomplish by coming here? And dammit, if he was going to sneak into her cottage, why hadn't he awoken her? Jane walked to the bed and fell back onto it to stare up at the knotty pine ceiling, undecided if she wanted to scream or burst into tears.

Alec had been here twice now and hadn't even said hello, just bringing her stuff back one or two pieces at a time. But *why*? What could he possibly be trying to prove? Well, other than that he really wasn't afraid of her father, she thought with a snort. For the love of Zeus; didn't he realize that with nothing more than a flick of a wrist, Titus could turn him into a dung beetle or a sea slug or a . . .

Jane bolted upright. Was Alec trying to send her a message by sneaking in past Nicholas's guards? Like maybe *she* could sneak *out* past them just as easily?

Then why hadn't he just taken her with him?

But then what? Were they supposed to spend the rest of their lives running? Jane threw herself back down. Not while wearing a shackle around her ankle, they couldn't, because Father and Mac and Nicholas would always know where she was.

Damn. She needed to find a way to contact Alec and tell him to stop trying to help her. Duncan, maybe? Could she ask him to deliver a letter to Alec? Or Sam? She'd only seen Sam once since she'd been back, but the man had acted rather aloof, as if he didn't want to be seen speaking to her.

Jane bolted upright again. The privy! If the helicopter had delivered the shelter yesterday, the privy should be leaving today or tomorrow. She could sneak over to the building site and place a letter inside where Alec would find it. "Yes!" she cried, jumping off the bed. She tapped a button on the sound machine until the room filled with ocean waves crashing onto shore, turned up the volume, and ran into the bathroom. After taking care of her morning rituals but too excited to dress, she rushed to the main room and sat down at the small desk, opened the top drawer, and pulled out a pen and several sheets of stationery embossed with the Nova Mare crest.

But then she stilled with the pen poised to write.

What to say? She snorted, deciding she should probably start by apologizing for lying about who she was—even if the scoundrel *had* known all along. And then maybe she would give *him* hell for deceiving *her*.

She stilled again, her mother's serene smile when she wanted to persuade Titus to see things her way suddenly flashing in Jane's mind. No, she would probably have a better chance of persuading Alec to stop coming to Nova Mare if she *didn't* tell him only an idiot would push Nicholas's and Mac's patience past the point of no return.

She sighed, and started with her apology.

Jane heard a knock on the door and straightened with a groan at the realization she'd been sitting bent over the desk for nearly an hour. "Just a minute," she called out, gathering up all the pages she'd filled and shoving them in the drawer. "Who is it?"

"For a woman who's been waiting over a week to get her hands on that Arabian mare, I'm surprised you're late, princess."

"Nicholas!" Jane threw open the door to find him holding her bedding, which he tossed onto the sofa when he walked inside. "I . . . I got involved in a book and didn't realize what time it was."

His eyes narrowed on hers. "What are you reading that's turned you pale, Lina?"

She pressed her hands to her cheeks and spun around. "No, I'm just shocked I forgot about my morning ride with Hashim. I'll just be a minute."

"Don't rush. I've heard keeping a man waiting is the first weapon a woman pulls from her arsenal if she's determined to catch his interest."

Jane stopped at her bedroom door to gape at him. "You

think I'm trying to catch the *Bedouin's* interest?" She snorted. "Hashim's not a buffoon; he's an arrogant, condescending son of a bitch. The guy thinks I should be honored if *he* decides to choose *me* to be his wife."

"He has good taste in horses."

Jane took a calming breath when she saw Nicholas's eyes turn sparkling blue and shot him a smile. "I hope he knows that when he leaves here *alone* right after the ball, the mare's staying."

"You're slipping, princess," Nicholas said with a chuckle, heading back outside. "I would have expected you to insist the stallion he also brought stays, too." He stopped just before closing the door, his eyes narrowing again. "Why am I hearing ocean surf?"

Jane gave a negligent wave at the bedroom behind her. "It's a digital sound machine I bought last year in New York City. I'd forgotten about it, but found it in the bottom of my satchel when I was looking for something to wear this morning." She shrugged. "Maybe now I can start sleeping in my bed again before my nose falls off from frostbite." She waved him away when his eyes remained narrowed on hers. "Go on, Nikki; I'll be along in a few minutes."

He took a glance around the interior of the cottage, then stepped back inside, walked to one of the chairs in front of the hearth, and picked up her iPad. "What's this?"

"That's just my computer," she said, backing into her bedroom. "I'll see you in the barn in twenty minutes," she added brightly, closing the door then leaning against it with a shudder. Damn, she'd never been successful lying to Nicholas. Even as a boy he had always seemed to know when she was beating around the truth, and if he suspected Alec had been here again, *Nicholas* would likely be sleeping on her porch.

Sheikh Hashim may have brought her a magnificent mare as a token of his interest in procuring *her* interest, but it had taken the man almost a week to let Jane do more than brush it, as he apparently didn't want her breaking her magnificent neck before he could wed and bed her—presumably in that order. Of her suitors, Hashim was by far the boldest, to the point of arrogantly saying, to her face, how honored she should feel that he was even considering her to be his wife— number *four*, he had accidentally let slip this morning while Jane had been brushing *her* magnificent mare.

Had her father lost his mind?

"I don't like that look in your eye, Lina," Nicholas said, walking beside her leading his horse as she led her prancing mare out of the barn. "What are you up to?"

Jane glanced over her shoulder to see Hashim unhooking the stallion he'd also brought through time—because he apparently wouldn't be caught dead riding anything but a magnificent Arabian—then shot Nicholas a glare. "I'm about to do wives number one, two, and three a huge favor, at the same time making sure I don't become number friggin' *four*."

Nicholas shook his head, although she could tell he was fighting a grin. "Not on my watch you're not." He pulled her to a stop. "A simple 'no' from you is all it takes."

"But I'm down to only three and a half suitors now with just nine days to go."

His mouth twitched again as he arched a brow. "Who's the half?"

"Niall," she said, breaking into a full-blown smile, "although I'm starting to count him out completely." She glanced at the barn then back at Nicholas. "Watching Jacoby and Soren get sent home got me thinking that if *all* of my suitors get sent home before the ball, I'll be off the hook without having to outright reject them. Don't look at me like that," she muttered, her smile disappearing. "I didn't bite Jacoby's horse's ass, and I certainly didn't push Soren off that cliff. But their unfortunate accidents made me realize that Daddy can't very well expect me to choose from *zero*."

"Not on my watch, and sure as hell not with this one," Nicholas growled, gesturing toward Hashim mounting his horse, the jerk apparently not even willing to do Jane the honor of helping her mount. "He's *not* a buffoon, and you could wind up on the wrong end of the next 'unfortunate accident.'" Nicholas grabbed her around the waist and tossed her up onto her mare, then clasped her leg to get her to look at him, his eyes having hardened to steel. "Your word, Lina."

"Well, fine then," she snapped as she started to spur her horse forward.

Nicholas grabbed the reins and held the mare in place. "What else aren't you telling me?" He suddenly stiffened. "You've seen MacKeage."

"Of course I have. I had dinner with Niall last night."

"*Alec.* You met him someplace and he gave you the sound machine and computer. Did Kitalanta take you to him?"

"No! I swear, Nicholas, I haven't seen Alec MacKeage. Nor Kitty since that day we saw him in the woods."

"Is there a problem?" Hashim asked, riding up beside Jane.

"I believe her highness should spend time in the paddock getting acquainted with her mare before we let her take such a spirited animal on the trail," Nicholas said. "I'm sure it would please Titus if you could give his daughter enough instruction to keep her from breaking her beautiful neck."

"It will be my pleasure," Hashim said through a tight smile, grabbing one of the mare's reins as he headed to the paddock. "I'm sorry for bringing you such a dangerous prize, highness, as I was led to believe you were an accomplished horsewoman."

Jane twisted around to see Nicholas standing with his arms crossed and his eyes narrowed in speculation as he watched her, and she shot him an obscene gesture anyone from any century would recognize before turning to Hashim. "I learned to ride before I could walk," she muttered, pulling the reins out of his grasp and trotting to the paddock.

Jane then blatantly ignored the SOB sitting on his stallion after he'd closed the gate and spent several minutes getting acquainted with her new mare. That is, until she noticed Nicholas striding toward the office pavilion leading his horse. Dammit, he was going to call his guards and give them hell for letting Alec sneak onto the grounds again. Or else he was going to tattle on her to Mac.

Jane eyed Hashim from the corner of her eye and then pushed the mare into a canter while gauging the height of the paddock fence, deciding it was time to show the arrogant jerk some real horsemanship. She collected the mare by gently pulling on the reins while tightening her legs into its sides, then released its pent-up energy in a burst of speed as she aimed directly for the fence.

"No!" Hashim shouted as the mare soared into the air without hesitation, clearing the fence with ease and surging into a flat-out gallop when Jane leaned over its neck and gave it free rein.

Nicholas spun toward her in surprise, then broke into a grin. "Enjoy your little rebellion, princess," he said as she raced by.

"Try to keep up, would you, Nikki?" she said with a laugh as he vaulted onto his horse. She glanced over her shoulder just in time to see Hashim also jump the paddock fence and come tearing after her—his expression not the least bit amused.

Oh yeah; the guy was no buffoon, and she didn't have any problem picturing him riding across the desert brandishing a raised scimitar. Jane gave a smiled nod at two startled guests as she galloped past, then turned up the cart path that she knew led to a beautiful high-mountain pond a few miles away.

Sweet Athena, it felt wonderful to break free, the sure-footed mare's equal joy to be racing like the wind palpable. She crested a knoll with a quick look back to see Hashim closing in on her with Nicholas about twenty horse-lengths behind him—the former's expression still not amused and the latter's too far away to read.

Well, at least she'd turned Nicholas's attention away from Alec.

Jane gave an exuberant wave at the guard sitting on a boulder as she galloped past, recognizing from his size and sun-bronzed skin that he was Atlantean. And judging by his grin, Jane guessed it wasn't the first time he'd seen Princess Carolina racing by on a horse with Nicholas in pursuit. Although back on Atlantis, Nicholas had always made sure his horse was faster—unlike today, thanks to her arrogant suitor.

Jane had no more than rounded a bend in the path when she gave a startled shriek, realizing that Hashim had caught up with her. She veered away when he tried to grab her reins, and then she pulled her mare to a stop with another laugh. "Ah, Hashim, this beautiful mare is magnifi—" He threw his leg over his stallion's neck and, reaching out and snagging Jane's hair, dragged her with him as he slid to the ground. "Hey!" she cried out in pain, shoving against him. "What is your prob—" She cried out again when he slapped her hard enough that she fell to the ground.

"You stupid bitch!" he shouted, bending to her.

But before Hashim could touch her again, Jane's stalwart protector sent the angry warrior sprawling onto his back with a well-placed fist to the jaw. "Get her out of here," Nicholas growled over his shoulder just as Hashim sprang to his feet.

Jane flinched in surprise when a pair of strong hands clasped her from behind and lifted her to her feet, then held her steady as she seemed to be trembling with shock or disbelief—or both. "Easy now," the man said, leading her away. "Come, highness," he said more firmly as she tried to turn around to see what was going on.

"He's got a knife!" she cried when Hashim suddenly pulled the weapon from his boot. She gave the guard a shove. "I'm okay. Go help Nicholas!"

"Lina, *go*," Nicholas snapped without taking his eyes off his opponent crouched to strike as sunlight glinted off the knife in his hand. "And take the mare *and* the stallion with you," he added in a provoking, almost bored tone.

"Highness, come," the guard repeated in perfect English, snatching up the mare's reins and handing them to her while still clasping her arm. And then the man actually grinned as he led her toward the stallion that had wandered back up the path. "I'm enjoying this particular tour of duty too much to insult Nicholas by helping him deal with one measly opponent." He gently tugged her forward when she looked back in time to see Nicholas deflect the slashing knife just before driving his fist into Hashim's face again. "Here, your lip's bleeding," the guard said, reaching in his pocket without breaking stride and pulling out a handkerchief.

Jane dabbed at her mouth while trying not to notice that her hand was shaking, and took another look back as they rounded a bend and saw Nicholas drive his boot into Hashim's belly. "Um . . . what's your name?" she asked, licking the cloth then carefully wiping the blood off her chin. Sweet Athena, she couldn't believe the bastard had actually struck her.

"Rowan." He finally let go of her arm, apparently deciding she wasn't going to run back and help Nicholas herself, and shortened his stride to match hers as they led the mare and stallion over the crest of a knoll. He shook his head with a chuckle. "I have no idea why the Bedouin was so angry. I used to watch you galloping all over Atlantis as a child, and you rode better than most warriors." He glanced over at her and winced. "There's a bubbling spring a short distance away," he said. "I think we should wet that cloth and cool off your cheek to slow the swelling." He shook his head again. "I can't believe the bast—the fool had the nerve to strike you."

Finding her trembling easing in direct proportion to her distance from Hashim, Jane snorted. "What about it can't you believe: that the ancient-minded bastard had the nerve to strike a woman or to strike Titus's daughter?"

Rowan snapped his gaze to hers, but then grinned again. "Actually, highness, I can't believe he didn't have the sense to know you would have struck him back if Nicholas hadn't come along."

Jane took one last calming breath, only to flinch when a clap of thunder suddenly split the air and shook the ground, then broke into a wincing smile when she realized she was now down to two and a half suitors. "So, Rowan," she said, sliding her arm through his, "tell me what your favorite thing is about this century."

Jane smoothed down the front of her fleece, patted her carefully made-up cheek, then opened the door of her parents' cottage and strode inside. "It was my fault," she said, causing four sets of eyes to turn to her—two sets glowering, one filled with concern, and one giving her a speaking glare.

"This is about me, Lina, not you," Nicholas said tightly, his glare intensifying.

"My getting slapped isn't about me?"

"Oh, Caro," her mother said, rushing to her. She held Jane's shoulders as she studied her face, then touched her swollen cheek. "I can't believe Hashim had the audacity to actually strike you." Her concern turned to an equally intense glare as she looked at Titus. "If this is anyone's fault, it's yours," Rana said, guiding Jane over to her father. "You've brought warriors here from centuries where women are considered nothing more than chattel. Look at her," she demanded when Titus lowered his gaze. "This stops now. You send the remaining men back *today* and stop this insanity."

"The men stay," her father said with imperial authority. "And if Carolina hasn't chosen one of them by the night of the ball, I will choose for her."

"Titus," Rana said on a soft gasp, her face flushing with . . . Jane couldn't tell if it was anger or shock.

Her father arched a brow. "Last time I checked, my word was still law in this family." He looked at Jane. "Choose."

"By the gods, Caro, just *pick* one," Mac growled. "The Crusader; marry the infidel-killing idiot so you can finally be free."

"Free?" Jane whispered, turning to face him. "How would going from a dictatorial father to an equally ancient-minded husband possibly make me free?"

Mac stepped closer. "Devonshire will head off on one of his Crusades the day after you announce you're with child."

"And if he decides to stick around to watch his child grow up?"

Mac waved that away. "You'll twist him in such a knot trying to please you, the bastard won't know if he's coming or going. Or marry Sir Garth. The chivalrous fool will be putty in your hands. Just *pick* one, so you can get on with your life."

"Well, fine then," she snapped, keeping her eyes locked on his. "I pick Niall."

He stilled. "The hell you will."

Jane spun toward Titus. "On the condition that we get to live in *this* century."

Mac turned his thunderous glare on Titus. "She's not marrying a MacKeage! Send him back. Today. Better yet, do as Mother says and send them *all* back and marry her to Nicholas."

Jane clutched her chest on a gasp. "What? No!" She shot Nicholas a frantic look, but when he merely lowered his eyes, Jane looked at Mac, incredulous. "Are you insane? Nicholas is more like a brother to me than *you* are."

"Enough," Rana said with her own quiet authority, wrapping an arm around Jane and giving her a squeeze. "Carolina still has nine days to decide, and no one—especially not you, Maximilian—is deciding for her." She gave her husband a barely perceptible nod. "Fine then," she said with utter calm, "you will learn Carolina's choice the night of the ball." She led Jane toward the door. "I only hope, husband, that you are prepared to live with the consequences."

"Mama," Jane whispered once they were outside. "What have you done?"

"I have no idea," she whispered back, guiding Jane down the steps. Rana took hold of her hand and continued walking up the path leading to the summit. "Well, other than buy us nine days," she said with a sigh. She shook her head. "But I know that look in your father's eyes, Caro, and he's not budging."

"But why is it so important that I get married?" Jane gestured angrily behind them. "It's not like he's dying for grandbabies; he has Henry and Ella of direct blood, and Sophie is just as dear to him. Why do I *have* to get married?"

"I believe he's scared," Rana said, shaking her head again. "I don't know of what, but there's something he's not telling me that's making him act so unreasonably all of a sudden. He gets this way sometimes; all closed up and unreadable, as if he thinks he's protecting me from . . . from whatever," she said with an angry wave. She started walking faster. "I swear one of these days I'm simply going to explode in sheer frustration and leave him."

Jane pulled her to a stop. "No! Father would die if you left him."

"I see; so you can run away, but I can't?"

"But I'm his daughter; I'm supposed to leave home. But you . . . Mama, you love Daddy more than life itself. And he loves you."

Rana started walking again. "Yes, he loves me so much that he treats me as if I'm some fragile, simpering woman who can't handle the truth—like now. Why in Hades won't he simply tell me what's going on?"

Jane captured her mother's fisted hand and swung it between them. "And you've never once protected Daddy by keeping your problems from him? Say . . . like the time that Roman emperor cornered you in our garden several years ago?" She glanced over with a smile. "Did Daddy never question why his houseguest suddenly packed up his wife and servants and left a week early?"

Rana lifted her free hand to her mouth to cover her laugh and shook her head. "He did wonder why the fool was walking funny when he left." She pulled them to a stop and threw her arms around Jane in a fierce hug. "We'll fix this, Daughter. Even if I fail to discover *why* Titus is being so pigheaded and Maximilian is siding with him for the first time in his life, I promise that you and I and Olivia will find a way to stop this." She leaned back. "Can you continue acting interested for nine more days, Carolina?"

"Do you really think Daddy expects me to after this afternoon's argument?"

Her mother looped an arm through Jane's as she once again headed up the path. "I think you should *double* your efforts on your three remaining suitors, as if you're desperately trying to decide before the ball. Trust me, Caro; it will drive Titus and Mac positively crazy."

Jane sighed. "And likely send Nicholas into uncontrolled fits of laughter."

Rana gave her arm a squeeze. "It was just like old times when you burst into the cottage to defend him," she said with a warm smile. "If I had a penny for every time you and Nicholas appeared before Titus defending each other, I'd be a rich woman."

"What was Mackie thinking to suggest that I marry him? He knows how we feel about each other. And I thought Mac *liked* Nicholas, so why would he want to saddle him with a brat like me?"

"Nicholas saddled himself with you the day you were born. The moment his mama set you in his arms in order to concentrate on saving my life, Nicholas fell in love with you." She squeezed Jane's arm again. "He was only seven years old, and I believe you became the baby sister he never had. I was told that for the entire three days that it was uncertain if I would survive, the only time Nicholas gave you up was to let the nursemaid feed you. You owe that man a lot, Carolina; the only reason you were allowed to run wild on Atlantis was because Nicholas was always with you."

"I know. I really missed his maddening grin these last two years."

Rana stopped walking just as they reached the summit, the sun reflecting off the sudden twinkle in her eyes. "Then I guess you should have been more alert these last two years, and you might have seen that grin only a few paces away."

"Nikki followed me?" Jane covered her face with her hands when her mother nodded. "Oh, Mama, he saw the jerks I dated. And kissed! He saw me kissing them!"

Rana sat down on a boulder, pulling Jane down beside her. "He wasn't always following you, baby. Nicholas just regularly popped in to check on you for us." She nodded toward Jane's feet. "The ankle bracelet was supposed to be all the protection you needed. Now come," she said, wrapping her arm around Jane and staring out at Bottomless, "and allow this beautiful autumn view to calm your heart. Tomorrow's a new day, Daughter; so let us go to that place deep inside ourselves and access our wisdom that we may find a feminine solution to our maddeningly male problem.

Chapter Seventeen

Suddenly finding he was walking the trail alone, Alec veered toward a large tree and stepped behind it, resting his hand on his knife as he looked around, trying to decide why the wolves had vanished. He slowed his breathing to listen, and finally heard the clank of a bit as a horse shook its head, the sound coming from his campsite just a hundred yards away. Damn. He didn't know if the wolves disappearing meant they knew his visitor and didn't want to be seen with the enemy, or if they'd spread out to guard his back. Alec continued down the trail and walked into camp as if he didn't have a care in the world, forcing himself not to set his hand on his knife again when he saw brotherly Nick sitting on the top step of the lean-to.

Not that his knife would have done him much good considering the bastard was polishing a goddamn handgun the size of a small cannon.

"I assumed I'd have a better chance finding you here around supper time," his uninvited guest said when Alec stopped in front of him, "since you seem to be rather busy at night." He slid the gun in a holster inside his jacket, stuffed the cloth in his pocket as he stood up and walked down the steps, and held out his hand. "Nicholas." He grinned. "A good friend of Jane Smith."

"Nicholas what?" Alec asked, taking his offered hand.

"Just Nicholas will do," he said, ending the handshake. He walked over to the fire pit, pulled a metal lighter from his pocket, then crouched down and lit the campfire he'd apparently prepared while waiting. "There's a sack of food from your uncle's camp cook on my saddle," he said, gesturing toward his horse before setting a couple of logs on the crackling fire. "Jeanine also sent some beer, but I think you might prefer what's in my saddlebag instead." He twisted while staying crouched and gestured for Alec to go look. "Your ancestor, Niall MacKeage, brought it from eleventh-century Scotland, but Rana thought you might appreciate it more than Titus would."

Alec walked to the horse and took the sack off the saddle horn, then unbuckled the saddlebag, reached inside, and pulled out a bottle of ancient liquid gold. He walked to the lean-to and climbed the stairs, set down the food and Scotch, and shrugged off his backpack.

"This is also for you," Nicholas said, reaching inside his jacket on the opposite side of his gun as he walked to the bottom step. His hand reemerged holding a long envelope, which he held out. "It's from Lina." He grinned again. "I saw her sneak up to the building site and go inside the privy they're supposed to deliver tomorrow, and figured she'd found an ingenious way to get a note to you. But it wasn't until I saw her return to the privy an hour later carrying another envelope that I decided to see what she was up to." His grin turned derisive. "This one's thinner than the first one she took back. The seal's not broken," he said, turning away when Alec took the envelope. "So I don't know if it's a love letter, a scathing lecture, or a heartfelt plea for you to stay away from Nova Mare. But knowing Lina, it's probably all three," he added over his shoulder as he walked past the fire before stopping and folding his arms over his chest.

"Show yourself, Kitalanta," he said toward the forest. "And you others as well."

The wolves stepped into the clearing from six different directions, their heads lowered and their tails tucked against their hind legs. No, only *five* wolves appeared, causing Alec to stiffen and scan the woods for the sixth one. He didn't think it had gone to the fiord, as they always fed in pairs. So where in hell was it?

Nicholas crouched to his heels as Kit stopped in front of him about ten paces away. "Titus recognizes your valor, my friend," he said, extending a hand, "and admires your loyalty to Carolina. Come, orca. It would appear you've earned your badge of courage." He ruffled Kit's fur when the wolf finally closed the distance between them. "What's this?" he asked, fingering the braid of Jane's hair. He gave a quick glance at Alec before looking back at Kit, and chuckled. "I suppose every warrior needs a token to remind him why he's in the fight. But know there'll be hell to pay if Leviathan sees that. As for you others," he said, standing up and looking around, "you would do well to emulate Kitalanta." That said, Nicholas shrugged off his jacket as he walked back to the fire and sat down, the wolves preferring to bed down where they were.

Okay; apparently the big bastard was settling in for a visit. Alec looked at the thin envelope in his hand, blew out a sigh, and stuffed it in his hind pocket as he went to the rear wall of the lean-to. He grabbed two tin mugs, snatched up the bottle of Scotch as he headed down the steps—again scanning the woods for the sixth wolf—and sat down an arm's reach away from Jane Smith's heavily armed good friend. Christ, he hoped the missing wolf didn't start something, because he really didn't see it ending well.

"Besides being an errand boy," Nicholas said as Alec poured Scotch into each mug, "I've come to ask your advice about a decision I'm trying to make." He took the mug Alec handed him, took a long swig, and wiped his mouth with the back of his hand. "Son of a bitch, that's smooth." He looked over and grinned again. "I can see why Lina likes you,

MacKeage, as I'm starting to like you myself. Hell," he said with a chuckle, "if she considers me a man of few words, she must find you truly refreshing."

Alec took a drink—damn, his ancestors knew something about Scotch—and refilled his and Nicholas's mugs. "What is it you're trying to decide?"

Nicholas stared into the crackling fire. "It appears I'll be out of a job in nine days, and I'm trying to decide what to do with the rest of my life." He looked over at Alec, his ocean-blue eyes direct despite his negligent shrug. "Once Lina chooses on the night of the ball, she'll no longer be my . . . worry."

"And if she doesn't choose?"

He shook his head. "She has no choice but to choose, which I believe Titus explained to you just last night," he said softly, grinning at Alec's surprise. "Which is another one of my errands," he continued just as quietly. "Titus asked me to come out here and explain that you no longer have to sneak around to see Carolina—or *Jane*, he said you kept calling her—because you're welcome to come to Nova Mare and openly court her with the others."

Titus had told Nicholas about their late-night conversation? "You can go back and tell him thanks but no thanks," Alec said, which he followed with a swig of Scotch to wash away the foul taste Jane's suitors left in his mouth.

Nicholas nodded. "I didn't think so. I told him your rather unique courtship was more effective, anyway." His eyes suddenly hardened. "Which is why despite the little chat you two had, I've given my men permission to use any means necessary to stop you from wandering in and out of Nova Mare seemingly at will." And just that suddenly he grinned again. "It took the guard you tied up last night until nearly noon to get free. And though that normally would have meant immediate dismissal, I somehow allowed Dante to talk me into letting him stay. So don't be surprised if he and the others are a little harder to sneak past."

"You're assuming I intend to."

"Another of my errands," he continued as if Alec hadn't

spoken, his voice back to normal, "is to warn you about what happened this morning. Rana's afraid you might get . . . upset when you notice the handprint on Carolina's face."

Alec stilled with his drink halfway to his mouth. "Who in hell hit her? Titus?"

Nicholas's eyes flared in surprise. "No," he snarled. "The Bedouin."

"And where is the bastard now?"

Nicholas dropped his gaze to his mug and shook his head. "Let's just say he's no longer here and won't be leaving handprints on any more women." He took another drink of Scotch, then looked at Alec again. "So, any suggestions as to what I should do with the rest of my life?" He waved the mug at the fiord. "I find myself liking this century with all its modern conveniences. And weapons," he said, grinning again as he nudged his arm against the gun in his shoulder holster. "And since Titus promised me a satchel of money and the choice of which century I wish to live in, I'm trying to decide if I want to stay in this one." He shook his head. "But I need to find something stimulating to get me out of bed every morning."

"Why don't you ask Mac?"

"Because Mac isn't exactly approachable at the moment. And if Lina chooses Niall MacKeage the night of the ball . . ." He looked back down at his mug. "Well, let's just say the little earthquake Spellbound Falls experienced two and a half years ago will seem like a minor tremor."

"What does Mac have against Niall?"

Nicholas downed the Scotch in his mug. "It's not just Niall he's opposed to, but any MacKeage, apparently. Only none of us can figure out why he's so adamant that Lina not marry anyone from your clan, especially considering he's such good friends with Duncan." He shrugged. "Personally, I think—"

"Nicholas? Are you through taking Alec's measure yet, because I'm beginning to get a bit chilled."

Alec stiffened even as Nicholas shot him a grin. "Another of my *errands*," the big bastard drawled, standing up. "Sorry, I guess I forgot you were here."

"You did not," Rana Oceanus said, striding into the clearing with wolf number six walking beside her, its tail wagging like a love-struck puppy.

Alec scrambled to his feet with a silent curse.

"Hello again, Alec," she said, sliding her purse onto her shoulder and extending her hand to him. "I'm so glad we were able to catch up with you this afternoon."

He took her offered hand and gave a slight bow. "Mrs. Oceanus."

She used their handshake to lead him back to the fire. "My, the sun sets early this time of year this far north, doesn't it?" she said cheerily, finally letting him go to hold both of her hands over the fire. "And the temperature drops so quickly." She walked to the jacket Nicholas had tossed on the ground and, giving the man an apologetic smile, sat down on it and settled her purse on her lap. She patted the ground next to her. "Sit here beside me, Alec. And please, I insist you call me Rana," she said, darting Nicholas a speaking look before smiling at Alec again. "Being Mrs. Oceanus is really quite tiring, and sometimes I just want to be . . . an ordinary woman."

Jane's mother was about as ordinary as her daughter, Alec thought with a stifled snort as he sat down beside her. "How about *your majesty* or *highness*?" he asked.

She reared away, horrified. "No, that's worse!" She leaned toward him and patted his arm—then left her hand there, he couldn't help but notice. "To you I'm *Rana*," she growled—though she was smiling. "I insist."

Christ, he really didn't see this ending well. "May I ask what brings you way out here on this chilly afternoon . . . Rana?" *Other than to make me crazy missing your daughter,* he silently added. Damn, Jane and her mother could be twins but for their ages. Not that they looked all that much alike, as Jane seemed to have inherited her father's height and eyes and dark hair. But their mannerisms, like their slightly lopsided smiles, no-nonsense strides, and demonstrative have-to-touch-you nature, were identical. Hell, they even smelled alike.

Still keeping her hand on his arm, Rana looked past Alec just as errand boy started to sit down. "Nicholas, could you go get one of the cups we packed so I can try some of that lovely highland gold Niall thoughtfully brought Titus?" She leaned toward Alec again when Nicholas straightened with a loud sigh and headed to his horse. "If the subject should ever come up around my husband, you never saw that Scotch," she whispered, giving him an intrinsically Jane smile.

Nope; definitely not going to end well.

"Now, Alec," she said, opening her purse and reaching inside. "I don't know if you're aware of it or not, but Olivia and Maximilian are putting on a private ball the evening of the day-long celebration of the hotel opening." Her hand re-emerged holding a bunch of thick vellum envelopes. "And with your being way out here in the wilderness, I decided to deliver your invitation personally to make sure you received it. I know it's here someplace," she muttered, fingering through what had to be a dozen envelopes.

Was she serious?

She'd definitely caught Nicholas by surprise, if dropping the silver cup just as he was bending to pick up the Scotch was any indication. "What are you doing?" he asked, crouching to glare across the fire at her—or, more specifically, at her lap.

Rana arched a very Janelike, perfectly shaped eyebrow. "I'm delivering Alec's invitation to the ball." She waved the envelopes in the air. "And tomorrow you can help me go into town and deliver the rest of these."

"All the invitations were sent out weeks ago."

"Yes. Well," Rana murmured, lowering the envelopes to her lap, "Olivia and I decided to invite a few more people. I could probably start feeling my toes again if I could get some of that Scotch down to them, preferably by way of my stomach," she continued, dropping her gaze to the bottle in his hand. "So, Alec," she said, turning her attention back to him when Nicholas picked up the silver cup and wiped it on his shirt before filling it to the rim. "I was also hoping you could give me some insights into some of the people Olivia suggested that I—that *we* might wish to invite." She started flipping through the envelopes, reading off the handwritten names. "Frank Duffy, Charles Vail, Nicholas Patterson, Richard Nason, Michael Byram—"

"Rana," Nicholas interrupted, handing her the cup full of Scotch, "does Titus know you're doing this?"

Up went that perfect brow again. "And just when did my husband start caring about the details of any ball I've put on—or, in this case, helped put on?"

"Since this particular ball was *his* idea. You've invited a bunch of local—and I'm assuming unmarried—men."

She lifted her cup in a semi-toast, her sudden musical laugh hitting Alec square in the chest. "Well, of course they're unmarried; that's the whole point of this stupid ball." And next came that lopsided smile. "I'm just making sure Carolina has several men to . . . dance with."

And as sure as a bolt of lightning might strike him dead, Alec realized where Jane had learned the art of acting clueless. He grabbed the Scotch and refilled his tin mug, then refilled Nicholas's mug and held it out to the apparently speechless man.

The three of them drank—long and heavily.

"I am nine days away from a hard-earned retirement," Nicholas growled into the silence broken only by Rana's soft gasps for breath. "And you're going to get me banished to some prehistoric hellhole."

"No, Nicholas," she rushed to assure him, not a drop of cluelessness in sight. "I'm not asking you to keep what I'm doing a secret from Titus, or Maximilian, or even Carolina." She smiled—somewhat smugly, Alec thought. "In fact, I plan to tell Titus tonight, after which I intend to point out that the men *he's* invited seem to be dropping like flies. Or haven't you noticed that we're down to only three?"

"Two and a half," Nicholas said, a corner of his mouth

twitching as he slid his gaze to Alec. "Lina counts Niall MacKeage as only a half, because your ancestor appears to be more enamored with this century than with her."

"Yes. Well," Rana murmured, looking at the envelopes. "So Alec, what can you tell me about Frank Duffy?" she said, holding up an envelope. "Olivia said you probably know more about him than she does, as he's part of Duncan's construction crew and lives in Pine Creek."

Seriously? She wanted him to help her vet husbands for Jane? Alec looked down at his mug to hide his glower. "Well, Frank's a fine enough fellow, if ye don't mind that he's been married three times and has six child—"

The envelope was tossed in the fire before he'd even finished. "And how do you feel about this gentleman, Charles Vail?"

"Charlie lives here in Spellbound, and I've spent more than a few hours in a boat fishing with him." He shrugged. "Good fellow from a good family, and strong as an ox."

That envelope got slipped in her purse. "Nicholas Patterson?"

Alec started to shake his head, but then nodded. "I would definitely invite Nick, especially if you're wanting to liven up the party."

She hesitated, then slipped Nick's envelope in her purse. "Richard Nason?"

"Aye," Alec said with another nod. "And Michael Byram, as well. Mike has a brother you might consider inviting, if ye don't mind that Raymond is in his early forties."

Rana reached in her purse, pulled out a pen and small notebook, and wrote down *Raymond Byram*. "I'll make Raymond his own invitation this evening, as I feel each gentleman deserves special attention even if they are from the same household." She looked over at Alec. "What do the Byram brothers do for work?"

"Mike's a logger. So was Ray, but a tree he was cutting landed on him a couple of years ago and left him partially disabled. He used the insurance money to buy a pontoon boat and now gives guided tours of Bottomless to tourists."

The poor woman looked down at her notepad, her shoulders slumping with her sigh. "Yes. Well. I suppose the important thing is that Carolina has a wide variety of men to . . . dance with."

Nicholas suddenly stood up just as the wolves rose to their feet. "Sounds to me like you won't have to wait to tell Titus all about your exciting plan," he said rather cheerily just as Alec heard pounding hoofs heading toward them.

How goddamned wonderful, considering how well things had turned out the last time a group of mounted men had stopped by for a visit. Alec started to get to his feet, but Rana grabbed his arm and pulled him back down with one hand even as she reached for the bottle of Scotch with the other. She filled her cup and his mug to their brims, then corked the bottle and gave it an impressively accurate lob into the woods, where it landed on a bed of moss. The woman then picked up her cup and held it up for a toast, her sparkling brown eyes dancing with laughter as she gave him a wink.

Christ, he missed Jane.

Not being the idiot everyone accused him of being, Alec clinked his mug to her cup, then hid his grin by taking a drink as he decided the safest place right now was sitting beside the wife of the king of the drùidhs. His decision was reinforced ten seconds later when Titus came galloping into the clearing followed by three men, the wizard looking meaner than Jane's imaginary bear.

Nope; not going to end well at all.

"Are you thinking to protect her," Nicholas asked Alec from across the fire, his eyes also filled with amusement as he nodded down at Rana, "or hide behind her?"

"That would be up to him," Alec said, using his mug to gesture at Titus just as the six wolves crowded up against the other side of Rana, making Alec wonder if *they* were protecting her or hiding.

"Wife!" Titus snapped as he dismounted and strode toward them, only to halt when brotherly Nick stepped in front of him, making Alec also wonder exactly who Nicholas was to the Oceanuses, as the man certainly didn't act like an errand boy.

"We left you a note saying we'd be back shortly after dark," Nicholas said calmly.

"Yet you failed to say *where* you were going," Titus growled while glaring at his wife. He turned that glare on Nicholas. "It's a damn good thing you told your guards."

"Titus, you remember Alec MacKeage, don't you?" Rana said brightly, slipping her arm through Alec's and leaning into him—making him wonder if she didn't remember that he and Titus had met quite recently, which he still had the loose teeth to prove. "Come try some of this Scotch he just poured for me," she added, holding up the silver cup. "Apparently the Scots know a thing or two about distilling spirits. Come on," she sweetly coaxed when Titus didn't move, "and I'll explain why I asked Nicholas to bring me out here today."

Alec saw the old wizard fold like a house of cards, but not before giving Nicholas one last glare as he stepped around him and strode to the fire. He took the silver cup from his wife, downed its contents in one swallow, then wiped his mouth. "That's really quite smooth," he said thickly, holding the cup toward Alec for a goddamn refill.

"Come sit down," Rana said, shooing the wolves away and patting the ground on the other side of her. "And I'll tell you all about the wonderful idea that came to me just this afternoon," she added, waving her handful of envelopes when Titus didn't move.

That certainly deflected his attention from a refill. "What in hell are those?" he asked, sitting down and snatching them away from her.

He started to open one, but Rana covered his hand. "No, don't ruin the seal. I don't have enough left to rewrite it again. They're invitations to the ball."

"Who are these men?" he asked, thumbing through the envelopes, only to still in surprise and snap a confounded glare at Alec.

"They're gentlemen who live in Spellbound Falls and

Turtleback Station." Rana took the envelopes from him and carefully arranged them into a neat pile again. "And some are from Duncan's crew."

"But we posted an open invitation to everyone in town," Titus said gruffly, eyeing the pile on her lap, "as well as to all the employees. So why are you giving these particular men engraved invitations?"

"Because I want these particular men to come to the ball. That's why I'm doing exactly as you did, and am delivering my invitations in person." She patted Alec's knee while still looking at her husband. "Starting with Alec here, because I think it's important that Carolina have a wide variety of *dance* partners to *choose* from."

Alec looked over his shoulder when he heard coughing and saw Nicholas's shoulders shaking as the man fiddled with something on his saddle. The three guards who had arrived with Titus had dismounted and were also busy adjusting their saddles.

Alec downed the rest of his Scotch, then stood up. "Could I interest the two of you in staying for supper?" he asked, deciding that if he couldn't have Jane, he could at least enjoy her mother's crazy antics. Damn, he had a thing for smart and sassy women. "Nothing fancy, I'm afraid, but I promise it'll be filling." He slid his gaze to Titus. "And I believe I have some stout beer on ice in my cooler."

"We would love to stay," Rana said just as Titus started to shake his head, her eyes sparkling in the firelight. "Carolina assures me that besides being a very good hairstylist, you're also quite a talented cook."

Now she decides to bring up the ten days he'd spent with her daughter, just when they'd all been getting along so well?

The woman looked around the darkening forest, her eyes widening as she looked back up at Alec with a lopsided smile—that sparkle intensifying. "The smell of cooking food won't bring a mean old bear nosing around, will it?"

His next nocturnal visit to Nova Mare, he was going to bind and *gag* Jane and lock her in a closet—naked. "No, ma'am," he said, striding to the lean-to before she said something else outrageous.

Nicholas joined him at the food locker. "May I ask what you're doing?"

Alec bent down and opened the locker, took out his tin of trail mix, dug two six-packs of beer out of the food sack, and straightened. "I'm making sure *this* visit doesn't end in more bruised ribs and loose teeth." He thrust the beer and trail mix toward him. "Here, these are for your men."

The bastard chuckled as he took Alec's offering. "Sorry, my friend, but plying them with food and liquor won't make them any gentler when they catch you." His amusement vanished. "Which, I assure you, they will."

"They certainly have my permission to try," Alec said cheerily, grabbing a frying pan off the back wall, then snatching up the sack of food as he headed back to his royal dinner guests—determined to make *this* visit end well.

"Mind telling me what that was all about?" Alec asked, using the vellum envelope Rana had just handed him to gesture at Titus and the guards disappearing into the darkness, Rana riding in front of her husband.

"That was a mother trying to get a handle on the man her daughter has fallen in love with," Nicholas said, lifting the stirrup on his saddle to expose the cinch.

"Jane's not in love, she's just infatuated with a ski bum who treated her like an ordinary, *grown* woman."

Nicholas gave a snort, tightening the cinch strap. "Keep telling yourself that, MacKeage, and maybe you'll start believing it."

"Two questions," Alec said, deciding to ignore that comment and move on. "First, why doesn't Titus just use the magic to come and go?"

Nicholas lowered the stirrup and turned to him. "The official story is that he and Rana made a conscious decision to live like normal, *ordinary* people. But unofficially," he said with a grin, "I happen to know that popping around the world and traveling through time upsets Rana's stomach, so Titus only uses the magic when he absolutely has to if she's with him. Next question?"

"Will you marry Jane and live in this century?"

Nicholas stared at him for several heartbeats. "Do you have a sister, Alec?"

"Aye, one, a couple of years younger than me."

"Then you understand my feelings for Lina. And I'm sure you also understand that I will do whatever is required to make sure she's safe and as happy as is possible."

Not particularly liking that answer, Alec asked another question. "Can you explain to me why Titus simply doesn't tell Rana and Jane about the birthday deadline? They're both strong, intelligent women, so what's he protecting them from?"

Nicholas hesitated, crossing his arms over his chest as he stared at Alec, then released a heavy sigh. "Titus nearly lost Rana when Carolina was born," he said quietly. "My mother was the island's midwife, and I was only seven at the time, but I've subsequently learned that up until that point, Titus hadn't believed he *could* lose Rana—or his children, for that matter. He was so shaken by that realization that he appointed my mother as the family's personal healer and moved us into the palace." He grinned. "My father was quite excited to be named royal gardener, and I was immediately given a bedroom next to Carolina's, along with the job of keeping the princess safe *and happy* until the day I turned her over to her husband."

"At age seven?" Alec said in disbelief. "You became Jane's bodyguard while still a kid yourself?"

"It wasn't exactly taxing for the first six or seven years, and I was fourteen by the time Lina was old enough to start roaming the island." He grinned again. "And by then Titus had made sure I was well trained."

"That still doesn't explain why he won't tell them *why* Jane has to get married."

"He's afraid, Alec. If Rana ever finds out that he made a deal with the gods to keep his daughter safe until her thirty-first birthday, and that in three months they'll be free to come after Lina, Titus is afraid the worry might be too much for her."

Alec snorted. "That woman is about as frail as a big old mama bear."

"I agree. But few people realize that Rana's actually a mortal, and after nearly losing her in childbirth, Titus lives in fear that even his considerable power won't be able to save her next time." He shook his head. "If anyone ever wanted to paint a portrait of what love looks like, they'd only need to have Titus and Rana pose for them." He chuckled, gesturing at the campfire. "You saw them tonight; even after thousands of years of marriage, they're still crazy about each other, and one of their greatest joys seems to be trying to outfox each other. You have to admit that Rana inviting her own suitors to the ball just to make a point was nothing short of genius." He turned and mounted his horse. "You were given a rare treat tonight, Alec. Rana rarely involves anyone other than immediate family in her battles with Titus, which tells me one of two things. Either she's getting quite desperate, or she's already decided you're family."

But then Nicholas sobered. "I really don't want to marry a woman I consider a sister," he growled. "And I also hope that Lina gets to stay in this century. But unlike Mac, I *prefer* she marry a MacKeage." He shrugged. "It doesn't matter if it's you or Niall, just as long as she's happy." He leaned down. "If you care at all for Lina, don't force her to sacrifice herself trying to uphold her father's position as king of the drùidhs."

"Are you saying she really won't say no to him?"

Nicholas straightened with a sigh. "I'm saying that Lina feels the same powerful duty to protect the drùidhs that Titus does. She understands that the Trees of Life are all that's ensuring mankind's survival, so even though she doesn't know *why* her father is demanding she marry, ultimately she will obey him. She might have come to you as Jane Smith, but at her core she will always be Princess Carolina." He softly snorted. "If there's one thing that Rana and Lina have taught me over the past thirty years, it's that men don't hold a monopoly on honor and duty. And the Oceanus women have spent their lives walking a precarious line trying to honor their own self-worth *and* their duty to humanity."

He spurred his horse forward toward the trail. "Marry Lina for me, MacKeage," the bastard said with a suspiciously cheery wave as he disappeared into the darkness, "and if I stay in this century, you can introduce me to your sister."

Alec stared after him, fighting the urge to throw up.

Christ, she was going to do it; Jane was going to marry one of those goddamn mortals in nine days. And even if he did manage to finish picking them off one at a time, she would just dutifully marry Nicholas—without even knowing *why*.

Something pressed heavily against his leg, and Alec looked down to see Kit staring up at him, the light of the fire reflecting in his lupine eyes, the braid of Jane's hair looking somewhat tattered as the wolf held the bottle of ancient liquid gold in his mouth.

Alec shuddered trying to dislodge the bus sitting on his chest, took the Scotch away from Kit, and walked to the campfire. He sat down, uncorked the bottle and took a long, long swig, then poured a bit in his hand and held it out. "Go on, you've earned it," he said, letting his thumb brush the side of Kit's snout as the wolf gently lapped the Scotch. He then reached over and grabbed a leftover can of beer, poured it into his and Nicholas's mugs, and set them out for the two remaining wolves—having seen the other three following Titus and Rana when they'd left.

Christ, his campsite felt emptier than ever and too damned silent without Rana's laughter—which had grown increasingly musical as the Scotch had finally worked its way to her toes. Alec picked up the vellum envelope and stared at his name written in bold yet decidedly feminine script, and softly snorted. He'd like to be a fly on the wall of the elder Oceanuses' bedroom tonight to see how their royal battle of wills played out behind closed doors.

Thousands of years of marriage, Nicholas had said, and Rana and Titus were still madly in love with each other.

And mother and daughter could be twins but for their age difference.

Dammit; Jane had no business loving him, because he sure as hell had no business thinking he could make an anything-but-ordinary woman happy for even ten years, much less thousands.

Alec leaned over just enough to reach in his hind pocket and pulled out the letter Nicholas had given him—that Jane had hidden in the privy. Well, the woman certainly didn't lack for creativity, he thought with a humorless chuckle. He unsheathed his knife and slit open the envelope, pulled out the single piece of Nova Mare stationery and unfolded it, and chuckled again at the salutation written in bold, feminine script.

Dear Idiot,

Stay the hell away from Nova Mare!

Sincerely,
Carolina Oceanus

P.S. Thank you for returning MOST of my belongings, but there appears to be one item missing from my jewelry pouch. I would like it returned as soon as possible, please, as I have a pressing need to USE it.

P.P.S. Oh, and thank you for the wonderful education, as I believe it will come in quite handy very SOON.

Okay then. Forget pissing off her father; *Jane* was ready to feed him to the orcas.

But then, he *had* promised to be her champion.

And last time he checked, *he* was strong and fearless and mortal.

Alec refolded the letter and slid it in the envelope with a heavy sigh, guessing it was time he shoved the goddamn bus off his chest and started courting Carolina.

Chapter Eighteen

Four long, tiring days of *doubling* her efforts to appear interested in her three remaining suitors, putting up with Aaron
and Sir Garth's posturing at the fading handprint on her
cheek as they swore to avenge her if they ever got their hands
on the infidel, and all but turning cartwheels trying to get
Niall MacKeage to just friggin' *kiss* her, was starting to take
its toll. Sweet Prometheus, it was time to start panicking.

Jane stormed into her cottage while shedding her jacket
and then rounded on Nicholas the moment he closed the
door. "Thanks for the help," she snapped, so angry she actually stamped her foot. "How in Hades am I supposed to
know which one to pick if you keep scaring them off just
when things start getting interesting?"

Apparently not the least bit impressed by her show of
temper, Nicholas also shed his jacket—exposing the modern
gun he probably wore to *bed*—and pulled an equally modern lighter out of his pocket as he strolled to the fireplace. "I
didn't want to be holding your hair back over the bushes
while you threw up after Devonshire kissed you," he said

with maddening calm as he crouched down and placed a few pinecones on the grate and set them on fire. He started adding kindling. "I'll make a deal with you," he continued, twisting on the balls of his feet to give her a grin. "In exchange for your doing me a favor, I'll keep my distance when Niall takes you fishing up at the high-mountain pond tomorrow afternoon."

Jane folded her arms under her breasts. "I promised Olivia I'd watch the cherub tomorrow afternoon while she runs some errands."

"Perfect," he said with a chuckle, turning back and adding a couple of logs to the snapping kindling. He stood up and faced her, his eyes crinkled with amusement. "Ella will probably make a better chaperone than me, anyway, and you'll get to see how Niall is with kids. So, do we have a deal?"

"That depends on what the favor is," she said more sweetly than she was feeling.

He sat down on the hearth and leaned forward to rest his elbows on his knees. "I want you to design a cottage like this one for me," he said, waving a dangling hand. "Completely self-sufficient like Nova Mare, using sun and wind energy and whatever that heat exchange system is that comes from the ground."

Jane dropped her arms in surprise. "You're going to move out of the palace? But that's your—" She clutched her throat on a gasp. "You think Daddy's going to kick you out when I get married, like you're . . . like yesterday's trash?"

He stood up and walked over and took hold of her shoulders. "No, Lina, he's not kicking me out. I'm kicking myself out." He pulled her into his arms. "I've pretty much decided I want to live in this century," he said against her hair. "And I'm going to buy a boat and a fishing pole and a cooler to keep my beer in, and get drunk and fish and nap in the sun all summer and hibernate like a bear all winter in my cottage. And maybe," he said gruffly, "I'll find myself a lady bear to hibernate with me."

Jane leaned away. "Ohmigod," she whispered, feeling her skin prickle as her vision suddenly blurred with threatening tears. "Oh, Nicholas, all these years you've put me before . . . You put your entire life on . . ." She smacked his shoulder, then struggled against him when he wouldn't let her go. "Dammit, Nikki! Why didn't you *say* you wanted a life of your own?"

"You were my life," he said, pulling her into a fierce hug. "It was *my* choice, not yours or Titus's or anyone else's. But you and I have known all along it wasn't going to last forever." His chest rumbled with his chuckle. "Hell, Lina, I couldn't have dreamed up a more exciting thirty years." He tilted her head back and shot her one of his maddening grins. "Or a more entertaining ending." He gave her forehead a kiss before turning away to walk back to the hearth, where he stared down at the fire. "I don't regret one minute of my life, so don't even think about making me out to be some long-suffering . . . buffoon," he said over his shoulder with another grin. "You just worry about making the choice that's best for *you* five days from now." He turned to her. "And design me a cozy cottage just like this one, only larger. Go on," he said, waving at the desk, "get out some paper." He headed toward the back rooms and stopped at the bathroom door. "You'll need to write this down, as I have several requirements that might challenge even your sharp mind."

Jane stood gaping at the empty hall when he stepped into the bathroom. Nikki was staying in this century? And fishing and getting drunk and napping?

And hibernating with a *lady*?

Sweet Athena, he'd been waiting for her to fall in love so *he* could fall in love.

But Nicholas had always been . . . well, Nicholas. He was also a *guy*. She knew he'd had lovers; heck, she'd even introduced him to some of them. But now that she thought about it, he'd never let any of them ever get emotionally close and had always broken it off if they'd started getting . . . clingy.

"Princess," he said in a tone that made her go utterly still, "could you come in here, please?"

She ran to the hall and stopped in the open bathroom doorway to see him standing in front of the vanity staring at the mirror, which appeared to have something written on it in lipstick and something taped to—

Jane gasped and ran in and snatched the packet off the mirror and tried to stuff it in her pocket. But Nicholas caught her hand and held it up between them, even as he looked at the mirror again. *"This had better still be unopened, lass, the night of the ball,"* he quietly read. He looked at her. "Mind telling me what's going on, *lass*?" he asked, his eyes as lethal as his tone.

Jane brushed down the front of her shirt with her free hand—since he wouldn't give up the one holding the condom. "I really don't think my love life is any of your business," she said as she fought down her blush, "any more than your love life is mine."

"Until the ball, everything about you is my business." He reached up and pulled the condom from her hand—after a small tug of war—and stuffed it in his pocket. "How in hell does the bastard keep getting in here?" he growled, finally letting her go, then pushing her ahead of him out of the bathroom.

Jane ran into her bedroom, trying not to let him see her frantically looking around for other signs that Alec had been there. "Maybe he met the employee bus in the parking lot at the bottom of the mountain this morning and asked one of the housekeepers to leave that message," she said when Nicholas followed her. She shot him a smug smile and decided to deflect his anger from Alec to herself. "I hid a note in the privy they flew out to Alec the other day, telling him to stay away from Nova Mare." She winced, only just now realizing her mistake. "Except I contradicted myself by also asking him to return the condom he . . . um, took out of my jewelry pouch," she ended in a whisper as she lamely gestured at Nicholas's pocket.

"And what were you doing carrying a condom in your jewelry pouch?" he asked really softly as she stared at a spot on the far corner ceiling.

"I was going to . . . I thought I might . . ." She snorted and glared at him. "Okay, look; I thought that if I wasn't a virgin, then Daddy couldn't marry me off to some power-hungry buffoon. I carried that stupid thing around for *two years*," she growled—only to suddenly hug herself on a shuddering breath. "Except I couldn't do it," she whispered, "because I was too fussy."

"Lina," he said thickly. "You know that instead of solving your problem, using that condom only would have compounded it."

She looked up, smiling sadly. "I know. I think that's what Alec thought, too."

Nicholas's jaw slackened in surprise. "You tried to seduce MacKeage? And he actually managed to keep his hands off you?"

Jane snorted and threw herself back onto the bed to stare up at the ceiling. "He didn't exactly— What in Hades am I lying on?" she muttered, jumping up and pulling back the quilt, only to gape at the fist-size rocks scattered all over the sheet.

"Son of a bitch!" Nicholas roared, grabbing one of the rocks. His jaw slackened again and he grabbed another one. "The damn things are still *hot*." He snapped his gaze to the closed window, then bent down and looked under the bed, then walked to the closet and opened the door. He slowly turned, staring in silence at the rocks in his hand for what seemed like forever, then held them toward her. "The bastard was here less than half an hour ago."

Having seen Nicholas's legendary temper surface only twice in her life, and really not wanting to hang around if this was about to become explosion number three, Jane bolted out of the room. Only he caught her just as she reached the front door, then simply grabbed their jackets and dragged her outside.

Partly because she liked to think she was pretty smart and partly because she was curious as to where he was taking her, Jane remained equally silent as he dragged her down the path toward the resort's common green. He suddenly shoved both their jackets at her without breaking stride or letting go of her arm and pulled a small walkie-talkie off his belt.

"Everyone," he snapped after keying the mike, "report in, beginning with Rowan, from north to east."

"I see Dante from where I'm standing, sir, and not so much as a mouse has walked between us," a voice Jane recognized as Rowan said over the small speaker.

"Dante here," another voice said, "and I see Cyril."

The radio squelched, and then, "I can see Ephraim not three stadions away," another voice she assumed was Cyril said, indicating the men were positioned about eighteen hundred feet apart.

And on the roll call went, until the radio suddenly went silent.

Nicholas stopped walking. "Who's next?"

Whoever he was, Jane felt sorry for him. Not because she was worried Alec had hurt him, but for what Nicholas was going to do to the missing man when he found him.

"Averill," Nicholas said quietly to the last man to report, "who are you next to?"

"Micah, sir, and I'm looking right at him. He's sitting against a tree not three stadions away."

"Then don't you think you should go see why he didn't immediately stand up when I came on the radio?" Nicholas said really softly. "Who's after Micah?"

Again, silence.

"Rowan and Dante, meet me at Micah's post. You others spread out to fill the void they're leaving," he said as he started dragging Jane again, turning onto another path she assumed led to Micah.

A little worried Nicholas didn't even realize she was still with him, Jane remained silent for fear he'd make her go back to the cottage. Because honestly, she wanted to see what was going on, as she couldn't imagine anyone being able to sneak past one of Nicholas's guards—especially not Alec. Alec might be good in a fight, and he'd served in the military according to Sam Waters, but the underachieving ski bum couldn't possibly outsmart the most elite fighting force on the planet from *any* century.

They'd just reached the man still sitting leaning against a

large tree when Rowan and Dante came running up to them. Jane tried not to flinch when Nicholas—still holding on to her arm—used his foot to give Micah's shoulder a shove, but she couldn't stifle a gasp when the man simply fell onto his side, apparently out cold. Rowan and Dante immediately grabbed his arms and lifted him to his feet, Rowan giving the guy's face a couple of brisk slaps.

Micah threw his head back with a snarled curse, then groaned, then finally noticed Nicholas standing in front of him. The soldier's eyes widened and he stiffened to a weaving attention. "Sir!"

Still holding on to Jane, Nicholas got right in his face. "Mind telling me how someone was able to sneak up and ambush you?" he asked really, really softly.

Micah shook his head. "He didn't ambush me, sir. I watched him walk toward me all the way from the office pavilion. I assumed he was a guest out for a stroll after dinner." He frowned. "Although I did think it odd, as he had quite a bad limp."

"He's hurt?" Jane said on a gasp.

Nicholas snorted and gave her a little shake without taking his eyes off the guard. "He's not hurt. MacKeage was just letting *Private* Micah think he was harmless. Then what?"

Micah dropped his gaze to the vicinity of his commander's chest. "The guy was startled when he saw me and came over when I stood up, and asked if I was hurt. When I assured him I was fine, and told him I was just enjoying the night air like you told us to tell the guests, he introduced himself as Darth Vader and shook my hand, and . . ."

Jane actually leaned away when she felt Nicholas's fingers twitch on her arm, expecting that explosion any moment now. Only he simply closed his eyes and dropped his chin to his chest. "And what?" he asked softly.

"And that's the last thing I remember, sir."

Jane saw Nicholas take a deep breath and look down the length of the tree line as he lifted the radio and keyed the mike. "Who's posted south of Micah?"

Again silence, and then, "Paul here, sir. I'm two down from Micah. Avery is posted between us."

"Would you please walk over to Avery, Paul," Nicholas all but whispered, "and kick the bastard awake?" He looked back at the three men standing in front of him—Rowan and Dante still holding up Micah—and keyed the mike again. "Did anyone else see a man with a bad limp out here tonight?" he drawled.

"I saw a male guest," someone said over the radio, "limping across the green, but then I lost sight of him when he went up one of the cart paths."

"I noticed a man limping past the lower hotel in the direction of the barn and employee apartments," someone else said. "Not half an hour ago."

Nicholas slowly uncurled his fingers from around Jane's arm, then turned and took the jackets from her. He silently stuffed Jane into hers, shrugged on his own, then took her hand and started walking back up the path.

"Sir," Rowan said, "any orders?"

Nicholas just kept walking as if he hadn't heard him.

Jane decided to also remain mute. They were all smart men; they'd figure out what orders to give themselves.

Although she did think about protesting when Nicholas turned onto the path leading to her parents' cottage, she decided against it because she still wasn't sure of his mood. Sweet Athena, what was Alec *doing*—other than making Nicholas really, really angry? Or maybe chagrined that *the bastard kept getting in here*?

Jane pretended to nonchalantly scan the woods to hide her smile. The scoundrel; Alec had brought back her condom— at the same time writing an unnamed threat in her lipstick— and warmed her bed with rocks just like she'd warmed his sleeping bag. She'd also discovered that he'd erased all the sex movies and books off her iPad. And he'd woven some of the hair he'd cut off her that first night into Kitty's fur, which meant he hadn't thrown it away like she'd thought.

She wondered if he'd made himself a braid, too.

But what in the name of Hades was compelling him to continue sneaking into Nova Mare and . . . doing stuff, but not even trying to talk to her? He obviously could get into her cottage whenever he wanted, so why not sneak in when she was *there*?

She wanted to touch him. Feel his arms around her again. Taste him.

And love him, dammit.

She'd actually told Alec she loved him in the first letter she'd hidden in the privy, saying she didn't care that he didn't have anything to offer her. She'd poured her heart out over six pages, explaining that all she wanted was *him*; his laughter, his teasing, his passion for life—and his passion for her. Except she'd gotten scared, worried that she'd sounded desperate and clinging, and so she'd taken the letter back.

But Alec must feel something for her, because why else was he still coming around? Wait; how did he know about the importance of the ball? Her mom had told Jane that she'd had Nicholas take her out to Alec's campsite to specifically invite him to the ball—to *dance* with her daughter—but did Alec know there were men her father had invited who were vying for her hand in *marriage*?

Jane glanced over at Nicholas, but still didn't quite dare break the silence that seemed to be calming him down, as his grip on her hand had softened. But it tightened right back up again when they approached her parents' cottage, and didn't lessen when he softly knocked on the door.

Her mom opened the door, only to stiffen with her smile half-formed as her gaze darted from Jane to Nicholas. "What's wrong?" she asked.

Nicholas reached out and took her mother's hand and wrapped Rana's fingers around Jane's wrist. "She's sleeping here tonight. She can go back to her cottage tomorrow, *after* I go over every square inch of it and post guards around its perimeter." He reached in his pocket and pulled out the condom even as he lifted her mother's other hand and dropped the packet in it. "And I strongly suggest you send someone back in time to Renaissance Italy for a chastity belt," he said, turning and walking down the stairs. "But you might as well give the key to Alec MacKeage for safekeeping," he said over his shoulder, "as the man appears to be either a saint or an idiot."

Nicholas unzipped his jacket to dissipate the heat radiating off him like an erupting volcano, and took his time walking to the employee apartments where he was staying. By the gods, he didn't know how MacKeage kept getting onto the resort grounds, and he sure as hell didn't like how easily the bastard kept taking his men by surprise. They were supposed to be the best of the best, and he trusted them with his life—and the lives of the Oceanuses. He'd even put the magic to work securing Nova Mare, and yet MacKeage was still able to walk in and out of here as if he owned the place. And he'd come in daylight this time and *still* managed to keep from being caught.

Nicholas stopped walking and stared at the dark path ahead. He knew *Duncan* had command of the magic, because Mac had given the Scot the energy of a mountain across the fiord. But did Alec also have the magic in him? Mac had told him no when Nicholas had asked. And Titus had told him there hadn't been any evidence of Alec having command of the magic when the old wizard had visited the Trees of Life to learn more about the man his daughter had fallen in love with.

That was one of the reasons Titus had invited Alec to openly court Carolina. The king of the drùidhs needed a strong and fearless mortal to marry his daughter, and even though Nicholas knew *why* the man had to be a mortal, Titus had said he suspected Alec also knew the secret of keeping Lina safe, but might not be aware that he knew.

Nicholas snorted and started walking again. When he'd asked Titus for more of the magic to stop people from waltzing in here, the wizard had assured him that Nova Mare was secure from the gods and demons, and that Carolina wasn't leaving here until she had a husband who could protect her. And when Nicholas had pointed out there was still one *mortal* kidnapper unaccounted for who apparently had enough magic to take off her bracelet, Titus had grinned and said that with all the acorns and stinging bees guarding Carolina, the third kidnapper was the least of his worries at the moment.

But MacKeage was starting to really piss him off. Nicholas let himself into his small apartment and flipped on the light, tossed his jacket on a chair, and unfastened the chest strap on his shoulder holster as he walked to the kitchen. Some days—usually days like today—he wondered why he was still in the game.

He stilled as he was reaching in the fridge for a beer and stared at the envelope sitting on top of the six-pack he had *not* filched from the restaurant's storage room. *"God dammit,"* he snarled, snatching the envelope and stepping back to close the door, only to reach back inside and grab the six-pack as well. He strode over to the table—his holster flapping against his side—and tossed the beer and envelope down, pulled out a chair and sat down, and hung his head in his hands with a curse.

How was the bastard *getting in here*?

Nicholas straightened with another muttered curse, jerked one of the beers free and popped the top, and chugged down half the can before setting it on the table and picking up the envelope. He lifted the unsealed flap and looked inside, then turned the envelope over to let the small piece of paper float to the table. He then picked up what looked like a newspaper ad, turned it right side up, and read the bold lettering that said: DIRECTOR OF SECURITY WANTED, NOVA MARE RESORT. The position would involve overseeing twenty officers to secure both the Nova Mare and Inglenook resorts, the ad went on to say. Experience in law enforcement was desired although not required, but management and people skills were a must. Contact Olivia Oceanus at Nova Mare Resort in Spellbound Falls, Maine.

Nicholas stared at the ad, wondering if this wouldn't

teach him to ask for advice, undecided if he wanted to roar or burst out laughing. Hell, if Olivia gave him the job, he should probably hire MacKeage, seeing how the bastard was already intimately acquainted with the grounds.

He dropped the ad and picked up the beer, but stared at the can instead of taking a drink. What had the rocks in Lina's bed meant? And the condom, he thought with a chuckle. How had Alec managed to keep his hands off a beautiful woman set on seduction? Because honestly, he didn't think a saint *or* an idiot would be able to resist Lina in full feminine mode.

Nicholas blew out a tired sigh and gulped down the rest of the can of beer, then popped the top on another one as he stared at the ad sitting on the table again. These last two years of having to keep Lina safe from a distance during her little temper tantrum had nearly killed him, which told him two things: He was getting too old for the game, and he probably shouldn't have children of his own, especially little girls. If it had been up to him instead of Titus and Rana, he'd have kept Lina confined to Atlantis until she was a thousand years old. As for her being happy . . . well, she could have married a nice island boy who also had a passion for science, and they could have had a dozen babies and planted enough wind turbines all over Atlantis to make it fly.

Yup, he sure as Hades better not have any daughters, because he really didn't think he could go through this again. And by the gods, nobody had better place another screaming baby princess in his arms ever again, either.

Nicholas set down the beer and picked up the job ad, carefully folded it, and tucked it in a slit on the back of his leather holster. Damn, he hoped Alec married Lina, because he didn't know two people who more deserved to spend the next ten thousand years trying to outfox each other.

Chapter Nineteen

———

Taking out the knight of the Round Table shouldn't have been anywhere near this hard, considering the guy was a strutting horse's ass, even though Sir Garth looked like he wouldn't have any trouble holding his own on a battlefield or tournament course. But honest to God, if Alec saw the knightly fool get down on one knee and expound on Carolina's beauty one more time, he was going to hit him right between his chivalrous eyes—and not with a silly acorn, either, but a goddamn rock.

How was Carolina managing not to ring Sir Garth's neck? The idiot had actually stepped away, looking horrified and quite apologetic, when *she* had tried to hold *his* hand while strolling down the resort road. Alec had turned his binoculars on Nicholas strolling behind them just in time to see the big bastard break into a grin.

Still, finding the opportunity to pick off the knight was proving nearly impossible—mostly thanks to Nicholas having *tripled* the guards. Was he bringing them in from Atlantis by the boatload? The man had even started sending small detachments out to patrol the wilderness trail, diabolically varying the hours day and night. But thanks to the wolves giving him plenty of warning, Alec had managed to stay one step ahead of the men—who he'd quickly realized were out for blood. Hell, once when four of them had hiked past the tree he'd climbed to hide in, he'd overheard them agreeing that a no-kill order didn't mean no-maim. And another time he'd heard them mention the money pool their thoughtful commander had said would go to the man who showed up with Alec's entire head of shaved-off hair.

Yup, brotherly Nick was one pissed off Atlantean.

And Mac was still roaring mad, according to Duncan. And like Nicholas, Duncan also couldn't figure out why the younger wizard was so opposed to Carolina marrying a MacKeage, and apparently Titus still wasn't telling his son that he had invited Alec to the ball. Alec wondered if Rana happened to mention *she* had personally invited him—as well as half the eligible men in two towns, he thought with a silent chuckle as he lowered his binoculars. He hadn't really expected Rana to follow through with her little charade, but the woman had hand-delivered nine more vellum envelopes to local men who were now strutting around like puffed-up baboons.

The whole of Spellbound Falls was abuzz with excitement over that goddamn ball. And he knew for a fact that Ray and Mike Byram, Charlie Vail, Rich Nason, and Nick Patterson had piled in Ray's tired old pickup and driven all the way to Bangor to rent tuxedos—all for the prospect of getting to *dance* with a beautiful princess. Hell, Ray had even bought a shiny new red aluminum cane to match his cummerbund.

Alec watched Carolina and Sir Horse's Ass stroll around a bend in the road with Nicholas strolling behind them, and sighed at another missed opportunity as he shoved the binoculars and slingshot into his backpack. He emptied his jacket pocket of small round rocks and slipped them into a side pouch, then looked up to check the position of the sun. One hour to dusk and a little under three hours to full dark-

ness, which was when he'd get a shot at the Crusader, Aaron
of Devonshire, since it appeared Sir Garth was dining with
Carolina this evening.

For three of the last four nights, Alec had seen Devonshire taking long walks off the resort grounds—in a different direction each night—the one night Aaron had missed
being his turn to dine with Carolina. Rather than following
him, Alec had merely timed Aaron's walks—that had been
over four hours long—while opting for a chance to take out
Sir Garth instead. Down to only two days before the ball,
Alec was starting to get more than a little pissed off himself,
and decided tonight was Devonshire's turn to fall out of
favor for Carolina's hand in marriage.

Alec carefully slipped his pack on his shoulders and
climbed down the towering pine he'd been perched in, the
four wolves scattered around the trunk sitting up and blink-
ing the sleep from their eyes when he finally reached the
ground. "Come on, ye bored lobos," he whispered with a
soft chuckle as he moved deeper into the woods. "It's time
we go find out if our fearless Crusader has an aversion to
imaginary bears."

Alec silently slipped into Titus and Rana's bedroom, quietly
snagged a chair from beside the bureau and set it next to the
wizard's side of the bed, then sat down straddling it with his
arms resting on the chair's back and waited.

He sensed the moment Titus woke, so he wasn't surprised when the bedside lamp suddenly snapped on. "By the
gods, MacKeage, you overstep your bounds!"

"Aye, that is one of my more maddening habits." Alec
gave Rana a smiled nod when she sat up with a soft gasp.
"I'm sorry to have startled ye out of your sleep, but I thought
you'd like to hear firsthand that your daughter is safe from
the third kidnapper." He slid his gaze to Titus and tossed
two small medallions on the blanket covering the wizard's
legs. "I took these off the dead men the day I caught them
chasing Carolina."

"And you decided to bring them to me *tonight*," Titus growled without looking at them, "in my bedchamber?"

Alec nodded. "I thought you'd want to know *tonight* that ye no longer have to worry about the third kidnapper." He shrugged. "Aaron was definitely a mortal, but he'd been given enough command of the magic to travel through time at *his* will, as well as find Carolina and take off her bracelet."

Titus clasped his wife's hand when she gasped, even as he paled to the roots of his regal white hair. "Are you saying the third kidnapper is Aaron of Devonshire? The Crusader I *brought* here?"

Alec nodded and opened his other hand to dangle a third, larger medallion from his fingers. "That's why she was blindfolded and he didn't speak around her, so she wouldn't recognize him when he rescued her. From what I overheard tonight, the kidnapping was just a ruse, and the real plan was to keep your daughter until after all your fearless warriors arrived at Nova Mare. Aaron intended to feign surprise when you were forced to admit Carolina was missing, and then vow he wouldn't rest until he brought her back to you." He shrugged. "But she escaped and then went missing, so he had to call on his magical partner in crime to help him come up with a new plan."

"But why kidnap her," Rana asked, "when he was *invited* to court her?"

Alec chose his words carefully, not wanting to reveal any of his first late-night conversation with Titus. "I'm afraid Aaron was as much a victim as Carolina, it turns out. From what I garnered, he was led to believe he'd end up the hero with your daughter as the prize," he quietly explained, sliding his gaze to Titus, "when in truth he was merely a means to put Carolina in harm's way in order to distract you long enough for your enemies to attack Atlantis. But I believe Aaron began to suspect he wasn't going to have a wedding night, which is likely what led to tonight's meeting with his magical benefactor." Alec gently swung the third identical but larger medallion he'd taken from the Crusader's broken neck. "Where I can only speculate who this symbol represents, I'm assuming you will recognize who gave Aaron the power to kidnap your daughter," he said, handing the medallion to Titus.

The wizard had barely taken it when he stiffened on an indrawn breath.

"Who is it?" Rana asked, taking the medallion away from him and also sucking in a surprised breath. *"Ares,"* she whispered, snapping her gaze to Alec. "The god of war is here? You actually saw him? *Here*, at Nova Mare?"

"Aye," Alec said with a nod, "only not on resort grounds because they're too well guarded, which is why Aaron had to hike several miles away. Or rather, *maybe* I saw this Ares . . . fellow," he said, giving a shrug. "I could only make out the shadowed outline of *something* talking to Aaron up by the high-mountain pond, and I couldn't tell if it was man or beast." He looked at Titus. "All I could see were pinprick eyes lit with fire, and I felt the air pulsing with what smelled like . . ." He rubbed the back of his neck. "I swear I smelled *fear*, only it appeared to be coming from Ares, not Devonshire."

"You smelled Ares and Aphrodite's son, Deimus," Titus said, his voice thick with barely controlled anger, "who is the manifestation of fear."

"But they're *myths*, which means they don't *exist*," Alec growled. He gestured toward the bed. "And for that matter, neither should *you*."

Titus stared at him for several pounding heartbeats, his voice turning gentle when he finally spoke. "We exist, Alec, because mankind imagined all of us—gods and demons alike—into existence. It matters not if we're Greek, Roman, Egyptian, Norse, Native American, Celtic, Chinese, Mayan . . ." He shrugged. "The deities became as numerous and varied as the peoples who populate the world, when every culture since the beginning of time sought to answer the primal question of *purpose*. And once a myth took root in the collective human psyche, we *became as real* as the people who created us." He smiled sadly. "We are, in fact, an exaggerated reflection of humanity's greatest good and vilest evil." He took the large medallion from Rana and tossed it onto the blanket beside the others. "So you see, it's by no means a stretch of the imagination that a god is pursuing a mythical princess, any more than humans—individuals and entire nations—continually try to force their wills on one another."

"It will take a very brave man to love our daughter," Rana said softly. "As well as one who's wise enough to understand that fear itself is only a myth."

Alec saw Titus cover her hand and give it a squeeze. "Were you able to learn what Aaron is now planning?" Titus asked, his voice growing enraged again. But then he suddenly threw back the covers to get out of bed. "Never mind; I will have the pleasure of asking the bastard myself."

Alec held up his hand to stop him, even while fighting to conceal his shock that the king of the drùidhs was wearing bright red pajama bottoms. "He's dead."

Titus reared back in surprise, his eyes locking on Alec for several heartbeats before he dropped his gaze and mutely nodded.

Alec stood up and set the chair back beside the bureau. "Ye needn't bother worrying about damage control, as there's no evidence that Aaron of Devonshire was ever here." He gestured toward the medallions that had fallen to the floor. "As for Deimus . . ." Alec gave a slight bow before turning toward the door. "I doubt you'll be hearing from him for a while, as apparently Ares's son has a *fear* of bees."

"MacKeage," Titus said thickly, making him turn back. "Thank you."

"It would appear your field of suitors is now down to two—not counting your man Nick—with only two days to go." Alec slashed the scowling wizard and his smiling wife a grin. "Would ye happen to know if Carolina favors one of them over the other?"

"My daughter—"

"*Our* daughter knows her heart," Rana said, cutting Titus

off. "And we both will support her decision." She in turn shot
Alec a very Carolina smile. "Although I'm afraid Maximilian is still doing his damndest to make up her mind for her."

"Wife!" Titus snapped.

Alec gave Rana a nod, not at all shocked by her direct-
ness considering whose mother she was. "I'm sure your
daughter is resourceful enough to eventually get her brother
to see things her way."

"Wait," Rana said as he turned to the door. "I also wish
to thank you, Alec. Not only for saving Carolina's life more
than once, it appears, but for telling me personally about
Aaron's treachery," she said, her smile disappearing as she
jabbed her elbow into her husband's side—which turned
whatever Titus had growled at her into a grunt.

Alec merely gave her a slight bow, turning away just as
he heard more muttering and another grunt, only to be
stopped when Rana called to him again. "Aye?" he said,
fighting a grin when he realized Titus was one second away
from tackling his wife with a pillow to shut her up.

"I'm just curious as to how you got in here tonight," she
said, arching an imperial brow. "When I mentioned my
worry about the . . . unfortunate accidents and strange oc-
currences happening here at the resort and on the riding
paths over the last few weeks, just today both Nicholas and
Maximilian assured me that even a mouse couldn't enter
Nova Mare without their knowing it."

"Then I guess they should turn their efforts to securing
the resort against acorns and bees and mere mortals instead
of mice."

"And bears?" Rana added, the lamplight reflecting off
her sparkling eyes.

"Aye, and bears," Alec said with a chuckle, stepping into
the hall and pulling the door closed on a muffled feminine
shriek.

Alec went down the short hall to the kitchen, slipped out
through the window and closed it behind him, then shoved
his hands in his pockets as he walked toward the small cabin
sitting up on a wooded knoll, Kit silently appearing from the

shadows to fall into step beside him. He stopped just short of being seen by the guards sitting leaning up against all four corners of the cabin, and broke into a grin when he heard the lulling sounds of a nighttime forest coming from the open window of Carolina's bedroom.

Aye, four down and only two to go—not counting brotherly Nick.

Chapter Twenty

Alec knocked on the door of the end apartment, then stepped inside the moment it opened, forcing Nicholas to step back with a muttered curse. "Ye help me take care of the mess your illustrious knight made of me, and I'll tell ye how I've been getting onto the grounds."

"Now what in hell did you do?"

"The man bled like a stuck pig from only a minor flesh wound." Alec tossed the tuxedo jacket he'd been holding in front of him onto the table, causing Nicholas to stiffen when he saw the blood on Alec's shirt. "I thought Titus gave instructions that Carolina's suitors were to come unarmed," Alec continued, pulling his shirttails out of his pants. "And what idiot puts an unsheathed dagger in his cummerbund, anyway, if he's a goddamn bleeder?" Alec tore off his shirt without unbuttoning it. "I couldn't take Garth's shirt because it's bloodier than mine, and it was the only one he had that wasn't covered in lace. Would ye have one I can borrow?" he asked, gesturing at the dress shirt Nicholas was wearing—under *his* safely holstered weapon. "Or what about the other suitors; Niall told me someone came up and measured all the men for modern formal wear. The Viking was close to my size, wasn't he?"

"Where is Sir Garth now?" Nicholas asked, not going after that spare shirt, Alec couldn't help but notice.

"He's having a nap in his room. I managed to get the bleeding stopped, and since the ropes wouldn't let him move much, he apparently decided he'd rather sleep than go to the ball."

"And Niall?"

Alec grinned, using the bloody shirt to gesture toward the southwest. "Last I saw of my ancestor when I dropped him off at Matt and Winter Gregor's house this morning, Niall was sitting in their hot tub, nursing a beer and playing with the whirlpool jets."

Nicholas didn't even so much as blink. "You do realize you still have one more suitor to eliminate, don't you?"

Alec shrugged. "His heart won't be in the fight, so I actually see that ending well. Mac, however," he said, dropping his ruined shirt on the floor and walking to the kitchen sink, "might be a problem." He turned on the tap, grabbed the towel off the oven door, and held it under the running water. "Do ye think Titus will be able to control him?" he asked as he wrung out the towel and turned to Nicholas. "Or am I going to have to fight the bastard in order to *dance* with his sister?"

"I think you might want to take along an extra shirt."

Alec winced and started wiping the splatters of blood off his pants, hoping that what he couldn't get off would blend in with the black fiber and not be noticeable.

"How have you been getting onto the resort without being seen?"

"Through the tunnels," he said, twisting to check the side of one pant leg and wiping another spot. He stopped in mid-wipe, pulled the small plastic bag full of blond hair out of his hind pocket, and shot Nicholas another grin as he tossed it to him. "Ye can give that to the two guards from the other night and the one I tied up, so they can claim the pot of money you put up for my scalp." He shrugged again. "I only went after them to make ye think that's how I was coming and going."

"What tunnels?" Nicholas asked, tossing the bag on the counter.

Alec went back to cleaning his pants. "I suppose it's hard to secure an area if no one bothers to mention there's a labyrinth of tunnels right under your feet." He looked up and grinned again. "And they're not man-made. Mac followed Carolina's blueprints exactly, conveniently cutting a couple of tunnels up from the fiord to run pipes to feed the saltwater swimming pools. Then there's a mess of them running all over the top of the mountain between the hotels and cottages and outbuildings to feed heat pipes and power lines to the entire resort. Most are large enough for a man to walk upright," he said with a shrug, "I assume to service the utilities as well as hide the mechanics." He grinned again and shook his head. "I suggest someone put a lock on the grate down at the fiord, though, to prevent all manner of vermin from getting in here."

Nicholas snorted and headed down the short hall off the living area. "I'll be sure to put that in my résumé when I apply for the job of director of security."

Near as Jane could tell, the entire indigenous population of Spellbound Falls and Turtleback Station, as well as seasonal camp owners, tourists lucky enough to be visiting the area this weekend, any number of curious Mainers willing to make the trek to the wilderness, and a small contingency of local and national news media, had been climbing off shuttle buses that had been carrying them up Whisper Mountain since noon. As they stepped off the buses, almost to a man, woman, and child, they would stand staring out at the Bottomless Sea more than two thousand feet below, then slowly turn in a circle trying to take in the breadth and scope of Nova Mare.

By nine that evening, it was standing room only in the

pool pavilion, the small conference center, one of the hotel segments and two of the cottages opened for display, and even the barn, as it appeared no one was in any hurry to leave. Although that probably had something to do with the unusually warm October night, as well as the picnic tables, camp chairs, and blankets that had been liberally distributed around the festively lit common green, along with tables laden with all manner of food and drink. Stronger libations were being handed out at stations strategically placed in the various venues, tended by servers Jane thought looked a lot like the crew from her parents' home away from home, which happened to be the huge submarine hidden in a massive cave at the end of the fiord—not very far, actually, from Alec's secret grotto.

Olivia was looking a bit overwhelmed, Jane decided as she handed her mother a second glass of wine then took a sip of her fourth glass; but then, this was her sister-in-law's first time planning anything with Rana Oceanus—who happened to know a thing or two about throwing a party.

"I see you managed to cajole Johann into making an appearance," Jane said to her mother, using her wineglass to gesture at Vienna's nineteenth-century version of a rock star, dressed in his signature white lace shirt as he stood watching the quartet playing the very appropriate *Wein, Weib und Gesang*.

Rana arched a delicate brow into her wispy brown curls artfully arranged around her understated tiara—which was only slightly more jeweled than the smaller princess tiara Jane was wearing tucked in her dark curls cascading past her shoulders. "And just when have you known Strauss to turn down a chance to hear his compositions being played by Atlantean musicians?" Rana asked. She shook her head, her smile smug. "Or ignore a request from me to do so?"

Jane smoothed down her floor-length dress that also matched her mother's except for being forest green instead of cobalt blue—both of their left arms fully sleeved and right arms and shoulders exposed—and looked around the room again. The private and more intimate ball taking place in the banquet pavilion was slightly less crowded but no less festive thanks to both the musicians and the open bar set up in the corner. Mackie was sitting holding princess hugs-a-lot, trying to keep her from crawling across the table to reach his friends from Midnight Bay: Kenzie and Eve Gregor and their toddler son, William and Madeline Killkenny and their toddler son trying to crawl to Ella, and Trace Huntsman and his recent bride, Fiona, and their twin infant girl and boy.

William's sister, Gabriella, and Rick Lane—who was also Maddy's brother—had their arms twined around each other out on the dance floor, moving in only a semblance of rhythm to *Wine, Women, and Song.* Not that Rick appeared to care that Johann Strauss was a nineteenth-century rock star, since he only seemed interested in the ninth-century young lady in his arms. Henry, however, seemed rather perturbed that Olivia wasn't intimately familiar with one of Strauss's more popular waltzes, as well as rather determined to teach his step-mum the art of proper dancing.

Standing next to the bar, looking as uncomfortable in tuxedos as they were to be the only locals attending the private ball, the suitors Jane's mother had personally invited kept giving Jane shy smiles—one of the men actually giving her a wink right after finishing off his second tankard of mead.

Rana leaned closer when she noticed where Jane was looking. "I really didn't think they'd actually come," she whispered. "But apparently mentioning I was worried you wouldn't have anyone to dance with was enough incentive to bring them en masse."

"He . . . I don't think he's coming, Mama," Jane said, knowing her mother knew who she was talking about.

Rana reached out and clasped Jane's free hand and gave it a squeeze. "He'll be here." She laughed softly. "He's probably trying to figure out how to tie his tie."

"Oh God, he probably doesn't even own a tie, and he's not coming because he doesn't have anything to wear."

Rana gave Jane's hand another squeeze. "Alec didn't exactly strike me as a man who would let the lack of proper clothing stop him from going after something he wants."

Her eyes twinkled in the chandelier light. "He's of high-lander descent, so I wouldn't put it past him to show up naked if he thought it would further his cause."

"Where do you suppose Sir Garth and Niall are?" Jane asked, fighting a blush at the thought of Alec's naked body as she looked around the ballroom. She gave a soft snort. "I can understand Niall dragging his feet, but when I saw Sir Garth this morning, he had such a triumphant gleam in his eyes that I was sure he'd be the first one here."

"Maybe he's not feeling quite so confident after seeing your father's other guests arriving this afternoon," Rana said, nodding at the table where Titus was sitting with several modern-dressed men and women, who were hanging on his every word.

Titus had invited some close acquaintances—most of them royalty—from various eras dating back as far as pre-biblical times, not only to show off his son's magically epic wonder, but to also encourage them to start going to Maximilian when they needed a theurgist to work out whatever problem they were having.

Her father sure wouldn't ask them to come see *her*, Jane thought, covering up her snort by taking another drink of wine. Because what would a mere woman know about repairing some natural disaster, discovering why animals or crops were suddenly dying, or stopping some stupid, senseless war?

And that's why William, Kenzie, Gabriella, and Fiona weren't the only time travelers attending the ball, although they were the only ones permanently living in this century. That is, besides several of the MacKeages from Pine Creek sitting with Duncan and Peg at one of the other tables—clear across the room from Mackie.

Jane choked on her wine and grabbed her mother's arm when Rana gasped just as a deafening clap of thunder suddenly rattled the floor-to-ceiling pavilion windows. The two women looked at each other and both broke into grins.

"Sweet Athena, I hope that was Sir Garth," Jane said, "and not Niall."

"It's okay, everyone," her mother said to the suddenly silent room. She laughed brightly and waved her wineglass toward the windows facing Bottomless. "It would appear the crew setting up the fireworks just ruined our midnight *surprise*."

The quartet began playing again and the room quickly filled back up with chatter.

Jane watched Sam Waters break away from the gaggle of local men and limp toward her. Olivia's father stopped and gave Rana a warmly smiled nod, then slid his gaze to Jane. "Would you care to dance with a gimpy old man, Carolina?" he asked, holding out his hand.

Jane handed her wineglass to her mom, took his hand, and let him lead her to a less populated section of the dance floor. "You're looking quite the princess tonight . . . Jane," he said, glancing up at the tiara in her hair as she set one hand on his shoulder and the other at his waist. He chuckled. "Which is intimidating your mother's personally invited dance partners. They've all spent the last hour trying to pour enough liquid courage past their tonsils to work up the nerve to even walk over and speak to you. And poor Ray—he's the one with the cane—is trying to figure out how to hold both it and you and dance at the same time."

"When we're done, you can walk me over and *I'll* ask them to dance." Jane winced. "It appears my manners are slipping, as I should have introduced myself to them long before now."

Sam looked around, then pulled her a bit closer. "Alec came into town a few days ago and asked me to have a new identity ready for you by tonight. It's—"

"Alec plans for us to run away?" she blurted in a whisper, her hand on Sam's shoulder bunching his jacket. "Wait, how did he know you made my *first* identity?"

Sam snorted. "He's known over a month. Apparently you tried to call me from his satellite phone the day after he rescued you, and he saw you'd called the trading post. He came to Inglenook to see me that night to find out what was going on."

Jane faltered in midstep, making Sam stumble before catching himself. "The night he left me in the boat he went to see you? And the two of you have been making plans to help me run away again?" she said past the lump in her throat, wanting to weep at the realization that Alec wasn't coming to the ball.

"I can't rightly say what he's planning, because the man's always played his cards close to his vest." Sam shrugged. "All I know is that he asked me to have a new identity for you ready to go tonight, but said it was only for in case plan A didn't work out the way he hoped."

"Only . . . one identity? Not one for him, too?"

"Just the one, Caro," he said softly, his gray eyes troubled as he gave a slight shake of his head. "I'm guessing it's because if plan A doesn't fly, he's figuring he . . . that he won't be in any condition to run off with you."

Jane stopped dancing.

Sam gave a quick glance around and started them dancing again, giving her a tender smile. "I'm betting you won't need the new identity, though, as I've never known Mac-Keage to have to resort to a plan B. But," he said on a heavy sigh, "if you do, then I swear this one is foolproof. Only in order for it to work, you're going to have to lose that ankle bracelet. I've got you booked on a flight out of Bangor International Airport at nine tomorrow morning that'll take you to Philadelphia, where you can pick any plane headed anywhere you want. I showed you how to get lost in a maze of flights the last time you disappeared. You remember how?"

Jane leaned closer, until her cheek was next to his. "I love you for caring enough to help me again, Sam, but I . . . I can't leave. I was acting spoiled and selfish last time, and shirking my duty."

"It's not selfish to want to control your own life," he growled, giving her waist a squeeze. "Don't give up on Alec just yet, okay? Let's see what plan A is before we—"

"Excuse me, but may I have this dance?" a gentleman asked, tapping Sam on the shoulder even as his gaze locked on a point somewhere past Jane's head.

Sam sighed. "I told you to give me the whole dance, Nick," he said, "*then* come over and cut in."

Jane kissed Sam's cheek and turned to the gentleman. "Introduce us, Sam."

"Carolina, this is Nick Patterson. He owns Angie's Bar and Grill in Turtleback Station. Nick, this is Princess Carolina Oceanus, and I know for a fact she's disabled more than one misbehaving dance partner with those four-inch spikes she's wearing, so be a gentleman or she's going to make you a gimp like me and Ray."

That certainly got Nick looking at her. Jane grabbed her apparently startled suitor and simply started dancing with him. "So, Nick, is it true Angie's has strippers every first Friday of the month? And do you allow women to come to your bar on those nights?" She widened her smile when he snapped his eyes to her again and mutely nodded. "Without *them* having to strip?" she whispered, only to wince when he stumbled and stepped on her toe.

Sweet Athena, why had her mother invited so many local suitors, Jane wondered half an hour later after dancing with local number eight—and a half, if she counted only swaying back and forth with Ray Byram and his cane. But the only one she wanted to dance with had apparently stood her up.

Jane plastered another polite smile on her face and let herself be handed over to the guy cutting in, only to stumble when a familiar set of hands slid around her back and pulled her into a very familiar chest that deflated on a long sigh of satisfaction. "Christ, ye feel better than I remember," he murmured against her ear as he used his chin to tuck her head against his. "Will ye tell me why in God's name your mother invited so many dance partners for you? I hate waiting in lines."

Undecided whether to scold him for being late or burst into tears at the feel of his arms around her, Jane simply melted into him with a groan of utter contentment. "Um, we should probably at least *sway*," she said thickly, "to appear as if we're not just standing here trying to figure out how to make love in the middle of the room."

"Don't tempt me," he growled, his arms tightening as he started them swaying. He chuckled. "Please tell me that's only wine in your mother's glass. Because the last time I had the pleasure of her company, she got a wee drunk."

Jane leaned away to smile at him, only to gasp instead. "You cut your—" He stifled her shout by pressing her face to his shoulder. "Hair," she finished in a mutter. She took a deep breath and straightened again, her eyes roaming over his short—but not too short—haircut, then his clean-shaven jaw—that she simply had to reach up and touch—then down to his perfectly tied tie. She leaned away to take in the breadth of the perfectly fitting tuxedo covering his broad shoulders and chest, his crisp white shirt, and . . . he had a tartan cummerbund? He actually *owned* one?

He chuckled again and pulled her back up against him, then started actually dancing. In fact, the guy could really dance. Really quite well.

Sweet Athena, she needed this.

"Do I clean up okay?" he asked, twirling her across the dance floor.

"You take my breath away," she whispered breathlessly. "You look so . . . so . . ."

"Civilized?" he finished for her, his amusement suddenly vanishing as Jane found herself waltzing backward through a door, only to just as suddenly be snatched to the side and pressed up against a wall by Alec's very hard body. "Run away with me," he said into her mouth, just before kissing the breath out of her.

Jane couldn't keep her hands off him, and apparently he was having a hard time keeping his off her, as she gasped in surprise when he cupped both her breasts and ran his thumbs over her nipples—making him have to press more intimately against her when Jane's knees buckled with her moan of pleasure.

The door slammed open followed by a snarled, "Son of a bitch!" Alec stepped away and turned, then used his back to press her up against the wall again—which muffled Jane's gasp of surprise when she saw Mac standing there, his jaw clenched as tight as his fists. "You get your hands off her," he said with quiet anger, "and leave before I kill you."

Jane felt more than saw Alec reach inside his tuxedo jacket. "I was invited," he said calmly as she leaned far enough to see him hand a vellum envelope to her brother.

Mac tore it open, read the card, then threw it on the floor with a snort. "Mother's invitations don't count. Are you going to walk out of here or have to be carried out?"

Alec reached inside his jacket again and pulled out another vellum envelope, then held it toward Mac. "Maybe this one will count."

Jane saw her brother stiffen and slowly take the envelope. He opened the flap and pulled out the card, then turned as pale as a ghost as he snapped his gaze to Alec. "Father invited you? When?"

"Two weeks ago."

Jane felt her knees buckle again. Her *father* had invited Alec to come to Nova Mare and court her? *Two weeks ago?* She smacked the back of his shoulder. "Then where have you been for the last two weeks," she growled, "while I was smiling my face off at a bunch of buffoons?"

"I was usually only a few yards away, watching you smiling at them."

"Why wasn't I smiling at *you* if Daddy gave his blessing for you to court me?"

"I did court ye, Carolina," he said, his back still pressing her up against the wall as he kept his eyes trained on her brother. "Didn't ye get my gifts?"

She gasped. "Did you just call me *Carolina*?" She smacked his shoulder again. "I'm *Jane*. To you, I . . . I'm Jane," she whispered, dropping her forehead to his back. "I want to be Jane."

The door slammed open again, and Jane lifted her head to see her mother come storming in with her father right behind her, followed by Nicholas—who then closed the door and stood against it, his arms crossed over his chest.

Chapter Twenty-one

Christ, he didn't see this ending well.

Alec stepped away from Jane, then caught her when she stumbled forward in surprise, pulled her up against his side, and wrapped a protective arm around her as he faced her parents and Mac. He eyed the door leading outside to gauge his chances of making a run for it, but decided that the three men in the room actually worsened the odds over three weeks ago now that he knew brotherly Nick a bit better. And Jane—damn, he was glad she still wanted to be Jane—wasn't exactly wearing running shoes.

Mac held the envelope in front of his father. "You invited Alec MacKeage? Two weeks ago? By the gods, *why*?"

"Because he fits all my requirements for a suitor," Titus said, smoothing down the front of his tuxedo. "And Carolina . . . wanted him."

"I invited him, too," Rana added, sounding somewhat bewildered as she lifted her gaze from the envelope in her son's hand to glare at her husband. "You let me play out my little charade when you had already invited him?" She turned to glare at Nick. "And you didn't say anything, either?" And then she turned on Alec. "Or *you*? You came here tonight carrying *two* invitations," she growled, pointing at her invitation Mac had thrown on the floor.

Nope; not ending well.

"I don't care who invited him," Mac snapped. "Carolina is not marrying a MacKeage. Where in hell is Sir Garth?" he snarled at Nicholas.

"Garth decided he wanted to go home about an hour ago," Nicholas said calmly, his arms still crossed, still guarding the door that led back into the ballroom.

Alec wondered if Kit could hear them and might be waiting at the back door like a good wingman, thinking the wolf could buy him enough time to toss Jane over his shoulder and make a run for it. At least that was the plan he was going with, until Jane suddenly broke free of his embrace and walked up to Mac. Alec sighed and silently walked up behind her as she faced her brother.

"Why, Mackie?" she whispered. "Why don't you want me marrying a MacKeage?"

Mac moved his gaze from Alec to his sister, his eyes suddenly softening as he touched her cheek. "All I've ever wanted is to see you happy and fulfilled and free to follow your passions, Carolina. But the only way that can happen is for you to marry someone who's afraid of the magic." He slid his finger to her lips when she tried to speak. "I can't stop your destiny, little sister, but having a husband who's in awe of us will at least give you the freedom you crave. Choose a warrior with more muscle than intellect, Caro," he softly urged, "because if you choose a MacKeage, you will be powerless in your marriage."

"If her husband's afraid of the magic, then he can't protect her."

Mac's eyes flared in surprise as they snapped to his. "You know."

"I know," Alec said with a nod. "But don't you think it's time *she* knew?"

Mac stared at him in silence, then slowly turned to his

father. Alec saw Titus hesitate, then give a nod just before he took his wife by the hand and led her outside—to finally tell her also, Alec assumed.

Mac turned back and gently clasped Carolina's shoulders, hesitated again, and took a deep breath. "The reason you have to marry a fearless mortal *now*, is that if you're not married and pregnant in three months"—Alec saw Mac's grip tighten—"every god and demon bent on destroying the Trees of Life will be free to pursue you the day you turn thirty-one, intending to seduce you in hopes of getting you pregnant with *their* child so Father and I won't retaliate when they attack Atlantis."

Carolina jerked away from him with a gasp, only to spin toward the door when a feminine shriek came from outside— which was immediately followed by Rana rushing back through the door, the look in her eyes fierce enough to stop a real bear in its tracks as Titus ran in behind her.

"Of all the pigheaded, arrogant assumptions you men have ever made," she all but shouted as she stormed up to Carolina and wrapped an arm around her, "this one is the most outrageous." She rounded on Titus, pulling Carolina with her to also face him. "Do you think *your own daughter* doesn't even have the brains of a sea urchin? Or that she doesn't have integrity? Or honor?" She turned just enough to include Mac while also giving Nicholas a speaking glare, apparently not wanting to leave him out of her little tirade. "All you had to do was *tell* us about this asinine deal with the gods, and we would have told you there *is nothing to worry about*." She snorted, shaking her head. "It was obviously a pact made between men, because if a woman had been involved, she would have laughed you all off the planet."

She shot her angry gaze around again—alarming Alec when she included *him* this time. "One," she said, her words directed at Titus, "we—no, *I* raised an intelligent, strong-minded, astute daughter Eros himself couldn't seduce, not some simpering miss who would be taken in by trickery or flattery. And two, there will be such a stampede racing after her that the idiots will go to war trying to stop one another from being the one to reach her, and Carolina will be forgotten in their madness." She actually laughed, although Alec could see she was far from amused. "Every woman knows that if you dangle a prize before a group of males, they'll start fighting one another to the point they'll forget *why* they're fighting."

His face darkening with either anger or chagrin, Titus brushed down the front of his tuxedo. "I wouldn't say all men are that single-minded."

"No?" Rana returned as she arched a brow. "You don't recall how the first time we met it took you *three days* to realize I was no longer even at the tournament?" She snorted. "You were so busy trying to impress me by challenging every competitor that you didn't even know *I had already left.*"

"It's not the same, wife," Titus snapped. "This isn't about—"

"Oh, it's the same, husband," Rana snapped back, cutting him off. "And just like *her mother*," she said, giving Carolina's shoulders a squeeze, "our daughter would simply walk away from your god and demon buffoons, laughing her head off." She glanced around at all of them again, and Alec saw her anger suddenly disperse on a heavy sigh. "We don't need strong and fearless men to fight our battles for us, Titus," she said softly, "or to protect us from life's worries. We want husbands who stand beside us, and who take our breaths away by treating us as equals." She lowered her gaze. "And up until three weeks ago, I thought that was the definition of our marriage."

"It was," Titus said gruffly, stepping forward and pulling her into a fierce embrace as he buried his face in her hair. "It *is.*"

Deciding he at least had the brains of a sea urchin, Alec took Carolina's hand and started leading her toward the outside door.

Of course she wouldn't go peacefully.

"No, wait," she said, pulling him to a stop. "You can't just walk off with me. You have to ask for my hand in marriage, and Daddy has to give us his blessing."

"But I don't want your hand in marriage, lass," he said, grinning at her surprise. He leaned closer. "All I'm wanting at the moment is your body," he whispered, "and I really don't think I should be asking your father for that." He shrugged when all she did was continue gaping, and turned away. "Okay, I'll ask him if ye want me to."

She caught the back of his tuxedo jacket, and Alec let her drag him to the far corner of the room, returning Nicholas's grin on his way by. "Are you nuts?" she hissed after spinning Alec around to face her. "I can't just run off with you without our being married. I'm a *princess*, and we do not have sex outside of marriage."

Alec sighed to hide his grin. "Ye need to make up your mind if you're Jane Smith or Princess Carolina so I can stay with the program."

"Dammit, I'm both," she snapped, actually stamping her foot—then nearly falling when her spiked heel broke off.

Alec caught her with a laugh and swept her into his arms. "So, was that a Carolina show of temper?" he asked, striding toward the outside door. "Because I'm thinking Jane would have taken a swing instead."

"Oh, look, husband," Rana said rather cheerily as he passed her still wrapped up in her husband's arms, "they're already bickering just like an old married couple."

"Wait," Nicholas said, making Alec turn to see him step forward and nod at Jane's feet. "You might want to lose the tracking device."

Jane gasped and started struggling, and when Alec wouldn't set her down she finally did take a swing, smacking the back of his shoulder. And when that didn't work, she pulled her dress up past her knee, waved the leg wearing the ankle bracelet, and looked over at her father. "Daddy, you need to take this damn thing off me. Mama, make him take it off," she pleaded in a growl, waving her leg again when Titus merely stood eyeing Alec speculatively.

Damn, he hadn't wanted to play his trump card unless he absolutely had to.

"M-mama," Jane repeated, this time in a whispered plea when Rana merely dropped her gaze—but not before Alec saw the uncertainty in the woman's eyes. "Mackie, please; *you* come take it off me." Jane twisted to look over Alec's shoulder when Mac also didn't move. "Nicholas, *help me.*"

"There's only one person in this room who can take off that bracelet, Caro," Rana said, looking directly at Alec. "So we will know you'll be safe under his protection."

Jane snapped her gaze to Alec. "You can take it off?" She looked at Titus. "But when you put this one on me three weeks ago, you said the gods themselves wouldn't be able to get it off."

"They can't, Daughter. Only a mortal can remove it, and then only if he understands the true source of the magic."

Jane slowly turned her head to Alec, her face having gone as pale as new snow, and started struggling again. He walked to a chair and set her down, knelt and rested back on his heels, and lifted her foot onto his thigh as she pulled her dress up to expose her ankle.

"T-take it off," she said thickly, pushing her foot against him when he didn't move. "Alec, if you can take it off, then do it." She leaned closer. "I'll be free," she whispered, pressing her mouth against his cheek. "I have the condom tucked inside my bra, and we can finally use it."

Alec dropped his chin to his chest on a sigh. "I can take it off, but I prefer not to."

She reared away. "What? Why not?"

He caught her fist heading toward his shoulder with a chuckle. "Because I prefer you take it off," he said, guiding her captured hand down to her ankle. He nodded at her surprise. "If ye truly want to feel free, lass, then you're going to have to free yourself."

"But I can't," she snapped, reaching down and tugging on the delicate chain, only to suddenly stiffen. "Wait; how do you even know you can take it off?" she asked, her gaze darting past Alec first to her father, then to where Nicholas was standing, then back to Alec as she leaned closer, the look in her eyes making him lean away. "Did you men work out some sort of deal behind my back?"

"I swear, Jane, we didn't," he said, shaking his head. "As for *how* I know," he went on with a shrug, "I'm really just guessing based on something your father told me, as well as something your mother mentioned." He snorted. "You people have a bad habit of talking your way around a subject instead of saying it straight out."

Alec heard another snort come from the general vicinity of Nicholas.

"What did they say to you?" Jane asked.

"Well, when I kept complaining that you all shouldn't exist because you're myths, they more or less kept agreeing with me. But then your father explained that mankind *imagined* all the various deities into existence, which in essence made all the gods *real.*"

Jane pushed her dress down over her legs with a snort of her own.

"And," Alec continued, pushing her dress back up over her knees, "something he'd told me earlier finally made sense. Your father said it's a misconception that magic-makers hold all the power, as it's the man who understands the source of that power who is the true force to be reckoned with. And your mother said that even fear is a myth." He slid off her broken shoe and held her foot in his hand as he fingered the bracelet. "Didn't ye notice that even the powerful magic Nicholas was using to secure Nova Mare didn't keep me out? And even though Mac got a few punches in the day he came to get you; have ye not wondered why, if he was so opposed to your having anything to do with me, that he didn't return and finish me off or at least drive me away? Think, Jane; is the question why *didn't* he or why *couldn't* he do anything to me?"

She silently looked past his shoulder again, her gaze darting between Mac and Titus before she looked back at him, and Alec saw the moment everything suddenly fell into place in that brilliant mind of hers. "He *couldn't,*" she whispered breathlessly. "And Daddy couldn't do anything but take me away from you that day, either. Theurgists and drùidhs can only use force to defend themselves or someone being directly threatened with bodily harm, as Providence forbids them from interfering in a person's free will. But even then they can't interfere if the person doing the harm is acting with a pure heart rather than malicious intent." She snorted. "The power isn't in the hands of the gods; it's in the hearts of mortals. And that's why the gods and demons are always fighting to keep mankind ignorant, afraid the knowledge that they really are nothing more than myths can just as easily *dis*believe them *out* of existence."

Jane looked at Titus and beamed him a smile, her eyes filled with pride, then lowered that smile to Alec. "And my father chose to champion mankind. Even at the peril of being made extinct by the very mortals he was trying to protect, Daddy built Atlantis and planted the Trees of Life to keep mankind's knowledge safe so as to ensure everyone's right of free will—including *mine*." She reached down to her ankle and took hold of the thin chain—only to stop and look up. "Will you be my boyfriend, Alec?"

He rubbed his thumb over the top of her foot. "Aye," he said gruffly, "if ye don't mind having to support a ski bum during the off-season."

"Oh, I can think of a way you can earn your keep," she said rather huskily as she looked down and slid the chain around to the small gemstone.

Alec saw her suck in a deep breath, hesitate a heartbeat, then effortlessly pull one end of the chain out of the setting. She straightened with a laugh as she dangled the bracelet over her head. "I did it!" she cried, throwing herself at him and wrapping her arms around his neck. "Thank you," she whispered in his ear. "Thank you for not doing it for me, Alec."

"My pleasure, lass," he said, hugging her back—only to have her suddenly pull away and jump to her feet.

She ran to her parents, kicking off her other shoe on the way. "Mama, look what I did! Come on," she said, lifting the hem of her mother's dress, "take yours off, too."

Rana pulled her dress from Jane's grasp and let it fall into place. "I don't want to take mine off, Caro," she said, leaning back against her husband with a tender smile as Titus wrapped his arms around her again. "I'm quite happy to wear it for several thousand more years." She nodded at the bracelet in Jane's hand. "But a twenty-first-century woman really has no need for magical protection, Daughter, as I believe women today are quite capable of taking care of themselves."

A loud gasp came from the other side of the room, and everyone turned to see Olivia standing in the doorway with Ella in her arms. After all but tossing Ella at Nicholas—who suddenly looked panicked when the child gave a squeal of delight and wrapped her little arms around his neck and kissed his cheek—Olivia ran up to Mac and stood on her tiptoes to better glare at him, even as she pointed at Jane's hand. "Did your mother just say Carolina doesn't need to wear that anklet because modern women are capable of taking care of *our*selves?"

"Don't ask Mac, Olivia," Jane said. "You can take yours—"

Not really seeing this ending well, Alec swept Jane off her feet and strode to the outside door, used his hip to push it open, then kicked it closed behind him just as Kit stepped out of the bushes. "Ye leave them alone to work that out, and focus on us," he said, although he practically had to shout to be heard over Jane's protests. "Did you say there's a condom in your bra?" he asked to divert her attention—which seemed to work, judging by her sudden stillness. He looked around, just now realizing he hadn't really planned beyond actually *getting* his hands on Jane. And her dress wasn't exactly outdoor wear, and she didn't have on any shoes.

"Carolina," Rana called out, rushing out the door—only to bump into them and make Alec turn. "Oh. Here, you forgot your backpack, Caro—I mean *Jane*," Rana said as she plopped the backpack on her daughter's lap, the added weight making Alec have to lean back to adjust his center of gravity.

He sighed, guessing he was lugging heavy luggage up

and down the mountain again. Wait; she'd brought a back-pack to the ball?

He had to readjust his stance again when Jane leaned over to clasp her mother's face and give her a kiss. "Thanks, Mom," she whispered. "I'll see you in a few days."

Where in hell did she think she was going? "Where are *we* going?" he asked.

Jane wrapped an arm around his neck while holding her backpack on her lap against his chest. "To the pool pavilion."

"Ye want to swim—oh," he said, feeling dumber than a sea urchin. He gave Rana an embarrassed grin because he was about to make off and then make *out* with her daughter just as the door opened again and Titus walked out, fol-lowed by Nicholas still holding Ella—who still had her little arms around the still panicked-looking man's neck.

"Bye, Daddy. Bye, Nikki," Jane called over his shoulder as Alec strode toward the pool pavilion—wondering why no one was stopping him from running off with their *unwed* princess. Hell, last he saw, they'd all been *smiling*.

"Well, that ended better than I was expecting," he said somewhat cheerily.

"You think so?" Jane said somewhat wistfully, resting her head against his. "Because in many of the fairy tales I've been reading to the cherub, there's usually at least some bloodshed before the prince gets to carry off the princess."

Alec saw all the people partying in the pool pavilion and walked around to the side of the building, then stopped at the utility door. "Open it for me," he said, bending enough for Jane to twist the knob. He carried her inside and set her on her feet, took her backpack and tossed it on a barrel, then clasped her face in his hands. "Are ye absolutely sure that you know what you're doing? And you're sure, Jane, that you're doing it for all the right reasons? Because," he went on, slid-ing his thumb over her lips when she tried to speak, "you're completely free now and no longer in any danger—not from the gods or a dictatorial father demanding you get married."

She reached up and gently slid his thumb away. "Do you

want me for all the right reasons, Alec? Not because I'm a princess, or because I'm wealthy, or because I have magical powers?"

He closed his eyes and rested his forehead against hers. "You're not helping me out here, lass. If you're all those things, then I have no business wanting you at all."

"What if I were just an ordinary woman? Would you want me then?"

"Aye," he said thickly, his head still resting on hers. "I could even love an ordinary woman, especially if she happened to be smart and sassy and passionate, and she enjoyed camping out in the wilderness and was willing to fight a bear for me."

"Alec?"

"Yes, Jane?"

"I'm getting cold feet."

He reared away. "After I just spent three weeks picking off all my competition, you're telling me *now* that you're getting cold feet?"

"Well, when should I tell you, when my toes start falling off?" she muttered, reaching for her backpack and unzipping it. "I didn't heat the floors of the utility rooms because that would have been a waste of good energy." She started shoving a pair of jeans and a fleece and lacy bright red underwear at him as she pulled each one out of the pack. Next she pulled out what looked like a new pair of hiking boots and tossed them on the floor, then dug around inside the pack and pulled out a ditty bag and set it on the clothes he was holding, then her iPad and solar charger, her hairbrush, a rock that looked an awful lot like one of the rocks he'd heated and left in her bed, and a thick, wrinkled Nova Mare envelope that she quickly shoved back inside.

"What was that?" Alec asked to cover up his little tirade for not knowing her *feet* had been getting cold.

"Nothing important," she muttered, finally pulling out a pair of socks.

"So we're starting out this relationship by keeping secrets from each other?" He snorted. "Ms. Jane Smith?"

She sat down on the floor and slipped the wool socks onto her feet—not looking at him, Alec couldn't help but notice. Although he did notice she was blushing. "I'll let you read it . . . after."

"After what?"

She stood up and turned her back to him. "Just after, okay? Will you unzip me?"

He set all her belongings on a shelf, then unzipped the back of her dress, giving a chuckle to disguise his shock when he realized she wasn't wearing underwear. "Did ye get dressed in a hurry this evening?" he asked, his voice sounding a bit high to him.

She let the dress fall to pool at her feet, then stepped out of it and turned to him wearing nothing more than her Jane smile, Princess Carolina tiara and emerald necklace, and the wool socks. "It's lined with a slip so it was decent enough, and I thought I might have to change in a hurry," she said, her voice sounding a bit husky to him.

"Wait; where's the condom?" he asked, glancing down at the floor. "Never mind," he muttered, feeling dumber than a sea urchin to realize she couldn't have tucked a condom in a bra she wasn't wearing. Alec grabbed her flaming red underwear, jeans, and thick fleece off the shelf and tossed them to her. "Then hurry," he growled, grabbing her other belongings and stuffing them back in the backpack. He picked up her dress and hung it on a hook on the back of the door with a rather harried—or maybe lustful—chuckle. For christsakes, he'd been waiting three weeks to get his hands on her again. "I'd like to be here in the morning to see the workers trying to figure out how the owner of this dress got home."

"You're going to be busy in the morning," she said— again huskily—as she pulled the fleece down over her head, apparently feeling the same way he did. She sat down and slipped into her boots and laced them, then looked up with a frown. "Didn't you bring a change of clothes?"

He grabbed the backpack, slung it onto one shoulder, then pulled her to her feet. "I was focused on getting *you*, not getting away," he said, leading her toward the hall that skirted the end of the pool room.

"Wait; Kitalanta," she said, trying to turn back to the outside door.

Alec kept dragging her. "He doesn't like the tunnels." He chuckled again. "He'll probably beat us to the campsite."

"But we're not going to the campsite," she said, rushing past him to open the pump room door and pulling him inside before turning and wrapping her arms around his neck and pressing into him. "We're going to the grotto."

Chapter Twenty-two

Alec stopped just inside the entrance to the grotto and dropped Jane's backpack in the sand when the beam of his headlamp illuminated the interior—or rather, the *furnished* interior—of the cave. "When did you do all of this?"

"Mom and I ditched Nicholas by telling him we were spending the day primping for the ball and then snuck down here this morning," she said, bending to pull something out of her pack. "Mom thought we should spruce the place up a bit. Do you like it?"

"Ye lugged all this stuff down the tunnel?" he said in disbelief, shining his light on what looked like a large feather mattress, at least a dozen fancy pillows of varying size, several puffy blankets, a Persian rug, wineglasses, and several bottles of wine, a wicker trunk—doubling as a table, he assumed, judging by the two pillows on each side of it—enough candles to light an entire house, and . . . was that a copper *bathtub*? "It would have taken two packhorses to carry all this down here, and that tub sure as hell didn't come through the tunnel. Where did all this stuff come from?"

"From Daddy's ship."

Alec whipped his head around, shining his headlamp out at the sheltered cove. "His submarine? The one Trace Huntsman nearly sank when Mac stole Henry from him? But I heard it was half the size of an aircraft carrier," he said when she nodded. "Ye mean it can fit through the underground river running up from the Gulf of Maine, and that it's out in the fiord right now?"

"No," Jane said, giving him a lopsided smile. She pointed at the north wall of the grotto. "It's in a really large cave about a hundred yards through the granite. And you know that steel door a little ways up the tunnel from the shoreline that you asked about when we came down just now, because you hadn't seen it on the blueprints? Well, it's locked because it leads to the dock Mac built for Daddy's ship. Mom got some of the crew to lug this stuff in for us, then she helped me make the place all cozy and . . . romantic." She shrugged. "The bathtub was her idea."

"Pretty damn sure of yourself, weren't you?" he drawled as she walked away and started lighting the candles sitting on tiny ledges jutting from the walls of the cave.

Once she had several lit, Jane shut off the lamp dangling from her jacket zipper, then pulled off Alec's headlamp on her way by him, tossing it down near the backpack as she headed to the other side of the cave. "I was pretty damn sure I'd be spending the next few days down here with *someone*," she said way too cheerily, shooting him a sassy smile over her shoulder and batting her lashes. She started lighting the candles on the other side of the grotto. "Although I had assumed he'd be my husband, not my boyfriend." She turned and walked up to him, that smile downright saint-tempting as the reflection of two dozen candles danced in her emerald green eyes. "But I guess that's the way it's done in the twenty-first century."

"Jane," he said on a sigh, "if ye need a ring— Wait, are you saying your *mother* helped ye stage this . . . ? That she . . . ?" Alec dropped his chin to his chest. "I can never, ever face that woman again. What mother *helps* her daughter seduce a man?"

"A mother who loves her daughter," Jane said, wrapping her arms around his neck. "And who realizes that sometimes saints and idiots need a little help making up their minds." She gave him another sassy smile. "But according to a very happy hooker I know of, sometimes all they need is the proper encouragement."

"And what . . ." He cleared his throat when she pressed into him. "What did ye have in mind?"

Jane lifted onto her toes, bringing her mouth next to his ear. "I stole a can of whipped cream from the restaurant," she whispered. "And I downloaded a couple of new sex books, and one of them mentioned that men have a particularly sensitive spot right under their—"

Well, that should teach him to ask, Alec thought with a shudder as he covered her mouth with his—even as he wondered if he shouldn't start reading more. Jane's reaction was immediate and no less enthusiastic than he remembered. Damn, it had been a long three weeks.

"Alec?" she whispered, breaking the kiss and leaning away just enough to look him in the eyes. "Can we finally both get naked at the same time?"

He started to speak, but stayed silent when the candlelight glittered off the single emerald in the center of her tiara, only to have Jane step away when she noticed where he'd been looking.

She just as silently pulled her fleece off over her head, took off her bra, pulled off her boots and socks, then took off her pants and panties, her gaze never leaving his. She reached up and took off her emerald necklace and tossed it in the general vicinity of her pack, then reached up again and pulled the tiara out of her hair and sent it sailing past his shoulder toward the beach.

And then she stood there, completely naked, facing him. "I love you, Alec."

And that, he figured, was about as naked as truth got.

Keeping his eyes locked on hers, Alec shed his jacket, his tie, cummerbund, and borrowed shirt, then lifted one foot then the other to pull off his shoes and socks. He unfastened his pants and pushed them down along with his shorts and stepped out of them, and stood in front of her completely naked. "I guess I love you, too."

"You *guess*?"

"Okay, I *know* I love you." He shrugged. "But I'm going to need a little time to get used to the idea, because I've spent quite a few years convincing myself that I *shouldn't* fall in love."

She crossed her arms under her breasts—which effectively pushed them up and toward him rather provocatively. "When would you *guess* you first realized you loved me?" she asked in an equally provocative whisper that sent the last firing brain cell he had down to his groin. "Alec?"

"What was the question?"

"When did you fall in love with me?"

He decided to focus on the curl of hair standing up from where she'd pulled off the tiara. Yeah, that was better. "I can't rightly say. But," he rushed on when he caught her scowl from the corner of his eyes, "I know when I finally *admitted* it to myself."

"And when would that be?"

"When I read the note ye left me in the privy," he said with a grin, only to hold up his hand to stop her when she started toward him. He went back to focusing on that curl. "Do you know the exact moment you fell in love with me?"

"That's easy," she whispered, the sudden gruffness in her voice making Alec drop his gaze to hers. "When you cut my hair."

He spread his arms and Jane barreled into him, and Alec lifted her off her feet and strode to the inviting bed she'd set up. He knelt with her still in his arms and pressed her onto her back, kissing her the entire way down, and settled himself between her thighs. Only then did he break their kiss to smile down at her.

"Would ye happen to know where you tucked that condom?" he asked, deciding he better use one on the chance Titus had gone ahead and magically *remedied* his little problem about getting her pregnant.

"I tossed it in the fireplace of my cottage."

He reared up. "Why?"

"Because I'd been carrying that particular condom around for all the wrong reasons. So," she purred as she reached under the pillow, her hand reemerging holding another packet—that he couldn't help but notice was already torn open, "I got us a whole box of new ones." Her sultry smile turned lopsided. "Which I can see was very smart of me, as I imagine making a baby might be a little too much for a man to wrap his mind around if he's still getting used to being in love."

He dropped his forehead to hers with a chuckle. "Are ye sure you weren't born in this century, lass?"

"Alec, are you stalling?"

"Aye," he said, not lifting his head.

He felt her go still beneath him. "Why?"

"Because you're a thirty-year-old virgin," he said softly, finally looking at her. "And it's not always . . . pleasant the first time."

"Then don't you think we should get the first time over with as soon as possible so we can get to the pleasant second time? And the third and fourth?" she whispered.

And that, Alec decided, was why he wasn't afraid to love Jane. "Aye," he said, just before he kissed her again—which, he quickly discovered, she took as permission to pounce.

It was more wrestling than lovemaking, with Jane often coming out the victor. Although Alec figured it was only because every last one of his brain cells had fallen under her spell. And he couldn't really complain, considering that losing to Jane was like winning the foreplay lottery.

But feeling she'd worked herself into a heady steam of passion, Alec finally slipped on the condom while she was busy looking for the particularly sensitive spot her new book said he was supposed to have, and wrestled her back beneath him and settled between her thighs again. Then he had to pin her hands down beside her head, and finally got her to quit squirming when he slowly pressed into her slick warmth.

He also stilled and smiled down at her. "Will ye be my girlfriend, Jane?"

"Aye," she drawled in a surprisingly good mimic of his burr, the candlelight reflecting the passion in her eyes. "Forever, Alec."

He pressed slowly but steadily forward, watching that passion ease slightly for the merest moment just before it flared with renewed fire and she lifted her hips into him with a moan. He withdrew and pressed into her again, sliding a little deeper and pulling a longer moan from her—which he answered with a groan of pleasure. Feeling her legs growing restless against his, and sensing her muscles beginning to tighten as she sought the pleasure she knew was hers for the taking, Alec increased the rhythm of his thrusts, only to lose himself in the storm with her.

He'd swear fireworks boomed overhead when she crested, even lighting up the sky behind them as Jane took him right along with her to that magical place they'd spent ten days craving to visit together. Hell, Alec thought as he lowered himself to his elbows to keep from crushing her so she could breathe—which they both were working very hard at, he couldn't help but notice—he could *still* hear and see fireworks.

"S-sweet Athena," she said in rasping pants, "if that was supposed . . . to be unpleasant . . . I can't wait . . . for the second time."

Alec carefully rolled away, and was about to tuck her up against his side when she sat up and yanked him up beside her just as another burst of fireworks broke over the fiord, causing him to sigh in relief that he hadn't been imagining the storm gods were rejoicing that he'd just *devalued* a princess.

Because personally, he felt she'd just added a whole lot of value to him.

"Oh Alec, could this night be any more perfect?" she said, slipping her arm through his and leaning into him with a sigh.

"Well, a bottle of my ancestors' liquid gold and a big juicy steak might help it a bit," he said, stifling a grin when she straightened away—to better gape at him, he figured. "Seeing how I spent the day dealing with your last two suitors, I only had a couple of donuts on the ride back from Pine Creek and missed lunch and supper." He looked over, and nope, she wasn't gaping but glaring. "What?" he said, pulling her back down just as another burst of fireworks broke over the fiord. He rolled on top of her, threaded his fingers through hers, and held her hands beside her head. "You want times two and three and four to be anywhere near pleasant, you're going to have to feed me."

Damn. Alec knew that smile she suddenly gave him, and he knew this really wasn't going to end well. But he'd trade having that goddamn bus off his chest for a thousand years of loving Jane any day of the week.

Jane turned from watching Kitalanta and his pod-mates, the rising sun glistening off their wet orca backs as they darted in and out of the cove playing keep-away with a large piece of driftwood, and saw Alec slowly fold the letter she'd given him ten minutes ago. Not knowing what to make of his silence, Jane guessed she probably should have thrown it in the fireplace the day she'd taken it back from the privy. Sweet Athena, forget that she'd declared her undying love for him; she had asked him to *marry* her.

"It would mean changing at least your last name again," he said quietly, sliding the letter back into the envelope, "and possibly never having children if an operation to reverse the vasectomy I had nine years ago proved unsuccessful."

Jane sucked in her breath. "You had a vasectomy? Why?" She saw him also pull in a deep breath and let it out slowly as he turned to her, his eyes unreadable. "Because I didn't feel I had any business being a father."

"But why?"

"Because while on a mission for my government, I killed a fourteen-year-old boy. He'd just killed my partner—a woman who also happened to be my lover—and was just turning the gun on me when I broke his neck."

Jane's skin tightened at the utter lack of emotion in his voice and guarded way he was holding himself. Sweet Zeus, did Alec think he was a murderer? Or that *she* would think he was? "Alec," she said, only to have to clear her throat when she realized he believed they shouldn't marry because he might not be able to give her babies. "That was self-defense." She snorted, determined to make this into nothing. "Do you think the six men Daddy brought to Nova Mare hadn't killed anyone?" She touched his arm. "Did my father know that you'd had a vasectomy when he gave you his invitation?"

"Aye," he said, still staring out at the cove. "And he knew about the boy, and he also said it was self-defense." He looked at her. "But that doesn't change the fact that the boy was just a kid."

"Who'd just murdered a woman and was trying to murder you, and who would have gone on to murder others. Alec," she said softly, "you can't judge yourself for something you did in the line of duty any more than I wouldn't have judged myself for marrying a man I didn't love to fulfill my duty. And I don't care if you can't give me babies. I *love* you." She smiled. "And anyway, if we decide we want children but can't have our own, we'll just adopt them. However many you want."

She saw his jaw slacken. "You're willing to adopt?"

"Of course. Nicholas was adopted, and look how wonderful he turned out."

Alec shook his head. "He told me his mother is your family's healer and that his father is your royal gardener."

She laughed. "That's because he was only about a week old when he was found on the beach, and Maude immediately took him in. Everyone thought it ironic that the island's midwife was childless, but apparently the moment Maude set eyes on Nicholas, she claimed him as her son."

"So brotherly Nick isn't an Atlantean? Then what is he?"

Jane shrugged. "Nobody knows. From what I've been told, everyone figured he'd been in a shipwreck when Leviathan found him and brought him to Atlantis."

Jane saw Alec take another deep breath and look down at the letter he was still holding. "I'm still just a ski bum."

"Then how come a ski bum owns a tuxedo, dances better than any man I've ever danced with, and appears to be as comfortable in a ballroom as in the wilderness?"

He tossed the letter onto the sand and wrapped his arms around his knees to stare out at the cove. "Have you ever heard of James Bond?"

Jane slipped her arm through his and leaned against his shoulder. "I have a couple of the older movies on my iPad, when Sean Connery played James Bond." She nudged him with her elbow, determined to lighten the mood. "Mostly because I love his Scottish accent. But what's that got to do with your owning a tuxedo?"

"For eight years, I was an American James Bond for my government. No one in my family knows; not my parents or brothers or sister, or even Duncan. Everyone thinks I was in the marines and served three tours of duty overseas, but . . ." He lifted his arm to wrap it around her, and then held her head against his chest as he took another deep breath. "I was known as the Celt, and it was my job to get in, get out with whatever information or person I was sent after, and not get caught or implicate my country. And sometimes that meant skulking around in dark alleys, and sometimes it meant attending formal functions at embassies and palaces."

"You mean like a spy?" She lifted her head in surprise. "You were a real-life James Bond?"

"I was an idiot," he said, pulling her back against his chest. "I was barely twenty-one when I signed up and twenty-nine when I finally *wised* up." He ducked his head to look at her. "It's not nearly as romantic as the movies, Jane, and it doesn't always turn out well in the end."

Jane straightened away in surprise as everything finally made sense. "Sam knows who you were. That's why he told me to go to you if I got in trouble."

Alec hesitated, then merely nodded.

"And you said Daddy knows, too."

He nodded again. "I think that's why he decided to let me court you, figuring I could probably do a better job of keeping you safe in this century, which he knew is where you want to stay."

She leaned against him again with a sigh. "Why couldn't he just tell me about that stupid pact he made with the gods? He created *more* problems by keeping it a secret." She snorted. "Which shows how little faith he has in me."

"Even though it involved you, keeping it a secret really didn't have anything to do with you, Jane," Alec said, twisting to push her down onto the feather mattress. He settled beside her, propping his head on one hand and cupping her hip with the other. "Your father thought he was protecting your mother from worrying herself sick. Did you know that he nearly lost her when you were born?"

"I know. But having a difficult birth doesn't make a woman weak; it just happens sometimes." She laughed. "Mama's the least weak-minded woman I know."

"But your father is a man," he said, giving her hip a squeeze, "and an ancient one at that. And being one myself, I know for a fact that our first instinct is to protect the women we love, which is why *we* become weak-minded at the thought of losing them."

Jane twined her arms around his neck and pulled him down until their noses were touching. "Promise that you won't ever keep secrets from me."

"Only if you remember that's a promise that runs both ways, Ms. *Smith*."

"Then I promise, if you promise I'll always be *Jane* to you."

"Aye, if you promise never to use your magic on me."

She snorted. "I'm fairly certain we've established you're immune to the magic. But," she said in her best sultry voice as she slid a hand down between them and wrapped her fingers intimately around him, "I'll promise to try not to, if you promise to always use *your* magic on me."

"Not a problem, lass," he said thickly, moving over her and slowly easing himself inside—without a condom this time, she noticed. He captured her moan of delight in his mouth, and Jane once again found herself in that wondrous place where time stopped and the world receded until only their passion for each other existed.

And her last coherent thought before Jane surrendered to the pleasure was that she'd give him a week to get used to loving her before she proposed again—in person instead of a letter, and definitely with both of them naked at the same time.

LETTER FROM LAKEWATCH

Autumn 2012

Dear Readers,

I would imagine that from reading my books, you've figured out by now that magic is my vehicle of choice for bringing you along on my journey into the realm of possibilities. I often compare telling a story to packing an SUV with my hero and heroine in the front seats, the back seats filled with a large cast of characters as they all head off on a road trip through a particular segment of their intersected lives. What's going on outside the vehicle—the weather, terrain, other travelers they might encounter—certainly has an impact, but the real story is what's happening inside that truck.

Ever find yourself trapped in a vehicle with someone you didn't particularly like? Someone who scared you? Someone you hadn't realized didn't like you? How about being trapped with someone you thought you absolutely adored only to discover they weren't exactly what they seemed? Yes, there's nothing like a nice long road trip to slowly me away the masks we hide behind. (Trust me; Robbie an spent five weeks trapped in an SUV and small camper two teenagers headed from Maine to Alaska. We made far as the Canadian Rockies and turned around; m sweet husband saying Alaska would still be there w boys finally moved out.)

I digress, but it was a very . . . memorable five

So back to my books and the role magic plays in my stories. I'll admit I have a tendency to get a bit outrageous—say, like when I rearranged the beautiful state of Maine to create an inland sea—but there is a method to my madness. You see, I want to make you stretch really far to suspend your disbelief, so you'll consider the everyday magic you encounter in your own lives to be real. Sound convoluted? That's the plan!

The magic is real, people; as real as the sunrise, the ebb and flow of the tides, the haunted call of a loon, that unseen fish tugging on the end of a line, the birth of a baby, the death of a loved one. The problem, in my opinion, is that these things seem so everyday ordinary that we forget how extraordinary they really are.

What guarantee do we have that the sun's going to rise tomorrow? We assume it is, because it's risen every day for the last . . . what, four and a half billion years? But what if it decided not to make an appearance tomorrow morning? What if the oceans stood still? What if every loon on the planet suddenly lost its voice? What if babies stopped being born? What if we stopped dying?

What if we woke up tomorrow morning and simply decided not to get out of bed?

That's what my stories are about: getting out of bed every morning—even on days we don't want to—and seeing the magic around us instead of . . . well, I'm not sure what the opposite of magic is. Maybe hopelessness? Despair? Indifference?

As the god behind the machine of my stories, I refuse to let my heroes and heroines give up. If they find themselves stuck in a vehicle with someone they don't particularly like, they're going to have to deal with it. Nobody's going to swoop in and rescue them by pulling that bogeyman out of the truck, or come along and change that flat tire in the pouring rain, turn all the traffic lights green, straighten out all the curves in the road, or roll back gas prices to a dollar a gallon.

(Well, okay; Maximilian Oceanus could, but he's not really real. I just made him up to make my point.)

And since I'm writing romance, I like for my hero and heroine to realize that if they would just team up, they could conquer the world. Or at least control—maybe even vanquish—most of those demons sitting in the seats behind them. (Didn't I have one of my characters—a hero, I think— in one of my stories say his mom or gram told him that a problem or burden shared was cut in half?)

And the "love conquers all" equation doesn't always have to involve the hero and heroine, either, as we learned in Charmed by His Love; *Duncan MacKeage's love for young Jacob Thompson certainly had the power to vanquish that little boy's demons.*

We're all in the vehicle, people; every one of us is on the same amazing journey and we're on it together. Our hopes and dreams and struggles and disappointments are shared by the people in our homes, living next door and down the street, and on the other side of the planet. And like my heroes and heroines, if we would just realize that by teaming up we could conquer the world . . . well, wouldn't it be a truly wonderful world to wake up to tomorrow? So share the love—in your home, down the street, and across the world—then see if a good number of those demons don't suddenly disappear and your burdens get cut in half. I promise it's a gift that will keep on giving, and you'll discover that smiles really are contagious.

Until later from LakeWatch, you keep reading about life and love and happily ever after, and I'll keep writing it.

Janet

P.S. My dad passed away last fall, but before you start worrying that I'm sad, please understand that I'm really quite happy for him. He was nearly ninety-four and actually quite eager to head off on another fantastical adventure. The only reason I'm even telling you is because at his funeral,

Dad's sister said she had discovered just last year—at the age of ninety-eight!—that she can write poetry. Of course I asked her to send me some of her poems, then asked for her permission to share them with you—to which she kindly agreed. So if magic is not real, then explain a ninety-eight-year-old suddenly waking up one morning a poet!

POEMS BY ETHEL F. TAYLOR

Crafty Gals

They gathered round the table
These gals so fair and neat
And became busy with their craft work
'Mid laughter gay and sweet.

Laughter and jokes were being exchanged
And gaiety flowed all around
With blissful feeling I watched them
Wishing it need not end.

Families are so endearing
More so as time goes by
May we all meet together in Heaven
And never have to say good-bye.

I'll hold this picture in my heart
When I'm once more alone
And cherish every moment
'Til the day that I'm called home.

Then at last the evening is ended
And we've exchanged a good night kiss
One day may we all meet in heaven
And not one of our numbers be missed.

Alethea

Alethea is a beautiful maiden
With a heart as pure as the snow
She fell in love with a handsome Marine
Many long years ago.

Now she wears his engagement ring
And her heart is full of joy
She counts the months 'til she graduates
Then she'll marry her Marine boy.

With a bit of sadness
Dad looks at his little girl
He has given her to another
And together they'll face the world.

The wedding feast has been eaten
And the guests have all gone home
Alethea and Steven run to their car
And the honeymoon has begun.

Mom and Dad wave their good-byes
With a touch of sadness in their hearts
Their little girl has grown so quickly
And from her it's hard to part.

They head across the USA
To their little home in the west
Where we all pray they'll live happily
Like two turtledoves in a nest.

Red School House

The little red school house
Where I went years ago
Brings back fond memories
Of the days of old.

We walked to school in winter
Although it was windy as well
Then huddled round the heater
Until teacher rang the bell.

The Lord's Prayer was always recited
Then Pledge of Allegiance too
Then out came our reading books
To show what we could do.

When the bell rang for recess
We'd all rush out of the room
The girls all played on one side
And recess was over too soon.

Beauty

The sun shone with an unearthly beauty
On the glistering trees below
One stood in awe at their majesty
And to think that God made it so.

If God makes such beauty here below
What splendor must be up above
Why are we reluctant to leave this place
And dwell with God above.

The snow will soon be melting
Then spring will once more be here
A time to get out and enjoy the sun
And see the stars so clear.

The birds will soon be singing their song
The grass will be turning green
God has given us so much beauty
Let us open our eyes and see.

Read on for a special preview of
Janet Chapman's next
Spellbound Falls romance

The Heart of a Hero

Watching through the windshield of his truck, Nicholas studied the three young men getting out of the late-model pickup on the far side of the employee parking lot at the base of Whisper Mountain. But the more the man sitting beside him explained why he'd asked him to come down here today, the more confused Nicholas became. Rowan was second in command of Nova Mare's small security force and quite capable of dealing with this sort of problem on his own.

"And the reason you simply didn't intervene?" Nicholas asked, darting an impatient look across the cab. He looked back at the three young men to see one of them lift a bicycle out of the of the pickup and lean it against a tree in front of the older, mud-splattered truck they'd pulled up beside. "They're on resort property, Julia Campbell is an employee, and last time I checked, keeping our staff safe was in your job description."

Apparently not the least bit intimidated by the growl in his boss's voice, Rowan shook his head on a soft snort. "If I've learned anything living in Spellbound Falls this past year, it's that Mainers don't particularly care to have strangers butting into their business—especially family business. Her brother's the one with the peach-fuzz beard." Rowan scowled at the young men lighting up cigarettes as they leaned against the shiny red truck they'd arrived in. "And I didn't intervene last week because I was afraid it would make things worse for Julia when she got home. Here she comes," he said when the bus shuttling employees down from the mountaintop resort halted in the middle of the parking lot.

Nicholas reached over and stopped Rowan from getting out. "Let's sit and watch for a while. You say he's here every Friday waiting for her to get off work, and that it's obvious he's hitting her up for money?"

Rowan nodded. "She usually has it in her pocket and just hands him some folded bills. Only last week he apparently wanted more than she was offering and grabbed her purse. They got in a small tussle, she lost, and he dug out her wallet, pulled out a fistful of money, and tossed the wallet and purse on the ground, then got in his truck and left." He snorted again. "The punk couldn't even be bothered to take her home, but left her to ride her bicycle in the rain. There, that's her in the red wool jacket and black pants, carrying those empty feed sacks," Rowan said, nodding at the workers stepping off the shuttle bus.

Nicholas saw the woman in red hesitate when she spotted the three young men leaning against the pickup, then watched her square her shoulders and head toward them— her brother straightening away when he saw her.

Julia Campbell was slightly taller than average for a woman and somewhat on the thin side, with a thick braid of light brown hair hanging halfway down her back that Nicholas suspected would spring into a riot of curls when let loose. It was dusk and starting to snow, so he couldn't make out the color of her large eyes set in an oval face on top of a gracefully long neck. Her posture was intrinsically feminine, her stride filled with purposeful energy despite it being the end of her workday. "She's older than I was expecting," he said, assuming she'd barely be out of her teens, judging by the age of her brother.

"I asked the shuttle driver her name after that little tussle," Rowan said, "then went back up to your office and checked her employee file. She turned thirty a few months ago, has been married but is divorced. And even though I've since learned her mother's dead and that she lives with her father between here and town, she listed a sister as next of kin to notify in an emergency. The empty sacks she's carrying were full this morning. Her family owns a cedar mill, and Julia supplies the resort with kindling and pine cones for the fireplaces to supplement her wages and tips. She works housekeeping Tuesday through Saturday, and from what I've gathered from quietly checking around, she asked to always be assigned the same eight cottages."

Nicholas glanced over at him, arching a brow. "Any particular reason you've become an expert on one of our female employees?"

"I'm *concerned*," Rowan growled back. "Sweet Prometheus, man, I'm old enough to be her father." He suddenly grinned. "And yours, sir," he drawled, just as Julia Campbell reached her brother, her hand already emerging from her pocket holding some money. "I don't like interfering in family business," Rowan continued, "but I also don't like seeing a woman being harassed. That's why I asked you to come down here today and help me decide what to do—if anything."

"Our authority ends at the resort's property lines, which means it's not our place to interfere in—" Nicholas stopped in midsentence when he saw Julia hand her brother the money then twist away when he made a grab for her. She stepped around him and pulled a set of keys from her pocket as she walked to the older pickup, but halted again when the other two boys moved to block her path.

Nicholas was out of his own truck and halfway across the parking lot when he saw Julia's brother start dragging her to the bicycle while trying to wrestle the keys away from her. "Come on, Reggie, it's *snowing*," Nicholas heard her say as he dodged employees walking to their vehicles. "Give me a ride home."

"I'm not heading back to town," the punk said, still dragging her. "Dad's drinking again, so I'm spending the weekend at Corey's camp." Finally getting hold of the keys, he gave her arm a shake. "You were supposed to leave the keys under the mat so I could get the truck this afternoon. I had to wait four freakin' hours in town."

She yanked out of his grip. "I kept them so you'd give me a ride."

"Not happening, sis. Peddal fast and you'll beat the storm. And while you're at it, you can figure out how to lug your kindling on your bike from now on, because you're not getting my truck again."

"Is there a problem?" Nicholas asked from directly behind the boy.

"Not that I know of," the kid snarled as he pivoted around, only to stumble back when he found himself glaring at a broad chest. "Who the hell are you?" he asked, taking another step back.

"Director of Security for Nova Mare," Nicholas said, matching him step for step. He looked past the boy to see Julia stop rubbing her arm when she saw him looking at her. "You in need of some help, Miss Campbell?"

Her eyes widened, apparently surprised that he knew her name, before she dropped her gaze and shook her head. "No, everything's okay."

"I'm outta here," the boy hissed, reaching toward his truck.

Nicholas placed his hand on the door to hold it closed. "I believe your sister asked you for a ride home."

"No, that's okay," Julia said as she suddenly headed for the trees. "I've decided I'd rather ride my bike." She set her sacks and purse in the basket attached to the handlebars, shot Nicholas a forced smile as she gave a nod, then walked the bicycle along the tree line before veering into the parking lot several vehicles away.

Suspecting Rowan was right about their interfering creating more problems for her, Nicholas turned to the boy. "I catch even a whisper that you've laid a hand on your sister," he said quietly, "on *or off* the resort grounds, you and I are taking a long walk in the woods together, you got that?"

"Are you freakin' *threatening* me?"

Nicholas leaned in, crowding the punk against the mud-splattered door. "Yes," he said succinctly, just before turning and walking to his pickup. "Take the shuttle back up the mountain," he told his second in command when the man fell into step beside him. "I'm going to give Miss Campbell a ride home."

"So much for not interfering," Rowan said on a chuckle as he headed to the bus with a wave over his shoulder.

He'd had to interfere, Nicholas decided as he got in his pickup, because he couldn't stand seeing a woman being harassed any more than Rowan could. He started his truck, but then had to wait for several cars to idle past before he was able to pull out behind them. And why was Julia Campbell letting some fuzzy-faced punk half her age push her around? If the little bastard wanted money, he could damn well break a sweat for it, not bum it off his sister.

Nicholas unclenched his jaw on a calming breath and turned on the windshield wipers to clear the swirling snow. "It's none of my business," he muttered, finally pulling onto the main road behind the procession of exiting workers. "I'm just going to make sure she gets home without breaking her lovely neck."

He'd been working at Nova Mare over a year now and still couldn't get a handle on the locals, which was confounding, considering there wasn't a country or culture he hadn't studied at length—some quite intimately. But Mainers appeared to be a breed unto themselves; maddeningly stoic, stubbornly self-reliant, and highly resilient. They were also deeply proud, especially the women.

Nicholas scowled out the windshield. Not only were the women proud, some of them were really quite bold when it came to pursuing something—or *someone*—they wanted. And apparently several of them wanted Nova Mare's unusually tall, blue-eyed Director of Security. Which was becoming a real problem, as he didn't particularly like being considered Spellbound Falls' most eligible bachelor—a title he'd heard whispered around with blatant regularity. By the gods, some of the women's antics were bordering on brazen.

Not that he had any intention of living like a monk if a lovely lady happened to catch *his* interest. He just preferred to be the one doing the pursuing.

So how had the decidedly lovely Julia Campbell escaped his notice?

Nicholas saw the vehicles in front of him swerve across the center line, allowing his headlights to land on Little Red Riding Hood walking her bicycle down the side of the darkened road in the nearly blinding snow. She'd pulled her hood over her head and was fighting to keep the bicycle's snow-caked tires out of the ditch, making him wonder why none of her coworkers were offering her a ride.

Tempted to hunt down her brother and take the punk on a *one-way* walk in the woods, Nicholas forcibly unclenched his jaw again as he drove past her and pulled to the side. He got out of his truck, but then had to snag the bicycle's seat when Julia merely veered into the road to go around him. "Take your purse out of the basket," he said as he grabbed the bike by the frame. "I'm giving you a ride home."

He lifted the bike when she didn't move—effectively making her snatch her purse with a startled squeak—and set it in his truck, but had to then snag Julia's arm and hustle her out of the road just as several vehicles swerved around them. He let her go when she bolted up the length of the truck and opened the passenger door, but then followed when she merely stood there staring at the chest-height seat.

She gave another soft squeak when he caught her around the waist and lifted her into the truck, and Nicholas closed the door before she could see him grin at the realization that Julia Campbell's eyes—their long lashes littered with snowflakes—were a rich hazel-gold. Feline eyes, he decided, with the potential to be warmly inviting one minute and stubbornly aloof the next.

And wasn't it interesting that he happened to like cats?

He walked around the front of the truck and slid in behind the wheel, checked his side mirror, and pulled back onto the road. "You'll have to tell me where you live," he said into the silence broken only by the thump of the windshield wipers.

"Just a few miles on the right. Um . . . thank you."

"You're welcome." He pulled off one of his gloves with his teeth and turned up the heater fan, then held out his hand to her. "Nicholas."

She hesitated, shook his hand without taking off her own glove, then went back to hugging her purse to her chest. "Julia."

What Nicholas liked most—and ironically least—about cats was their fierce independence, while he considered their most endearing quality to be their general lack of vocalization. And although he only suspected Julia Campbell could be stubbornly independent, judging by her determination to walk home in a snowstorm rather than ask a coworker for a ride, she was also proving to be a woman of few words. "How long have you worked at Nova Mare?"

"Since May."

Only six months. "And before then?"

"I waited tables at The Drunken Moose weekends and worked at my family's cedar mill through the week."

Wow, a whole sentence. "So were you living here when the mountains moved and the earthquake turned Bottomless Lake into an inland sea three and a half years ago?"

"No, I was living just north of Bangor. But we felt the earthquake down there."

"You work in housekeeping, don't you?"

"Yes."

Nicholas felt his jaw clenching again with a whole new appreciation of the women who complained that talking to him was like pulling teeth, and tried to decide what about this particular woman was bugging him. "You enjoy working at Nova Mare?"

"Very much," she said, adding a slight nod when she obviously heard the edge in his voice. "Mrs. Oceanus is a wonderful boss. That mailbox is my road." She set her hand on the door handle. "You can drop me off here. I live only a short ways in."

Nicholas turned onto the road and kept going, stifling another grin when he heard his passenger release a barely perceptible sigh. "It looks as if your days of riding a bicycle to work are coming to an end. You don't own a car?"

"I . . . It's being repaired."

Must be quite a major repair, since Rowan had told him Julia had been pedaling to work for months now—except on Fridays, when she apparently borrowed her brother's truck to bring her kindling and pine cones. And the woman's idea of a *short ways* was an understatement, considering he'd already driven down the rutted forest road over a mile without seeing any signs of a house yet.

And he still couldn't figure out what was bugging him. It wasn't anything she was saying or *not* saying or doing, just that something was . . . off. Not that it was any of his business, since he was only making sure one of their employees made it home without getting run over by a snowplow.

She really was as quiet as a cat, and just as— That was it; Julia Campbell wasn't *moving*. She didn't fidget, hadn't pushed back her hood or even wiped the melting snow off her face, and had managed to avoid any real eye contact with him. Nor had she questioned his showing up to give her a ride or protested his manhandling.

Nicholas felt his gut tighten with the knowledge that the first defense an abused woman learned was how not to draw attention to herself—especially unsolicited male attention. For the love of Zeus, she'd let a virtual stranger toss her into his truck without even so much as a scowl.

Granted, everyone who had anything to do with Nova Mare knew him on sight, and Julia probably figured that if she couldn't trust her employer's chief security guard then she couldn't trust anyone, but she should have at least questioned why he'd intervened in the parking lot today and taken her home without even asking.

So, did Julia Campbell simply pick her battles, or was she afraid of men?

Not that it was any of his business.

He finally spotted the house setting *two miles* off the main road, and pulled up behind a fairly new pickup that was as muddy as her brother's. He shut off the engine when he saw the porch light come on, then quickly reach over when Julia opened her door. "Wait and let me help you down," he said, getting out and walking around the front of the truck, not surprised when she didn't protest. "I've been meaning to have a set of running boards installed," he continued, guiding her to the ground. "Careful, there's ice under the snow. Let me get your bicycle out of the back and I'll walk you—"

"Julia! That you, girl?" a heavy-set man called out as he came down the porch steps wearing slippers and no coat and carrying a tall glass in his hand. "Who's that with you? You send him away and tell the fool we close at noon on Fri—"

"Daddy, be careful!" Julia cried, bolting for the house when the man missed the bottom step.

Nicholas dropped the bicycle and ran after Julia as her father stumbled toward a tree only to end up sprawled face-down in the snow—pulling Julia down with him when she tried to break his fall.

In what was starting to feel like a comedy of errors, Nicholas ended up in a small tug-of-war when the man tried using her to pull himself up before Nicholas finally wrestled Julia free and stood her out of the way. "Let me help you," he said, catching the man under the arms and lifting him to his feet.

"I told that Christless girl to spread the stove ashes out here this morning," the man grumbled, staggering forward to hug the tree he'd missed earlier. "And where in hell is she, anyway? She's supposed to come straight home from school and cook me supper." He pointed at Julia as she straightened from picking up her purse. "It's your fault. Ever since you gave her that truck, she ain't never home."

Julia shot an uneasy glance toward Nicholas then walked to her father. "Trisha told you she had band practice this afternoon," she explained just as a small SUV pulled up beside Nicholas's truck. "There she is now. Come on, Daddy, let's go inside and I'll cook you some eggs and pork."

Her father batted her away. "I spilt my drink," he growled, pointing at the empty plastic tumbler on the ground. He then glared up at Nicholas. "And I ain't going nowhere 'til I meet your boyfriend."

"Jules," a young woman said, rushing up only to slip on the ice and grab Julia's arm. "What's going on? What's wrong?"

"Both you girls are due for an attitude adjustment," their father snarled, his eyes narrowed against the swirling snow as he pointed an unsteady finger at them. "And don't either of you think I won't do it, either, just 'cause it's been a while."

Nicholas once again forced his jaw to relax, this time also having to unball his fists as he stepped up to the obviously inebriated man. "Let me help you to the house, Mr. Campbell," he politely offered, his grip—and likely his size—squelching any protest.

"I expect a man wanting to date my daughter to ask me first," he muttered as Nicholas maneuvered him up the steps.

"I'm not dating Julia, sir. I just gave her a ride home from work."

The man yanked to a stop at the door and pulled free, the porch light revealing his bloodshot glare. "You think you're too good for my Julia, is that it?"

"Dad," the woman under discussion hissed, opening the door.

"Come on, Daddy," her sister said, pushing on her father as Julia pulled. "Let's get you inside before you catch a chill."

Mr. Campbell shrugged off both girls, then grabbed Julia's arm and gave her a shake. "This is why you can't get another man," he growled. "And why you lost the good one you had. How many times I gotta tell you to show some proper gratitude when a man's nice to you." He pushed her in front of Nicholas. "I say driving you home in a snowstorm deserves a kiss."

Julia and her sister gasped in unison and Nicholas stiffened at the realization the man was serious. And if Julia's father had placed her in an untenable position, he'd put Nicholas in a quandary. If he simply turned and walked away, the drunken idiot would likely get angry at *her*. And if he leaned down, instead of slapping his face she'd feel compelled to kiss him.

"And not some shy peck on the cheek, either," Mr. Campbell continued, nudging his frozen daughter hard enough that she stumbled forward.

"Daddy," her sister growled, grabbing Julia's jacket to tug her back.

Well, hell. Nicholas pulled Julia into his arms, lowered his head as he lifted her onto her toes, and kissed her—making sure to linger just long enough to satisfy the bastard that she was properly grateful. "You're welcome," he murmured as he released her and straightened away. He gave a slight bow then turned and walked down the steps, got in his truck, and backed around and drove out the road.

Definitely not his business, he decided as he touched his tongue to his lips—which he noticed now held a taste of peppermint.